I0763289

Intersections

John Doriot

Intersections

This is a work of fiction. All of the characters, organizations and events portrayed are either products of the author's imagination or are used fictitiously.

ISBN 978-1-7332528-5-0

Dedication

For Edmond, Edgar,
and Maggie

About the Author:

A lover of horror stories since he was a very young boy, John began pursuing his dream of becoming a writer after he retired. The stories were always there, waiting for a chance to get out, and now that the door has opened, he hopes that they will find an audience. Other than the psychiatrists.

John lives in Georgia with his wife and dog in a secure facility. Feel free to contact him at madcow26@comcast.net and let him know your opinion about the books. He welcomes your feedback.

Table of Contents

Wheeler Road 1
Walton Way 9
State Street 19
Holston Avenue 28
Cunningham Road 45
S.C. 25 80
Washington Road 100
Tamer Lane 109
I-75 249
The Old Brown Dog 265

Wheeler Road

He went by the cemetery every morning on his way to work, unless he was called into the hospital to take care of a baby that was unconcerned with his daily routine. But it didn't matter if he was delayed in going. He went there every day without fail. Whether it was at lunch, or on his way home, he always found time to go. The cemetery was peaceful and he could sit on the bench underneath the weeping willow and talk to his wife. Tell her about his day.

And though the cemetery was quiet and peaceful, he still didn't feel at peace. He thought that would have changed over time, but it didn't. He missed her as much now as on the first day that they were separated. He still felt the pain of that loss and it seemed to echo through his body as if he was a hollow shell. It never went away and was a constant reminder that life was precious, even though his job cried that out to him every time he helped bring a new one into the world.

From his freshman year in high school, he knew that he wanted to be a doctor and, more specifically, an obstetrician. He could tell you the day when he realized that. It was December 1, 1961, a Friday. He and his mother were returning home from visiting his father in the hospital. He knew his father was dying and he couldn't think of a better way to honor him than to become someone who brought life into the world. He knew he would have liked that.

His father had worked hard all his life as a traveling salesman and his mother was a housewife. He remembered that his father had always come home at night no matter how far he had to travel each day. It was a promise he had made to her and one he always honored. It might have been after supper or sometimes after she had gone to bed, but he always made it home.

When his father was still a young man, he became too sick to travel. In fact, he became too sick to work at all. The cancer grew without restraint, and the last month of his life was spent in the hospital and then at home. He never got to tell his father that he was going to be a doctor but he always felt a familiar presence around him as he progressed through medical school. One that felt proud when he graduated.

Believing that his father was aware of what he had accomplished provided him comfort and closure.

He met his wife in college. She was working in the laboratory as a medical technologist and he was an orderly working on his pre-med classes. She was sitting alone in the hospital cafeteria reading a book and he walked up to her and asked if he could sit down. She smiled and nodded her head. He remembered the book she was reading that day: “To Kill a Mockingbird” by Harper Lee. She told him she loved the movie and had wanted to read the book. He liked that about her.

He liked a lot about her. She was pretty. Funny. Very smart and very opinionated. They didn’t always agree on things and they both tried their best to win the argument. Sometimes the arguments lasted for days but those were the best kind because they always ended up being decided in bed. He didn’t care that he never won those arguments.

He remembered when he asked her to marry him. They were in the cafeteria where they had been having lunch together for about a month. They had never gone out on a date after work or even seen each other away from work, but it didn’t matter. He knew she was who he wanted to marry and he was hoping she felt the same way.

When he asked her, she just shook her head no. He was surprised at her response until she started smiling and asked what took him so long to ask the question. He remembered telling her that he was afraid she would say no. She smiled again and shook her head and told him that he needed to get more in tune with what women were thinking if he was going to be looking around in their hoo-ha. He laughed when she said that and he laughed every time he remembered it.

While he was in medical school, she often worked double shifts so that they would have enough money to get by and when he could, he worked on the weekends as a phlebotomist in the hospital. After he became a resident, she continued to work extra shifts and he sometimes worked forty-eight hours straight, but he made a promise that he would always find a time to be with her each day. Sometimes it was for a meal and sometimes it was after she went to bed and he would wake her and they would have a cup of tea or coffee and talk. Or sometimes she would just want him to lay with her for the short time that he had before he went back to work. No matter what, they never went a day without seeing each other.

Delivering babies never became routine for him. It was always a significant event. He had seen other doctors treat the work as "just another day at the office," but he could never do that. They were the same doctors who had a condescending manner with the nurses and even their patients and he wondered why they would act like that. He tried to talk to them about their behavior, although most of them dismissed his constructive criticism as an intrusion and ignored him. But some changed the way they acted and thanked him for the feedback. And it was because of them, that he never stopped trying.

The nurses loved working with him and the way he stood up for them. His patients, the soon-to-be mothers and fathers, saw him as much more than a doctor. He felt like a member of their family and they were glad that they "had a family member who knew how to deliver babies." He was someone who was trusted and respected, not only within the hospital, but also throughout the community.

The births were always special even when they were difficult. He thought those moments were probably the most significant times in his career because they always reminded him of the challenging nature of the world and that sometimes just taking a breath was an extraordinary event.

He had made it a point to remember every baby that he had ever delivered. Their names and the date they were born were written in a little spiral-bound notebook that his wife had given him when he started his residency. He always carried it in the pocket of the white lab coat that he wore.

His wife had stitched his name and the evidence of his determination into seven white lab coats. She gave them to him at the same time she had given him the notebook. Across the front top pocket were the words: Edward Stephen Kaplan, M.D. She had used orange thread to complement his white jacket so that the combined colors would denote the university from which he had graduated.

Occasionally, he would look through the notebook and read the names of the babies. He could see the baby's face and the smiles of relief and love of the tired and determined mother, and the smiles of nervousness and love on the apprehensive and proud father. Most of the parents would send him cards with pictures of their children as they grew up and that meant a lot to him.

The only ones who didn't send him updates about their children had a reason not to. A reason that he and his wife understood much too well.

He and his wife had tried to have a child as soon as he started his practice. But they were not successful. Over a period of ten years, she had three miscarriages and two failed in vitro fertilization procedures. After the last unsuccessful attempt, she told him she couldn't handle the disappointment anymore. He told her that he understood, and though he didn't want to admit it, he couldn't handle it anymore either.

Though hurt and disappointed, neither one of them thought that life was being unfair to them because they couldn't have children. It would be selfish of them to think so. They had so much. Because each day he got to witness a miracle and when he shared those experiences with his wife, she saw the enchantment that sparkled in his eyes and that provided her consolation and happiness.

Even after he started his practice, he never failed to keep the promise he made as a resident, to see his wife every day. When she became sick, he felt like he should have been home more but she wouldn't allow him to change his routine. She told him that keeping a routine was important to her and it made her feel normal, even though her body was being torn apart by the disease that was trying to kill her and the medicine that was trying to save her.

He remembered those evenings when he came home late and she was sitting at the dinner table forcing herself to eat some soup. He again told himself that he should have been there with her because she had too many meals by herself. But she would look up at him and smile and ask him to sit down and tell her about his day. As he talked, he would see the hope return to her eyes and it helped him understand why she was doing things her way. After telling her about his day, he would ask her questions that she didn't want to answer but he asked them anyway.

"What did the oncologist say today?"

"Nothing has changed, which is a good thing. There was no growth in the tumor but it hasn't reacted as well to the chemo as he thought it would. He wants to try some more chemo."

"What did you say?"

"I asked him if it would make me sicker."

He didn't need to ask any more questions. He already knew the answer. It would. He had stopped asking her if she was in pain because he knew the answer to that question too. She would always say "No" even though he knew that was not the truth. He had to force her to take her pain medicine and he would coax her to drink milkshakes as she lay in his arms on the couch watching some of her favorite movies.

He didn't mind watching those movies over and over because what was on TV didn't really matter. The fact that he could hold her and attempt to make her feel better was all that was important. He would try to make her laugh and smile. Making her laugh was harder than making her smile because all he had to do to make her smile was tell her about the beautiful baby he had delivered that day.

He remembered her laugh but he only heard it now when he visited the cemetery. He could talk to her there in the quiet, and though she just listened most of the time, on occasion, he heard her talking to him. Even if he didn't hear her voice, he could always hear her laugh and see her face and it provided him solace.

Over the years, he watched many changes come to the hospital. Staff changed. The nurses who had always worn white began wearing colorful scrubs. Older nurses retired. The faces of the staff got younger and younger, but that youth was reflective of exuberance and a wisdom that exceeded all of his expectations. New supervisors and managers were hired and though that combination of change could have been troublesome in this very intense environment, it actually became a strength of the unit and benefited everyone. Technology changed. The ultrasound technology used in the obstetrical area became much more sophisticated. What were once grainy gray images became clear three-dimensional pictures. Laboratory tests provided much more timely data now, especially with information that would let the doctor know when the mother was in danger of losing the baby or if there was something wrong with the child.

The miracles that he witnessed became even more awe-inspiring over time. Babies who were born prematurely when he first started practicing had very little chance of survival. Now, babies born at twenty-three weeks were surviving in the neonatal intensive care unit. He loved to tell his wife about those babies and how they fought to survive. He could think of nothing else that showed how precious life was and he knew his wife would agree. Even in death, when he looked at the faces of those small babies that he delivered, they were always smiling at him. Letting him know that everything was okay.

On his way to the cemetery this day, he decided to take a different route. It was a beautiful summer day and he had his car windows down and he smelled the fragrant flowers that saturated the landscape. He found himself on a road he didn't recognize and something told him to stop at a house. The house at 1917 Arden Road. He pulled over and parked and got out of his car.

As he walked toward the porch, he looked around for something familiar but he didn't see anything that he recognized. There were beautiful azaleas and tea olives around the porch and he could tell the yard had recently been mowed. In the grass was a bicycle. It looked like the one he got for his birthday when he was a little boy. There were streamers and remnants of balloons scattered around the bike and on the ground. It looked like there had been a celebration of some sort. He walked up to the front door and knocked but no one responded. He opened the screen door and yelled "Hello" as he walked in and looked around.

Portable card tables had been set up around the dining room and den. There were empty colorful plates and cups on the white paper table cloths. The cups had a picture of Harry Potter holding a wand pointed outward with the caption, "Have a Happy Hogwarts Birthday!" He also saw a big chocolate cake on one of the tables. He was right - there had been a celebration. A birthday celebration.

He called out "Hello" again but still no one answered as he continued walking through the house. He heard children laughing and he looked out the window and saw them running around playing some game holding onto brooms that were between their legs. Probably has something to do with that Harry Potter movie he thought. He turned around and walked back toward the living room. As he did, he noticed the pictures on the wall.

The pictures showed a family in different places around the country. In each photo, he saw a young boy at various ages but he didn't recognize the parents or the child. He got out his spiral notebook and looked through the names, hoping they would help him remember, but they didn't. Then he saw her. He saw his wife holding a little boy in her arms. In other pictures, he saw someone who looked like his wife but was much older and holding another young boy in her arms. He went back and looked at those first pictures another time, and this time when he looked, he saw that older woman again.

He felt someone grab his hand and he turned around. It was his wife. He knew he must be dreaming because his wife had been dead for thirty years. But he didn't care, it was a nice dream and it felt real.

"What are you doing here?" he asked.

"Looking for you," she replied.

"How did you find me? Do you know whose house we are in?"

"You weren't hard to find. You have always been on my mind. I have never really left you. I was always there with you. I knew you were there with me. You never left me."

"Do you know this house, the people that live here?"

"I do. This is our son's house. He is a very successful salesman for an orthopedic company. He sells knee and hip implants. And that boy outside celebrating his ninth birthday is his son. The young boy's name is Stephen and his father's name is Edmond. They were both named after their grandfathers."

"What a wonderful dream I am having," he said as he looked at his wife. "Anything is possible in a dream, isn't it?"

"It is, Eddie. My sweet Eddie," she said as she looked up into his eyes and rubbed her hand across his cheek. "But it's not a dream. You see, I adopted Edmond almost thirty years ago."

He looked at her, unable to speak. Unsure of what she was saying. Unsure of what to even ask.

"Come, let's go for a walk," she said as she led him out of the house and down the street.

After they had walked past several blocks of unfamiliar large homes, they turned the corner and he recognized the road. They were on Edgemont Avenue, where the cemetery was located.

He smiled at his wife. She was walking with him back to her resting place. This is a nice dream, he thought. He hadn't been by the cemetery today so he realized he must be doing so in a dream this time. But things looked a little different as they approached the weeping willow and the bench where he usually sat. Her marker appeared different too. It looked new and white; not gray from the years of harsh weather that came from all the winters that had visited it.

He looked at the weathered marker next to hers and saw his own name. He shook his head as he bent down to make sure he was reading it correctly.

Edward Stephen Kaplan, M.D.
Born June 26, 1945
Died June 23, 1985

Dedicated husband and physician. Loved by many. Missed by many.

"For those who are led by the Spirit of God are the children of God." Romans, 8:14.

He looked confused – he didn't understand. She smiled and pulled him tighter and he looked over her shoulder at her marker again.

Jean Marie Kaplan
Born June 23, 1947
Died June 26, 2015

Dedicated wife and mother. Loved by many. Missed by many.

"For those who are led by the Spirit of God are the children of God." Romans, 8:14.

"What is going on?" he asked. "I've been delivering babies for over forty years. I lost you a long time ago."

"You did lose me a long time ago Eddie. And you were there delivering babies, as you say. For ten years you delivered thousands of babies, but then you couldn't anymore. You became so sick that you died before I had a chance to get well. You were gone way too soon, Eddie," she said as she paused for a moment.

He saw the tears falling down her face as she continued.

"But you weren't ready to go. And so, you didn't. I could tell when you came by the house. Your presence gave me reassurance and serenity. You never stayed long, because you couldn't. I knew they needed you elsewhere so I never asked you to stay. You were needed in the hospital. And you were there in the delivery room just like you said. But you were a whisper then, a whisper that the residents heard when they were in there; in the delivery room, sitting in front of all those hoo-has."

He smiled when he heard her say that but she said it more for herself than for him. She needed to say something that would steady her legs and keep her from crying.

"You were there, my love, telling all the young doctors what to do. Helping them learn. Helping them overcome their fears and helping them figure out ways to save those that were in trouble. Those that struggled to live. Those whose first breath was always a miracle. Those that reminded you of your father and of me."

He suddenly realized he was like his father in more ways than he knew. But he was okay with that. His life had made everything okay. She had made everything okay.

"You were waiting on me," she said. "You always said you couldn't rest unless I was at home with you. I came home today Eddie. I am here with you now."

Walton Way

He was very tired. Working two jobs was overwhelming but he knew they needed the money. His wife was in the middle of her nursing school clinical rotations and was only able to work a couple of days a week now. She was also eight months pregnant and those twelve-hour shifts were exhausting. Sometimes she struggled to even work one day a week and he knew that, so he didn't ask her to do any more. It was up to him to carry the load now.

After the baby was born and she was working as a nurse, they would be okay. Eventually. At least that's what he told himself. He had insurance through his job but even with that, they would be close to $10,000 in debt after the baby came and they already struggled to get by now. It would take them a while to pay that off. He had thought about taking out a loan but when he did, all he could see was the Twilight Zone spiral and hear Rod Serling's voice talking to him, as he fell down into the black and white vortex.

He had watched the show so many times that he had memorized the opening monologue. In fact, they had made a tradition of watching the Twilight Zone marathon every New Year's Day for the past six years. One year before they got married and every year since. Neither of them really cared too much for football and they both loved sci-fi, so watching the Twilight Zone marathon was something of a "no brainer" that they both looked forward too.

Smoking dope was also a "no brainer" while watching that marathon and they did that every year until his job and her school and pregnancy required them to stop. They snacked all day while they enjoyed the strange and nightmarish stories of the Twilight Zone, washing down the munchies brought on by the marijuana with either wine or beer until it was time to cook the steaks out on the grill. That had also become a tradition but it was one they wouldn't be able to afford this year. The only way they could even afford cable now was because he told himself he could go a few days each week without dinner. He would tell his wife that he had already eaten something at work and just wanted an apple. And so he ate a lot of apples.

Fortunately, his full-time job at the hospital allowed him some flexibility with his work schedule and he was able to pick up extra shifts at Amazon that no one else usually wanted. But he had now worked almost thirty-eight hours straight and his body was telling him it needed sleep. In fact, on his way home that early morning, both his body and his car were telling him that. He wasn't sure how many cones he hit before he swiped the first orange barrel which jarred both the car and him awake.

He was heading for another orange barrel and hit it too before he slammed on the brakes. A glance in the rear-view mirror showed a line of orange cones behind him that looked like a storybook tornado had come through and knocked all of the gnomes to the ground. But he saw nothing else - no workers, no blue lights. He backed away from the barrels and drove out of the work zone as fast as he could. He checked the rear-view mirror for blue lights but still saw none and let out a deep sigh just as he ran through a red light.

"Fuck!" he yelled out loud as he looked around, but again there were no cars and no people to witness what he had done. All the way home, he watched for blue lights and thought about how lucky he had been.

He pulled into the driveway as far as he could and parked. He grabbed a small penlight from the glove compartment and examined the front of his car. There were a few orange streaks on the very bottom of his door and a small scratch on the fender but there was nothing else that would provide evidence of his accident. He grabbed a towel from the kitchen and came back outside to rub away the crayon-like orange marks and then smiled. "Damn, I got lucky," he said to himself as he walked back toward the house.

The paint was now peeling away in many places on the small, white frame home. When it was built, it would have been called a row house and was the last one of a series of them on the street. The houses had been built in the 1920s for people working in the large hotels that were the epicenter for the rich during the 1920s through the 1940s. Two of those hotels were still standing on Walton Way. Their architecture reminded everyone who saw them of the wealth and opulence that once existed in that part of town. One of them still served as a hotel, but the one closest to their house had long since fallen into disrepair within its magnificent walls and had become section 8 housing.

Their home was on Azalea Avenue, just off Walton Way, and it sat below the grand building that now served as housing for the impoverished. They were lucky to have found it since it was a fluke it still even existed. Two small 600 square foot homes had been turned into a 1200 square foot home by a local contractor in the 1950s. At that time, the renovated home was a nice rental, but over the years and with the changing dynamics of the city and the lack of interest by the owner's children, the house had become barely rentable.

At first, she was as excited as he was when they found the house. The convenience to the coffee shops and bars downtown complemented their bohemian lifestyle. Even after several break-ins, she wasn't deterred from living there. When she was attacked though, all of that changed.

Her husband was working late and she was coming home from working a twelve-hour shift at the hospital. It was dark and she didn't see the man waiting for her in the shadows. As she opened the door, he shoved her into the house and slammed the door shut. His head was covered by a toboggan face mask, but he saw the gun she pulled from her purse. After the break-ins, her husband had recommended that they both get a Georgia concealed weapons license and she was glad he had done so.

She didn't even have to pull the trigger. She just said, "Come a little closer mother-fucker so I can make sure I shoot off your pecker and balls at the same time." And with those words, the man ran out of the house, hoping she wouldn't shoot. She never bothered to tell her husband about the attack but that night changed her forever. All she told him was that she stopped a break-in with her gun.

Perhaps she didn't tell him because there was nothing he could do about it. Perhaps she didn't tell him because the wine made her forget. Wine, she knew she shouldn't be drinking because of the baby, but was needed to lessen her anxiety. Or perhaps she didn't tell him because she was becoming disillusioned with everything about her home, life, and marriage. Yep, she told herself as she went to sleep that night. It was all of those things.

As he walked up to the porch that early morning, he remembered how good things were when they first moved there. They loved being with each other and they loved everything about the house - the location, the style, the cost. It was all perfect for the life they were living then. They frequented the coffee shops and bars downtown and it was close to where they both worked. It was even convenient for her school and so they stayed even though they realized their environment was not always safe.

It was 3 a.m. that morning when he got home, and all he wanted to do was get in the house and sleep. He didn't bother to take off his clothes or even make it to the bedroom. He dropped down on the couch and closed his eyes. But instead of his mind turning off, he thought about what he was doing and why he was doing it. The baby had been a surprise for both of them. His wife appeared excited when she got the news, but the excitement he demonstrated was not real. His mind never seemed to shut off as he worried about their future together with the baby and wondered what he was going to do. Those thoughts traveled along his neurons until one of them would short out and he would be able to stop thinking about anything and just sleep.

He didn't hear his wife get up and go into the kitchen the next morning and begin making breakfast. He didn't hear anything until his phone rang just after 6 a.m. He tried to ignore it but knew it might be the hospital, so he had to answer it. He was right in his assumption. The pathologist was calling to tell him there was a body in the morgue that needed an autopsy. He told him the name of the body was Kate Smith and he repeated the name back to the pathologist and said he'd be in after he showered and had breakfast.

He sat up on the edge of the couch with his head in his hands and tried to clear his head. It was like trying to clean up a can of spilled paint. No matter how much he wiped up, he kept finding some spots he missed. He wondered if he would ever free his mind up enough to do his job. His wife brought him a cup of coffee and sat down next to him.

"You look like you haven't had any sleep in days," she said. "And you don't have to respond to that statement because you and I both know that's true. You're killing yourself. How much longer do you think you can do this?"

He took several sips of the coffee before he responded. "As long as necessary, I guess. What other options do we have? You can't work much and we need to put some money away. We're sure to have more expenses after the baby comes and I don't want to worry so much about paying our bills."

"Aren't there some other places where we can cut some costs?"

"Like what? We don't go out to eat. We live in a house that is just barely safe enough and cheap enough. We can't give up cable. Those old shows - The Twilight Zone? No, we're not giving that up. Once you get through nursing school and after the baby is twenty-one, we should be okay."

"Twenty-one?"

"He should be out of the house by then, don't you think?"

She smiled and started to say something else but she didn't.

"Look, I can cut back some of my hours at Amazon and still keep a job there. Don't worry. I only need three hours of sleep a day."

"Really?"

"We are about to find out," he said as he finished his coffee and patted her leg with his hand.

"Do you even remember the name of the body that the pathologist just told you?"

"Kate uh…Jones. No, no. Smith. Kate Smith."

"In your state, don't be surprised if the bodies start talking to you. Sleep deprivation can cause a lot of things to happen to your conscious mind."

Fuck. What a nice thing for her to say, he thought to himself. Great, now I will be thinking about that the entire time I'm in there. Thanks a lot, Lyndsay.

"I'll be fine. No worries."

Lyndsay nodded her head as she watched him walk toward the bathroom.

"Would you make me another cup of coffee? Only this time, put some caffeine in it?"

"Sure," was all she said as she got up and headed to the kitchen.

He stayed under the shower for what seemed like an hour but was only five minutes and when he came out, he felt like some energy had returned to his body. Cold shower, some coffee, and I should be good to go he told himself. He put on his scrubs and walked back into the living room, where his wife was holding his large Yeti cup of coffee.

"Be careful Josh," she said as she handed him the cup.

"Not to worry. Kate Smith. See. I remembered. That shower and coffee gave me a burst of energy. With this cup, I should be good for another four or five hours and then I can come home and go to sleep. I'm not working at Amazon tonight."

She acknowledged his response with a smile as he turned around and left the house. A glance at the car reminded him of what he had done earlier that morning, as he got in and drove carefully to the hospital. Within fifteen minutes, he was opening the door to the morgue.

"Ah, what a beautiful smell that is," he said as he took several sips of his coffee. "I love the smell of formalin in the morning. It smells like victory," he laughed as he remembered Robert Duvall's line in "Apocalypse Now" about the smell of napalm.

He placed his cup on the countertop and put on the paper waterproof pants and lab jacket. He then added two sets of gloves and his face shield. He opened one of the three morgue coolers and found a body covered with a sheet. He pulled it back to check the toe tag.

"Yahtzee!" he yelled out. "I need to buy a lottery ticket on the way home." He then pulled out the metal stretcher upon which the body identified as Kate Smith rested.

He pushed the cart next to the autopsy table and removed the sheet from the body.

"Fuck." He had seen a lot of shocking things in this job but for some reason, he wasn't prepared today for what he saw. She was a small white woman with larger than normal breasts and a very athletic body. He could even imagine her being very good looking before whatever happened to her had removed half of her head.

He studied her chart and saw that she had been in a car accident. He was amazed as he read through the nurse and physician notes that she had lived several days in the ICU. The right hemisphere of her brain was gone along with one of her eyes and ears. She looked like someone had sliced through her skull and cerebral cortex with a Samurai sword in one of those Japanese ninja movies he liked to watch.

"How in the hell did you live two days?" he asked. "And why am I doing an autopsy? I believe I can tell you the cause of death."

He locked the morgue cart wheels and picked up the body's legs and placed them onto the table. He then walked over and shifted her upper torso onto the table. He was amazed at how easy that was. "Damn, I have more energy than I thought," he said to himself. He pushed the empty cart back into the cooler and removed one set of his gloves as he took another drink of coffee.

He assembled the saws and blades he would need to begin the autopsy and looked over at the body again while taking one more sip of coffee. When he saw the eye open, he dropped his cup onto the tile floor and fell back against the counter.

He closed his eyes and shook his head remembering what his wife had told him. Fuck you, Lyndsay, he said to himself. He opened his eyes and saw the eye staring back at him.

"I'm sorry. I didn't mean to scare you, but you were getting ready to destroy evidence. That needle mark in my hand. That wasn't there for an IV. It was used by my husband to inject potassium chloride into my body. He's a doctor so he knew what he was doing would put me into cardiac arrest and well, as you can see, I don't need to tell you how successful that little act was."

Joshua didn't move or say anything. God damn. What the fuck am I supposed to do now?

"My mind is kind of fuzzy. I have a little memory loss but for some reason, I feel like I know you. Are you the pathologist?"

Memory loss? Half your brain is gone, he thought. Just talk, Josh. You need to get through this by talking to it and then the hallucination will go away. Talk to her as if she is really talking to you. Then you can regain your sanity when you realize how silly all of this is. Just get it out.

"No. I'm a diener," he replied.

"What the hell is a diener?"

"A morgue worker responsible for handling, moving, dissecting and cleaning the corpse. The word comes from the German word Leichendiener which literally means morgue servant."

"Oh, that's just fucking wonderful. You don't even know what to look for. I was poisoned and no one will ever know because I am being taken apart by the fucking morgue's hired help."

"If I were you, I wouldn't be trying to piss off someone who is standing over you with saws and scalpels while you lay there on a cold steel table."

"Good point."

Joshua nodded his head and shrugged his shoulders at her comment.

"I'm really thirsty. Can you give me some water?"

What the hell, Joshua thought. He filled a styrofoam cup with some cold water and walked over and held up what remained of her head. She opened her mouth to drink the water but most of it fell out of a hole in her cheek.

"I guess I need to drink really fast. Can I have some more?"

"Sure," Joshua replied. He refilled the cup and poured the water down her mouth.

She struggled to swallow but got a lot more down this time and she smiled up at him. "Thanks."

"No problem. And by the way," he said, "Unless he gave you a ton of potassium that would show up in your organs, there would be no way to tell. The blood in your body starts hemolyzing as you die. It would be high in potassium because of the hemolyzed blood."

"But what about blood I had drawn a week ago? Could you compare that to my blood now?"

"No. As I said, the potassium in your blood now is not a true representation of its real value."

"Fucking asshole," she said.

"I couldn't agree more," he replied.

"Why?"

"Oh, I wasn't talking about your husband. I was thinking of the person who put this idea of a talking corpse in my head. Shit, what am I doing? I am trying to explain myself to a corpse. A dead body with half a head. Fuck this!" he said as he turned around and opened the large metal door.

"Where are you going?"

"Outside to have a cigarette. I'm hoping that something that looks familiar, smells familiar and tastes familiar will help me regain my sanity, which appears to have gone missing due to lack of sleep."

He opened the door and took off his gloves as he pressed the foot lever on the trashcan and threw them into the red biohazard bag. He walked over to a tree on the edge of the campus and lit up a cigarette. The familiarity of the cigarette made him feel better but he wondered how he was going to be able to do an autopsy on someone who was talking to him.

"This is really fucked," he muttered as he finished one cigarette and lit up another. The woman on the table looked familiar for some reason. He had seen her before but he couldn't remember where. It's just your fucking mind playing tricks with you he told himself. The corpse is talking to you so you think of it as a real person. You need to pull it together before you go back in there, Joshua.

He took several more puffs on the cigarette and watched the smoke float up into the trees and that image and the nicotine calmed him. He walked back into the morgue and once again put on his gloves.

"Have you wondered why morgues have such large metal doors? Are they trying to keep people out or things inside? I mean, let's consider what's in here. Dead bodies and body parts. God forbid the hospital burned down but everything in the morgue remained intact," she said.

He ignored her. He told himself that he would not hear anything else as he began preparing for the autopsy. This was just an auditory hallucination brought on by lack of sleep. He would probably hear her scream when he started cutting through her but he just needed to do his job. He picked up the Stryker saw to open her chest cavity and looked down at the body.

"I wonder if it's a state law or something," she continued.

"I am not listening to you," he said as he turned on the saw.

"What do you plan to do with that saw?"

He didn't say anything as he looked at her chest.

"Hey bud, eye up here," she said and when she did, he started to laugh.

Something triggered his memory when she smiled at him. That smile. Even on that head, he told himself, I know that smile.

"By the way, these breasts are real. Not the $10,000-for-two special at the plastic surgeon. These are the real thing."

He dropped the saw and stumbled backward toward the steel door of the morgue.

"You know, you never told me your name. You know mine by the toe tag. So, what's yours? I should at least know that before you start cutting me up."

"Your name is Kate, right?" he asked as his voice trembled.

"No," she replied. "My name is Karen, Karen Evans."

Joshua felt the cold steel of the door through his clothes as he fell against it. It felt like icicles were forming on his back and his body began to tremble. He bent down and tried to take off his shoe covers but his hands were shaking too much. He looked back up at the woman on the table and his eyes allowed him to see who she was for the first time.

"My name is Joshua. Joshua Adams. I know why you had a blood test a week ago. You were checking to see if you were pregnant. You were checking to see if you and I were going to have a baby."

Tears rolled down her cheeks. She knew who he was now. He had just visited her a few nights ago in the ICU. His brain had been trying to protect him from the truth but it couldn't anymore. The doctor, her husband that she spoke about. The one that she said killed her. He was his boss; the pathologist. He had changed the toe tag. He knew about their affair.

He couldn't say anything else as he opened the steel door and stumbled outside. He found his car and started driving, unsure where he was going. The lights of the cars and stoplights didn't seem real. He wasn't even sure if he was driving. He was unable to feel his body or the steering wheel.

He saw the orange cones but he couldn't stop the car from running over them. He saw the men jumping out of his way as his foot pressed on the accelerator. He hit several orange barrels before his car went over the side of the bridge. The same bridge they were trying to repair from the last time a car went over it. He felt the car hit the ground and his body flying through the windshield and the glass cutting into his head and face until he didn't feel anything else.

Dr. Evans was the last person to leave the wake that was held for Lyndsay's husband. He wanted to speak about Joshua at the wake, but she wouldn't allow it. She told him it wouldn't be right even though the real reason was that she had felt very strange about everything since his death. She didn't like being alone in the house anymore and was glad she would soon be out of it. She poured herself a glass of water and another scotch for him before they sat down on the couch.

"They didn't find any excess potassium in her blood. She died due to trauma. Her heart just gave out," he said, sipping his scotch. "And by the way, the acid idea was pure genius. And priming its effect by suggesting that one of the dead bodies might start talking to him before he went to work that morning when he was so tired. Absolute genius. With the lack of sleep and then the LSD, he really didn't have a chance, did he?"

"No, probably not," she replied. "But him crashing into the same place where your wife drove her car off the bridge. Don't you think that was a little weird?"

"He was probably drawn to it by his subconscious mind. It was very possible that was the only part of his mind that had any control at that point."

"I suppose so." She reached over to grab her purse and a small white envelope fell out. The glass of water dropped from her hand.

"What's wrong?" he asked.

She opened the envelope and looked up at him.

"The LSD. It's still here," she whispered. The envelope floated to the floor and she began to hear her dead husband's voice telling her that he knew what they had done.

"No!" she screamed as she heard the matter-of-fact and familiar voice of Rod Serling talking to her about another dimension. She covered her ears as she heard the chilling theme 'na-na-na-na; na-na-na-na' over and over in her head but she couldn't block out the music or Mr. Serling's voice. The voice that welcomed her through a portal to a very unique and very real world, where she could spend an eternity screaming and trying to leave, only to realize she never would.

State Street

The street was aptly named. On one side was Virginia. On the other was Tennessee. People that visited took pictures standing in the middle of the street all the time. It was always easy for the locals to pick out the visitors to the town.

The town was situated in East Tennessee and was surrounded by beauty from lakes, rivers, and mountains, but the town was known for four things. Three of them - the NASCAR speedway, the Rhythm and Roots music festival, and the downtown area that was split down the middle by two states - the townspeople were happy to talk about. One of them, they never wanted to mention. Some people would go as far as to lie about it saying they had no idea about what they were being asked. But everyone who lived there knew about it.

It was called the East Tennessee Regional Medical Center and from its name, it sounded just like any other hospital. But the name concealed its true mission. Not many people went to East Tennessee Regional Medical Center to get well. Most people went there because it was the only place they could live. Some of them, due to misaligned DNA or the presence of additional chromosomes, were content to live there. Some of them, due to their heinous crimes and inability to control their gruesome desires, were placed there against their will for the rest of their life. And some of them lived there because their brains heard or saw things which no one else did.

It was the last group that sometimes found the help they needed and were released back into society to function like everyone else. To achieve that freedom, however, they had to accept that they were not like everyone else. It seemed counterintuitive to success but it was necessary. The released patients were required to check back in with a mental health professional on a frequent basis to verify that they had not become a threat to themselves or to society again. Sometimes those mental health professionals made an error in judgment. The town believed Bassett Reginald Reynolds was one of those errors.

With a name like Bassett Reginald Reynolds, you would think that his family had a lot of money. The name just sounded like someone who had everything money could buy and if you thought that, you would be right. His friends called him Hounddog because of his first name and his proclivity for spending his parents' money. Those that say money can't buy friends are wrong. Hounddog had lots of them because he paid for everything when they were with him.

To say that money can't buy real friendship is true though, because as Hounddog got older, his reckless and uncontrolled behavior increased and those around him shared in the blame. At first, it was a non-issue, because whatever trouble was realized, money paid for it to go away. But eventually, the disobedience of a juvenile became the crimes of a young man and he was accused of killing a man in an alley after he had been drinking and smoking PCP all night.

When the police came to pick him up at his parents' house the next morning, he first told them he didn't do it and that he couldn't remember anything that happened the night before. But when they asked about the blood on his clothes, he remembered. He told them the "shadow woman" instructed him to kill the man and if he did so, he would be protected for the rest of his life. So, he followed her instructions. Everyone knew what he was saying was delusional, but Bassett believed that the shadow woman saved his life that night.

He didn't tell anyone that the shadow woman spoke to him in a language he had never heard of before. She said it was an ancient language that very few people still remembered; one that was primitive and mythological in nature. When he asked why he could understand it, she answered that it was because she had been drawn to him and wanted to share with him what others had shunned or had spoken of only in frightened whispers. Hearing that, he knew with certainty that she was the woman he would be with for the rest of his life.

At the trial, as soon as he declared that the "shadow woman had told him to kill the man," the family money and influence could only protect their son so much. That and the fact that the man who was killed had a criminal background. He was a serial rapist, and Bassett's attorneys tried to spin the story that Bassett had done the town a favor. But Bassett's insistence that the shadow woman had told him to do it, and the fact that he cut off his victim's head, could not be overcome. Though the verdict kept him out of prison, it required him to become an inpatient at the East Tennessee Regional Medical Center.

Bassett went through numerous rehabilitation classes at the hospital and had many mental health professionals helping him try and find his way back from the dark places in his mind. They helped him realize that the shadow woman didn't really exist and was just a product of his mind and the drugs he had ingested that evening. After several years of sobriety and an admission of his guilt and remorse for what he had done, Bassett Reginald Reynolds was released back into society.

Bassett was a changed person when he returned home and his family encouraged him to go away to college to make a fresh start. He was wary of that idea because he feared falling back into old habits if he was on his own. His parents realized that might be true and suggested attending the community college in town. That seemed like a good compromise to Bassett, and so he applied, and his parent's money and influence once again came to his aid and obscured the unfortunate past of their son, such that, his application was accepted.

Bassett thrived in community college. He became a good student and people could see that he was trying to straighten up his life. In his second year of college, he met a girl named Patricia Jean Smith and without a doubt, everyone who knew him would say she was the best thing that could have ever happened to him. But those who met Patricia Jean Smith didn't see the real person beneath her beauty and charm. Her face was a mirror image of the shadowy figure who had spoken to Bassett in an alley almost three and a half years ago. And as she said then, Bassett knew she was there to protect him.

His parents loved seeing him with Patti, the name that she preferred. Patti called Bassett, "Reggie," and they did everything together. Patti loved being outdoors and she and Reggie took advantage of the mountains and rivers that surrounded them. They hiked, kayaked, camped, and went on white water trips as often as they could and neither one of them could have been happier.

Even the health care professionals who met with Bassett could see the enthusiasm he had for life now. They wrote in their notes, "there is a redemptive spirit about him that emanates like an aura around his body" and they were quite pleased with their success. After his appointments with them each month, he always heard, "keep up the good work" as he walked out the door and it made him laugh. It didn't matter to him what they said. He knew he was safe now because of Patti.

Patti's favorite holiday was Halloween. She loved visiting haunted houses and looking for ghosts and wanted Reggie to go on a haunted ghost tour in downtown to celebrate the holiday. Bassett was concerned that the tour might make a stop at the alley where he had killed the man and he wasn't sure he could handle that in such a public manner. He mentioned his concerns to his parents and his therapists, but they viewed the fact that he was bothered by it as a positive change and convinced him that he could manage anything that occurred that night. So, he agreed and booked them the haunted trolley tour for Halloween night.

Most people on the tour that evening were in costume and Patti looked at Reggie and said next time they would need to dress up. He nodded his head and laughed, trying to hide his nervousness about what they might encounter. Once everyone was aboard the trolley, the guide introduced herself and the driver and announced that the tour they were about to embark on would be "Spooktacular!" Instead of groaning at the stale joke, everyone on the trolley cheered, excited to venture into the haunted parts of town on "All Hallows Eve," as the guide referred to the night.

They drove around town and stopped every few minutes while the guide talked about the old buildings and the paranormal activity associated with them. At each stop, the guide would shine a flashlight on some aspect of the building and tell them about what supposedly happened there, denoting whether a paranormal scientist had actually verified the claim.

The guide described elevators going up and down in buildings that had no electricity; and an old newspaper building where the typewriters would start typing without anyone in front of them. She showed them an old schoolhouse that was built in 1886 for the poor by a wealthy industrialist. The crypt that housed his remains was located at the front of the building, just as you opened the front doors. She said he still walked the halls of the long-since abandoned schoolhouse and many people told stories of hearing his footsteps.

The tour then stopped at the entrance to the alley. Patti could tell something was suddenly wrong with Reggie. The hand she was holding turned ice cold and there was no color in his face. She shook his arm several times and called his name but got no response until the trolley headed to the next site. As soon as they left the alley, the color returned to his face and she felt the warmth return to his hand and he smiled at her.

"What happened back there? Did you see a ghost?"

"I did," he said.

"Really?" she asked in an enthusiastic manner. "What did it look like?"

"Just a shadow really."

"Damn," she said as he put her arm around his. "I wish I had seen it too."

He didn't reply to her comment. He just stared out the window as they drove to State Street where the trolley pulled off the road and stopped. The guide told them they were now at what was known as the "haunted pillar," a lone concrete structure that had once been part of a cotton storehouse where slaves worked. She said that a Quaker priest came to town in the early 1800s and witnessed slaves being chained to that pillar and then whipped. He told the slave owners that if those cruel actions did not cease, the building would be destroyed and everything in it would be cursed.

The slave owners dismissed the preacher's warnings and told him to leave town and so he did. The very next day, a tornado came through the town and destroyed several buildings, including the old cotton storehouse. The guide even gave the date of the tornado and encouraged the trolley riders to look it up on their cell phones to verify the story. When they found the reference and saw what she was saying was true, they were even more inclined to believe what she said next.

"Everything in the area was destroyed in the tornado," the guide began. "Everything except the pillar, which remains standing today." The guide added, "But the pillar was cursed and legend has it that any person who touches it will suffer ill fortune." She then invited anyone who wanted to challenge that legend to do so. The driver opened the doors, upon that cue, as everyone got out and walked over to the pillar. They all looked at it, though no one attempted to touch it.

Patti grabbed Reggie's arm and together they walked toward the pillar. "What do you think?" she asked. "Are you brave enough to touch it?"

"I don't think that's a good idea," he replied. "You of all people should know better than that."

Patti looked at Reggie in an odd manner. "Why should I know that?"

He leaned over and whispered into her ear, "Because you promised to protect me."

Patti looked at Reggie and nodded her head. "Yes, I know," she said as she leaned over and touched the pillar.

At her touch, everyone cheered and yelled. Patti ran around and raised her arms as if she had just won a race. Another man who had been sitting quietly at the back of the bus walked over and also touched the pillar. Again everyone yelled and cheered. The man looked at Patti and Reggie and smiled. Reggie thought he saw something familiar as he looked into his eyes. It scared him and he told Patti that they needed to get back on the bus.

Reggie was frightened but Patti told him that he had nothing to worry about and though he wanted to believe that, it was difficult for him to do so.

Reggie didn't hear anything else the guide said for the rest of the tour, as he kept looking back at the man who had also touched the pillar. Every time he glanced back, the man was looking out the window but Reggie sensed that as soon as he turned back around, the man would be staring at him and Patti.

After the tour ended, Patti suggested that Reggie come back to her house and she would surprise him with some special Halloween treats. When she whispered in his ear what that meant, he couldn't say no. Several days later, Bassett Reginald Reynolds was sent to the East Tennessee Regional Medical Center for the rest of his life. After the coroner released her body a week later, family and friends mourned the death of Patricia Jean Smith.

It didn't take Jim Donner long to find a job or a place to stay when he moved to that town in East Tennessee. His roommate kidded him about working at the "nut house" but Jim had heard all of that before and it didn't bother him.

"Have you seen him yet?" his roommate asked Jim.

"Who are you talking about?"

"Him. Reggie the Ripper. He cut off the head of a man in an alley and then did the same to his girlfriend. They say they found her head in his bed the next morning like that scene from "The Godfather." Only this wasn't a horse's head, it was his girlfriend's. They say if you stand just outside the hospital gate, you can hear him yelling in torment every Halloween as he is reminded of what he did. And this is Halloween night, dude. Believe me, a bunch of us are going over there at midnight and see if we can hear him."

"You're wasting your time. And no, I haven't seen him. He's in a special locked down unit that I don't have access to yet. Still have to undergo some more training. But what you're saying he did or does now every Halloween, I'm sure is not really true."

"Well, you and I, my friend, should be able to find out tonight. Don't you work an all-nighter?"

"Yep."

"Well, I guess we'll see then, won't we?"

When Jim got to work that evening, he was paired with a new trainer. She introduced herself as Tricia and told him that she had been working at another facility in Georgia for several years and was transferred to this one due to family circumstances. "You ever worked in a psych hospital on Halloween night with a full moon?" she asked him.

He shook his head no.

"Well, there's something about the full moon that makes a lot of the bad ones very agitated and the fact that this is Halloween, well, I'm afraid it might get real loud tonight. I promise you, we won't be bored this evening."

"That's fine with me," Jim replied.

"Well, let's get started doing our checks," she said. They went through the ward helping clean up those that needed it and overseeing recreational activities throughout the evening. It was near midnight by the time they helped everyone to bed.

"You haven't been in the locked ward yet have you, Jim?" Tricia asked.

"No."

"Well, tonight is your lucky night!"

She led him to the elevator and gave him directions to not do anything that she didn't tell him to do and he told her he understood. He noticed she wasn't wearing a Taser and asked her about it.

"No, I don't wear one," she replied. "I know some of the other supervisors do, but I've realized that I don't need it. Just remain calm, alert, and don't do stupid things, and you will be fine."

"Good to know," Jim replied as the elevator doors opened and they got in.

She put her key in the elevator plate, pushed "six" and the doors closed. When they reached the sixth floor, she moved her key to the locking mechanism for the elevator and they entered the locked ward.

Walking down the hall, they looked into the windows of the rooms and checked on the patients. Many of them were pacing in their rooms and several came charging toward the doors at them, banging on the windows. But Jim noticed that each one of them calmed down and went back to their beds as Tricia whispered to them through their windows.

"What are you saying to them?" he asked.

"Just telling them that they have nothing to worry about and to rest."

They continued to walk down the hall and soon came to the room where Bassett Reginald Reynolds resided. As Jim looked into the window, he recognized him and smiled to himself.

"You know who that is?" Tricia asked.

Jim shook his head no.

"That's Reggie the Ripper. Decapitated a man in an alley and people say they found his girlfriend's head in his bed. Seems kind of harmless now, doesn't he?"

Jim glanced at Tricia and smiled as if he agreed with what she was saying.

"What they say about him isn't true though," she said. "His girlfriend's head wasn't found in his bed the next morning. It was in the toilet and her headless body was in the bathtub. He fell into a ball on the floor after he went in there to use the bathroom and lifted the toilet lid. During the trial, he could only repeat the words "shadow woman" as if he was talking about some ghost. They said he was mad as a hatter and should have never been released back into society. Hospital caught a lot of shit for that. Do you believe in ghosts, Jim?"

"No. But I do believe in revenge," he replied as he grabbed Tricia by the throat and began choking her. "And I know about the head in the toilet. I was the one who put it there," he said as a smug smile formed upon his face.

She coughed as her face turned red and he tightened his grip around her neck like a python. He watched Reggie beating his hands against the window and smiled when he could tell she was no longer breathing. His smile widened when he let go of Tricia's neck and Reggie screamed when he saw her body disappear as it hit the floor. Jim grabbed the keys from her waist and opened Reggie's door. Reggie stumbled back to his bed, muttering words that Jim didn't understand.

"That was my brother you killed in the alley, you piece of shit, and we were very close. Both of us were born with rattlesnake blood in our veins, I reckon, cause when you try and corner one of us, or try and hurt one of us, you usually end up dead. I still don't know for sure how you got the best of my brother. He must have been real drunk for you to have done what you did to him, but you are going to pay now. I been waiting two years to get to you," Jim said as he stood there just inside the room.

"You shouldn't have touched the pillar that evening, Jim," he heard someone behind him say. When he turned around, Tricia was standing in the doorway. She looked different though and then he recognized her. He now saw the face of Reggie's girlfriend; the one he murdered that night two years ago. The face that stared up at him from the toilet.

"The pillar is a portal, Jim. One that awakens those within the shadow realm. The people who live inside these walls know all about the shadow people. Some of them are tormented by us, and some of them are protected by us. It's strange, isn't it? How those that are deemed crazy are the ones that can actually see the truth?" Tricia asked.

"What fucking truth, you stupid bitch? I killed you twice and I'll kill you a third time along with this crazy-ass mother-fucker."

"You're not the brightest bulb in the pack are you, Jim? Not to diminish my own presence mind you, but to think you passed a background check is horrifying. You are having a conversation with a person that you said you have killed twice, but yet, she is standing here talking to you. Your brother was killed in the alley that night because he touched the pillar too and then tried to kill Reggie. I came to his aid and showed him how to send someone like your brother straight to Hell. I plan to do the same thing tonight with you. I promised Reggie long ago that he would always be protected and he will be. I visit him often in here. And we always have a celebration on Halloween. Tonight will be even more special."

Before Jim could move toward the woman standing in the doorway he felt something cold against his neck. He reached out his arms toward her and felt himself falling forward. For a few seconds, his head and his body moved in tandem as they fell downward. The last thing he saw was his outstretched arms on the white tile that was disappearing from the blood that gushed forward from his neck.

There was an investigation into the death of Jim Donner and though the hospital tried to keep it out of the newspaper, they were not successful. The paper told a sordid story of how Jim Donner had obtained a job as a mental health technician in the hospital with the sole intention of killing Reggie the Ripper in retaliation for killing his brother in the alley. They never learned that Jim was the man who killed Patti, but that was because neither Reggie nor Tricia wanted that known.

Patti's brief existence in this world was Reggie's gift for doing what was asked of him years ago in that alley. Though he didn't know it, Patti touched the pillar that night to save his life, because she was aware of Jim Donner. She saw him that night on the trolley too, but she didn't want Reggie to worry. She knew what would happen but she wasn't concerned with the physical vessel which she inhabited temporarily because over time it wouldn't matter. Within the walls of the East Tennessee Regional Medical Center, she knew the one she swore to protect would be safe and would always be with the shadow woman that he had loved.

Eventually, the "Spooktacular All Hallows Eve" trolley tour added the hospital as one of their stops. The tour became even more popular as it told the story of the brothers, Mike and Jim Donner. The guide always made a point to tell everyone that it was believed that both of them had dared to touch the haunted pillar and because of that, both died a gruesome death. The paranormal scientists that visited that pillar many times backed up that belief.

The guide also talked about Bassett Reginald Reynolds and his girlfriend Patricia Jean Smith. The guide was right when she said Patti, as she liked to be called, touched the pillar and was killed in a horrible manner, but she was always wrong when she told those on the tour who killed her. It was a trivial fact in the mind of Reggie. The fact that his girlfriend could walk through the halls unseen by those who worked there was more significant and always amazed him.

Holston Avenue

The trees were on fire this morning. He sat and imagined he could feel the heat from the radiant, multi-colored leaves reaching out onto his porch, even though he knew it was only the sun. Nevertheless, he still smiled. The flaming reds, oranges, and yellows of the leaves were as vivid on the trees in his yard, as they were on the trees in the cemetery that was across the street. The trees that captured his entire field of vision reminded him of a color wheel for a paint store. Sherwin Williams was good but still an amateur, he thought as he noted the variations of the leave's colors on nature's palate. Yellow, faded into gold or orange, which turned into peach or apricot. Red was transformed into crimson or maroon, or sometimes absorbed by the yellows to create a pink or coral. The shades and hues seemed endless and the evergreens even took on various shades of green as if they knew they would be overlooked if they didn't, by all the color that saturated the air around them.

He loved fall more than any other season. Over time, he began to understand why. He disliked spring because he was drafted then to go fight a war in a place that he had never heard of; a place where the spring rains resulted in torrential downpours that went on for days. He hated summer because it reminded him of the heat in that jungle and the memories of sweat that permeated every part of his body. Sweat that never went away and caused things to rot. He resented winter because there was no winter over there and now winter reminded him of all the holidays he had missed. Yes, he now understood why he loved and looked forward to the fall season. In fact, fall was the only time he went outside these days.

He couldn't do things for himself anymore. When he turned sixty-eight, he was diagnosed with ALS. Just like that country he hadn't known anything about, he wasn't aware of what ALS was either. Even when they gave it the name of a sports hero, it still meant nothing to him. Only when they sat him down and explained what would happen as the disease progressed did he understand what the letters ALS meant.

He was seventy now and confined to a wheelchair. Any part of his body that required a muscle to act, was no longer functioning. He couldn't move. He couldn't talk. He couldn't even blink. But he could still see and he could still think and he told himself that he wouldn't allow this monster to destroy his will. He had already gone through a battle of wills with several other demons in the jungle that had tried to destroy him and he had overcome each one of them. He would be god-damned if he would allow this fucking three-letter disease to do him in.

That's why he loved sitting there in his wheelchair on the porch. The cool weather and the colors of the world at that point in time reminded him that there was a reason for living. There was still beauty in a world where beauty didn't exist for him for a very long time. The nurse who now cared for him seemed to understand that. She sat on the porch with him and talked about her life and how beautiful the trees looked. He liked listening to her talk about both.

He had his breakfast, lunch, and dinner out there on the back porch during the fall even though the only way he recognized it was meal time was when he saw the nurse put the liquid into his feeding tube. At first, he missed tasting food, but over time he remembered some of the things he had to eat in the jungle and he convinced himself he wasn't missing anything. For the moment, he still had control of his mind and eyesight and every day he had to remind himself, that neither the jungle nor the three-letter disease would ever take those away from him.

The nurse's name was Robin. Considering the last two nurses that the VA had sent over, he would describe her as a "keeper." He always found the use of that word very interesting. It was used by fisherman to refer to fish and by people to describe the man or woman they were trying to catch. And in the fish's case, the hook was real and not just a hypothetical piece of metal with a sharp barb on the end of it. He knew women didn't like to be compared to a fish but they usually didn't mind the "keeper" reference. Perhaps not Steven Hawking type of material but still something to contemplate he told himself. And though he couldn't demonstrate it, he was laughing at the thought of it and the reference to Hawking. He believed he would have found that funny, coming from an ALS "brother from another mother."

Robin treated him like a real person. His past two nurses were either immersed in their phone or a book all day and did the bare minimum to be considered nursing care. They acted as though he couldn't hear them so they didn't bother to even try talking to him. They did describe to him what they were doing, such as feeding him or changing his catheter, but that was it. Robin wasn't like that. She talked to him as just another person and somehow they were able to carry on a conversation.

She was a no-nonsense type and he liked that about her. The first day they met, she said that she would never lie to him or try to spin things in a manner that sounded more pleasant. She had taken this job because she was a nurse who had a lot of experience with death. She told him she wasn't a hospice nurse and that she would try and keep him alive as long as she could, but the end was coming. It was not said in an uncaring manner. She said it as if he understood that was the truth. And he did.

He knew she was telling him these things so that he wouldn't be scared as things got worse. The words were helpful, direct, sincere, and empathetic. He couldn't ask for any more than that. He appreciated what she told him because he recognized that what she was talking about was beginning to happen. His body had begun to tell him the same things. He realized that this would be his last fall and he was glad that Robin was the one who would spend it with him.

He also liked the fact that Robin smoked. Neither his doctors or her supervisors would have approved, but she still placed the cigarette in his mouth and let him inhale as much as his lungs would allow. It had tasted good in the jungle and it still tasted good now. The three-letter monster wasn't able to take that away from him, yet. Smoking after a meal had been a long-time routine for him and it helped him believe for a moment that his life was still normal.

"So, I guess with a name like Abel, your parents were Bible thumpers?" she asked. She sat down across from him and began to eat her breakfast.

He wanted to smile and tell her that his father was a preacher and his mother was the choir director in their church, but he couldn't. It didn't seem to matter as Robin somehow could sense what he was going to say.

"I knew it," she said, as she took a bite of her chicken biscuit and drank her coffee. "Mine were too for a while. Up until I was about ten. I really enjoyed going to church with them, but then everything changed. When my mother started seeing things, my father did too. She saw things in people's palms, tarot cards, tea leaves, and auras. My father saw things in people's wallets. Green bills. They made a good living off of my mother's 'gift' as they would say. My mom still does. It helps supplement her social security money. But my father is dead. Died of alcoholism."

Abel knew many soldiers who struggled with alcohol. He never did. He preferred more exotic ways to forget and there were many different paths over there in the jungle to achieve that goal.

"Yep, found in bed with an alcoholic's wife and the drunken son of a bitch shot him straight between the eyes."

Abel laughed so hard it made him pee. "I can tell you're laughing. Your catheter is telling me so," Robin said as she smiled.

Abel didn't believe that about the catheter but it didn't matter. She was right. He was laughing.

"Anyway, they made enough money to send me to nursing school, so I can't complain too much. But, you know, when I became a nurse, my relationship with the church waned. I couldn't tell you what caused that. Don't get me wrong. I still believe in God. I see evidence of his work every day. But I don't know. I just didn't feel that the church did anything for me anymore."

He felt the same way after he got back from the jungle. He believed God had a role in helping him survive, but he lost something over there that he never got back. Just like Robin, the church didn't do anything for him anymore. Especially now. He didn't want a bunch of people looking at him, telling him how much they cared about him. Their words may or may not have been genuine but it didn't matter to him. He didn't want to be in that environment.

"And before you ask, no, I don't have the 'gift' like my mom. I am not a 'seer' as she calls herself. Not sure I believe in them. My mother doesn't do anything but tell people what they already know or want to know. She is very good at reading people by the look in their eyes or on their faces. She can tell when they're anxious or worried about someone or something in their life. Or that they just need a person to vent to and hear words that replace their anger with hope. She is good at that. I guess you could call my mother a human placebo. Because when it comes right down to it, if you believe in the untruth, then whatever you say has an opportunity to become the truth."

Abel wanted to tell her that she was more like her mother than she knew but he couldn't. At least he didn't think he could.

"Something is telling me you believe I do have the 'gift,'" she said as she raised her eyebrows and stared into his face.

Yes, you do, Abel said as loud as he could. The soundless words of his voice tried to escape his lips, only to break apart against his teeth into tiny fragments that dissolved within his mouth like tasteless tictacs.

"Okay, I guess you do make a good point," she said as if she heard him reply. "I am good at reading people. It has helped me a lot in my nursing job.

I've been told more times than once that I can tell what someone is about to say before they even say it. So, okay. I'll give you that one."

Amazing, Abel thought. He could sit out here on the porch all day with Robin. Others in the same wheelchair might be cursing their life right now, but he wasn't about to. The scenery and the conversation with the person who was sitting just a few feet from him was something he might have missed if he hadn't become ill. So, *"Fuck you ALS!"* he screamed again in silence.

"From what I can tell, you have lived here a long time, haven't you?"

The blank stare of his face tried to say yes, but nothing happened.

"And there was no Mrs. Dorset, was there?"

Again, the blank stare agreed.

"Believe me, It doesn't take a rocket scientist to figure any of that out," she said. "Your house has nothing that says a woman has lived in it. No pictures. No little doo-dads on the wall or in the kitchen. Nothing commemorating a special day or anniversary. If there was one that you may have loved and lost for whatever reason, there's always something, somewhere in the house, that remains of them, once you have established that level of intimacy. And for whatever reason, you can't hide it. It's impossible to put away. I don't know why that happens but it does. And there isn't a thing in this house of yours that suggests that happened. I am sorry about that, Abel. You appear to be a good man and I don't know why that didn't happen for you."

It's happening now, Abel replied. Every muscle in his body tried to convey that to her and for a moment, he thought he saw her face redden but it went away as fast as it appeared. It was just the sunlight and its reflection off the color of the trees he told himself. Regardless, he wished he could make her understand that she was becoming that special woman in his life and would be the one she had just described.

"Your house and your neighbor's house are the only two homes on this side of the street. Once that new church gets built this part of the street will be a parking lot. I wonder if that's the church or God telling you something."

He wanted to laugh and though he couldn't, she could see something in his eyes that told her he was. "Find that funny, do you? I sure hope they keep the trees in your yard even though I bet they don't. But if they were smart, they would. They are so big and beautiful at this time of the year. I know they've been here a long time."

Probably close to a hundred years, he thought. He had bought the small house in the early 1970s after returning from the war, and they were already big then. The house was built in the 50s and he had done all the upgrades in the house himself. He refinished all the floors, knocked out some walls and opened up the great room and kitchen. Updated both bathrooms and put in bigger closets in both bedrooms. Put in a new ceramic tile kitchen with granite countertops and new appliances, and painted every room in the house. What was a nice house, he believed he had made into a great house. When he had moved into it, he said it would be the house where he died. Though he had doubts about that when he said it, all doubt had been removed now.

Unlike most people, he didn't mind living across the road from a cemetery. He liked the peaceful nature of it and what it represented. So many of his friends in the jungle never found a quiet place to rest. There was very little evidence that they ever existed except in the memories of their family. They died in that God-awful jungle and it made him sad to think about it. He tried to imagine those soldiers were over in the cemetery across from him. On certain nights, he believed he could see them out there - resting against the trees, smoking a cigarette. Only this time, not having to worry that the orange flame on the end of the cigarette was a target for a sniper.

The neighbor that Robin had referred to, Steve, had also been in the jungle and made it back home too. Even though they shared a common bond, Abel knew deep down, they were very different. The bitterness in his neighbor's soul never left and he remained angry at the world.

Abel and Steve were very friendly at first. They drank beer and listened to music together. They even got high together. But his friend wanted to relive all the battles he had fought in the jungle once he was drunk or high, and Abel didn't want to hear any of the gory details that he seemed to delight in describing. Steve and others like him wore the body parts of the enemy around their neck and he could understand why they did so. They believed it was necessary in order to survive the hellish environment in which they had been placed. But he abhorred the practice and he disliked Steve for doing it, and even more so, for seeming to gloat about it.

The problem with soldiers like Steve was that they didn't understand what they were doing wasn't going to help America win the war; it would only ensure that the war would go on forever. Unless you were willing to commit genocide and wipe out the entire country, butchering the soldiers they fought against only provided their enemy with a greater will to fight.

When you peeled away everything else that was going on, it was just that simple. Something you should have learned from your parents; that two wrongs don't make a right. His father had taught him that lesson at an early age, and that along with some other words of comfort from his weekly letters, helped him survive that jungle. His guidance and his words helped Abel find a way through all of the horrors he encountered every day. They helped him fight the demons which took many forms over there and that were all around him, and at times, inside of him. With his parent's constant encouragement and words of love, he overcame every one of them before he came back home.

His parents both died five years ago. Although he missed them, he was glad they weren't around to see him in the condition he was now. While they both had great inner strength, he was afraid if they had seen him in his present condition, that strength would have been sorely tested if not lost altogether and he didn't want that for them. He already knew what that felt like and that should be enough for one family to endure, he thought.

"Well, Steve is getting it cranked up early this morning," Robin said as the sounds of Santana's "Soul Sacrifice" came blasting from his back door.

Abel didn't need to have Robin turn his wheelchair around for him to know that Steve was sitting on his back porch smoking a joint. That was how Steve started his day, every day. With a joint and loud music. Santana, The Doors, and Creedence Clearwater Revival seemed to be his favorites. He wanted to ask Robin if he was drinking a beer too, but he didn't have to wait on that answer.

"Shit, not even 10 a.m. and he is already drinking a cold tall one," Robin said as she returned Steve's wave.

Abel saw Robin waving and he knew Steve would be walking over to his porch soon. Though he pretended to come over to check on him, Abel knew he was only coming over to try and get to know Robin. He didn't care anything about him anymore. He was just someone who lived next door that Steve once got high or drunk with, but that was okay. Abel wouldn't have been his friend anyway once he got to know him.

It did piss Abel off though to see Steve killing himself with drugs and alcohol when he had an otherwise healthy body. For a moment, he would feel sorry for himself but then his anger and determination to not let the monster win would overtake whatever he was thinking and he would just look at Steve and feel sorry for him. Though not sorry enough not to yell *"Fuck off you drunk bastard"* in his expressionless manner each time he came over. It made him laugh and feel better about himself. Each time he did that, he moved his eyes a millimeter and he could tell that Robin somehow knew what he was screaming. It had to be that gift she inherited from her mother, he told himself, and then he laughed some more.

After about an hour and several more beers and another joint, Steve strolled over through their backyards and walked up onto Abel's porch. "What's up my man?" he asked as he bent down and looked into Abel's eyes.

You piece of shit. Don't pretend to pay attention to me so that Robin thinks you care. She knows better. Fuck you and get the hell off of my property. If you could only read my eyes, you sick son of a bitch.

"How's he doing this morning?" Steve asked Robin as he stood up.

"He told me he wanted to go out for a ten-mile jog in just a few minutes. You interested in joining us?" Robin asked.

Abel laughed and this time he knew Robin could see the piss in the catheter move.

"Wish I could join you but you see I don't believe in running anymore. Got no reason to run anymore, so I don't. In fact, I hate running. God damn how I hate running. Got enough of that in basic training to last a fucking lifetime. In fact, ole Abel here is lucky in that regard too. He won't have to run ever again either. Aint't that right, brother?" Steve asked and raised his hand for Abel to high-five it.

What a stupid fucking asshole, Abel thought. When he saw Robin's eyes, he could tell she was thinking the same thing.

"My bad, my bad," Steve said as he took down his hand. "Forgot. Sorry, Dude."

"What do you want, Steve?" Robin asked. "Abel and I were about to go in and do his arm and leg strengthening exercises."

Abel wanted to burst out laughing. *That was a good one. And something Steve would believe. I think I am falling in love with this woman.*

"Just being neighborly, that's all," Steve replied. "Well, when you're done with the exercises, let me know if either one of you wants to get high. I got to hand it to those slant-eyed bastards, they make some kick-ass dope."

Robin knew there was no point to try to correct Steve's derogatory language so she didn't. She just replied in a manner that she hoped would make him leave.

"I'm not sure we need to. We can almost get high smelling it from over here."

Steve laughed. "I know you give my man some smokes every now and then. So you just let me know if either of you wants to try some of this shit? Okay?"

"I don't. But I'm not sure about Abel. Why don't you ask him?"

Steve looked at Robin as if she was joking and started to laugh. But when he saw she wasn't laughing he stepped back and paused for a moment before responding. "Fucking good idea," Steve replied as he turned toward Abel and bent down in front of his wheelchair. "Want to try some of this shit, my brother?"

Quit calling me your brother, you dumbass. I don't suppose you heard me the first time. Get the fuck off my porch. And you don't need to bend down each time to talk to me. My ears are not location dependent.

"What's he saying, Robin?" Steve said as he stared into Abel's eyes.

"You really want to know?"

"I asked the fucking question, didn't I?" Steve said angrily and he turned around like he was going to hit Robin. She saw his aggressive posture and backed up, ready to defend herself. Steve realized what he was doing and smiled.

"Sorry. Sometimes things just come over me that I can't control. Some PTSD shit, the doctors say, even though the god-damn war was forty years ago. Forty fucking years ago, goddamnit and I am still paying for it. But anyway, I'm sorry if I scared you. I wouldn't do anything to hurt someone as pretty as you."

That's a fucking lie, Abel said over and over in his head. *If you can read my face Robin, read it now. He would hurt you if given a chance. It's not just PTSD. It's something inside of him that's wrong. Look at me,* Abel screamed. *Stay the fuck away from him.*

Robin didn't respond to Steve's apology. She just walked by him and stood in front of Abel and started talking. "First of all, he said quit bending down in front of his wheelchair to talk to him. It isn't necessary. He hears just fine. He doesn't need to read your lips, but considering the moustache that covers your lip, I doubt he could anyway. He said you should also try taking a shower every once in a while, and cleaning that shit out of your moustache and eliminating the body odor that sometimes overwhelms the pot smell clinging to your clothes. He then said he didn't want any pot this early in the morning. It fucks him up too much and he enjoys just looking at the trees. The color he sees with a clear mind is better than an altered one from the dope."

"He said all that, did he?" Steve asked in a sarcastic manner.

"Every word."

"Fuck. I didn't know I was living next to Shakespeare. God-damn. But that's cool. Just trying to be a good neighbor and all you know," Steve said as he turned and walked down the porch steps.

"And just so you are fully aware," Robin added as he stopped at the bottom of the steps. "You and I are never going to get together. I have a license for a concealed weapon, which I am not afraid to use, if and when I feel threatened. So be careful how you act around me in the future. Who knows, I might just go PTSD on your ass, you know?"

“Be careful, bitch,” Steve said as he formed his hand into a gun and pulled the finger trigger. “I got things wrong with me and I would be careful not to get into my head. It’s dark in there. Abel knows. He’s been there. It ain’t a place you want to be. Sometimes you can’t find your way out and you just end up dead and forgotten.” He turned and walked back to his house.

Abel was thrilled and frightened at the same time by what Robin said to Steve. He wanted to warn her that she needed to watch herself, but again, she saw what he was thinking in his face.

“Don’t worry. I’ve handled worse assholes than him in my life. Even had one as a boyfriend for a short period before I realized that I didn’t look that good with a broken nose and black eye. Imagine my face with a broken nose and a black eye. Just messes up all that natural beauty, doesn’t it?”

Abel laughed but he also wanted her to know that Steve was more dangerous than she thought. He didn’t know how he could convince her of that but he knew he needed to do something.

“Look, we’re going to go inside for about thirty minutes and make that asshole think we’re doing some exercises and then we’ll come back outside and enjoy the rest of the day. It’s supposed to get up to about seventy-three degrees this afternoon. It should be gorgeous.”

For the next half-hour, they sat inside and she told Abel about the failures of her love life. While he listened to her, Abel started to hear something else. Something he had ignored and never really heard before now. He was anxious to get back outside and just as thirty minutes passed, Robin rolled him back out onto his porch; out of the sunlight but with an unobstructed view of the trees.

“It is beautiful out here, Abel. Truly beautiful.” She sat down next to him and held his hand.

As Abel sat and looked at the trees, he heard the sounds that had always been there among the trees but had often gone unnoticed. Up until now, he had ignored them as background noise, just a part of nature. But as he listened today, it became something else. Though it couldn’t be what he thought, he really believed that the squirrels were talking to him. *Listen to yourself, Abel. Listen to what you are saying. The fucking squirrels are talking to you. This is an auditory hallucination. That’s all it can be. Your body is just sending you another sign that the end is coming. Deal with it, man.*

But no matter how much he tried to deal with it and dismiss what he was hearing, he couldn’t. The clicks and chatters sounded like a language he had been taught before. A pattern of sounds that meant something. Something he learned before he went to the jungle. A language he understood.

“Though the Master said that the humans have dominion over us, do you think it means he can do anything to us that he wants?” he heard one squirrel ask another. Abel redirected his vision upward as much as he could toward the limb of a large Maple tree and thought he saw the squirrel that was talking.

“No, I don’t,” the other one said as it scraped its feet on the bark of the tree.

“Then why doesn’t anyone do anything about this human? The one that has foul burning grass in his mouth all the time? He shoots our friends and family just for the fun of it. Not for food as the Master intended. And he tries to bury his anger in the ground where we have our food. The ground rots from his anger and destroys our food. Why doesn’t the Master do something about that?”

“I don’t know,” the other squirrel said as it looked down at Abel and scratched its stomach. “But his anger is much like the dog that catches one of us. He rips the other humans apart like the dogs do to us. I run away when I see it happening.”

When he saw the squirrel looking right at him Abel became convinced that he was losing his mind and that the end was coming very soon. He loved the idea that he could understand what the squirrels were saying, but he believed it was just another sign that he didn’t have much longer. The thought of not having much more time with the woman he had fallen in love with made him sad, and he gripped her hand as hard as he could, thinking about how much she meant to him.

Robin felt Abel’s hand move. She wondered if it was a muscle spasm at first, but as it continued to strengthen, she jerked her hand away and stood up. She saw Abel looking at her and he was blinking. “Shit,” she yelled out. “What the hell are you doing?”

Almost as soon as she asked the question, she knew the answer. Terminal lucidity. It was a phenomenon that occurred rather frequently in terminally ill patients. Right before they died, they would exhibit signs of normal behavior for a brief moment of time. Things that they couldn’t do before like move or speak, they could do now for a short period. And she was seeing it with Abel. He had gripped her hand and he was now blinking his eyes.

“What are you trying to tell me?” she asked repeatedly, and each time, he would blink his eyes. It didn’t take long before she noticed that he blinked in the same manner, in the same pattern, to her question. This isn’t random, she thought. Something about this seems familiar. “You’re trying to tell me something with those blinks, aren’t you?” Suddenly, she remembered.

"Abel, I need to leave for about an hour and then I'll be back. I'm going to leave you out here on the porch. You should be fine. It's about two now, and I will be back before three. The weather should be good. No rain. Just the sun and the trees. If you can understand me, can you blink once for me?"

Abel blinked once.

"Shit," he heard her say as she went running down the porch and jumped into her car. Within an hour she was back and had brought someone with her. She wheeled him out onto the porch and positioned him in front of Abel.

"Abel," Robin started. "This is my grandfather, Robert Graham. He was a signalman in the Navy during World War II."

"Hello, Abel," Robert said.

Abel blinked his eyes several times and Robert smiled.

"You were right, little girl. I always told your grandmother you were the smartest Graham cracker in the box. He said, "Hello Robin," in Morse code. He is using his eyes to send you a message."

Abel blinked his eyes again and said thank you to Robert.

"My pleasure, Abel. What do you want to say to my little girl?"

As Abel blinked, Robert told Robin what to write down. Within about ten minutes, they had recorded everything Abel wanted to say. Robin looked at her grandfather and nodded her head as if she was saying thank you for trying. When Abel saw that he became so angry that he was able to move his foot. He stamped it so hard on the wooden deck that his wheelchair moved.

Robin knew Abel was mad. He understood that nod to her grandfather meant she didn't believe what he was telling her. She looked at him and took a deep breath before she started to talk.

"You do realize you just told my grandfather that Steve over there is a serial killer and has been burying bodies in his back yard. And that you know that because the squirrels told you."

Abel blinked his eyes once indicating that was correct.

"Abel, squirrels can't talk to you. You aren't Dr. Doolittle and perhaps that's a bad reference considering he didn't really exist either, but I know you get my point. You're a smart man, I know that. And you know what your disease can do to you. That's what is happening now. That's all it is and I hate to be the one to tell you that, but you know I told you I would never lie to you."

Abel looked at Robert and started blinking another message to him. Robert told Robin what he was saying. "Get the Bible. Read Job, Chapter 12, verse 7-10."

Robin found the Bible and read the passage aloud, "But ask the animals, and they will teach you, or the birds in the sky and they will tell you, or speak to the earth, and it will teach you, or let the fish in the sea inform you. Which of all these does not know that the hand of the Lord has done this? In his hand is the life of every creature and the breath of all mankind."

"Of course, you of all people would be quoting from Job. But really, Abel? Squirrels? To think they are talking to you is just bat-shit crazy, don't you think?"

Abel blinked his eyes twice and then started another message to Robert. "Read Romans, Chapter 1, verse 20," he instructed.

"For since the creation of the world God's invisible qualities - his eternal power and divine nature - have been clearly seen, being understood from what has been made, so that people are without excuse."

"You are pulling out all the stops, aren't you?" Robin asked. "Your parents were more than just Bible-thumpers weren't they? Your father was a preacher, wasn't he? So regardless of what I continue to say about how crazy all of this is, you are going to just keep quoting from the Bible about what is truly possible?"

Abel blinked his eyes once.

"Okay, let's say you're right. Somehow and some way your brain heard something suggesting that Steve has bodies buried in his yard. What do you expect me to do, go over there with a shovel and just start digging around, looking for some evidence?" she asked sarcastically.

Again, Abel stamped his foot down and moved his wheelchair. This time when he blinked his eyes he was even able to move his head downward.

Robert looked up at his granddaughter and smiled. "Don't dismiss a dying man's last words, granddaughter."

"How do you know he's dying?" she asked angrily even though she knew what he was saying was true.

"Because he told me."

"Okay, Batman and Robin, say you two are right. How am I supposed to know where to dig in that two acres of a backyard he has, without him seeing me? And even worse, say I'm over there and he does see me digging around. What do you think he is going to do then? I know and you know what he will do then, Abel. He will hurt me - and you. And by hurt, I mean maybe kill both of us. I know for fucking sure, he is capable of doing that."

Robert looked at Abel and Abel blinked his response.

"Tonight, when it's dark, his friends will show you where to dig. Just dig where you see the glowing embers."

Robin stood there and pulled out a cigarette.

"Hey - I want one of those," her grandfather said as he reached up and removed the oxygen cannula from his nose.

"You have end-stage COPD and you want another cigarette? Hell, why the fuck not?" She rolled her eyes as she turned off the oxygen and gave her grandfather a cigarette. As she stood there smoking her cigarette, she thought about everything she had just heard.

"Always smoked Lucky Strikes during the war," Robert told Abel while he took a puff on the cigarette and coughed and then spit out some blood. "But these Camel filters aren't that bad."

Robin just shook her head as she watched her grandfather choke down the cigarette she had given him and tried to think. After a few drags on her cigarette, she placed the cigarette in Abel's mouth and watched him take a very deep puff as the smoke exhaled from his nose. Terminal lucidity. Should go well with my terminal lunacy she thought as she finished her smoke. She walked over to Steve's yard and looked around for several minutes before coming back to the porch.

"Okay. Let's just see if these glowing embers show up like you say they will," Robin said as she took hold of her grandfather's wheelchair. She put his cannula back in his nose and then turned his oxygen back on.

"I'm going to take him home and then I'll be back. With a shovel I suppose," Robin said as she started to wheel her grandfather away.

Before she could get off the porch, her grandfather stopped her by grabbing Abel's arm. She looked down and saw her father meet Abel's eyes. He raised his other arm and saluted Abel before he let go of his arm. She looked up at the sky, trying to control the varied emotions that circulated through her mind, and said a silent prayer as she rolled her grandfather's wheelchair back to the car. As she drove away, she said another silent prayer, hoping that nothing else happened before she returned.

She got back to Abel's house just as the sun was setting. She walked out to the porch with a shovel and just shook her head as she looked at Abel in his wheelchair. He blinked his eyes several times and she thought she saw a smile, but she knew that wasn't possible. At least she didn't think it was possible, but perhaps it was considering everything else that had happened today.

"So what now?" she asked. "We just wait?"

Abel blinked his eyes once telling her yes.

They sat there in the dark and Robin noticed it was getting a lot colder. She checked the weather app on her phone and saw that it was supposed to get below freezing during the early morning hours.

"Damn." She turned the phone toward Abel so he could see it. "Below freezing later tonight. I need to get you some blankets."

He blinked his eyes twice.

"What do you mean, no?" she asked. "You will die out here if…." and then she stopped her sentence. She turned her head so he wouldn't see her tears. She wiped away her eyes and then looked back at him.

"Though I doubt there will be any glowing signs over there in Steve's yard, if anything did happen to me when I went over to that asshole's yard, and I am not able to get back over here, you will die from exposure. But you know that don't you?"

Abel blinked his eyes once.

"Crazy-ass people with ALS. They think they control the fucking world," Robin said. She put the shovel down and pulled her chair next to him and held his hand in hers.

Abel laughed as hard as he had ever laughed. He really loved her sarcasm. Together they sat there and watched the sun go down. It soon became very dark and very cold. Robin put on her jacket and though he objected, she placed a blanket around their shoulders while they sat and waited. After almost two hours she decided that what they were doing was ridiculous and told him she was going to take him inside. Abel did not respond; he just stared. And within a few minutes, she felt his finger drag across her hand in a forward motion and she then saw three glowing embers over in Steve's yard.

"What the fuck?" She looked over at Abel but couldn't see him in the dark. She turned on her flashlight app and pointed it toward his face. He closed his eyelids and then opened them several times as if he was warning her to put the light out.

"Okay, I see them, I see them!" she whispered as she picked up her phone and called 911. "I can't believe this is really happening." She gave them Steve's address and told them of a domestic dispute and that it sounded like someone was being killed and then hung up.

She turned the light on her phone to a dim mode and held it up to Abel's face. She smiled at him and saw him blink once. She leaned over and kissed his cheek and then turned off the light. She picked up her shovel and trudged toward Steve's yard as if she were approaching a room to tell a patient they were dying. The glowing embers disappeared as she reached the yard, but she remembered where the closest one was and started to dig as quietly as possible.

She had removed quite a lot of dirt by the time she heard Creedence Clearwater Revival coming from Steve's porch. She heard John Fogerty singing about a bad moon rising and thought how fucking appropriate that was. Steve was drunk and high as usual, but he still retained the ability to sense things in the dark that he had learned in the jungle, and he knew someone was in his yard, in a place they shouldn't be. He pulled out his gun and without asking who was there, fired several times.

Both bullets hit Robin and she fell to the ground. The first went through her abdomen and the second grazed her skull and was the one that knocked her to the ground. As Steve began to walk toward Robin, he heard the sirens coming down the street and he took off running. But he was too high to realize he was running toward the police and not away from them. When he failed to drop the gun, they shot him.

Abel heard the gunshots from his back porch and knew Robin was injured. He heard the police shoot Steve and heard him cursing as they placed him in handcuffs. He could only hope the police would search Steve's house and yard for the other "imaginary person" Robin mentioned when she called 911.

His hopes were soon answered as he saw the floodlights begin moving back and forth across the yard.

Within a few minutes, they found Robin lying on the ground and saw what she had unearthed. There was a human hand in the dirt and they called for the EMTs to help Robin while they continued to look around the yard.

Abel heard the police talking about the need to rope off the crime scene that Robin had exposed. He smiled as he thought about everything Robin had done for him and what she had meant to him. He wondered if she would ever listen to squirrels in the same manner and he laughed. He would miss the fall afternoons with her.

Robin moaned and the EMTs watched her move her head and open her eyes. She realized that she was looking toward the cemetery and thought she was seeing the woods in summer with hundreds of fireflies flying around the trees. The paramedic starting her IV heard her mumble something and his partner asked him what she said. When he replied that he thought she said "mislabeled," they both agreed that didn't make sense, but that they needed to get her to the hospital fast. She was losing a lot of blood and they hung another IV and a bag of O-negative blood.

Just before Robin's medication knocked her out, she thought she saw Abel getting out of his wheelchair and walking down his porch steps over to the cemetery. She saw him waving to her and though she tried to wave back, she couldn't. The EMTs were holding her arm down as she went to sleep.

It snowed that night. Abel felt the cold flakes on his face but he didn't care. He remembered the jungle and how it had rained for two weeks straight and how he never got dry. This cold was nothing compared to that feeling of always being wet and hot and he welcomed it. His body was soon covered in snow but he didn't feel the cold anymore. The snow felt like a warm blanket wrapped around him and he looked forward to falling asleep.

When the EMTs arrived at the hospital with Robin, they learned that she was a nurse. One of them began thinking about what she had said as they were putting her on the stretcher. When he asked the other nurses about her, they said that she did home health work for the terminally ill. He suddenly realized she wasn't saying "mislabeled"; she was saying "disabled," and he called her supervisor and asked where she had been working.

The EMTs rushed to Abel's house and found his body on the back porch covered in snow. His body was still there even though Abel had left it some time ago. He had walked over to the cemetery. Upon arrival, he met a nice man who offered him a cigarette and a lighter. Abel thanked him and as he lit the cigarette he noticed the Signal Corps emblem on the lighter. It was two crossed flags with a flaming torch of gold in the middle and the initials R.G. engraved underneath. He handed the cigarette lighter back to the man and smiled as he realized that they were both smoking Lucky Strikes.

Cunningham Road

They bought their first house on October 1, 2012. It was a small brown contemporary-style house out in Sevier County, about twenty miles southeast of Knoxville, with a view of the Smoky Mountains in the distance from their front yard. There were several small farms located off the road to their house and each of them had a red barn with "See Rock City" painted on the sides. Jane and John Smith had lived in Tennessee their entire lives but neither of them had ever been to Rock City. Both of them remarked at the exact same moment as they drove by the barns that they should go there one day. They laughed and shook their head as they thought about how often they did that with each other.

Near their house, on a side road of gravel and dirt, there were abandoned trailers anchored like ships that had run aground; still standing defiantly across the road from new trailers where people now lived. Large fields with tall wheat-like grasses filled up the space between all of them and grew unchecked amidst pockets of large trees of dogwoods, redbuds, and oak.

John had driven down that road many times while watching their house being built and those fields had always made him think of Africa. It was easy to think that way because of the tall grasses that swayed back and forth with the smallest evidence of a breeze, and the fact that those fields looked like the place the narrators on NatGeo talked about when they mentioned elephant graveyards, provided you could envision that the abandoned old trucks and cars were elephants. He fully expected to see a pride of lions resting in the shade underneath one of the clumps of trees but he never did. Even with his strong imagination, it was very difficult to imagine lions when you saw two or three awkward-looking cows lying in the shade next to the remains of a rusted-out old car.

But none of that mattered to the new homeowners. They were too excited about their new home to be concerned with the other things around them that could affect their property value in the future. None of that was important now. They were too young to be concerned with the future.

They also were unaware of the neighborhood covenants that existed, as there were none in the myriad of documents that they signed at closing. But there were neighborhood covenants out there in the country where they had decided to build their home. Covenants made 175 years ago did not seem relevant in today's market and had long since been forgotten. And though irrelevant for the unaware, they were nevertheless, still in effect.

It was raining on October 21 when they moved into their house. It was a Thursday and they both took off from work to give themselves a long weekend to move everything from their apartment to the new home. It took them all day, with the help of a friend, and numerous trips with the U-Haul and their cars to get everything moved. Their anticipated six-hour day ended up being a thirteen-hour day as they did not make the last trip until 10 p.m. They were too tired to do much more than toast their work with a hamburger and a beer before their friend left to go home and they placed a sheet on the mattress and went to sleep.

The next day, they woke up and started to unpack their belongings and wondered aloud to each other, again at the same time and with the same words, why it took so long to move when they had so little furniture? They laughed and this time when day turned into night, they were done. They celebrated by grilling some steaks and toasting their feeling of achievement with a bottle of champagne.

There were no trees or shrubs or plants of any kind in their front yard. They had to convince the builder to put sod down, or they would have had a house surrounded by dirt. But he acquiesced and they had a yard and one large tree in their backyard. One beautiful large tree in their back yard. It was a Live Oak and though they didn't know its exact age, the builder told them it was at least two hundred years old and maybe even older.

Two people holding hands could not put their arms around the trunk of the tree and some of the lower limbs were also too big to realize a full embrace. The tree from top to bottom was about forty feet in height but some of its limbs were even larger. Their property was almost an acre and the tree encompassed at least half of it. In fact, that tree along with a few clumps of brown grass and small patches of wild raspberries and blackberries was their entire backyard.

They didn't have a large front porch so that they could enjoy the view of the mountains, but they did have a deck on the back of the house and they could sit and enjoy that tree throughout the year. Live Oaks in East Tennessee were not common but they were unaware of that until they moved in and noticed people driving up and down the road behind their house and stopping to take pictures of their tree.

If someone was writing a story about the couple, it would have been a simple one, but one that made people smile when reading it. They had pilgrim-like names: John and Jane Smith. Their jobs had a greater calling than being referred to as just a job. She was an elementary school teacher and he was a medical technologist working at the University Medical Center. They were realizing the American dream of owning their own land and house and in this case, on a piece of property in rural America with a pastoral view of the mountains. And then there was the tree, the enormous old Live Oak. One of a few that had survived the hard winters within a very small southern town that was usually just a bit too far north for a Live Oak to survive, must less flourish, but it had done both.

And so someone did. The small weekly newspaper, the Seymour Herald, published a story on the couple that built a house on the property where the old tree lived. Everyone in Seymour, in fact, most everyone in Sevier County and Knox County had heard of the tree, so when the article came out, it generated even more cars coming by and people taking pictures of the tree.

Neither Jane nor John was too concerned about the interest in the tree or the increased traffic that came by their house because, after about a week, it went away. "So much for our fifteen minutes of fame," she said and they both laughed.

Over the next month, John spent every weekend planting trees and shrubs in the front yard and Jane spent every weekend, making the inside of their house look like someone lived there. She wasn't sure of the exact day when she met her neighbor for the first time, but she knew John wasn't there. She was sure he wasn't there because the man frightened her and she would have felt safe knowing John was at home.

She heard someone knocking on the front door one afternoon while John was making one of his many regular trips to the Home Depot. When she opened the door, she saw a man with a Tennessee cap on his head. Though she didn't want to stare, she couldn't help herself when she saw the childlike face that smiled at her.

She knew normal adults had thirty-two teeth and she was certain that the person standing there in front of her screen door had only half that many, as it appeared there was a gap between every other tooth. But it was as if he wasn't aware that was a concern or something that people would notice because it did not deter his smile that day and she doubted if it ever did. She wondered if it might hinder his ability to eat, but after she began talking to him, she was certain that it didn't. Between sentences, she watched him gnaw on a piece of beef jerky he had in his hand.

"Morning, Miss," the man said as he reached up and tipped his hat toward her. "Name's Audie Newell. Family lived in this part of Tennessee for as long as I knowed. Probably at least 200 years. We lived down the street in a log cabin that my pa built, but he died and the family had to sell some of the land and the cabin and moved into trailers on the other part of the land that was still ours."

Jane smiled but she couldn't stop staring at the man's lack of teeth. That is until she noticed his eyes. Both eyes were brown. Hazel, if someone from an optometrist office was defining the color, but that was insignificant. What was significant was that the pupils never looked in the same direction as he talked. If one eye was looking straight at her, the other was looking left or right or up or down. Only by accident did they align themselves and only then, for a few seconds before they were again moving in opposite directions.

"Hello, Mr. Newell. My name is Jane Smith. My husband should be back any minute from Home Depot," she said nervously. She couldn't help thinking there was something strange about the man other than his teeth and eyes.

"Yes ma'am, I knowed who you were. Read that story in the paper the other day. They spoke highly of you and your husband."

Jane just kept smiling as she reached up and locked the screen door as silently and unobtrusively as she could. If Mr. Newell saw or heard her lock the door, he didn't mention it as he continued to talk.

"I reckon since you and the husband built this house and done gone and started planting shrubs and trees here in the front yard that you both plan on staying here?"

That was a strange question for him to be asking. Hurry home, John, she thought as she checked her watch. He should be driving up the road any moment now she told herself anxiously.

"Did you ever get to thinking why no one ever built here before you and your husband?"

"No. No, we didn't." Where are you going with this she asked herself? This surely can't be a floodplain. They have to declare that in the closing, I know that. Maybe the ground won't percolate she thought. But the builder assured us that the tests he did for the septic tank were good. Unless he lied.

"Bet the land was cheap, weren't it?"

"Yes," Jane replied. "We thought we got a good deal."

"Well, ma'am, I hate to be the one to tell you this and my brothers would have told me not to, if'n I had asked them, but as good neighbors, we ought to tell one another things, even if they might not be things you want to hear. At least that's the way that I feel. You feel that way too, Miss Smith?"

"Yes, I guess I do," Jane replied apprehensively.

"Well, you ought to know that this here land was cursed back in the pioneering days, 1785 to be exact, and that tree in the back there, well it was cursed too, back in the early 1800s. July 21, 1827, if 'n you want the exact date."

Shit, Jane thought. Superstitious folklore. Remember where you are Jane. This is the country and even though it's 2012, there are still people that hang on to the backwoods beliefs and myths.

"My great-great-great uncle was a man by the name of Samuel Newell. He established this place, Seymour that is, back in 1783. Was a learned man. Went to Harvard and the Andover Theological Seminary. Was one of the very first missionaries. Anyways, before he went back to the east, he tried to convince some of the settlers out in this part, to try and work with the Cherokees who called this land theirs. Which if you think about it, it really was theirs seeing how they lived here before us. But they didn't listen to him. There was an Indian shaman, an old woman by the name of Ah-gah-tana that was killed here on this property right beside that tree out back. Just before she died, she cursed this land so that nothing would ever grow here 'cept that big ole Live Oak in your backyard."

What about the wild raspberries and blackberries and the shrubs and trees that John had just planted Jane wanted to ask, but didn't. She just allowed Audie to continue with his story as she checked her watch again.

"Am I keeping you from being somewhere, Miss Smith?"

"No."

"Are you sure, ma'am? 'Cause you keep looking at your watch."

"Sorry, just have to be somewhere later today and I need to do some things around the house before I get ready to go." Though that wasn't the truth, Jane didn't think it was inappropriate considering what she was hearing.

"Well, as I was saying, this place is cursed. Back in 1827, three black men were hung from that tree. Accused of stealing chickens and horses from some farmers who caught them and killed them. Come to find out, they wasn't the ones that did it but it was too late. Their wives cursed the men that killed their husbands and brothers and said that tree would always be there as a warning to others and anyone that tried to cut it down, would die a horrible death. Seems like several folks didn't believe them women and tried cutting it down. Story has it that they were trying to cut some of the limbs down, and when they did, the limbs fell on them and crushed two of the men. Impaled another one. One of the top limbs, one of them that they call a widowmaker, well it lived up to its name and supposedly went right through his head. Ain't that something?"

"Yes, it sure is," Jane said as she saw John's car coming and waved to him. "There he is, Mr. Newell, my husband. He's coming down the road."

Audie saw the car and then turned back toward Jane. "You always get this excited to see your husband coming back from the store?"

Shit, Jane thought to herself again. He's a lot smarter than he appears to be. "Just glad he came back so that you could tell him what you were telling me," she replied.

"Why would I want to do that? Ain't you going to remember what I was saying?"

"No, I will remember. Just thought it would be nice for you two to meet," she answered. I want him to see your face so he can be aware and on alert. Because you sort of frighten me, Jane thought as she opened the screen door and ran over to the car. John stepped out and Jane hugged him tightly.

"Shore is nice to see that," Audie said as Jane turned around to see him standing next to the car. "Wish my family would have welcomed me home like that. If it weren't for that old beagle of ours, I don't think anyone would even know when I left or came back."

"John, this is Audie Newell, one of our neighbors from down the street."

"Nice to meet you, Mr. Newell," John said, shaking Audie's hand.

"Mr. Newell was just telling me how the land we own was cursed by the Indians and then again by some black women back in the early 1800s."

John looked at Jane in a puzzled manner and then back at Audie. He wasn't sure what to say and Audie recognized the confusion on his face.

"Yes sir, I know them's strange words to hear but that's the truth. Anyone that's lived out in this area for any time at all would tell you the same thing. That's the reason no one ever bought this land or tried to settle here. Like I was telling your wife, this sure is an awkward way to meet your neighbor but I knowed I needed to tell you."

"Audie, is it?" John asked and he nodded his head. "I appreciate you coming to tell us all of this, but why wouldn't you tell us before we moved in or even started building the house?"

"I wanted to, but I reckon I never got up the courage to do so until now. I know my family, especially my brothers, wouldn't be happy at all to even know I was here. But I figured it was the right thing to do, even if it does come after you built the house."

"You wouldn't be interested in buying this property for yourself now, would you Mr. Newell?" John asked.

"No sir, and if that's what you figure the reason for me being here is, I'll just be telling you good day and hope things work out for you and the missus," Audie said as he nodded his head toward Jane and turned and walked away.

"Do you really think that was the best way to handle that John?" Jane asked. "We don't know anything about his family and from what he told me, it sounded like there were a bunch of them that lived out here. We really don't need to get in some battle with our neighbors."

John put his arms around his wife and hugged her. "We have nothing to worry about," he said. "Just old wives tales. Surely, you don't believe in all those old superstitions and curses, do you?"

Jane looked at John in a somewhat annoyed manner. "Says the man who has an appointment with a psychic next week that he made almost two years ago."

"That is the Wears Valley Psychic, to be precise. Been written up in the newspapers several times. I believe that gives the person I have an appointment with some credibility."

Jane nodded her head as she rolled her eyes.

"You know I did that on a dare. But seeing how I am going to be there, I will now make sure to ask the person about the cursed land upon which we now oversee and standeth upon."

"Yes. Make sure you ask him about it using that word 'standeth.' I'm sure that will make quite an impression," she said as she began to laugh.

"Look," John said as he took his wife in his arms. "The fact is, that none of what Mr. Newell told you or what the psychic tells me really matters. You only believe what you want to believe and I don't believe in psychics or Mr. Newell's warnings. And you don't need to worry. Okay?"

He held her close to him and kissed her forehead. Jane looked down the road but couldn't see Mr. Newell anywhere. That was strange. The view was unobstructed for almost two miles before the road turned and went up a hill lined with trees on both sides.

How is that possible? There was no way he could have already walked two miles in the short time that she and John had talked but there was no one on the road. She wanted to say something to John about it but she held back. He would just dismiss it anyway. It wasn't really impossible for him to be at the curve already or perhaps somewhere else along the road, she told herself. She walked inside and locked both the screen door and the front door and told herself that she would keep both of them locked from this point forward.

Even if all of what Audie said wasn't true, there was still something about him that bothered her.

That evening after dinner, Jane got out her I-pad to look up the name Samuel Newell and was surprised by what she saw. Everything that Audie alluded to was true. At least that's what she thought, not realizing she was ignoring the fact that some of the things that Audie told her were not mentioned anywhere in the reference material she had found.

"Look at this, John," Jane said as she showed him the information on Samuel.

"Okay," he replied. "So he existed. Seems to have been a good guy according to this information. I don't see anything that says this land is cursed. Am I missing something?"

"No, you aren't missing anything. It doesn't mention the Indian massacre or the death of the Indian Shaman, Ah-gah-tana either, but history often omits that type of information."

"An Indian Shaman named Ah-gah-tana? Really, Jane?"

"I want you to ask the psychic about her. Promise me you'll ask him."

"Yes, I'll ask him if you will just calm down."

"Don't tell me to calm down," Jane said, taking back her I-pad. Laying back against the pillow, she thought she heard something outside. Something moving around close to the windows. "Did you hear that?"

"Yes, I heard it. Don't tell you to calm down."

"No! Next to the windows. There is something out there." Jane got up and peeked through the window blinds. She saw something moving next to the shrubs that John had planted. She couldn't make out what it was but it looked big to her.

"What are you doing over there?" he asked, but Jane didn't respond verbally. Without turning around, she motioned for him to come over to the window. John shook his head and joined her.

"Look out there," she whispered. "Tell me what you see."

John pressed down on the blinds and peered through them for a minute.

"Holy shit!" he said as he jumped back with Jane holding on to his arm.

"What is it?" she yelled. "What is it?"

"I just remembered! I didn't water the shrubs today."

Jane looked at him as if she might get a knife from the kitchen and stab him. "Asshole." She punched him in the shoulder and looked through the blinds again.

"Shit!" she cried. The face of the man she had met earlier that day was looking in the window at her. Well, at least one of the eyes was looking in the window at her.

"Nice try," John said as he sat down on the couch. "Won't work."

Jane looked again, but the face was no longer there. She ran to the front door and turned on the outdoor lights. John then realized that something really had scared her. He told her to get back as he opened the door and walked out on the wooden front steps. He asked Jane for a flashlight and within seconds she returned with one.

John walked all the way around the house and Jane stayed inside near the phone. She was ready to dial 911 at the slightest indication that something was wrong, but after a few minutes, John came back to the front of the house, shaking his head. "I'm not sure what you saw, but I don't see anything out here," John said as he walked back into the house.

"I saw him. Mr. Newell. He was looking in our window," Jane said as she grabbed her husband and pulled him close to her. John felt her trembling body and knew something had scared her, even if he wasn't sure it was Mr. Newell.

"It's okay, Jane. I promise you. It's okay. I will make sure you are always okay."

John held his wife until she stopped shaking. Then he told her to sit on the sofa and he would make her a cup of hot tea. When he handed her the tea, he gave her a Xanax too.

"Take it," he said. "I think you need it."

"I concur," she agreed.

John turned on the TV and put his arm around his wife. Neither of them was ready to go to bed so they watched a couple of episodes of "Shark Tank." When Jane began getting drowsy, John told her it was time that they went to bed. He made sure she saw him check the locks on the door and he even looked out the window for her one more time.

"Nothing there," he reported as they walked back toward their bedroom and got ready for bed. Jane went to sleep as soon as her head hit the pillow but John stayed up reading more about the Newell family on the I-pad. Again he said to himself; Samuel Newell seemed like he was a good man. Not sure how that carries over, genetically, but I guess time will tell.

He then looked up the name Cunningham and found out that a Nehemiah Cunningham, from Ireland, settled in Virginia in 1641, somewhere in the Shenandoah Valley. It was believed that one of his sons, Alexander Cunningham was one of the earliest residents of Tennessee, living in and around the area where they now lived. He had a granddaughter Jean, who lived in Massachusetts and was tried as a witch in Salem in 1775. Shit. Need to erase all this information. A granddaughter who was tried as a witch.

That's all she needs to see he thought as he looked over at his wife before he turned off the light and went to sleep.

The next several days were uneventful. John wanted to drive down the road and look up the Newell family, but Jane asked him to stay away from them and he did as she requested. On Wednesday of the next week, Jane and John traveled to Wears Valley for his appointment with the psychic. They drove up to a split-level brick house. "So, this is where a psychic lives?" John asked sarcastically. "It's sure not as I imagined it. I sort of expected some, I don't know, some runes or some unknown symbols etched into a rock or on the house."

"Runes and symbols?"

"Yeah, something like that."

"Said the non-believer," Jane laughed. "Well, maybe there will be a hobbit there just behind the metal door, to welcome you into the seer's lair."

"Funny," he replied but he knew she was right. His words betrayed him. Even though he had made the appointment on a dare, he could feel the anxiousness within his body; some level of excitement as they got out of the car and walked toward the unknown.

They opened the door and came into a room that contained a sofa and a woman sitting behind a desk. That was all. No pictures, nothing that would suggest this was anything but a very ordinary room on the bottom floor of the house.

The woman looked up and asked if he was the 5 p.m. appointment and John nodded his head yes. "That will be $150. You brought cash, correct?"

John nodded his head again. She didn't even bother to ask his name. In fact, that's one of the things that gave some level of believability to this meeting. When he had made the appointment two years ago, they didn't ask for his name then either. He was just assigned a date and time to come. There was no way they could have done any background check on him. All the articles that he had read about the man and the people who visited him suggested he did indeed have some power to see the future of those who met with him.

John gave her the money and sat down next to Jane. He could tell she was enjoying all of this. He was about to say something to her when the telephone rang and the woman answered it and said okay. She glanced up and told John to go through the door and sit in the chair across from the desk. She warned him it would be rather dark in the room but that there would be enough light for him to see the chair.

John looked apprehensively at Jane and she whispered to him that she would be praying for him and then kissed him on his cheek and started laughing. He whispered back to her that she was very funny and then opened the door that the woman had pointed toward. The light in the room was dim but he saw the chair and the desk and someone sitting at the desk. He also smelled something. There was incense burning. It smelled sweet, like honeysuckle and roses.

The man sitting in the chair said nothing as John sat down across from him. His eyes were closed and his head tilted back. Just like the house, there was nothing about the man that suggested he was some sort of mystical seer. He had brown hair that hung down onto his shoulders and he had a normal looking face. If you saw him on the street, you would probably walk right by without even noticing him. But when the man opened his eyes and looked at him, John felt something. His eyes were blue, but not a shade of blue he had ever seen before or could describe afterward. They were ethereal, not natural.

The man had a pad and pen in his hand and he began writing as he looked at John. He wrote for several minutes before he said anything.

"I do not tell people when they will die. I read auras. Everyone has different colors that radiate from their body and their interaction with each other; the colors, they all tell me something about you. I will write down everything I see today and after I have told you everything that I can see, I will allow you to ask me some questions."

John didn't say anything. He just nodded his head.

"You have very interesting colors around you. None of them are distinct except for the dark yellow one. They are all muted. Blended. That is very unusual. You just bought a house. The first house you and your wife have ever owned. It's out in the country. The house is structurally sound but you will have water problems."

"Is it okay to ask questions as you talk?"

"I would prefer that you didn't," the man replied as he continued.

"You have met your soul mate. That is rare. Both of you help people. That will continue for as long as you both work. And even beyond that. Both of you like living in the country and being outdoors. It's as if you are both old souls in that regard. If you believe in reincarnation, you were pioneers that lived in this area long ago."

"So, you don't believe in reincarnation?" John asked.

"I believe that I don't completely understand all of what God is capable of doing. I am not ready to say reincarnation doesn't exist anymore that I am ready to say that it does exist. But I can see a link to you and to the past."

Hell, you could say that about anybody, John said to himself. I paid $150 for this and waited for two years. Well, what did you expect? Just continue to listen. It will be over soon.

"There are issues with things that you eat. Stay away from onions and dairy. You suffer from abdominal issues but otherwise, your overall health is good. There is cancer in your family and there is a good chance that you will get it too but cancer will not kill you. In fact, you will get sick from something at your house. Beware of the black widows."

Shit, John said to himself. Spiders? Black widow spiders? Jane will freak out. Well, I know for sure now, I can't let her read all this stuff he's writing down.

"There is a large tree in your yard. It is over four hundred years old. And though it looks healthy, there is death all around it. Its roots are strong but its limbs, they weep. It would be wise to listen to the shadows that surround the tree."

"Okay, I really have to stop you there, because I don't understand what you are saying. It's as if I am sitting across from Master Yoda. Listening I am, but hearing I'm not."

John thought what he said would bring a laugh from the man who had never introduced himself. But it didn't.

"I don't understand what you mean by Master Yoda?"

"Star Wars. You go to the movies, right?"

"No. Never. I only go out into the mountains. I don't watch TV. I read books, read the Bible every day, and hike in the mountains. One can learn a lot about what is going to happen around them by looking into what nature provides you. She leaves many clues out there. And I doubt I will find anything more beautiful to watch or see than the Smoky Mountains."

Well, he is right about the Smoky Mountains. But what the heck does he mean by listening to the shadows? "How am I supposed to listen to the shadows of a tree? I was never taught that language."

"I cannot tell you that. But I can tell you that the tree has a spiritual nature around it. You can perhaps learn about it or the land that it is on from the recorder of deeds or from the library. There is someone whose name starts with A who can share her knowledge of the tree. There are also other women who can tell you about the tree. They have a very distinct accent when they speak. They do not come from this country."

A woman whose name starts with A. Surely to shit he isn't referencing Ah-gah-tana. "Are you talking about a woman by the name of Ah-gah-tana?"

"That name is unfamiliar to me but as you said it, the yellow aura around you intensified. She does mean something to you."

"What about Newell, does that name mean anything?"

"Again that name changed the aura around you. The black aura around you."

Black aura? John thought. That can't be good. "What does that mean?"

"The black aura has two meanings. It can suggest a long life or suggest your life is going to go through a major change."

"What kind of change?"

"I don't know, but if it is indeed changing, your life will forever be altered."

John wasn't sure what that meant but he knew he wouldn't get anywhere asking any questions about it now. He would have to just let him continue and do some more research on the Newells on his own.

"You like music. A particular type of music. Your blue aura lights up when I say music. You love listening to the blues. Your wife likes music too. Not as much as you do, but you have fun together at concerts. You are close to your friends. Once they become your friend, they are friends for life. I see lots of pictures around you. You may become a photographer. Or paint. Your wife. She may paint or write. She has an ability to see what is in nature that few others do. Her name is Jean?"

"Jane."

"I see someone named Jean. She wants to talk to you and your wife. Drugs and alcohol are around you but you will not be affected by them. Racism is around you. Not in you or your wife but it is around you and has meant something to you in the past. It will mean something to you again. Be careful how you deal with it. That is all that I see. What questions do you have for me?"

Well, he is right about the racism statement. We experienced that with the foster child we had. Never thought it would happen to us in the place we lived or the school he attended but it did. I can't tell Jane about that either because it might influence her decision to foster or even adopt another child later. I just need to keep that to myself.

"Should I cut down the tree? You said its limbs weep. It's a Live Oak so I can see how you would say that because of all the curvature in the limbs but does that mean something else besides just the normal way it grows?"

"You cannot cut down the tree. Those that have tried have regretted it. There is a person whose first name starts with an E who knows a lot about that tree and will explain things to you or perhaps your wife. She will tell you about the tree and what it means to you and your wife."

"You said the only color that was distinct for me was the yellow one. What does that mean?"

"It represents the path on which you walk in this life."

"What does that mean?"

"It suggests you are a good person."

John knew that wasn't everything it meant. He could tell the person sitting across from him was holding something back. "It is a lifeline, isn't it?"

"Yes."

"So, you can see when someone is going to die?"

"Sometimes."

"And is this one of those times?"

"I told you I don't tell people that. It changes the way they live their life. Sometimes for the good and then sometimes for the bad."

"What does it say about me? I want to know."

"I will only say that your life has significance. Meaning. It has importance."

Shit, he is telling me I am going to die. Ask him, John, just ask him. "Are you telling me I am going to die?"

"All things die."

"Yeah, I know that. But are you telling me I don't have long before I die?"

"All I will say to that is those accused were innocent until those accused were guilty."

John got up and was walking out of the room when he heard the psychic continue talking.

"Go with God. He is with you. He protects you and will welcome you home. Those that protect the innocent have a special place at the table."

He looked back at the psychic and saw he was again sitting with his head tilted back and his eyes closed. Wait a minute - the notes. He said he would give me the notes he was writing. He walked back in the room and saw the papers sitting on the edge of his desk. When did he put them there? I didn't see anything. Must have been when I was walking away. Why didn't he just hand them to me? Shit, this has been an interesting encounter he thought as he folded the yellow notepad papers and placed them in his back pocket.

When he came out of the room, the woman at the desk was gone. John looked somewhat surprised to find his wife sitting alone in the room. "She said you were the last client and for us to just lock the door on the way out."

John shrugged his shoulders as he walked out and Jane closed and locked the door. They hadn't made it to the car before she started peppering him with questions.

"Well, how was it? What did he do when you talked about the ground on which we standeth? I bet he knew he wasn't fooling around with just any old country bumpkin when you asked him that question," she said as she laughed.

"It was different," John said quietly.

They got in the car and started driving home. "What do you mean different?"

"He sees auras. Different colors mean different things to him. And before you start to ask me a thousand questions, let me just tell you what he told me. First of all, I didn't use the word standeth, so before you get on me about that, let me tell you he did say I had met my soul mate and that was rare."

"Okay, I'm liking this so far."

"He said we had just bought a house in the country but that we were going to have some type of water problems. He said we both had jobs where we helped people and that we always would even after we stopped working."

"Really? He said that? That's kinda eerie, don't you think?"

"I have to admit, he got a lot of things right though I'm still debating that one about the soul mate."

She punched John in the arm and he laughed. "Keep talking mister," Jane said. "Or I start kicking your shins."

"That will be hard to do in the car," John said as he saw his wife sliding over toward him.

"Okay, okay," John laughed. "He knew about my food issues. Told me to stay away from onions and dairy. That was interesting I thought. He said that there was cancer in my family and that I might get cancer but I would not die from it."

"Are you kidding me?" Jane asked.

"No, like I said, he told me some things that really made me wonder about the abilities he had. Anyway, he knew I liked the blues and that we enjoyed going to concerts. Said that when I made a friend, I had that friend for life."

"Boy, that hit the nail on the head. Think about all your friends from high school you are still friends with. That's amazing."

"He also said he thinks that one of us will take up photography or painting. Or that you may become a writer."

"Oh – that sounds interesting. I hope he's right about that."

John paused as they came up to a red light that would allow them to turn on to Chapman Highway.

"Is that all?" Jane asked. "You did ask about Ah-gah-tana, right?"

"I did. He didn't know of her and couldn't tell me anything about her. But he did mention that we had a tree that weeps in our yard and someone with a name that begins with A has knowledge about that tree."

"Damnit, John. Just like Audie said. Ah-gah-tana, she put a curse on the land and that tree."

"Hold on there, Elvira, mistress of the dark. It could also mean Alice, or Amy, or April, or Allison, or any number of people whose name starts with

A and works at the County Registrar of Deeds. He said we should look into it at that office or at the library."

"You can look, but I already know," Jane said as she looked out her window at the beautiful rural countryside.

Yes, I know you think you know, John said to himself. That's why I'm not going to tell you about the black widows, or how the mention of the Newell name affected my black aura. And why I am not going to mention what I found about Jean Cunningham or the discussion of racism that the psychic mentioned. That will just have you believe even more in what Newell told you. I'll have to check all that out on my own.

"He did mention something about reincarnation," John added. He knew that would catch his wife's interest.

"He said we were old souls. Could have been pioneers in the day if we believe in reincarnation. When I asked him if he did, he said he wasn't sure of it or not, but with God, anything was possible. He doesn't watch TV or do anything except read the Bible and other books and hike in the mountains. He did seem very spiritual in that manner."

"Interesting," Jane replied as she smiled at her husband before she turned back toward her window. I am sure we were here long ago, she said to herself. I felt that the first time we came out here but I was afraid to say anything to you. You would just say I was nuts. But I'm not nuts and the Wears Valley Psychic just confirmed that but I am not going to tell you that. Not yet at least. "So are you glad you went?"

"Yeah, I guess I am. He got a lot of things right. It was different. Entertaining. But I wouldn't do it again. Just don't see the sense in doing it again." And let's just hope the other things he mentioned don't come true, he said to himself.

The next day, as John was showering, he felt something painful on the back of his neck. At first, he thought he had slept wrong and had a pinched nerve but as he moved his head around, he realized it wasn't that. He had a horrible headache too and felt like his heart was going to jump out of his chest. He called Jane into the bathroom to look at the back of his neck and she said, "Damn!"

"What does damn mean?" he asked apprehensively.

"It means that you got bitten by something. It's all red and full of pus. Do you feel bad?"

"Yeah, sort of," he replied.

"I think a doctor needs to see this." She called into work and told them she wouldn't be there because she needed to take her husband to the emergency room.

John didn't argue with her. He was feeling a little achy and sick to his stomach now. As soon as the doctor saw the bite, he told them it looked like a spider bite. John immediately thought of what the psychic had said. The doctor said that there was nothing that they could give him for the bite, not knowing what kind of spider it was; and that the best thing that they could do would be to manage the wound and make sure the ulcer didn't worsen.

He prescribed oral antibiotics and an antibiotic ointment and warned them that if the wound got worse he should come back to the ER or see their primary care physician immediately as he might need some hyperbaric therapy. He also prescribed some pain pills and recommended that John take the next couple of days off.

Jane took John home and he swallowed a pain pill and went back to bed while she sat next to him. After a short time, Jane knew that John would probably sleep for the next two or three hours, so while he slept she went out to the back porch and sat, looking at the tree.

A weeping tree. She heard the words John said and repeated them over and over in her head. I wonder if you weep for a different reason she asked herself. "And what is it about you that makes me believe that I know you from another time?" she asked out loud. She heard someone reply and she looked around, puzzled by the response.

"Not sure," was what she heard and when she got up, she saw Audie examining the shrubs and flowers that John had planted around the house.

Seeing him there, Jane realized that she no longer felt threatened by him. In fact, she almost felt like apologizing to him for thinking he was strange but she didn't say anything about it. Just move forward, she told herself as she looked down at him from the porch.

"Were you here the other night?" she asked.

"Reckon so," Audie said. "I was checking on them plants in the front yard."

"In the dark?"

"Don't matter if it's light or dark. You can tell a lot about plants by just feeling them. Smelling them. Checking the ground at their feet."

"Why were you doing that?"

"'Cause I told you things don't live in this soil and I was surprised to see these plants living. But as I figured, they's all dying now. A lot of them got root rot. Too much water. Few of them out front, those two maple trees, they got ambrosia beetle. You need to burn them. There ain't nothing that can kill that dang bug. The ones with root rot, I doubt you can do anything for them either, but you don't have to burn them."

"Thank you, Audie. I'll tell my husband about that when he wakes up."

"He ain't ailing, is he? Awful late to still be in bed."

"As a matter of fact, he is. He was bitten by a spider the doctor said. And though the doctor didn't say it, I think it might have been a black widow."

"Yes, ma'am. They's around here. Just need to keep the wound clean and it should heal up in time. Never knowed why people were so afraid of them. Hardly ever kill anyone 'ceptin if it was a youngun or someone already sick."

"Have you ever heard of the Wears Valley Psychic, Audie?"

'Yes ma'am, I have. He's got the power to see things about people that no one else can."

"Yes, that's what we've heard. He told my husband that we had a tree that wept in our yard. Why do you know so much about that tree, Audie?"

"Great-great-grandmother told me about it right before she died. Rest of my family didn't much care for her because she was so old, but I liked being around her. She told me lots of things. How to not get lost in the woods. What plants would make you sick and those that would help you. I loved listening to her tell me about all the plants. Always took a liking to 'em. Knowed some plants that I'd rather be around than some people. You know, poison ivy never bothered me. Could lay around in it and not get the least bit of irritation. My older brothers didn't have that same ability, much to their consternation," Audie said as he smiled and looked up at Jane.

This time when he looked at her, both eyes stayed focused on her until she replied to him. "You didn't get along with your brothers, did you, Audie?"

"No ma'am, not that good. They had a mean streak in them. Much like my papa. I often wondered if I was kin to them and I think they wondered the same thing."

"Should we be worried about your family, Audie?"

"If it was me, ma'am, I would stay as far away from them as possible. Ain't nothing good gonna come from you getting to know them. They ain't the neighborly type."

Jane knew the answer before she asked it but she asked the question anyway.

"You were here the other night, just checking on us, weren't you Audie? You just came by to make sure we were all right."

Audie looked down at the ground when she said that. He didn't reply, just nodded his head. Before she could say anything else, he looked up at her, with one eye focused on her and one looking at the tree.

"You need to go in and check on your husband," Audie said. "He's starting to stir around a bit. Probably be a good time to check on that bite too. I can try and find some marigolds for you and you can use them on the wound. They are real good at helping to heal things. Just mash the petals up in water and wash the wound with it."

Jane started to ask Audie how he knew John was awake when she heard him call out her name. She went to the door and told him she would be right there. When she turned back to thank Audie he was walking away into the woods. Before she could call out to him he had vanished behind a tree.

She opened the bedroom door and found John awake. He asked her for something to drink, a Pepsi if they had any. When she returned, his hands felt warm as she handed him the drink.

"I think you're running a fever." She got him some Tylenol, cleaned his wound and applied the antibiotic ointment again. She thought the wound looked worse than it had this morning. The redness around it had spread and the ulcer seemed to be getting deeper. I'll really have to keep an eye on this, she told herself. We'll have to see how it looks tomorrow. "How do you feel?" she asked.

"It hurts. Really hurts," he replied. "Much worse than this morning."

"Well, you aren't supposed to have another pain pill for a couple of hours. Let's give that Tylenol some time to work and if it's not better in an hour, I'll give you another pill."

John winced as he nodded his head. "Shouldn't do that," he said as she propped up his back with more pillows so he could drink the Pepsi.

"Guess who came by while you were asleep?"

"The mortician?"

"Funny. Though I did find the number on the internet. There is one in Seymour by the way. You know, just in case."

John managed a weak smile.

"No, it was Audie," she said but before John could ask any questions, she let him know she wasn't concerned. "I misinterpreted him and his actions. I bet that happens all the time, unfortunately. We are all too prone to judge people by the way they look. Anyway, he was here checking on the plants. Said your flowers and shrubs are suffering from root rot because of too much water and the two Japanese Maples in the front yard have something called ambrosia beetle infection. Said the only thing we could do was burn them. He didn't think the other plants would survive but we didn't need to burn them."

"Problems with water," John said in a robotic manner as he looked at Jane.

"Does appcar so, doesn't it? Kinda creepy isn't it?"

If you only knew. A black widow bite and now this, he thought. Shit.

"Do you want me to burn the trees?"

"Before you do, can you call the agricultural extension agent and ask them about this amber beetle?"

"Ambrosia beetle, and yes, I will. Are you hungry?"

"No, still a little nauseous. I'll just lie back down and try and rest." He took another sip of Pepsi and then handed her the glass.

Jane sat on the edge of the bed for a moment and watched her husband sleep. He looked kind of pitiful. I hope Audie brings back those marigolds, she thought, before she got up to call the agricultural extension agent. He sounded very worried and asked if she could bring one of the trees to him so he could inspect it. She said she wasn't sure she could do it today, but she would try. She wrote down the address and then went back to check on her husband one more time.

She felt his head and he didn't feel hot anymore. No fever, that's a good thing, she said to herself. Jane realized she couldn't do much for him while he was sleeping and then thought again about those trees. She felt that John would really want her to find out what was wrong with them, so she went outside and cut down one of the saplings and put it in the back of his truck. She went back to check on John once more and gave him a quick kiss on his forehead without waking him. She left a note beside the bed telling him what she had done and when she should be back home.

It took her about thirty minutes to get to the agricultural extension office in Strawberry Plains. "Son of a bitch," he said as he looked at the tree. "Excuse me, ma'am. Didn't mean to say that, but I was hoping you were wrong when you called. You're over in Sevier County, right?"

"Yes, Seymour."

"And you have another tree just like this one with the same holes and little trails of sawdust coming out of them?"

"Yes."

"Well, we are going to burn this tree for you and when you get back home, dig up the roots on this one that you cut down and dig up the other tree and burn them. I will notify the state about its presence. These little bugs have a pretty name but it ain't pretty if they get established anywhere. They will take down an entire forest."

"Wow," she replied. "I had no idea. Could it harm other trees and plants in our yard?"

"Sure could."

"I have a beautiful large Live Oak in the back yard. I would hate to see it damaged."

"You bought the property with the Sevier County Live Oak?" he asked, sounding somewhat surprised.

"We did. In fact, I was hoping someone could tell me more about the tree and the property. Could you or could you recommend someone? And also tell me what I need to do to protect it?"

"The best thing you can do is burn those trees and keep your fingers crossed. If that Live Oak is healthy and from the last time I saw it, it was, it should be okay, but the sooner you burn those trees the better. Regarding the history of the property, there is an elderly lady, a retired professor from the University of Tennessee, who doesn't live too far from here. She taught history there for so long, I think she became a part of it. If she's up to it, she will talk to you as long as you want to talk. If she ain't, then you won't even get her to answer the door. But, please promise me you will set fire to that tree and the roots of this one today."

"Yes, I promise. And thanks for the information." Jane got in the truck and entered the address the agent gave her into the GPS. She soon found herself on an old dirt road surrounded by pasture land. Unfenced and beautiful, with a view of the Smoky Mountains in the distance. Just like the land was intended to be, she thought. The open pasture land changed to thick woods as she crossed a small wooden bridge over a rushing stream. And as she drove over the quaint little bridge, all she could think was "over the river and through the woods to grandmother's house we go."

After another mile, she saw the log cabin in a small clearing. It looked like a scene on a postcard advertising Tennessee and she parked in front of the house and got out. She knocked on the door and looked at the two rockers on the front porch. She thought about how she would like something like that at her house one day. She snapped a picture on her phone to share with John later.

She knocked once more and was afraid the woman wasn't home or like the agent said, didn't want to talk, but the door opened and before her stood a woman who could be the grandma she was thinking about as she crossed over that stream.

"Hello, Ms. Bass. My name is Jane Smith. I know you don't know me, but the man at the agricultural extension office, Jack, told me about you. My husband and I just bought the house in Sevier County with the Live Oak and I had heard some things about the property and I wanted to know more about it and so I had some problems with a maple tree, ambrosia beetle the agent said, and so he told me to burn it and I have another at home I need to burn, and then he told me about you and how you know so much about history around here and that's what led me to you here today," Jane said and was about to say more when Ms. Bass held up her hand.

"Do you always talk like that? Because if you do, I'm not sure I can keep up with you."

"No, ma'am. I am just a little nervous. Jack said..." she started but Ms. Bass stopped her.

"I know what Jack said. He said I can be a bit persnickety at times, but you got me on a good day. Especially since you just told me that you bought the property with the Sevier County Live Oak. Come on in Jane and sit down and let's talk."

Jane closed the door and followed her inside. There was a sofa with a southwestern design, two leather chairs, and dreamcatchers along the wall. A variety of Indian bowls, moccasins, shawls, and knives decorated the room. There was also a large six-foot-tall display case in the corner of the room filled up with even more items, highlighted by background lights in each area.

"Some of those things you are looking at are old, five to six hundred years old. I found them out in the woods. They're out there if you know what you are looking for. By the way, my name is Edith and I'd prefer you to call me that. Would you like a cup of coffee or tea? I'm going to get a cup of coffee."

"Yes, a cup of coffee would be nice," Jane said as she continued to look around the living room. Within a few minutes, Edith returned with the coffee and sat down.

"I'm impressed that you bought that property considering all the history associated with it. Lots of country folk believe that land to be haunted. Got to admit, lots of city folk do too."

"Well, we didn't know anything about it before we bought it. What do you believe, Edith?"

"I know some bad things happened around that area. As a result of that, people start believing in things that try and help them cope with the reality and brutality of what happened in the past. Instead of learning from it, they would prefer to allow the past to haunt them so to speak. By doing so, they assign everything to the supernatural, and thus, they believe it is beyond their control to change."

"I heard there was an Indian massacre there. Is that true?"

"There were Indian massacres all throughout the land as the white man moved them out of their homelands. Some of what the Native Americans did was quite gruesome in retaliation but they were only defending what was once theirs. It was impossible for those leading the way, and by that I mean financing things, to realize that they should work with the people whose land they were taking from them. I say it was impossible, because, at that time in history, they didn't know any better. History hadn't taught them anything.

Though we have evolved and learned a lot from those interactions, we still see those in power making the same mistakes and still treating people in a cruel and inhumane manner.

"But enough for my soapbox, to answer your question, yes an Indian massacre happened there. A settlement of Cherokees was attacked by a group of pioneers in 1785 who were living in Fort Knox, which as you can guess, later became Knoxville. Probably about fifty to seventy-five men, women, and children were killed from what we can tell. Shame too. A man by the name of Samuel Newell tried to make peace with the Cherokees and had some success with them before he moved away. Became a very successful missionary over in Africa.

"Now this is when the first supernatural reference begins. A diary was found in amazing condition, written by one of the men in that battle, an Alexander Cunningham. There was a reference to a great healer within that Cherokee community who cursed those that day and said the 'Hand of God' would forever be a warning to anyone who lived there; that they would be unwelcome on this land and that the land would not be fertile. Alexander Cunningham was a grandson of a Nehemiah Cunningham who was one of the first to settle in Virginia in the middle 1600s, over there in the Shenandoah Valley."

"Wow! That's so interesting. We actually live on Cunningham Road. What is the 'Hand of God' and was there a name for that healer?"

"Oh, I would have liked to have you as a student in one of my classes instead of those freshmen that were trying to sleep off a hangover and just there because they needed an elective credit," Edith sighed as she took a drink of her coffee. "Yes, according to the diary, her name was Ah-gah-tana and the 'Hand of God' she was referring to was that Live Oak in your yard. Knowing how slow Live Oaks grow, I would say if she was calling it the 'Hand of God' in 1785, it was already a massive tree so I am thinking that tree is at least 350 to maybe 400 years old now."

Just like Audie said, Jane thought. I cannot wait to tell John. I'd like to bring him out here to meet Edith. Provided she lets me come back. "You said that was the first supernatural reference, meaning there are others?"

"You may have been my A+ student. All attentive and asking questions. I love it. Yes, Alexander Cunningham, for whom the road is probably named, though it could have been named after many prominent Cunninghams that lived in that area, had a granddaughter named Jean. She had an affair with one of the slaves that lived around that area. A man called Aron Bone. He was from West Africa, so we have no idea what his real name was, but according to Alexander, who was still living at the time, we know his name to be that what I said. He feared for his granddaughter's life when news of that illicit affair became known and sent her to Massachusetts, where she was later accused of being a witch and shunned by everyone there. She committed suicide according to Alexander's diary."

"Why was she accused of being a witch?"

"She could see and talk to spirits according to her grandfather. Perhaps she talked with Ah-gah-tana, but we will never know. But just as Alexander feared for the life of his granddaughter, he also feared for the life of the slave. He even said as much in the diary, which for a white man of wealth and power in that time, was most impressive. He was right about both of them. One of his last entries in his diary was about three black men being accused of stealing some chickens and being hanged on that tree in your yard. One of them was Aron Bone, the one I mentioned earlier, and the other two were his friends, an Elijah Gates and Samuel Smith. Their wives cursed the people that hung their husbands telling all that would listen that they were innocent. And Alexander, in a very brave moment, confirmed that. I wrote what he said down because I found it to be so profound."

She pulled out the folded piece of paper and read the quote. "I fear those women of color to be correct in their assertion that those three men were innocent. I believe the prejudice that is in men's hearts precludes them from seeing that and for that reason, their warnings should be heeded, and a wide berth given to that property.'"

Edith was leaning back in her chair as she contemplated that quote of Alexander's, and when she looked up, she saw Jane was looking somewhat overwhelmed.

John was awakened by a sound at the door and, assuming it was Jane, he called out to her that he would be there in a minute. He didn't get too far before three men burst into the bedroom and shoved him back onto the bed. The one who pushed him was fat and short and smelled like he hadn't taken a bath in weeks. The putrid smell made John throw up.

"Fuck, look what that shithead has gone and done! What the fuck is wrong with you mister?" the short fat man yelled as he wiped off his pants with the blanket.

"Damn, Dauber, he looks like he's sick," the taller blonde-haired one said. "Are you sick, Mister Smith?"

John thought fast and nodded his head. “Yes, I have a very bad case of the flu. I am highly contagious. I wouldn’t recommend being around me. If you see anything you want, just take it and leave.”

“Shit, Estes,” the blonde-haired man said as he turned to look at the third man, who seemed to be surveying everything. John knew right away that he was the leader. The one who would determine how things progressed.

“You weren’t supposed to be home, Mister Smith, and that’s created a little dilemma. That little man standing next to you, probably catching the flu, if that’s what’s really wrong with you, would just as soon stick you with that knife of his than not. Sometimes I can stop him and sometimes I can’t. What reason would I have to tell him not to do that, Mister Smith?”

“If you go look in the closet, behind the clothes hanging up, you’ll find a box. It has highly valuable coins in it. Worth at least ten thousand dollars. Take them. That’s all I have of value besides what I have in the bank and I can’t make it to the bank. I can write you a check but I don’t think you want me to do that.”

“Go look in the closet, Buford. And, Dauber, you might want to stand back just a bit. From the way he looks, he ain’t going to do anything to you. Without a doubt, he’s a sick man and has probably got something contagious.”

Buford returned from the closet with several boxes and opened them to see the coin collection.

“Well, that’s real friendly and smart of you, Mister Smith. You are correct about us not wanting to cash a check from you. This coin collection seems like enough for now. We may come back when you are feeling better though. You ain’t going to tell anyone about this little visit, are you?” Estes asked.

“No, not a word.” John felt like he was going to pass out and fell back onto his pillow.

“Damn, Estes,” Dauber said as he noticed several pictures that were hanging on the wall and then looked back at John. He walked over to the wall and stared at one particular picture for a few minutes. Then he yelled at Estes and Buford. “Hey you two, come over here. Don’t this little nappy look familiar?”

The three men all stared at the picture. They instantly recognized the black child sitting on John’s lap. Estes turned around and when he met John’s eyes, they both knew. The black child who was killed that day: the foster child that John tried to save, was killed by these three men in his bedroom.

All John could tell the police that awful day was that three white men attacked him and Bryan. He told the police that he didn’t think they intended to kill anyone at first. But Bryan fought back as they hit him, and John knew by the way they were hitting the child and by the ugly words they uttered, they wanted to kill him just because he was black.

Estes said nothing as he leaped over and grabbed a pillow while Buford and Dauber held John down on the bed. Within a few minutes, the pillow that Estes held over his face took away all the oxygen from John's body.

"Shit," Buford said as they looked at the lifeless body on the bed.

"It probably was the best thing that could have happened," Estes said. "I don't think he was the kind that would have just sat back and allowed this to occur. You know how hard he fought us that day. Anyway, look around and see what else we can take and then we need to get the hell out of here."

"What's wrong?" Edith asked.

"My maiden name was Gates. And I married a Smith. And I..." Jane started to say before Edith interrupted her.

"I know what you're thinking but before you get too excited, let's take a look at a program I developed at the University. Some of the algorithms and data banks I developed were bought by some of those ancestor tree companies that I am not allowed to tell anyone about. The university made a lot more money than I did but I can't complain. I got my cabin in the woods," she said and smiled at Jane.

They got up and went into a little room off the kitchen where Edith had a computer. The desk was in front of a window overlooking a large rock formation. A small waterfall trickled down from a grayish-black crevice in two of the boulders that otherwise seemed fused together. "How lovely!" exclaimed Jane.

"When the rains come, that little waterfall becomes quite spectacular, but that's for another day," Edith said as she logged on to her computer. "Tell me your father's and grandfather's names and if you know your great-grandfather's name, that would be a nice bonus."

"My father's name was Harold. My grandfather's name was James and my great-grandfather's name was Nathaniel."

"Yep, you would have definitely been my A+ student," Edith smiled as she entered the names in her computer and together they watched the algorithms begin to flash across the screen and the list of names begin to align with a percent sign next to them.

"The percent sign indicates the likelihood of this being an ancestor," Edith said. "With more information - wives, cousins, uncles, etc. - we can increase that likelihood."

As they looked down the list, they saw the name Elijah Gates and a 76% number beside the name.

"Goodness," Edith said. "That's a pretty high likelihood of that person being related to you based upon just three names. In fact, I would say it's almost a certainty. Seems to me like you have a strong ancestral link to that land."

Jane couldn't believe what she was hearing and wanted to rush home and tell John but then paused as she began to understand the significance of what Edith had just said. Her ancestor didn't own that land. He was murdered on that land. She was related to a man, a black man, that was killed on that land. As soon as she realized that a feeling of fear hit her and she knew she needed to get back to John quickly.

"Ms. Bass, I mean Edith, I can't tell you how much I appreciate you talking with me today and showing me this information. I need to leave though. I want to stay and ask you more, but I need to leave. My husband isn't feeling the best and I need to get back and check on him. Thank you so much though, and if it's okay with you, I would love to come back with my him and learn some more. I know he would enjoy it as much as I have."

"You can come back anytime Jane," Edith said as she led her to the front door. She handed Jane a piece of paper with her email address and phone number on it and told her if she could provide more family names, she would be happy to continue researching for her.

On the way home, she couldn't help but think that John was keeping something from her. Something that the Wears Valley Psychic told him that he didn't want to tell her. The historical data shouldn't have been obscured from the psychic. I bet he saw something and told John about it and he's not telling me, thinking I will overreact.

She saw that the garage door was still open when she drove up and realized she must not have closed it when she left. She drove into the garage and walked into the house. Upon entering the kitchen, she noticed that the back door was also open. That's odd she thought, but maybe John was feeling better and went outside for a moment. She checked on the back porch but didn't see him there before closing the door.

She walked into the bedroom and saw her husband lying on the bed and knew something was wrong. She ran to him, yelling as she shook his shoulders but she got no response. She pulled out her cell phone and called 911 and started performing CPR on John as soon as she hung up.

"Wake up. Goddamnit!" she screamed as she pushed on his sternum and provided him mouth to mouth resuscitation. She heard the ambulance drive up and met them at the front door to lead them back to her husband. She watched as they felt for a pulse and then used some sort of device to try and detect one. “It’s very, very faint,” she heard the man with the device say and then say, “we need to go quickly” as they lifted him onto a stretcher. As they were driving to the hospital, they began asking Jane questions about his health. She told them about the spider bite and they examined the wound and saw that it was very infected.

Jane sat next to John in the ambulance, holding his hand all the way to the hospital. She heard, “we are losing him,” as one of the EMT’s brought out the defibrillator and told her to sit back as he shocked him. She watched as they gave him adrenalin and shocked him several more times, but the monitoring device suggested their lifesaving actions weren’t working. When he was rolled into the ER, one of the nurses led her to a private room while they took John away. Within minutes, the same doctor who treated John for the spider bite came into the room with the nurse and sat down beside her.

“There was nothing we could do for him.” With those words, the tears came flowing down her face, and she felt empty inside. Like there was nothing in her body that could enable her to breathe or allow her heart to beat. She heard them calling her name as she closed her eyes and then she didn’t hear anything else.

She woke up in a patient room on a stretcher and though she felt like it had been hours, only a few minutes had passed since they brought her back from the syncope that she experienced. That was the medical term for what had happened but it failed to describe the physical and mental trauma Jane had experienced when she was told her husband was dead.

“I am very sorry, Jane,” Dr. Ray said as he held her hand. “Do you remember me?”

“Yes, yes, I do.”

“I know this is a lot to try and comprehend right now, but I don’t think your husband died due to the spider bite. Though the bite is indeed infected, I don’t see any reason as to why a strong young man like your husband wouldn’t have been able to overcome that, especially with the antibiotics we had given him. Something just doesn’t add up.”

Jane looked at Dr. Ray in a confused manner.

“If it’s okay with you, I would like to order an autopsy on your husband. To find out what he actually died from. I just don’t think it was a spider bite that killed him.”

Jane wasn’t sure if Dr. Ray was trying to protect himself or was showing genuine concern for her husband. But when she glanced over at the nurse, there was something in her eyes that told her she should do what the doctor requested. "Bring me the papers," Jane said as the nurse patted her hand and left the room. "You think he was killed, don't you, Dr. Ray?"

"I think that is a strong possibility. I think we should call the police and have them escort you back to the house and let both of you look around. You don't have to agree to that, since we don't really know the cause of death, but I would recommend it."

"Yes, I am okay with that. Call them. And while we are waiting on the police, can I go say goodbye to my husband?"

"Of course," Dr. Ray replied softly.

The sight of her husband, so still on the bed, took her breath away. She couldn't stop the tears that filled her eyes and made everything a blur. Jane took John's hand and sat down beside him. She tried to wipe the tears away and started talking softly.

"There was so much we were going to do, John. I know you weren't ready to leave. We had places to go. Hadn't done even a third of the trails in the Smoky Mountains. Never made it to Mount LeConte. Never made it to Hawaii or the Pacific Coast Highway. I can tell you this. The psychic was right about soul mates. I know you were always mine. I knew that from the first time we met. And I know that's how you felt too, even though you might not have said it. You would have loved meeting Edith Bass. The history professor I met today. I think you two would have hit it off and we would have enjoyed her company for a very long time. She told me some things about the land we are living on. I think we were both linked to that land by our ancestors. I didn't tell you that, but I always felt that way. There are other things I haven't told you yet either. I was waiting for the right time, but now you just need to know. I believe you can still hear me. I am pregnant, John, and I promise you that this child will live a good life and know everything about you. I only hope he is as good a man as you were. I appreciate you wanting to spend the rest of your life with me. I feel so lucky to have been with you even though the time was so short. I will never stop loving you or missing you. Rest in peace, my love," she said and kissed him on his forehead.

When she turned around, she saw the policeman standing in the doorway and the nurse beside him was crying. The nurse hugged Jane and told her again how sorry she was. Jane thanked her and told the policeman that she was ready to go. On the way back to Seymour, she said, "I forgot. I forgot to tell him that I would take care of the trees. I wonder if I should go back," she said in an uncertain manner as she looked at the Knox county policeman. "No, no, that's ok. I'm sure he can still hear me," and Jane told him to keep driving.

The Knox county policeman told Jane that he had no jurisdiction in Seymour but the Sevier County police would be waiting for them at the house. When they arrived, they were met by two officers. They asked Jane to tell them everything she could remember about the scene before they entered the house. She told them all she could recall as the detectives made notes and then indicated they were ready to go inside.

They followed Jane around the house while she looked for things of value that might have been stolen. She noticed right away that John's coin collection was missing. The police taped off the closet and called their forensics specialist to come and check for prints and DNA. Jane looked in the drawer next to the bed and saw that the pearl handle .38 was gone but she didn't mention that to the police. She remembered John had gotten that from a friend just before they moved out there and he had told her the serial number on the gun had been filed off, so she kept that information to herself.

After going through the entire house, they found nothing else missing. Even all of her jewelry was untouched. The police thanked her for her help and asked if she had someplace to stay while they completed a more thorough investigation of the house. She said she could stay with a friend in Knoxville and they waited while she gathered a few things and left the house.

The drive to her friend's house was difficult and she cried so much that she had to pull over several times to compose herself. While sitting on the side of the road, her phone rang. She didn't recognize the number but answered it anyway. It was Edith and though Jane tried to hide it, Edith could tell she was very upset and asked her what was wrong. She was shocked to hear that Jane had found her husband dead when she got home. Edith told her how sorry she was and that she would call her back another time, but Jane wanted to know why she called.

"Well, I got it mixed up a little earlier today Jane," Edith started. "The affair that Jean had was with Elijah Gates, not Aron Bone. It appears your ancestor had the affair with Jean Cunningham. I think your connection to that property is even stronger than we thought."

Jane wasn't sure what to think when she heard that, but she thanked Sarah for calling and told her she would let her know when the service would be held. Edith again said she was sorry and to stay strong and that she would be thinking of her and praying for her.

She stayed at her friend's house for several days until she got a call from Dr. Ray who told her that he was very sorry to have to give her this news, but his assumption had been correct. Her husband died from suffocation, not a spider bite. They were ready to release his body now. She thanked the doctor for letting her know as her sadness turned to anger. She called the

Sevier County police department and was told they were almost finished with their inspection of the house. They had found a few footprints on the back steps but no fingerprints anywhere and no DNA.

Her friend insisted on taking care of the funeral plans after Jane wrote the obituary and selected the place she wanted John buried. She knew that John wanted to be cremated and his ashes spread in the Smoky Mountains. There was a place right off the road that they always went to when they visited the mountains. It was private and had its own waterfall and they had called it their "special place."

Jane wrote the simple obituary in just a few moments. It said:

John Evans Smith
32 years young
Husband and Soul Mate.

She gave the obituary to her friend, thanked her for all her help and told her she would be going home the next day. As soon as she got home, she started searching for the notes from that psychic reading. She still had a strong feeling that maybe John had been keeping some information from her. She looked all over the house and then suddenly remembered about the trees she had never taken care of. Jane went outside and cut down the other maple, dug the roots of both of them up and set them on fire. When replacing the shovel in the garage she happened to lift up John's toolset that was sitting on a steel storage shelf and found the notes from the psychic.

She took the notes and sat down on the front steps while she watched the Maple trees burn. She read about the first home and the water problems. She saw the note about being soulmates and the fact that they both liked the outdoors. She saw the reincarnation reference to the pioneers and she now realized how true that statement was. She read about the food problems and cancer and then saw the warning about the black widows.

I knew it. You didn't tell me that because you knew how much I hate spiders. But there it was. Another true and prophetic statement. She then read what he wrote about racism and how it affected them in the past and would affect them in the future and she started to tremble as she thought about Bryan. She saw the references to a person whose name started with A who had something to do with the tree and also someone whose first name started with E who could tell them about that tree. She read about the woman named Jean who seemed to have information to share with them. How could he know so many of these things? She saw the statement about listening to the shadows of the tree and that he felt the tree had a spiritual nature but he also saw death all around it. Then there was the quote. "Those accused were innocent, until those accused were guilty." She knew what all of that meant now. As soon as she read it and said it out loud, she knew that referred to her ancestor Elijah Gates and his friends. They were innocent of the crimes they were accused of and hanged unjustly

She watched the trees burn until they were just ashes and then doused the fire with the water hose. She got up to go back in the house and noticed a jar of water with some marigolds in it. Audie. He must have come by and she smiled at the thought. But then she suddenly remembered what he had said about his brothers. She got in her car, filled with anger from her husband's death and the way his brothers treated the kind Audie she had gotten to know. She made sure she had her taser in her purse as she drove down the road and around the corner until she came to three trailers with the name "well" on each one.

I bet the N and E fell off, she thought as she went up to the first trailer and knocked. Estes opened the door and came outside and Dauber followed him.

"Can we help you?" Estes asked. And though he knew who she was, he didn't use her name.

"Yes. I want to know where Audie is?"

"Audie?" Estes replied and then looked over at his brother and started laughing.

"That dimwitted googley-eyed bobblehead ain't been around here for a long time. He died about ten years ago. Fell off one of the cliffs in the Smokies. But we can help you. We can help you with a lot of things," Estes said as he and Dauber leered at her.

"If either one of you come near me, I will call 911 after I shoot both of you. I have a gun in my purse and if you don't believe me, try me."

Estes backed down when he looked in her eyes and realized she was not scared. "Well, sorry we couldn't help you today, but maybe another day," Estes said as he and Dauber went back into the trailer. Jane hurried back home and locked every door in the house. She sat down with a bottle of George Dickel and poured a big drink, knowing she shouldn't drink it, but hoping it would calm her nerves and her body which was shaking with fear, anger, and confusion.

How could I be seeing and talking to Audie, she asked herself as she poured another drink. He's dead. But he's as alive as the people I was just talking too. It's in my blood she told herself. Elijah Gates and Jean Cunningham. She saw spirits. If John was here, he would say I was crazy but it's all so true. Everything makes sense now. We were led to this place. For some reason, we were meant to be here.

Jane finished off half the bottle before falling asleep and only woke up when her friend called to tell her all the funeral arrangements were made and she had the urn with John's ashes. Jane thanked her and told her she would send out directions to their family and friends of when and where they would spread his ashes. She did not expect any family at the service. They were both only children and both of their parents and grandparents were dead. There were a few cousins, and though she sent them the notice of the funeral, she doubted they would come.

As she sat there framing the email message, she heard someone stirring around next to the shrubs. She picked up her taser before she peeked through the blinds and saw Audie. The spirit of a kind soul was out there looking at her plants. She had to say "spirit of a kind soul" again for it to sink in and she went over and poured another drink. She drank it and then walked outside. "Hello Audie," she said.

Audie looked at her with one eye as the other one looked at the plants. "I'm real sorry about your husband, Mrs. Smith."

"What do you mean?" Jane asked.

"You said he was sick the other day, with the black widow bite. I hope those marigolds that I left you helped."

"Thank you for bringing them, Audie, but they couldn't help him. Someone killed my husband."

"I was afraid of that. Lots of bad things happen on this land and in this area. Especially when my brothers get an idea about something and start drinking."

Jean just stared at Audie. She knew what he was saying. His brothers had killed John and she wanted revenge. When she looked at Audie and thought about the brothers she had just interacted with, she thought how far his brothers had strayed from the family tree. They were like leaves blown miles away by unforgiving winds, while Audie, the dead person she was speaking to, was what Samuel Newell envisioned when he had children. And now she wasn't scared talking to Audie. In fact, she liked having the ability to see people that others couldn't.

"Audie, have you ever seen the black women you told me about when we first met?"

"Yes, ma'am. Them and the Indian woman have never left this place. They are still here, but not many folks see them. And those that do, often regret that they did."

Jane shook her head and smiled. "Do you think the plants with root rot will make it?"

"They might. They are not getting worse which is a good sign."

“Thank you, Audie. I hope you can come to John’s funeral. It’s this Sunday in the Smoky Mountains. I am going to spread his ashes into a creek that we both loved to visit.”

“I wish I could ma’am, but I can’t go back to the Smoky Mountains. If I do, I won’t ever be able to come back and I like visiting with you. And a few others that are around here.”

“I think I understand, Audie,” Jane said, but just before she went inside, she heard him call out her name. She turned back around toward him.

“Bryan wanted me to tell you he’s okay. He really likes where he is now and he wanted to thank you and your husband for being so kind to him.”

Jane couldn’t see Audie anymore after he said that. She was unable to see anything. She just nodded her head and went inside and buried her face in a pillow and cried.

There was a large crowd at John’s funeral in the Smokies. Lots of people from his workplace and hers attended. Many of their friends came. Jane didn’t say much at the funeral but told everyone that John would be happy knowing he would forever be in a place that he loved as she sprinkled the ashes into the water. After that, everyone embraced Jane and told her how much she and John meant to them.

The following weekend, Jane was sitting out in her front yard in a lawn chair looking at the mountains. She had a bottle of wine and planned on watching the sunset and toasting the memory of her husband. She enjoyed the sunset so much, that when the full moon replaced it, she got another bottle of wine and opened it so she could sit and gaze at the moon and continue the very personal wake.

Around midnight, the Newell brothers came flying around the corner of the road, just down from her house and suddenly swerved as if they saw something standing in the middle of the road. The Ford 150 flew off into a deep ditch, rolled over on its side and got stuck between several trees. Jane began walking toward them and heard them talking as she got near.

“Why in the hell did you swerve off the road, Buford?” Estes yelled. “That was just a couple of darkies in the road. Hell, we would have been doing the world a favor if we had just run them over.”

As Jane neared the crash, she smelled gasoline and something else really strong. The back of the truck was loaded with gallon jugs of moonshine. Some of them had been punctured and were leaking too.

“Looks like you boys are in a shitload of trouble,” Jane said as she bent down and looked into the car. “With all that gasoline and moonshine leaking, the least little spark and BOOM! Then Hell’s got a new trio of fuck-ups to clean up the puke and shit that covers the floors.”

"Fuck you!" Estes yelled. "As soon as we get out of here, we'll show you who is going to Hell."

He tried opening his door but it was stuck. It was then that Jane saw the three black women. They were there with her making sure the doors wouldn't open. "Beware of the black widows," she said and then started to laugh.

"Get ready for a glimpse of your future boys," Jane said. She pulled out her lighter and walked back until she found the end of the gasoline flow. She flicked the lighter to life and dropped it to the ground. The flames followed the gasoline trail and when it reached the gas tank the truck exploded. With the additional mixture of the dripping moonshine, it quickly turned into an inferno. She heard the men screaming as they tried to get out and could see their bodies catching fire. She went back to her chair and poured herself another glass of wine before she called 911. She told them there was a crash near her house and it looked really bad. The truck had exploded and was in flames. She gave them her street address and put her phone down as she took another sip of wine.

"This will be the last alcohol I will drink for a while, Johnny," she said as she rubbed her stomach. "Hope you don't mind it too much tonight, but it's been a hell of a week. But things are looking up. One day, we will have a big porch out here and we can sit and look at the mountains and think about how lucky we are to live in such a special place. The home your father chose for us, and where our ancestors lived and died. But all of them are resting easy now, John. Everyone is resting easy and is at peace. Including me. And with the 'Hand of God' in our backyard and with friends all around us, who could ask for much more?"

S.C. 25

The well-traveled road didn't have a name. It was not unlike many other rural roads in South Carolina. It simply had a number: South Carolina State Highway 25. It was still a dirt road up until twenty years ago when it became asphalt, but even now, there were still a few sections of it that were only dirt and gravel.

There were not a lot of houses on the road or very many businesses either, even though the dirt road had been improved. The state and local politicians had promised that paving the road would bring more houses and businesses along with it. But as was often the case, those who held political office were wrong with their assertions and affirmations.

S.C. 25 was just always going to be one of those roads that people used primarily to get from point A to point B and there would always be only a few destination points on the road. Currently, there were only four along a ten-mile stretch of the road if you counted the elementary, middle school, and high school as one. The second destination was Stumpy's mini-mart. Anyone living in and around that ten-mile area, stopped at Stumpy's to get gas, beer, cigarettes, and lottery tickets. Stumpy and/or his wife were always there and they knew most everyone that stopped in there.

All the locals knew Charlotte and Elvin Daniel, the owners of Stumpy's and the genesis of the name Stumpy. Elvin was born with symbrachydactyly on his left hand and he liked to use that term when strangers stared at his appendage that had small projections where his fingers and thumb should have been. "When I saw this store was for sale, I had to buy it," Elvin would say and then hold up his hand and together, he and the customer would look at it. The stranger would nod their head in agreement until Elvin would start laughing, and then they would laugh together, and often, the customer would linger a little while longer and start a conversation with Elvin about current events, or their family, or college football. Almost everyone wanted to talk about college football, especially after they noticed the autographed picture of Elvin with Steve Spurrier that hung on the wall, just to the right of the cash register. Whether you loved him or hated him, the picture of the "ole ball coach" was very good at generating a discussion.

The name Stumpy never bothered Elvin. In fact, he took great pride in it because he believed he had something that others didn't. His parents had taught him to think that way and as a result, Stumpy never met a stranger in his entire life. Even if you didn't know him when you walked in the store, you left knowing him and thinking how nice and how funny that man was with the hand caused by the term that they had never heard before and always mispronounced.

The third destination point on that stretch of highway was Spanky's. After 6 p.m. on every Friday and Saturday evening, the parking lot was full. The owner of the establishment was supposedly a distant cousin of Spanky, the young boy who was in the "Little Rascals" shows that ran in the 1920s and early 30s. He had a picture of the Little Rascals over by the bar and another signed picture with Spanky and Pete the dog next to the cash register. But unlike the innocent nature of the Little Rascal shows, Spanky's on Highway 25 provided the customers a more mature level of entertainment.

And then there was the funeral home. Everyone who died within a fifty-mile radius used Thurmond's Funeral Home to plan their funeral. It had been in the same place for fifty-one years. Robert and John Thurmond started the family business and though both of them were now dead, John's daughter Estelle inherited the business and kept it in operation. She got her associates degree and mortician's license just before her father died and never considered doing anything else.

Even as a teenager, Estelle helped her father and uncle at the business and watched as her father implemented changes to keep it current. Just before he died, she promised him she would make sure the crematorium service would be finished and she made good on that promise. In fact, his was the first body cremated there. She kept the urn in her office and said good morning and good night to the ashes of her father each day when she came and left work. Though she never told anyone, she always heard him return her greeting.

Unlike her mother, Estelle's only child, Janice, did not enjoy working at the family business. Her mother required Janice to start working there as soon as she turned thirteen and though she protested to her father, he could not change Estelle's mind. Janice's father was a truck driver and was gone for weeks at a time so he wasn't there much for his daughter. He loved her and his wife but he allowed Estelle to run the home as well as manage the upbringing of their child.

Janice tried at least once a year to convince her mother that she didn't belong at the funeral home and now that she was fifteen, soon to be sixteen, she thought it was time to try it again. "Why do I have to work there at the funeral home? I don't like it."

"Because that's what our family does and it will be good for you to learn the business."

"What if I want to do something else? Say, become a scientist or maybe even an astronaut."

"You're not going to become a scientist or an astronaut. You don't have the aptitude nor the perseverance required for either of those disciplines," her mother sighed.

"Well, what if I want to do something else, say, become a policeman?"

"Do you really want a job as a policeman?"

As soon as she heard her mother's response, Janice thought she sensed a small weakness in her mother's defense. "Yes, I really like the idea of it," she replied even though she was overstating her true feelings for the job.

"Well, when you are old enough to make that type of decision, then we will see. Until then, you will work in the funeral home."

There it is, Janice said to herself, a crack. A willingness to consider her opinion. That has never happened before. I need to keep trying. "I really hate the way it smells. The embalming fluid makes me nauseous."

"I admit it does take getting used to. I try and keep you out of that area. There are many other things you do around there to help me out."

"I don't like the way it feels either, momma. I don't know what it is really, but I feel like I am being watched all the time. It's really creepy."

"Death is just a part of life, Janice. We help people move on. We help them celebrate the lives of their loved ones. We help them say goodbye. There is nothing creepy about that. It's an honor that they allow us to take care of their loved ones, one final time. And you are not being watched."

Estelle said that last sentence with as much conviction as she could, even though she didn't believe it herself. She wasn't about to tell her daughter that she still felt her grandfather's presence within the building every day.

Janice looked at her mother's face and knew there was nothing more to say that at this point that would help change her mind. But that was okay she thought. At least she had made some headway.

Estelle took Janice to school every morning and picked her up every afternoon. There was no sense in riding the bus since the funeral home was only a couple of miles from the school. Often on the way home, Estelle would stop at Stumpy's for some gas or milk or bread. Janice always enjoyed stopping there. She loved talking to Stumpy and the way that Charlotte doted on her. Charlotte called Janice their "little girl" and always took her up in her arms when she was little, and never let her get out of the store without allowing her to pick out the kind of candy she wanted.

The fact that Charlotte called Janice their "little girl" never seemed odd to her and she never questioned anyone about it. It wasn't until she was in the first grade that she understood why. Her mother told her that she reminded them of their own daughter who died at an early age from the flu. The next time they stopped there, Janice went up to Charlotte and Stumpy and told them she was sorry that their daughter died, but that she knew with parents as nice as them their daughter was surely in Heaven. After that, Janice could have walked out of the store with anything and everything she wanted.

It wasn't long after Janice had challenged her mother again about working at the funeral home that they stopped at Stumpy's one day after school. Now that she was fifteen, she was used to the fact that they didn't always go straight home after school. If the funeral home was busy, Estelle would bring Janice back with her for a couple of hours while she tried to get the necessary tasks done before a funeral service. Depending on what those tasks were, Janice either helped her mother or did her homework. Neither of which were chores Janice enjoyed doing.

When they stopped at Stumpy's that Friday evening, Estelle asked Janice to go in the store and tell them that she wanted to get twenty dollars of gas. Janice nodded her head and went inside to see Stumpy sitting behind the cash register, smiling at her. "How do, Mr. Stump; put 20 on the pump," Janice sang out as she opened the door.

He smiled at the rhyme. "Are you going to be one of them rap singers?" Stumpy asked as he turned on the pump for Estelle.

"I doubt I have what it takes to do that Stumpy," Janice replied. "I'm really not that good of a singer."

"From everything I have heard, that doesn't really matter."

She laughed. "Where is Miss Stump?" Janice asked just as Charlotte came out from their office.

"There's my little girl!" Charlotte said as she came over to hug Janice. "My you have grown! Every time you come in here, you seem to have grown half a foot. And in other ways that would suggest you aren't a little girl anymore. Won't you be sixteen on your next birthday?"

"Yes. But for now, I'm still relying on mom or dad, if he's home, to get me around this place."

"Don't be in such a hurry to grow up," Charlotte said as she brushed back Janice's long black hair back from her face. "Has your momma given you the talk?"

"What talk?"

"You know, about girls and boys and..."

"Whoa, Mrs. D!" Janice said as she held up her hands. "Just because I'm starting to get boobs now, doesn't mean that someone needs to give me the talk. I learned all about that type of stuff four years ago."

"Goodness, look at you," Charlotte replied. "So young and so mature all at the same time. Just wasn't like that when I was growing up.'"

"What wasn't like that when you were growing up'?" Estelle asked as she came into the store and handed Stumpy a twenty-dollar bill.

"Learning about the birds and the bees in school. Used to be, that information came from your mother or grandmother as soon as they saw their girl becoming a woman, in a physical way. They knew they needed to fill her head up with all the right information so her knowledge wasn't outpaced by her body. Of course, even back then, the information sometimes came too late," Charlotte said.

Estelle looked at her daughter with a confused scowl on her face and Janice knew she needed to say something to her mother before she was asked a dozen questions. "In the fifth grade, in health class, they told us about puberty and all of that other stuff. Believe it or not, I do know how babies are made, Mom. And before you go all Robocop on me, no, I haven't done anything like that. I haven't even kissed a boy. I'm not ready." Janice didn't add she hadn't found the right boy either, but she didn't feel that information was necessary at this time.

Estelle looked over at Stumpy and shrugged her shoulders. "Don't you worry none, Estelle," Stumpy said as he looked into her eyes. "You don't need to worry with your young lady. You brought her up good."

Estelle looked at her daughter and then back at Stumpy. He was right. Janice was a good girl. The fact that she was starting to speak up for herself, even if it was about not working at the funeral home, was really a good thing. She was becoming an independent thinker, even though she knew that some part of that independence reflected the rebellious nature of teenagers.

"What do you want today?" Charlotte asked as she took Janice's hand and led her down the rows of candy and snacks.

"Well, mom and I are going back to the funeral home to work some before we go home, so could I get a couple of bags of chips for us and two cokes?"

Before Estelle could object, Charlotte responded. "Of course, you can." Janice smiled and kissed Charlotte on the cheek.

Estelle pulled out a five-dollar bill and tried to give it to Stumpy but he wouldn't take it. "On us, Estelle. It will always be on us. We love spending time with you and our Janice. We will always be there for you and your family. Always."

"Thank you, Elvin. I truly appreciate the kindness you've shown our family over the years."

"It doesn't come close to how comforting you were to us. So kind and caring for her and us. We will never forget that."

Estelle knew Stumpy was referring to the loss of their child. It was fourteen years ago and she could tell it was still like yesterday for him. I don't guess you ever get over the loss of a child, she said to herself. No, I don't have to guess. I know you don't. She reached over and squeezed Stumpy's hand. She was one of only two people that called Stumpy, Elvin. The other one was his wife and she only did that when she was mad at him.

"Thank you, Mrs. D, Mr. Stump," Janice said as she gathered up the drinks and chips. On the way out, just behind her mom, she looked over at Stumpy and asked, "What do you think about the Gamecocks this year"?

"Probably win at least ten games," Stumpy predicted.

"Hope you're right, Mr. Stump. Bye!"

As they drove away, Estelle looked at her daughter and started to reprimand her for asking for something every time they were at the store. She told herself that when she was little, it was okay. She understood why the Daniels did what they did. But now that Janice was a young woman, soon to be sixteen, she didn't think it was appropriate for her to keep taking things from them. But before she said anything, she remembered Elvin's words: "It will always be on us," and she stopped herself. Just like her daughter working at the funeral home, there were just some things out of one's control she told herself and she started to laugh.

"What are you laughing at?"

"Just wondering how you're going to react when I take those barbecue chips from you," Estelle said as she leaned over and tried to grab the bag of chips.

"Oh no," Janice said, pulling back. "You always want plain Ruffles and so you get plain Ruffles!" Janice threw the bag at her mom and laughed.

"Yep, you're right," Estelle agreed. "This evening, I need you to mop the marble floors and then make sure the bathrooms are clean. I need to do some things in 'that place' you don't like to go into," Estelle said as she ate her chips.

"The bathrooms? Really?"

"I know, I know, there isn't anyone on this planet that likes cleaning bathrooms, but they shouldn't be too bad. Just clean out the toilet with the scrub brush, clean the sink, make sure that the towel dispenser is full and mop the floor. That's not too much to ask. Come on, I'll show you a trick about the marble floors," Estelle said as they got out of the car.

"I can't wait," Janice groaned. She followed her mom into the funeral home and back to the janitorial closet. She loaded up a cart with all the supplies Janice would need and then accompanied her to the main chapel.

"Most people think you need Pine-Sol or some exotic mixture of vinegar and lemon juices to keep marble floors shiny, but they're wrong. Just need a good soap, water and a soft microfiber cloth that's on the end of this mop. This spray bottle is filled with dishwashing soap and water. Just spray it on the floor and then use the mop. After you've done that, you can take care of the bathrooms. Okay?"

"I am tingly all over," Janice said as she rolled her eyes at her mother.

Estelle smiled and told her that she should be finished in about an hour and a half, but if she needed her to come and get her. Janice shook her head and began cleaning. She finished with the marble floors in about thirty minutes and the bathrooms only took twenty more. What am I supposed to do now, she asked herself after she took the supplies back to the janitorial closet. She sure didn't want to study. She began walking around the building, looking at the furniture for what seemed like the hundredth time, as she went through the lobby and toward the other small chapel at the end of the building.

I know this furniture has been replaced several times but the sofas and chairs always look the same, she thought. They are always some dark velvet fabric. What's up with that? It's like they told everyone in mortician school that velvet fabrics have some unique properties to comfort those that sit in them. Velvet is so lame. I'm going to tell mom that she needs to just get some regular furniture. Make people feel like they are at home. That would be what I would do. I'll tell her that on the way home today.

Janice kept walking down the back hallway toward the small chapel. She saw the white wrought-iron easels outside the chapel doors. There must be a funeral tomorrow she realized. There was no announcement or picture on them yet but Janice knew that was something her mother usually did on the day of the funeral.

The doors to the chapel were open and she saw the casket at the front of the room, with the top open. She couldn't tell if there was a body in it but she suspected there was. She walked down the center aisle toward the casket.

In the smaller chapel, the pulpit stood atop two small semi-circle shaped floors that looked like setting suns. It was designed to look like a little country church, with shiny wooden floors and pews. Janice had always thought it was much prettier than the main chapel. The pews were dark walnut and she remembered her grandfather telling her mother that they were very expensive but they were worth every penny. He was right. All the woods complemented each other and made you feel like you were in a church that had been around for a long, long time.

It was odd that she remembered that particular statement now since she usually didn't really care what her grandfather and mother talked about when it came to the family business. But he was right. They looked beautiful sitting there atop the dark oak floor.

As she neared the casket, she could see a girl laying in it. She remembered hearing about a young girl who had drowned a few days ago. She was only seventeen. She fell off her horse and hit her head on a rock as they were jumping over a stream. Janice was surprised by how alive the girl still looked lying there in the casket. Even though she had tried to avoid it over the years, she had seen a lot of dead bodies in caskets and she always thought they had looked like mannequins. But not this girl, this young woman. She looked like she was just resting there for a moment.

Janice stood right beside the casket looking down at the girl, trying to remember her name. Then she heard a voice in her head. It was telling her the name was Mary Lynn but that most people just called her Mary so it wouldn't be confused with Marilyn. Janice quickly turned and looked behind her to see who was talking, but she was all alone. She heard the same voice again; only this time it came from in front of her.

"What's your name?" the voice asked. Janice looked all around and then backed away slowly from the casket. She thought about running out of the chapel, but the tone of the voice sounded lost and sad and made her want to stay and help the person that was speaking to her.

"Janice," she whispered as she looked down at the girl. "Please, please, don't open your eyes if it's you in the casket that's talking to me. I don't think I can handle that."

"I can't move my body anymore, Janice. My eyelids won't open but you are right. I am talking to you. I haven't said all my goodbyes yet, so I am still here. After tomorrow's service, I won't be able to talk to anyone. I will miss my family dearly. And my horse, Duchess, and my dog, Maggie. Maggie tried to pull my head out of the water, but when I hit my head on the rock, there was nothing she could do. But she never left my side. She stayed there until my parents came and got me after Duchess came home without me and they started looking for me. She led them straight to me and Maggie. They were both wonderful animals."

"Why are you talking to me?" Janice asked.

"Because you're here and you seem to have a kind nature about you. Do you work here?"

"Yes. My mother owns the funeral home and she has me helping her with small jobs. But no dead person has ever talked to me before. Oh - I'm sorry I said dead person. What am I supposed to call you? I don't mean to say anything that would be offensive. I am just not sure what I am supposed to say or do. I'm not even sure if this is real or not. Oh my, I hope I'm not going crazy," she said as she placed her hands over her eyes.

"It's okay Janice. You don't need to do anything. I was just happy you stopped by and allowed me to talk to you. It's made me feel better."

When she heard the soft voice again, she removed her hands from her eyes and looked down at Mary, who continued talking.

"My parents are still too upset for me to say anything to them. I doubt I'll be able to do that until tomorrow. I have visited with Maggie and Duchess though. They both can tell when I'm around and they let me pet them, though I'm not sure how I can do that. I think they both just pretend that I am petting them, though they are both looking straight at me, just as if I was there."

"Are you comfortable? Can I adjust your head or anything?"

Mary started laughing. "I can't feel my body anymore Janice, but thank you for asking. Your mother took very good care of me and of my parents. You must have inherited her kind and caring nature."

Well, I never really thought about it Janice said to herself. She felt like they always seemed to butt heads these days, but as she stood there and thought about what Mary said, she realized that wasn't always the case. She actually did like being around her mother. It was only in the last year or so that they seemed so different. Maybe Mary is right. Maybe we are more connected and alike than I realize.

Mary didn't tell Janice that she could hear everything she was thinking because she knew how uncomfortable it would make her. And it really wasn't necessary she thought. She had seemed to work everything out in her head anyway. "How old are you Janice?"

"Fifteen. Well, I will be sixteen in January, which is only four months away."

"Where do you go to school?"

"Outland Valley High School. I'm in the ninth grade."

"I wish I had been able to go to public school. My momma home-schooled me. She used to be a teacher but when my twin brothers were born, she didn't want to do anything but stay home with me and my brothers. And believe me, they are a handful, especially now since they just turned twelve. I don't know what momma will do without my help trying to watch over those wild ones. Momma says they are like feral dogs and she is right. They aren't afraid of anything and will get into everything."

"What does feral mean?" Janice asked, almost embarrassed that she didn't know.

"Wild."

"It seems like your momma was a pretty good teacher. Probably better than any I've had."

"I'm not sure about that, but my mother was a very good teacher. And she loved us all so much. Daddy works at the paper mill. He is a shift supervisor out there. The house and the land we live on were given to him by his Daddy, so in many ways, we were very lucky. Even though I said I wished I could have gone to public school, I really have no reason to complain. We had so much, and I loved living out in the country. It was so pretty there; no matter what season it was. I couldn't even tell you which one I liked the best. There was something special about all of them."

Janice could hear the sadness in her voice again. The words seemed to hover in the air for a moment before they went away as if she was trying to hold onto them and bring them back to her.

"I am so sorry, Mary."

"You don't need to be sorry, Janice. I hope my words don't make you feel that way. I can't help but miss things right now, but I know that there is an even more beautiful world waiting for me. I have seen glimpses of it. But I just want to say goodbye one more time and then I'll be at peace and over time, so will my parents. The boys, well they'll be fine. In fact, I think they may be a source of comfort for my mother and father. They seem to be doing that now, though I don't expect their inclination to control themselves will be something that they can do forever."

She is seventeen years old, barely two years older than me, but she sounds so mature. It feels like I'm talking to my mother. How is that possible, Janice asked herself. Was she that way before she died or does wisdom come with death? And then she heard her mother's words speaking to her: "Death is just a part of life. We help people move on and celebrate the life of their loved one."

Just as her mother's voice was drifting way, Janice heard Mary's voice as if she was finishing her mother's thoughts. "Death complements life in many ways, Janice. They are both full of mysteries and answers. Neither one can exist without the other." Mary's words made her mother's statement even more significant and they resonated with Janice in a powerful way.

"Did your mother teach you that?" Janice asked.

"She did. She was, as you said, very smart. As are you, Janice. You just don't think you are, but you are. You will see. And caring about others comes as natural to you as your beautiful black hair or the color of your eyes; which by the way, are a beautiful brown. They remind me of pecans."

Janice wasn't sure what to say when she heard someone other than Charlotte complimenting the way she looked and so she said the only thing that came to her mind: "Thanks."

"You're welcome. And by the way, I do agree with you about the velvet. I don't like it either. Your idea of making it feel much more like home is a good one. I like this chapel. It's so much nicer than the other one. This one makes me feel like I'm in our little church out there in the country, in a field all by itself. As if someone told God that this little piece of land in the middle of nowhere needed a church. Maybe the person that put it there knew that in the spring and summertime, the field and the cemetery fill up with wildflowers and that little white church looks like a painting. I know it sounds like I am making everything up, but I'm not. I can tell you how to get there if you have a mind to see it."

"You heard me thinking about the velvet?"

"I did. I can hear everything in here if I want. If I don't, I can just cut off the sounds somehow and I am somewhere else. Somewhere that feels comforting and I don't worry about hearing or seeing anything. I am just content."

Janice felt a little weird that Mary could hear the thoughts in her mind and she remembered how she had told her mother that she felt like she was being watched all the time and it started to creep her out. But then she realized how much she had enjoyed talking with Mary. She thought about how much she had learned from her and how she had made her feel so much more at ease about being in the funeral home. Even more at ease about life in general. She sighed and smiled as she looked down at the beautiful young woman in the casket.

"What color were your eyes Mary? I bet they were blue, weren't they? Dark blue, like blueberries."

"Yes. You are very intuitive, Janice. I can sense that about you. My father used to have something he'd say when I was little and he'd pick me up after coming home from work. Blueberry eyes and blueberry pies for you and I. He loved blueberry pies. And my mother made a lot of them. He would never eat any until he was sure I had a bowl of pie and vanilla ice cream too so that

I could eat it with him. And he would say that stupid little saying again as we ate: Blueberry eyes and blueberry pies for you and I."

"Sounds like he loved you very much, Mary."

Mary's voice wavered for just a moment as she responded. "He did. I had a very loving family. I was blessed. I think you are blessed too. One day I know you will realize just how much."

Janice's eyes welled up and she reached up to wipe the tears away as she turned her head.

"Your mother is finished with her work now. She's coming to look for you. I appreciate you taking the time to talk with me this evening. I wish I had gotten to meet you in real life. I think we would've been good friends. But now is better than never."

Janice wiped her eyes again and gathered herself as she smiled at Mary. She wanted to believe the conversation that had just occurred was real, but a small part of her still questioned everything. "Before I go, Mary, and I know this sounds a little wack considering everything that we have talked about it, but can you reassure me that I am not going crazy?"

"Is telling you that you're not going crazy all it will take to convince you of that, considering it's coming from the same voice that makes you think you are going crazy in the first place? Are you sure that's what you really want from me?"

"Well, maybe not, seeing how you put it that way."

Janice heard Mary laughing and she began laughing too. She turned to walk out of the chapel but hadn't gone more than a couple of steps when she turned back around and asked for the address of the little country church.

"101 Cades Cove Road, Edgefield County, South Carolina."

"Thank you, Mary. Rest peacefully." Janice repeated the address several times within her head so she would remember it.

"Goodbye, Janice, and thank you for coming by. I hope you enjoy the flowers next spring," Mary whispered and then her voice was gone.

Janice turned around and saw her mother standing in the doorway. Estelle walked over and put her arm around her daughter as they gazed at Mary in the casket.

"We can never know His plan, can we?" Estelle asked in a rhetorical manner. "But he has one. I have to believe he has one. Such a beautiful young woman, Mary. Struck down and yet still so much life in front of her. A beautiful young woman and from what I understand, not just beautiful on the outside, but kind and compassionate too. And such wonderful parents. Even the boys, her brothers, were so well-mannered."

Janice remembered what Mary said about the boys "controlling themselves" and she smiled at what her mother had just said about them.

"Yes, she is beautiful. She doesn't look like anyone else I've ever seen in here."

"Yes, I know. I don't think I did that much really. It just appears that a natural beauty radiates from her, unable to be suppressed even in death."

Janice started to say that sounded like something Mary would have said, but she caught herself. She wasn't sure how her mother would react to the fact that she had been talking to the young woman lying there in the casket. But she wanted to tell her all that she had said and how appreciative she was of the way her mother took care of her and her parents. And about the velvet. Well, I can at least tell her about that, she thought.

Walking out of the chapel, Janice started a conversation, hoping that it would lead to a discussion about Mary. "Mom. I think this chapel is prettier than the other one. The wood is so beautiful. The oak floors and the dark walnut pews. Didn't grandfather buy those?"

Estelle was taken aback for a moment by her daughter's comments. She had never said anything about the funeral home that wasn't some sort of complaint up until now. What's changed? Did seeing Mary in the casket resonate with her in some way? They weren't that far apart in age. That's very possible she thought, but regardless, she wasn't going to quell her interest.

"Yes, your grandfather did buy those pews. They were expensive even back when he bought them. They were $300 a pew, but today, they would probably be ten times that much. And you're right, this chapel is so pretty. It's my favorite, too."

Keep going, Janice told herself. "But all the dark velvet, mom. I really don't think people like that. I think it reminds them they are in a funeral home. Wouldn't it be better if they felt like they were in their own home? Nobody has velvet in their home, except maybe a few rednecks that have some velvet Elvis up on their wall."

Estelle started laughing. "What's gotten into you?" she asked.

"Just giving you my opinions. You want them, don't you?"

"Absolutely I want them. I've never really even thought about the dark velvet in this place. But now that you mention it, I think I may have to agree with you. I was just doing what I had learned from my father. Yes, I think as we start to replace furniture, we could get rid of the velvet and make things look more like home. Thank you, daughter. Very good ideas and I appreciate you speaking up."

They walked out of the funeral home and got in the car. As they drove home, Janice knew that this was the time to ask about Mary.

"Mom, have you ever heard anyone talking to you in the funeral home? I mean someone who wasn't really there? You know, one that has passed on?"

Estelle paused before answering that question. Just a week ago her daughter was saying that she felt like she was being watched as an excuse to not come to the funeral home to work. And now tonight she shows some interest in the place and has something positive to say. What is she doing? Was that just a way for her to lead into this question? A way for her to make another request to stop working?

"No," Estelle finally replied. She really didn't believe she was telling her daughter a lie when she said that. She couldn't be positive that she heard her father talking to her. Guiding her. Listening to her and giving her advice. She couldn't say for sure it just wasn't a way she used to work things out in her own mind. Talking to her father and remembering what he taught her and the advice he had given her in the past. No was the right way to respond to that question, she told herself.

When she heard her mother's response, Janice knew for sure what her mother would say if she brought up her conversation with Mary, so she kept quiet about it. But she did want to go back to the funeral home and see if it happened again. Though she wanted to believe she actually had that conversation with Mary, she was still concerned that she might not have and she would be that girl that everyone whispered about when they walked by her. So, she wasn't really sure if hearing Mary's voice again, or not hearing Mary's voice would be better for her mental well-being. The only way she would know for sure would be to go back to the funeral home.

She asked her mother if she could come with her tomorrow to finish the arrangements for Mary and her mother was even more confused by that question. But again, she reasoned, it would be better for her to try and cultivate this current interest in working there. So she told her she would love to have her help. They would need to be there early to make sure all the flowers and pictures that her family wanted were set up and arranged appropriately.

Her father wasn't home that evening, so Estelle made dinner for just the two of them and it was one of the best meals that they ever had together. They talked a long time about her grandparents and the funeral home and Janice asked a lot of good questions. Estelle couldn't wait for Jim to get home so she could tell him about the change in their daughter's attitude.

The next morning, she let Janice set up the pictures on the easels while she worked on the flower arrangements. Estelle complimented her on the job she did and gave her a hug. Janice was hoping she would hear Mary thank her for the way she arranged everything but she didn't hear her voice at all.

Together, she and her mother sat at the back of the chapel after all the family and friends were seated and listened to Mary's memorial service. Janice saw how distraught her parents were as friends and family talked about how kind and thoughtful Mary was. Many people in the chapel got up to speak and each of them had a special memory of Mary that they shared. She also watched her brothers sitting like little gentlemen next to their parents and she remembered again what Mary said about them and smiled. She hoped Mary would be able to say goodbye to her parents today and provide them some comfort.

She and her mother watched them load Mary into the hearse and drive away. When they had all gone, Estelle thanked her daughter for helping so much. Janice smiled and told her that she wanted to start helping out more at the funeral home. Janice even said she would go into the embalming room and wanted to see how the crematorium worked. Estelle took her daughter in her arms and said she would be happy to show her everything. On the way home that afternoon, Estelle drove Janice into town and took her to eat at the Pizza Hut. Pizza was her daughter's favorite food and Janice said if Pizza Hut was one of the perks for working more, she was ready to "bust a move" at Thurmond's. Estelle laughed and said she was sure that they could make it some sort of regular get-together.

Over the next month, Estelle taught Janice everything about the funeral home business. She even showed her the embalming and cremation processes and she could tell her daughter had a hard time with both of them, but she still stayed there with her, listening and learning. Janice helped with many funerals over that month. She did anything and everything her mother asked, except the embalming and cremation, which required a license and wasn't anything she really wanted to do anyway.

In all that time, Janice never heard any of their lifeless clients talk to her and she began to wonder whether she had really heard Mary's voice at all. She thought about the conversation with Mary all the time and it began to bother her. She started to question her mental state. Several days later, the nightmares about the funeral home began.

The nightmares were always the same. Three young men had broken into the funeral home looking for a place to hide from the police. They found Janice inside and she was all alone. She didn't understand why her mother had left her there by herself and she called out to her as the men approached. She looked behind her and saw the casket and knew if she had hidden in there she would have been safe but she didn't have time now. She then saw the crematorium door and the insides of the furnace. She felt the heat and saw the flames burning skin and bones away as if they were made out of paper. The pain she felt was unbearable, like a thousand nails being hammered into her body all at once and she screamed until she awoke.

Though she was screaming in her sleep, she wasn't making a sound that anyone could hear. She just woke up and sat on the edge of the bed and tried to clear her mind of everything. Sometimes she would go downstairs and get a glass of water, and watch some TV, but she never fell back asleep. And soon, the lack of sleep began to take a toll on her body and made the doubts she had in her mind even more prominent and troubling.

It wasn't long before Estelle noticed how tired her daughter looked and asked her what was going on. Janice just told her that she was having trouble sleeping. Worrying about a test or some essay that she had to write because she wanted to do better in school. Her mother said that perhaps she was working too much at the funeral home and she might need to cut back. But Janice told her no and that she was sure she would be better once this semester was over. And so her mother left it at that.

But nothing changed. In fact, it just got worse. The nightmares became even more vivid. She could see the three faces of the men so clearly, that she found herself looking around for them when she was at school or at work. Now when she woke up, the screams turned into tears as she lay there in bed and worried about her well-being. Some nights, she tried to stay awake and read or watch TV as long as she could but eventually, she would fall asleep and when she did, she would fall into that frightening world again, always awakening in a harsh manner.

She retreated from everyone at school and even became unresponsive to questions that were asked by her teachers. Her classmates at school started to call her "The Walking Dead" and asked her if she enjoying partying with her friends when she went to the funeral home. Their kidding only made Janice feel worse and she withdrew even more into her own world. One where she couldn't hear any of her classmates or teacher's words. It was as if she made herself deaf and she began to question how long she could do this.

Eventually, the principal called Estelle to talk about Janice, explaining that her teachers were worried about her and asked if she thought her daughter was doing drugs or if anything traumatic had happened at home.

Estelle told him that Janice wasn't doing drugs and that she felt she was probably just working too much at the funeral home and as a result of that and the pressure to do better in school, she was having trouble sleeping. She said she would make her stop working and she was certain that things would soon return to normal. The principal advised her to keep Janice out of school for a week and also suggested that she might want to consider taking her to a mental health professional.

When she picked Janice up from school that day, Estelle said she wanted her to stop working for a while and even stay home from school and rest. This time Janice didn't object, though she wasn't sure that would help. She could not rationalize the conversation that she had with a dead body and was convinced that she was going crazy. Though she wanted to, she had never been able to tell her mother about what was really troubling her. Nevertheless, she wanted the nightmares to stop so she was willing to do whatever her mother wanted.

Estelle was relieved that Janice agreed to her requests. She knew she should take her straight home, but she had just a few things she needed to finish up for an early funeral service the next morning. She told Janice that she was sorry and asked her if she would be okay with staying in her office and resting for a little while so she could complete her work and Janice nodded her head yes. When they reached the funeral home, Estelle walked Janice to her office and said she could lay down on the sofa. She gave her a blanket and sat down next to her as she brushed her hair back from her face. "You know I love you very much, don't you?" Estelle asked.

Janice smiled and nodded her head.

"And if you don't want to work at the funeral home, you don't have to. It's not for everyone. It will be okay, sweet girl. You don't need to worry about it anymore. You do what will make you happy."

Janice reached up and hugged her mother and said she was sure she would be better soon. She kissed her mother on the cheek and laid her head back down on the sofa. Her mother smiled and told her she would hurry and then they would go by Pizza Hut on the way home. Janice didn't reply. Her eyes were closed as if she had already fallen asleep. Estelle left the office door open and went to the embalming room to finish the preparation of the body.

Janice found herself in the same dream again, but this time things felt different. She felt there was someone else there in her dream, ready to help her should she need it. She soon saw the three men and then the crematorium. And this time when she saw the flames, she saw something that frightened her even more than the flames.

She gasped as she sat up suddenly, feeling disoriented as she looked around. She suddenly realized she was in her mother's office and a sense of panic seized her. She ran to the embalming room and grabbed her mother by the arm. "What are you doing?" Estelle asked.

"Just come with me. Quickly. Please."

Estelle wasn't sure what was wrong but she could see the look of determination in her daughter's face so she went with her. Janice took her mother into the small chapel where there was an empty casket. She told her mother to get in and to not say anything and Estelle quickly did as she asked.

"Don't worry, mom, but don't say anything. Everything will be okay. I promise."

Running back into the lobby, she heard glass breaking from the side door in the main chapel and saw a hand come through the window and open the door. One of the men in her dream walked through it, followed by the two others. Janice screamed and ran toward the crematorium, hoping she could get there and lock the metal doors before they could catch up with her.

The three men chased her through the funeral home before a gunshot rang out. She felt the bullet go through her spine and her legs crumpled beneath her just as she got to the crematorium door. She looked up at the men as they stood over her and she heard one of them say they couldn't let her live. They picked her up and pushed her into one of the furnaces and closed the door. Janice didn't feel the flames though as she heard Stumpy's voice, telling her to let go and that he would catch her.

Estelle thought she heard a gunshot and was halfway out of the casket when she heard Stumpy whispering to her that he was there and to stay quiet. She then heard a voice yell, "What the hell!" and heard multiple gunshots. She lay there, terrified and unsure of what to do until the casket was opened a few minutes later by a police officer.

"Are you okay, ma'am?" he asked.

"Yes, I'm fine, but where is my daughter?" Estelle cried out as she ran to her office. The policemen ran with her but they found the office empty. She looked at the officer, confused and scared.

"What happened here?" she demanded.

"These three men robbed Stumpy's and went looking for a place to hide. We got a call from his wife Charlotte, telling us they had been robbed and that her husband had been shot. She told us there were three of them and that they went east on 25. We sent a car to the store and several more down 25 when we saw someone waving a flashlight in front of the funeral home. When we got here, we found the three men. Two of them were dead and one of them was muttering something about some man with one hand who had shot them."

Estelle burst into tears. As the police officer tried to console her, she noticed the note on her desk. She wiped away her tears and began to read.

"Dear Mom and Dad: If you are reading this, I didn't make it back to the crematorium in time, but don't worry about me. I am fine. Better than fine. I know I will be in a beautiful world. One Mary told me about some time ago. Please spread my ashes at 101 Cades Cove Road in Edgefield County in the spring. When you do that, you will understand what I am talking about. I will always love both of you very much. Thank you for loving me. I now know just how lucky I was. Janice"

Estelle fell to her knees, sobbing, and the police officers called the EMTs. After reading the note, they checked the crematorium and found the furnace that was still on and blood on the floor. They turned the furnace off and walked away, fighting back their tears. When Estelle awoke in the ambulance the note was still clutched in her hand. She folded it up and placed it over her heart.

Her husband was waiting at the hospital and he held her hand as they rolled her into the emergency room and the doctor examined her. Within a few minutes, the police officer who had been with her at the funeral home asked if he could talk to her a minute. She agreed and told him everything that she knew. The officer said that they had a very brave and courageous daughter and he was very sorry for their loss. Though unable to talk anymore, they both tried to smile and acknowledge his comment as he left the room.

The police officer wasn't sure what to put in the report after he heard Estelle tell him about Stumpy telling her to be quiet while she was in the casket, and then shooting the three men. What she said coincided with what the man that survived had said though. But how was that possible? Stumpy had been killed when his store was held up by those three men moments before they went to the funeral home. So he thought for a moment and then put in the report that the men were shot by Elvin Daniel in self-defense. That was the truth. He didn't know how, but he knew the answer resided somewhere above his paygrade and he let it go. The report was never questioned.

Estelle showed the note to her husband and told him that she wanted to go back to the funeral home after they released her. The police officers escorted them back and watched as Estelle collected her daughter's ashes and left.

Estelle only performed one more cremation before she sold the funeral home. Charlotte asked her to cremate Stumpy and she honored her request. Estelle shared Janice's note with Charlotte, who asked if she could accompany them to that place in the spring and Estelle said she thought Janice would like that very much.

She signed the papers that placed the funeral home into the hands of a new owner and shared the suggestion that her daughter had made. He liked the idea and said that he would work on replacing the velvet furniture. He also told her that he didn't plan to change the name of the funeral home. He knew what that name meant to this community and as long as he owned it, the name would remain the same. His comments gave Estelle a great deal of comfort and she thanked him as she fought back her tears in an unsuccessful manner.

On the first day of May, Estelle, Jim, and Charlotte went out to 101 Cades Cove Road in Edgefield County. They had to stop the car as soon as they saw the little white church and the field that was covered in wildflowers. None of them could speak as they gazed at the beautiful setting.

They drove into the church parking lot and walked into the field next to the cemetery. Estelle and Charlotte opened the urns and watched as the ashes floated in the air like pollen and then settled down amongst the flowers as if they were always meant to be there. Estelle remembered Stumpy telling her that he and Charlotte would always be there for her family and she smiled, though she was still unable to truly understand what had occurred that night.

She then heard a girl's voice, one she didn't recognize, talking to her. Telling her that "death complements life in many ways. They are both full of mysteries and answers" and then she heard her daughter's voice telling her that was her friend Mary speaking to her. Janice told her she had met a lot of people in this new world, and they all appreciated the way her mother had cared for them and their families when they had passed on and that made her very proud to be her daughter. She then said, "I think it will help you to understand to know that He was there that night for me too."

As they stood in the beautiful field, a woman with two young boys holding her hands walked over to Estelle and introduced herself and told her how sorry she was for her loss. Estelle heard Janice telling her that was Mary's mother and that she could use some help taking care of those two little boys. And then Estelle remembered and smiled as she began to understand the mystery.

Washington Road

It was a well-traveled road that had become a main thoroughfare for the town. The first road that linked the city to the ever-expanding growth that was occurring to the west. Sixty years ago, it was a road of asphalt and gravel and dirt as the road improvements only went so far. But that changed on a daily basis until very few people living there knew anything but the modern road they traveled on thousands of times in a year.

Drivers and passengers seldom noticed the large metal drain covers off to the side of the road unless they were tearing up the road and installing new, larger drain pipes or repairing the existing ones. During those times, especially when stopped at a red light, the drivers and passengers could see people wearing white plastic hard hats and fluorescent green or orange vests standing around a small plastic barrier encircling the drain hole. Very few of them saw the workers descend into or rise out of those holes but they did. And when that occurred, he hid.

He watched them from the dark, always out of their light until he knew they were gone for the day. He didn't like it when they came down into the pipes. The pipes had been his home for so long that he could not say with any certainty just how long it had been.

He didn't keep track of the days of the week any longer. Most of the time, he knew when a day had passed, but sometimes in the winter or on really stormy days, he couldn't tell you when the day had come or gone. But time down there in the large concrete tunnels was irrelevant. The only thing that mattered was that he knew where the old one was. And though he knew he shouldn't, he felt safe around the old one.

He remembered the day he met the old one. The absence of his left hand reminded him every day. And that greeting established the ground rules that he lived by. Stay away from the old one and you would be safe. If he moved, you moved. When he slept, you slept. When he ate, you ate. He was comfortable with that living arrangement. The war he was in prepared him for that type of lifestyle.

He was taught to live in the jungle alone for weeks at a time. The officers told him that his mission was to infiltrate the enemy's position and to gather information. But the true mission was unspoken. Unspoken but understood. Gather information and kill as many of the enemy as possible.

He thought he would have trouble killing another person, even when he knew they would kill him if given the opportunity. But he didn't have any trouble at all. In fact, it became too easy. He didn't know how many he killed in the eight years that he was there. It was not important to him. His job was to gather information and kill people. They didn't tell him to keep track of how many people he killed.

The faces of the people he killed became unrecognizable. Even the face of the first person whose throat he cut so deep that the knife scraped the cervical spine as he moved it from one ear to the other. That face had no eyes, no ears, no nose, no mouth. Nothing that would tell you it was a human being. He knew that seeing his enemy in that way was critical for his long-term survival. Otherwise, he would not have been able to rest. Even though he could go up to three days with minimal sleep, if he went beyond that, his ability to protect himself became unpredictable.

When he came back from missions in the jungle, he found it difficult to associate with the other soldiers. He stayed to himself and the other soldiers learned very quickly to leave him alone. He watched the other soldiers use drugs and drink to help them cope with the world in which they now lived, but he never enjoyed doing drugs. He had tried them once but he felt exposed and unable to protect himself, so he never did them again. He did drink whiskey though. He liked Jim Beam and no matter how much he drank, he maintained a level of awareness around him. A circle of safety that he could rest within and if penetrated, still be able to show the careless person how sharp his knife was and how lucky they were to still have everything on their face.

When the war was over, he went home. He never thought about staying there in that jungle. He didn't believe he could handle seeing the faces of his enemy in his routine daily life. He knew that would create a problem for himself that he didn't want to encounter.

He didn't have any brothers or sisters. His father, he never knew. He didn't remember ever seeing him and had no idea why he wasn't around until his mother told him on his twelfth birthday. As she was cutting his birthday cake, she said that his father died when he was two years old. She stated that a large concrete pipe broke free from a crane and killed him and two other men. The company paid her $50,000 for his father's death.

She told him that she never expected his father to amount to much and was amazed when she received that large check after his death. She bought the house they were living in with that money, along with some new furniture and clothes. She used the rest of it to live on. The birthday cake they were eating and his birthday present represented the last of that money. His birthday present that day was five ten-cent Marvel comic books.

She also told him that she would be starting work the next day, so she would no longer be home when he returned from school each day. She would be working in a bar from 3 to 11 p.m., waiting on tables and serving drinks. She shared that news as she poured them each a drink of whiskey, Jim Beam, to be exact. That's why it didn't shock him that he liked Jim Beam. The taste for it came naturally.

After getting his discharge papers and taking the bus home, he thought about the reception and welcome he would receive when he got there. Unfortunately, he wasn't surprised by it. There was none. No one was there to greet him and say welcome home. His mother had left him a note stating that there was some meatloaf in the refrigerator if he was hungry. That was it. Not welcome back or looking forward to seeing you or glad you are okay. Just that there was a meatloaf in the refrigerator. When he read that note, all the memories of the evenings he spent home alone came rushing back to him like he was watching the pages of those five comic books flipping by page after page. He remembered all the times he spent at home reading those comics over and over and listening to the radio. And then he realized why he was so comfortable living in the jungle, isolated and alone most of the time. It came naturally.

The house looked the same, but some of the furniture was different and there was a new TV in the den. He sat down in a large brown recliner and turned on the TV with the remote control he found on a small table beside the chair. He flipped through the channels and saw the soap operas and game shows and then turned it off. He didn't like watching anything except sports. He enjoyed the football games that they had been able to watch over there when he was resting before heading out on another mission.

When he opened the door to his room it was like he had stepped back in time. Nothing had changed. The bed, the chest of drawers, the nightstand, even the blanket on the bed was the same. He placed his duffel bag on the floor and sat down on the edge of the bed. He opened the bottom drawer of the nightstand and smiled when he saw they were still there. The five comic books he had received for his twelfth birthday. The last birthday gift he ever got. He picked them up like they were delicate manuscripts and looked at them as he lay back on the bed.

Even though he knew every word of every story, he read them again and this time they were even more enjoyable. The Fantastic Four, Hulk, Ant-Man, Giant-Man, Iron Man, The Wasp, Doctor Strange, Captain America, The Howling Commandos, and Prince Namor - The Sub-Mariner. They were still there, allowing him to escape into another world with heroes who defeated the enemies that threatened society and mankind.

He unpacked his duffel bag and went downstairs. He took out the meatloaf and made a sandwich and poured himself a glass of milk. He had to admit it tasted a lot better than the food he had been used to eating. Much better than anything he caught in the jungle. He never acquired a taste for bugs and worms but it really didn't bother him to eat them. Whatever it took to survive. He was very good at doing that.

The next day he was up and dressed early. He had heard his mother come upstairs around 2 a.m. and he walked over to her bedroom and looked at her laying crossways on her bed. He didn't bother to wake her as he left the house and started walking. The houses he saw were a mix of both new and old. His old high school looked the same but the elementary and middle school were gone. He wondered where they went as he continued to walk around the town.

Everyone seemed to be in a hurry to get somewhere, whether they were walking by him on the street or driving by him in their cars. He heard a lot more beeping from the cars and people yelling at other drivers. He wondered why they were doing that. They didn't understand how lucky they were, he told himself and shook his head. He soon found himself at a construction site and stood there for a moment as he watched the large crane lowering a concrete pipe to the ground. He heard someone yelling at him and motioning for him to come over and so he did.

The man introduced himself as the foreman of the project and asked if he just got back from serving over in Nam. He wondered how the man knew that and then realized he was wearing his army fatigues. The foreman noticed the patch on his sleeve and asked if he was in the Special Forces and he nodded his head. He asked him if he needed a job and though he hadn't really thought about it, he nodded his head yes. The foreman asked when he could start and he told him tomorrow.

“Great”, the foreman replied. “I can use a good man like you.” He took him over to a trailer and gave him a hard hat and a fifty-dollar bill. “Go get some work clothes, some good leather gloves, and some steel-toed boots and show up here tomorrow at 7 a.m. We work ten-hour days, five days a week, and you get ten hours of overtime, at time and a half, every week. Your starting hourly rate is $7.20 an hour and that will go up as you learn more skills. You good with that?”

He shook his head yes.

“By the way, never got your name,” the foreman said as he held out his hand.

“Jakub, uh, Jakub Plotniak,” he said hesitantly as he shook the foreman’s hand.

“Glad to meet you, Jakub. My name is Brian Lancaster. See you tomorrow at 7:00 sharp.”

“Yes, sir,” Jakub said as he turned around and left.

As he walked around downtown, he thought about what all the other soldiers had said as they were headed back home. How they had heard it was difficult to find a job and that the economy was going in the tank. If he had remembered their names, he would have written them a letter and told them to move to his hometown. It wasn’t hard to find a job here he thought as he walked into the clothing store to buy the work clothes. He found the shirts and jeans he needed, but the man who helped him said he would need to go over to Bob’s Hardware to get the gloves and boots. He told him where it was and which bus to take as it was several miles away.

Jakub just looked at the salesman and told him to point him in the right direction and he could get there. The man smiled and gave him the directions and Jakub started walking. He took his time and within an hour, he found the store and got the gloves and boots. He still had seven dollars left and headed back toward town to get something to eat before he went home. He knew exactly where he wanted to go and found the place still there on the corner of Main Street and 2nd Avenue. Hoskens Drug Store.

He had only been to Hoskens a couple of times with his mother, but each time he went, he thought the food was some of the best he had ever eaten. He arrived just before they stopped serving lunch and he ordered two egg salad sandwiches, a bowl of chili, and a slice of homemade chocolate pie. The waitress was happy to wait on him and when she brought him his food, she asked if he had just gotten back from the war. He nodded his head. She asked him how it was over there and he looked up at her, not sure what to say.

He said the nicest thing he could think of and that was "Wet" and then began eating. It was even better than he remembered and he savored every bite. Though the lunch was not quite three dollars, Jakub left the entire seven dollars for the waitress and thanked her for the meal on the way out. She thanked him for the tip and told him to come back, even though as soon as he left, she began telling her coworkers how strange he made her feel. But if he was going to leave a tip like that every time, he could come in wearing just his underwear and shoes and she'd be glad to wait on him.

Jakub heard his mother come in that night around midnight, but this time she opened his door and looked in before she closed it and went to bed. He could smell the alcohol and heard her stumble several times as she got into her bed. He left her a note the next morning telling her he had a job and left for work. He got there at 6:45 a.m. and Brian was there waiting for him.

"I knew you'd be early," he said as he took him into the trailer again and had him fill out some paperwork that he needed for the payroll folks and the government. "Uncle Sam's taking too much of the money Jakub, but there isn't much I can do about it," and Jakub just shook his head saying he understood. Brian introduced him to several men on the job and told them all what to do and Jakub started working.

The men he worked with complained about everything going on in their lives during the entire time they were working. They complained about the government and taxes. The high cost of living, especially gas. Their lack of sex with their wives or girlfriends. He very seldom heard any of them mention anything they were happy about and most of them always had a headache from the beer or liquor they had been drinking the night before. They didn't seem to be happy about anything, except when they talked about sports.

Jakub didn't join in their conversations unless they were talking about sports and even then, his comments were very limited in their scope. Over time, they stopped even trying to include Jakub in their conversations but that didn't bother him nor them too much, because Jakub did two to three times as much work as the others. He knew that he was carrying the load, but it didn't matter to him. He liked having something to do and it kept his mind off of other things he didn't want to think about.

Every week when he got paid, he left fifty dollars of his check for his mother in an envelope on the table. He knew she would spend very little of that on food, so he did most of the grocery shopping, which usually cost another thirty to forty dollars. He calculated that if he saved his money, he could save $20,000 in two years and that was his plan. Though he liked the job and his boss, he didn't like the people he worked with. He didn't like being around the people in town either. And he didn't like living at home. It had never been a home and was never going to be.

Over the next two years, he saved his money and began buying items he knew he would need to live where he was going. Waterproof boots, several knives, manganese and flint, and any waterproof clothing he could wear over his fatigues. Everything he needed would have to fit into one backpack. He was very adept at knowing what to place in that backpack and making sure he had what was necessary to survive. He had learned in a world that would have killed him if he hadn't.

When he had saved up $20,000 and had everything he needed, he got up and walked downstairs after his mother came home one night and stumbled into bed. He placed the comic books and $10,000 in an airtight, waterproof container and put them in his backpack along with the other things he had packed. It was 2:30 a.m. when he looked at his watch and wrote the note to his mother, leaving $10,000 in an envelope next to it. The note read: "Thanks for the meatloaf." He walked out the door and toward the construction site.

Brian came to the house after Jakub hadn't shown up to work in a week. He met Jakub's mother and wasn't surprised that he had left. He asked her if she knew where he had gone and she shook her head no. That response didn't surprise him either. He gave her his card and asked her to call him if she saw him and she promised she would. "Godspeed, Jakub, wherever you are," Brian said as he walked to his truck.

Jakub hadn't noticed that his hair had turned white because he kept his head and face shaved. He knew by doing so, he could minimize the lice infestations. Though he didn't know it, his body had a very strong immune system and he was able to resist infections that most people acquired every year. He had read an article some time ago where Dr. Linus Pauling suggested that maintaining high levels of vitamin C would help your body's overall health so he took a high dosage of it every day.

He figured the scientist who won a Nobel Prize for chemistry knew what he was talking about. He also liked the fact that he won another Nobel award for speaking out against the war and so he always kept several bottles of vitamins with him and never got sick. That's what he needed the $10,000 for when he went down into the concrete pipes to live. That and the other things that wore out over time. He came out of the pipes when he needed to buy something, often waiting until just before the store closed to minimize his exposure to everyone. He couldn't remember when it happened, but at some point, the stores that sold the vitamin C and other supplies he sometimes needed, started staying open all night long. When that happened, he often shopped in the middle of the night and was gone before anyone really noticed him.

It wasn't difficult to find food down in the large concrete pipes. There were always small animals coming down into the pipes and they were not hard for him to catch and eat. Most of the time he cooked the animals, but if it was too wet where he was that evening, because of the old one's location, he ate the animals without cooking them. He always made sure he didn't contaminate the raw meat by removing the gut of the animal with a precision that had been learned from his years of experience in the jungle.

Though he wasn't sure how many years had passed since he had gone down into the pipes, he began to realize that his body's ability to react was slowing down. Sometimes he found himself sleeping and unaware that the old one was getting too close. But for the time being, he had always been able to wake up in time and move away. He knew that there would come a time when that didn't happen and he began to wonder what it would be like if the old one got hold of him like it did the rats that passed by it. He realized it wouldn't be that bad of a way to die. At least it would be quick, he thought, as he looked down at his hand.

He didn't know what day it was when he heard a strange sound coming from a place somewhere in the pipes that he hadn't been to in a long time. He looked over his shoulder at the old one and it seemed interested in the sound also. Jakub started walking toward it, always looking behind him, as the old one followed him in its slow and methodical manner. He had walked about a mile when he saw what was making the noise. It was a small child who had fallen down into the pipes. The little boy was in a section of the pipe that Jakub knew people couldn't get to from above but was very accessible to the old one if he decided that he wanted a larger meal than usual.

The little boy started screaming when he saw Jakub walking toward him. He raised his hand up toward the boy and when he did, the child screamed even more. It made Jakub worry as he looked back to check on the old one. He put his left hand down and held up his right hand and put his finger toward his lips and shook his head. The young boy stopped screaming as he looked at the person standing there.

"Are you Captain Hook?" the little boy asked.

For a moment he didn't understand what the boy was asking but then he remembered. Somehow, he remembered what the boy was referring to as he looked down at his left hand.

"Yes, I am and Peter told me to come get you out of here. Is that okay?"

The little boy nodded his head and Jakub looked over his shoulder one more time before he moved toward him. He saw the old one approaching them and he knew he didn't have much time. Jakub started running as fast as he could through the knee-high water until he reached the little boy and pulled his knife out. He didn't have time to explain to the child what he was doing as he cut through his belt and jacket so he could remove him from the pipe. He heard the boy screaming and he turned around as he felt the bump against his leg.

He drove his knife into the large log numerous times as he held the boy behind him. On the last thrust into the wood, he twisted the blade and then pulled it out. The little boy was scared and wasn't sure what the old man was doing but Jakub turned around and told him that they would be okay now. He took the little boy to a place in the pipe where he knew there would be people above and helped him climb up the steps until he could get out. He heard him running toward the people yelling that Captain Hook had saved him from the crocodile.

Jakub retreated into the pipes knowing there would be a few people who would come down there and look around and he knew he needed to go where they wouldn't find him. The old one was dead now and he didn't have to worry about it. In fact, he felt like he didn't have to worry about anything else anymore. Whether it was the images of the war or the images of the people that looked at him in a strange manner when he came home from the war, staring at the two metal clamps where his left hand used to be; those images were now gone. Suppressed into a dark place in the back of his mind and no longer available for viewing.

He would live out his life in solitude because that is where he had always felt most comfortable. He still had his comic books and he still enjoyed reading them. Even more, now that he didn't have to worry about being in a place where he was not wanted. He was just like the superheroes he thought; those in his comic books. He had defeated that which had threatened him his entire life and had now saved a little piece of mankind. It just came naturally.

Tamer Lane

He lived at the corner of Redbud Lane and Mercy Street, just one street over from a part of town that people avoided going into unless they lived there. Those within the drug community knew him as Bix. Those within the town and across the state knew him as Reuben Broadwater, and he was well known throughout both as one of those that "came from old money."

He had always thought that the name of the street that ran parallel to the undesirable community was a contradiction for what occurred in that part of town. There was very little mercy shown to those that lived there. Their life was hard; filled with poverty, poor living conditions, and very little interest in changing the way things were. It was predestined to be that way he had determined, considering what he knew of its history.

While he was doing research required for his doctorate in history, he found that Mercy Street was given its name by an early Jesuit priest, Antoinis de Ippolito, when he established the first and only Jesuit settlement in Georgia in July of 1718. But like their sister settlements in Louisiana and Florida, they found it difficult to survive and prosper there among the Native Americans.

Father Antoinis was burned at the stake by the Chickasaw tribes in 1723. Ten years later, James Oglethorpe brought more settlers into Georgia and in 1735, the Augusta, Georgia settlement was permanently established. The Jesuit settlement, though destroyed, was not forgotten because of a diary the priest had kept. Due to his work and his documentation, the name Mercy Street was maintained. A historical marker was even placed not far from Reuben's house that designated the land as an early Jesuit settlement. The marker did not mention what caused the demise of the settlement, nor did it mention the burning of the priest. Historical markers are reluctant to denote the savage outcomes that often occurred during the birth of a nation.

His home was built by his great-grandfather, Absalom Wood, a successful merchant, in 1908. A spiral staircase curved over the front door from both sides of the large house. The door at the top of the stairs was used primarily for an exit from the bedrooms, as a safety feature, like the fire escapes of the large apartment buildings in New York where he had grown up. Those fire escapes were not only effective, but they also served as a unique design element for the home. The door beneath the stairs was the main entryway into the house.

It was one of the few homes in the downtown area that survived the Augusta fire of 1916 which destroyed over twenty-five blocks of the town. Two years after that fire, Absalom died and left his wife Hephzabah an immense fortune. She was an astute businesswoman and, along with her four sons and two daughters, increased the wealth left to her by her husband.

Two of her sons seized the opportunities that prohibition brought to the area and increased the family fortune with their mother's blessing. She enjoyed a cocktail in the evening and never saw anything wrong with making money off of untaxed whisky. She ensured that the whisky they made or bought was of high quality, which meant it wouldn't kill those who drank it. She even allowed her oldest sons to build a tunnel leading from the house, underneath Mercy Street into another small home that was entrusted to one of their loyal staff members to live in. His sole job was to keep the house clean and inconspicuous to the community. He did his job very well and passersby always remarked how nice his azaleas looked.

Hephzabah was very active in the Augusta society up until World War II broke out. Two of her sons enlisted and were killed in the liberation of France, and from that point forward, she never again left the house. It was said she died of a broken heart that she never recovered from on September 3, 1945, the day after the war ended.

The other two sons and daughters continued their success in the liquor business after the war, only this time in a legal fashion, as they opened bars and restaurants in Augusta, Savannah, and Atlanta. One of the brothers moved to Savannah and the other to Atlanta where they lived until both of them were shot in arguments that occurred over a business deal, a day apart from each other. It was reported in the respective local papers, as well as the Augusta Chronicle, that alcohol was involved in both of those arguments.

The two daughters were extremely close and maintained the large home. They opened up many other businesses within Augusta as it continued to grow. One of them never married but she had a very close female friend who lived with her in their family home. She died while they were out horseback riding one day. Her friend soon left and moved to California. The other daughter, Katherine, married late in life and had one daughter that she named Marigold.

Katherine's husband, Jack Sumpter, was from South Carolina and had vast holdings of land and farms in and around Edgefield County. He enjoyed farming and Katherine helped him grow his agricultural business while acquiring more land in South Carolina and south Georgia. The Georgia land was used primarily for the timber industry and provided wood to the paper mills that, at the time, were thriving in Augusta.

Jack loved being outdoors and truly enjoyed working with "his crew" in south Georgia. After a challenging week, Jack was often known to throw large bar-b-que parties for the men, with enough food for them and their families and plenty of beer and whisky for anyone who wanted it. Jack enjoyed drinking large amounts of whisky with "his crew" and though they tried, none of them were ever able to drink their boss under the table. Katherine warned her husband that a tree was going to fall on him and kill him someday, but she was wrong. He was killed by one of the largest timber rattlesnakes that had ever been seen in Georgia. Stretched out, it was as tall as Jack and he was almost six feet tall. The picture of the snake was shown in the Augusta Chronicle.

After Jack died, Katherine turned more of her attention to Marigold and began to teach her everything she could about all of the family businesses. Marigold was an astute student and never forgot anything that Katherine told her, often questioning why things were done a certain way. Even though she was young, she challenged old ideas and brought up new ones that long-time managers and supervisors had never even considered. Katherine realized her daughter had an aptitude for business that exceeded anyone within her family.

Her mother never tried to hide the family's participation in what she said could have been considered illegal business at the time, though she told Marigold that the federal government really never had the authority to restrict what people could or could not drink. "As long as people aren't drinking poison," she added, as if that one condition justified the family's activities during the Prohibition Era.

Marigold nodded her head as if she understood what her mother was telling and teaching her. And she did. She was learning that as long as there was an opportunity to make money, then the activity should be considered. Even though there may be government restrictions against the activity, one needed to evaluate whether that was something most Americans should be allowed to decide on their own. Life, liberty and the pursuit of happiness, Marigold thought. It's right there in the Declaration of Independence, she said to herself as she smiled at her mother and made mental notes that she stored in her reference catalog-like mind.

Katherine sent Marigold to Wellesley College to obtain her business degree and Marigold excelled in school. After graduation, Katherine started the process of moving Marigold into the management of the family businesses. Katherine thought that her young daughter would meet resistance from the many men that she had to deal with on a daily basis, but she and those men quickly learned that Marigold could hold her own with any of them. With each negotiation, she offered up ideas and suggestions that they couldn't ignore if they were smart. If they were stubborn, she showed them how much she didn't need their input and how wonderful competition was in the free market.

Within ten years, Marigold had taken over all of the business activities and Katherine enjoyed her days of leisure in one of their homes in Charleston or Savannah when she wasn't at home in Augusta. Katherine was atop the societal hierarchy within each town and when she died of lung cancer in 1985, it was prominent news. She had ignored the warning labels on the cigarettes for twenty years. "Just more government interference," she often told Marigold.

Marigold, like her mother, married late in life. Simon Broadwater was a very handsome man whose father owned several car dealerships. Though his own family was well off, Simon was unaware of just how rich and powerful the woman was that he married. Together they had one son, Reuben.

Just as her name might suggest springtime and sunshine, Marigold's personality was jubilant and carefree, within the confines of societal functions. But within the management of her businesses, her personality changed. The people who dealt with her called her as ruthless as Jacob Marley or Ebenezer Scrooge and then would laugh. Describing Marigold as ruthless in business, though, wouldn't be a fair assessment. In fact, it would be an insult. She was much more unforgiving than either of those fictional characters.

Soon after they married and long before Reuben was born, Simon had too much to drink one night and was arrested and thrown into jail for DUI. Because of her influence within the community, Marigold was able to go to the jail and retrieve Simon without the standard requirement of recording the incident in a legal manner.

When they returned home, Simon, still drunk, hit Marigold in the face after she berated him for embarrassing her and the family name. Soon after that, the servants heard a man screaming and went running into the study.

They had to restrain Marigold from killing Simon with a poker from the fireplace. Simon stayed in the home until he recovered and he never again did anything that would incur Marigold's wrath.

After that incident, Simon understood clearly who ran the businesses and their marriage and that she simply allowed him to share in her wealth and social standing. She told him that she could make him as wealthy as any man in the state and that he would also benefit from the many sexual pleasures that she enjoyed and was very proficient and adept at performing. She assured him that would all be his, provided he understood and maintained that level of understanding and loyalty to her throughout their marriage. If he didn't, however, and if she ever caught him with another woman, he would wish that he died that day when she almost beat him to death with a poker. Simon was a very smart man. He never again questioned Marigold's actions. In fact, after that incident and once his face had healed, the staff said Mr. Broadwater smiled a lot more than usual.

Reuben Broadwater was born two years after his grandmother died. Marigold was thirty-nine years old and his father, Simon, was forty-two. Marigold doted on Reuben when he was a baby and young boy, and the home on the corner of Redbud Lane and Mercy Street was full of laughter and grand parties to celebrate Reuben's birthday each year.

Guests invited to the birthday parties for Reuben were always leaders in the community and it was their good fortune to have children who were close in age to Reuben. Marigold found those parties an excellent way to conduct business, especially after the men started drinking. She made sure that her husband kept the drinks full for their guests and there were many deals made and finalized during those parties.

So, she started having even more parties. There were parties welcoming spring and the Master's golf tournament, which was beginning to grow in popularity. There were anniversary parties, birthday parties for her and Simon and some of their closest friends. There were parties welcoming fall after getting through the hot humid weather of summer in Augusta, and then there were always several parties around the Thanksgiving and Christmas holidays. Those who worked with Marigold would even say she softened a bit during those years, and perhaps to a certain degree, she did. But those who made deals with her during those parties often ended up wishing the next morning that they had one less scotch the night before.

Marigold knew her son was very smart and sent Reuben to private school. He inherited her catalog-like mind and never forgot anything she told him. He was a voracious reader, already reading at a third-grade level before he started school. He had only been in the first grade for a month when the teachers called Marigold and Simon and advised them that Reuben should skip the first and second grade and start in the third, even suggesting that they could consider moving him into the fourth if they so desired.

Perhaps for the first time in her life, Marigold listened to Simon that day as he suggested that their son should not be placed beyond the third grade. He reminded her that even though their son was very smart, he was still just a six-year-old. There wouldn't be that much of a social or emotional difference between him and eight-year-olds, but placing him with nine and ten-year-olds could put him at a disadvantage and inhibit his social growth.

Though Simon's heart was in the right place and Marigold agreed with him, they were both wrong about their son being at a disadvantage with the older children. He was never at a disadvantage within a social setting, regardless of where it was. It was as if he had an innate ability to disarm anyone around him and make them think they were friends. Sometimes it was sincere, but often it was just an act to ensure he got what he wanted. As he got older, Marigold realized that her son could turn that gracious and welcoming side of his character on and off like a switch within his mind. Though she never let him or her husband know, she wondered how that would manifest itself over time.

Reuben excelled in the third grade. Not only was he at the top of his class with his grades, but he was also well liked by everyone. Even the teachers told Marigold each time that they met, that her son was going to be one of those "movers and shakers" when he grew up. Marigold always smiled and said thank you to them in a polite manner. She was certain that what they were saying was true, but she also knew that there was something about her son that made her pause and think about the success and power that he would inherit and wield. She knew power to be both an aphrodisiac and a dominatrix and she understood it would be up to her to show her son the limits of both.

During the school year, she made it a point for the three of them to eat dinner together each night. She always asked her son to tell them about school and what he was studying. It was quickly evident how much their son enjoyed learning about history. His references to what the teacher had taught that day made it seem like they were there in the class with him. His interest in history never waned. By the time he was ten years old and in the sixth grade, he already knew more than what was being taught to those in high school.

Both she and Simon knew he would be bored in high school history class, so when Reuben began the seventh grade, they made the decision to hire a tutor who could supplement Reuben's interest in history. Neither she nor

Simon wanted to let him skip any other grades. They didn't want him to be "that child" in high school. They feared he would be picked on and made fun of by the older kids and they were right. They just didn't know that their son would have been able to handle it. Regardless of what they did or didn't do from that point forward, their son's view of society had already begun to take shape. It would be molded even more when Marigold began teaching her son how to manage the companies.

When Reuben turned thirteen and was a freshman in high school, Marigold began taking him with her to their businesses as much as she could after school, and always during school breaks in the spring. He was finished with school by 2 p.m., so there was a good four-hour period each day in which Reuben learned about the management of their diverse businesses. Reuben had been unaware that his mother and father owned so many different types of businesses. There was a floral shop, a bakery, and two clothing stores, one for men and one for women, and two restaurants.

When he asked her one day about how she and his dad had acquired so many stores, Reuben learned his first business lesson: know who the boss is. Marigold told him that his father didn't have any ownership in those businesses; everything belonged to her and that it would all belong to him someday. Reuben asked her why his dad didn't own the businesses with her and Marigold just smiled when she told him, "he doesn't need to." He learned his second lesson in business with that statement: do not surrender control of the business - regardless of the societal arrangements that you engage in.

She then showed him the two car dealerships that his grandfather owned. Reuben asked if he would inherit those too and Marigold told him no; she was sure that he would leave those to his aunt's children, his cousins Victor and Pamela. She said that his grandfather knew that he would be well taken care of and would not need the car dealerships. "Makes sense," Reuben replied in a matter of fact manner which made Marigold smile. He understands what I am telling him, unraveling the complications of family dynamics as if they were nothing more than a ball of string. People will underestimate my child at their own peril, she told herself, as she looked over and ran her fingers through his thick brown hair. I think one more lesson is needed today, she told herself as she drove to one of their restaurants.

The restaurant she took Reuben to was their hamburger joint located downtown off of Eighth Street, about three blocks from their house. They were only open for lunch and though it didn't exactly cater to the working class, it was designed to feel as if you were stepping back into a diner from the 1950s. In fact, that was the name of it. A pinkish- red neon sign reading

"*The Fifties*" hung over the door. She knew the restaurant was closed now and that the staff should be gone. She was hoping the manager was still there and he was, counting and balancing the afternoon receipts.

She unlocked the back door and asked Reuben to follow her. She stopped by the kitchen and looked around for a moment before they walked into the manager's office. He looked up, somewhat surprised to see her, but smiled when he saw Reuben.

"Bienvenido, Joven jefe!" he said and then looked at Marigold. "Hello, Senora Broadwater. How are you today?"

"I am fine, Rodrigo. How was the lunch crowd today?"

"Bien. Very good, as a matter of fact. The round and flank steak burgers are a big hit with the lunch crowd. It's a very good sandwich. It was a great idea and people don't mind paying a dollar and a half more. The price you negotiated with the vendor only drives our costs up a few cents. You are an amazing negotiator, Senora."

"Yes, I am very good at that," Marigold replied as she looked over at Reuben. "I would have thought that since we have been selling those for the past four months that our profits would have increased eight or nine percent by now, but they are only up about two percent. Did you raise the salaries of the cooking or wait staff without telling me?"

"No, Senora. I would never do anything like that without asking you first. You know that. I have been working for you for ten years. I will have to investigate more. Perhaps the cooks are throwing too much away. I will look into it."

"Do you mind if I see the records?" Marigold asked as she walked over and stood behind Rodrigo.

"Si, Senora. Here are the records."

As soon as he opened the ledger, Marigold slammed a meat tenderizer mallet on Rodrigo's right hand several times before he had a chance to move it. Reuben thought he heard some fingers crack but he didn't look away. He was mesmerized by what he was seeing. He watched as his mother put the mallet down on the desk and walked away so that she was standing in front of Rodrigo.

"Reuben, go into the kitchen and put some ice in a plastic bag and bring it back in here. Quickly. The swelling and bruising on Rodrigo's hand is becoming quite pronounced."

Reuben did as he was told. His mother placed the bag softly on Rodrigo's hand and told him to hold it with his other. Reuben watched as Rodrigo looked up into his mother's face. He could tell that he was mad but he could also see that Rodrigo was afraid of doing anything to retaliate against his mother. How is that possible, Reuben wondered.

He had never seen his mother do anything like that to someone, but he wasn't frightened by her actions. He was fascinated and wanted to understand what she was doing. He listened to every word she said as she talked to Rodrigo.

"Now tell me the truth, Rodrigo, because you need to get that hand to the hospital. They will need to put some of your fingers in splints. I am pretty sure I didn't break any of the bones in the palm of your hand but they will have to do an x-ray to make sure. But the sooner that you get there, the better."

"Mi hermana, my sister. She was in trouble. She needed money. I have been helping her. She is pregnant and cannot work. Thc doctor put her on bedrest or she will lose the baby."

"Why didn't you just ask me for help?" Marigold replied.

"I don't know. I wasn't thinking."

"Well, now you know. I trust you, Rodrigo. I gave you a job after you had been in prison because I believed in you when others wouldn't. You were once a cook here and now I have made you the manager. I shouldn't be someone that you steal from, should I?"

"No, senora. Lo siento. I am very sorry, Senora. I will pay you back. I promise."

"I don't expect you to pay me back, Rodrigo. I expect you to do what I hired you to do. Manage this restaurant. If you do that, we will never have a problem again and I promise you, you will enjoy the benefits of helping this business become even more successful. Now, let's go to the hospital."

"No, Senora. I will drive myself. I am ashamed to be with you and su hijo. I will be here at work tomorrow. Do not worry. I will make this place the best hamburger restaurante in town," Rodrigo said as he got up from behind the desk and left quickly.

"Let's go home," Marigold said as she walked into the kitchen. She cleaned off the mallet, put it away and then locked up the restaurant before heading out the back door. On the ride home, Reuben wasn't sure where to start but he was almost ready to explode to ask his mother what had just happened. Before he could ask, though, Marigold began to tell him what she wanted him to learn that evening.

"In business, you sometimes have to make some hard decisions. Now, I could have fired Rodrigo today, but what would that have accomplished?" she asked rhetorically.

"There would be another unemployed person, with limited skills, out on the streets, looking for the government - and by government, I mean people like me who help pay over ninety percent of the government's taxes – to give them a hand out. It doesn't make sense. If I could provide what had been a loyal employee for a very long time a life lesson, and then gain an even more loyal employee, wouldn't that be the best way to handle things? I could have sent him to jail, but again, what does that accomplish?

"People in jail only learn two things. One is that humans will have sex with their own gender if that is their only option and two, thieves learn how to become better thieves. But if you give the right person a chance, especially one who feels like he has very limited opportunities, you develop a relationship between employer and employee. All the management books you will ever read will tell you that is the most important thing you can do in order to have a successful company.

"Employer-employee relationships. They are the key to success. Those business books you will read someday in the very near future will also tell you that you should not manage with fear. That those days are gone. I would say yes and no to that type of philosophy. You certainly don't want people to be afraid to see you every time you say hello to them, but they need to know that you have the power to fire them as well as to promote them for their loyalty and hard work. I make it a point to know all the people that work for me. I have a mind that allows me to do that. You son, have that same ability. I have seen it. You are thirteen now, so it was important that you saw and learned all of what occurred today."

Reuben's mind was indeed cataloging everything his mother was telling him; storing away what he had seen and what she had said in files he labeled as "life lessons." He started asking questions that he believed he needed to know to complete "his files."

"Thieves are in prison because they are thieves. Dishonest. How do you know that they are the right person and are not deceiving you since that ability seems to be second nature to them?"

Marigold smiled as she heard her son's question. Underestimate him at their own peril she said to herself again.

"I personally interview each person when one of my managers wants to give someone a second chance. I ask them about their family. If they cannot tell me what has occurred with each of their family members, for the entire time that they were in prison, then I don't hire them. If the family wants to keep that person involved and he wants to stay involved with them while he is incarcerated, then I believe that he wants to do better with his life. That he still cares.

"No matter what people say, not everyone deserves a second chance, at least in my business. I am not God. Just like you saw today with Rodrigo. He will be someone I can trust forever now. He will not want to disappoint me again. Not after the chance I gave him to begin with and not with the chance I gave him again today. He knows I could have sent him back to prison but I didn't."

"But why use the mallet to crush his fingers?"

"He needed to be reminded that I am the head of the household and that I am very aware of what is going on in my house. His fingers will heal. I didn't ask for repayment and he will not have a hospital bill, but he will always have a reminder of today when he looks down at his hand. And he will remember who I am and what he promised."

Reuben re-opened the file within his mind on employee loyalty and relationships. He added an asterisk to the lesson. Sometimes pain is involved in establishing the connection between employer and employee to enhance the loyalty. He then moved on to some other things his mother just referenced.

"You just said that if faced with their only option, people will have sex with their own gender. People have sex with their own gender when they have options, outside of prison."

"Yes, they do. In fact, your great aunt was a lesbian. I never told you that. You do indeed have choices but it becomes harder for you to succeed in business if you are a homosexual. I didn't write the rules of business, I am just telling you how things are."

"It's okay mom. I'm not a homosexual. I like girls. I just didn't want you to think I didn't know about sex and homosexuals. And by the way, you've never really told me about the family. All I know are my father's parents and my cousins. What was the name of my lesbian great-aunt?"

You did what you told others not to do, Marigold told herself. You underestimated him. And you do need to tell him about the family. What have you been waiting on? He's ready. He didn't wince at all at what you did with Rodrigo. He stood there and watched and did what was told. He is ready to understand the history of the family.

"Her name was Meredith and she was very close to my mother, your grandmother, Katherine."

"What happened to Meredith and my grandmother?"

"Meredith died of a broken neck. She fell off her horse one day. It was heartbreaking for my mother. Your grandmother died two years before you were born of lung cancer. She smoked a pack of cigarettes a day for as long as I knew her."

"So, you learned everything about the family business from grandmother?"

"Yes. But I also went to a very good business school. Your grandmother wanted me to have every advantage possible as it was not easy for women back then to have a place of authority at the business table, so to speak. At least in the eyes of some men it wasn't. But they learned."

"Like Rodrigo learned?"

Marigold looked at her son and shook her head. "No, not like Rodrigo. I don't go around intimidating potential business partners with force. You need to do that with better ideas. Show them better ways to do things to enhance profits and if they don't want to participate, then show them they were wrong by finding other partners and then allow the free market to decide. In the free market, I will always win. I will always win because I have the best employees and I know what I am doing in every aspect of the business. The business theory I learned in school helped. My mother's mentoring helped. And my experience has helped. All three together have helped us become very profitable and rich. You do realize you are very rich, don't you?"

"I know you are very rich. I just reap the benefits," Reuben replied. Always know who the boss is, Reuben said to himself as he saw the smile on his mother's face. Lesson learned.

"Is that what you meant about business books that I would soon be reading? That I need to go to a business school like you did? Maybe that was the case back then, but I don't see how I could learn anything in those books that you couldn't teach me."

"It is important that you learn business law, Reuben. Things continue to change with our economy and our country and you need to know the law to stay ahead. And accounting. Both of those disciplines change over time. It's important that you learn them as well as marketing, finance, and economics. All of them are important."

"But I'm only thirteen. Couldn't you teach me all of that over the next three years, before I'm ready to go to college? I want to get a degree in history. In fact, I think I would like a doctorate in history. It fascinates me, as you know. That's all I usually talk about at the dinner table.

"And now, I'm beginning to really love American literature, too. James Fenimore Cooper and his Leatherstocking Tales, Nathaniel Hawthorne and his Tanglewood tales, which is really a re-writing of Greek myths, which I love reading about too. Washington Irving and his Legend of Sleepy Hollow and Edgar Allen Poe. I love everything I have read so far by him. You know he wrote what is considered the first detective story. And his poetry - The Raven and Annabel Lee. I love them."

"I can and will continue to teach you over the next three years, but you still need to go to college and get your business degree and probably, in today's world, a law degree as well. I'm starting to see joint programs for an MBA/JD degree spring up, at very good schools. I think those joint degrees would be an asset for you. And by the way, Poe died out in the streets of Baltimore, from alcohol and drug abuse."

"Yes, he did, but so what? It just means a genius died way too early. And I don't think I want to pursue that degree that you are talking about. Sounds boring and unnecessary. No, I'd rather get a joint degree in literature and history. I think a Ph.D. in both would be appropriate."

The life lessons for Reuben didn't end that day when his mother pulled into their driveway. Just before he got out of the car, Reuben learned that his mother wasn't used to hearing the word "No."

"Reuben, let's do this. I'm thinking of opening another small diner out in south Augusta. There's a lot of industrial business growth out there and very few opportunities for dining. While the restaurant is being built, I will teach you what you should know to run that restaurant successfully."

"Like when to use the mallet?" Reuben interrupted.

His mother smiled at his attempt at humor but he could tell she didn't really think it was funny.

"No mallets necessary. You and I will interview the staff but you will make the final decision on whom to hire. Once it is up and going, it will be yours to manage. If you make it successful, I will not require you to go to business school. You can pick out whatever you wish to study in college. But if the restaurant fails, then you get the business degree as I suggested. Deal?"

"Deal," Reuben said as he ran into the house, saying hello to his Dad as he passed him in the hall. He got on his computer and began studying successful interviewing and the key elements for restaurant success.

"What's up with Reuben?" Simon said as he looked at Marigold.

"Will you fix me a drink and join me out in the sunroom?" she asked as she leaned over and kissed Simon on his cheek.

He fixed her a scotch and water and poured his scotch over ice and accompanied her out onto the large porch. She told him about everything that they had done that day and then told him about the challenge she had given him.

"Knowing our son, he is upstairs on the computer finding out everything he can about running a restaurant," Marigold said as she finished off her drink. Before she could ask, Simon got up and made her another one.

"Marigold, he is thirteen," Simon said. "He is still just a boy."

"Simon, he has never been just a boy. And you know that. He is a year older than I was when my mother started teaching me about running the businesses. And when I look in his eyes, I don't always see a young boy. Sometimes, I see a young man, being held back only by his chronological age. Mentally, he is way older than thirteen."

"He is very smart, Marigold. Just as you were and are. His mind is like the steel trap that you possess. Once the information goes in, it never goes away. But he still needs to have fun. Remember how much fun we had when he was younger. He still needs that. I'm afraid otherwise he will not learn important social and life skills. Like all worry and no play makes Reuben a dull boy."

Marigold smiled at her husband. She patted the empty space on the sofa and Simon sat down beside her. She grabbed his hand and kissed him.

"Promise me something, Simon. You will always remind me of that."

Simon nodded his head and kissed his wife. She reached over and grabbed his crotch and then got up and locked the sunroom door before she reminded Simon of how skillful she was at things other than business.

Over the next six months, Reuben was invested in all things regarding the restaurant. He selected a staff of twelve, a supervisor, the menu, the advertising plan, and the hours of operation. He decided that the restaurant would be open for breakfast and lunch only since most of the working population in that area were shift workers. Once more people came toward that neighborhood they would consider a dinner operation but for now, just breakfast and lunch.

Both she and Simon were impressed with what their son had accomplished but that was not the main lesson that Marigold wanted to teach her son. After a few months, she told the food vendors who supplied the restaurant to raise their prices by twenty-five percent. They did as instructed, telling Reuben their costs had gone up.

Within a few weeks, Reuben realized he needed to raise his prices or he would soon start losing money. So, he raised prices and his business began to diminish. Though he didn't want to, he found it necessary to eliminate twenty-five percent of the staff. Even that wasn't enough of a cost reduction to bring back the margins he needed to stay open since the staff made most of their money from tips. After another month had passed, the restaurant was losing too much money and he told his mother that they would need to close.

Marigold sat down with Reuben and explained to him how she had instructed the vendors to raise the prices of the food. The vendors he was using, she told him, were subsidiary companies owned by her, and he had failed to take that into consideration. She also discussed material and labor costs with him and how that impacts small restaurants.

Reuben didn't get mad or show any emotion at all when she explained what she had done to cause the restaurant's failure. But she might as well have used the mallet on his hand, it made such an impression on him. It was just as effective. He looked into the catalog in his brain and re-opened the life lessons file cabinet and placed another asterisk with an exclamation mark beside the file that said always know who the boss is. Especially if it is your mother.

That summer the family traveled all over Europe for vacation. Reuben had a wonderful time, taking a special interest in the art and architecture of each new place. He enjoyed it so much that he convinced his mother to extend their trip another two weeks so that they could visit Greece and Cyprus and even some of the former communist countries. As they watched Reuben soak up everything around him, Simon leaned over and whispered into Marigold's ear how "all this play" was good for their son and for her. She nodded her head and smiled as they followed Reuben to some other building that he was insisting they needed to see.

When they returned home, Marigold took Reuben out to the restaurant she had given him to run and he was surprised to find it was still open and doing a bustling lunch business. He didn't need to ask anything. She was just making another point with him. She never said a word about what she did to keep the restaurant open. She didn't need to. He had learned everything he needed to know for the time being.

When he started his junior year in high school, Reuben became very interested in a young girl. His first real interest in a girl. Sarah was a cheerleader and when he met her for the first time and learned her name, he thought of Sarah Royster, an adolescent sweetheart of Edgar Allen Poe. It's meant to be, he thought, as he started arranging "bump in" meetings within the hallway. They shared Chemistry class together and he tried to be her lab partner as much as possible.

She was two years older than he was, but he could tell she liked being around him. He was only fifteen and didn't have a driver's license. Other boys who were trying to win her affections were picking her up in their own cars. But he soon realized that he had something they didn't have. His father had a Rolls Royce Phantom and his parents had more money than anyone else in town. He thought that might sway her decision in his favor when he asked her out. He knew he was good at reading people and he assumed that she would be impressed by the car and the money. He was right.

She was also impressed with sports. Though he preferred to talk about literature or something historical in town or something that he had seen in Europe, she preferred talking about other more mundane subjects that didn't really interest him. One day she looked at him and told him that he should try out for the wrestling team. Reuben had never really exercised but he was in fairly good shape. He was five feet nine inches tall and weighed 150 pounds. He liked the idea of wrestling. It had a historical relationship that interested him.

He researched wrestling and found that it was one of the oldest forms of combat. It was referenced within the Iliad and depicted in 15,000-year-old cave drawings in France. Some of the moves used today were used by Egyptians and Babylonians a thousand years ago. Greece trained its soldiers for hand to hand combat with wrestling techniques. So, he told Sarah that he was going to try out for the wrestling team in November. He could tell she was excited by the news because she placed his hand on her grapefruit sized breasts as she kissed him. He had his first wet dream that night.

When he told his parents that he was going to try out for the wrestling team, they both knew why but it didn't matter. They felt the competitive aspect of the sport would be good for him. Simon hired a personal trainer for his son, and each day after school for two months, Reuben worked out with him and practiced wrestling moves. By the time tryouts began in the middle of November, Reuben's body was a well-toned 148 pounds. His muscles weren't as developed as the other young men that usually also played football, but he was quick and well-schooled in effective wrestling maneuvers.

He tried out for the 152-pound weight class and made the team, beating out three other boys. Throughout the wrestling season, Reuben continued to work out several hours a day and added muscle weight and started winning matches. The more matches he won the more excited Sarah became when they went out on dates. He learned that Sarah was very proficient at performing several sex acts that up until then, he had just heard or read about.

He qualified for the regional championship and was competing against the previous year's state champion. No one gave Reuben a chance to win but Sarah encouraged him in a way that made him want to win and he tried his best that day. But the young man hit him in his testicles as he was initiating a takedown. Reuben had never felt pain like that before and found it hard to breathe as he was thrown to the mat and pinned in less than a minute.

His coach argued that the young man intentionally hurt him but the referees disagreed and Reuben lost. Reuben never forgot the match with that young man and it influenced the way he thought about competition and relationships from that point forward. He never wrestled again either. He had done it and done it well. That was enough for him. He had accomplished everything that he wanted to and over the next month, he and Sarah drifted apart. But that was okay. He had learned a lot from her too.

Reuben continued to do well in school and decided to join the chess club after reading that the game originated in India just before the sixth century. He knew being a member of the club would impact his social standing within the high school, but he didn't care. Being called a nerd or chess-geek didn't bother him. He loved the aggressive nature of the game. He thought it was even more competitive than wrestling. He studied books on technique and strategy and became so skilled at the game that when the state tournament started, he was ready.

He won game after game, advancing to the regional finals, just as he did in wrestling. The sponsor for the chess club was the Spanish teacher and Reuben didn't care for him. The teacher told Reuben that he was certain he would win if he used the Alekhine Defence against his opponent in the regional game. Reuben didn't agree with the teacher's suggestion and he also didn't like being told how to prepare for the game. He lost the game in ten moves, and his teacher just shook his head when Reuben smiled and shook the hand of his opponent.

Marigold overheard the teacher coaching Reuben about how to approach the game. As she sat there in the bleachers and watched her son lose, she knew he had done it on purpose. And she was right. Reuben enjoyed demonstrating to the teacher who was in charge. The teacher failed to understand what his mother had taught him. Rule number one: know who the boss is. But Marigold understood.

At the end of his junior year in high school, Simon suggested that the family go to Africa on a safari. Reuben began studying where they should go and within several days had mapped out an entire itinerary. This didn't surprise Marigold or Simon but they were surprised when Reuben asked if they were going on a photographic safari or would actually be hunting animals.

Marigold looked at Simon without an answer. She had always assumed they would be going on a photographic safari, spending much of their time in Egypt, considering all the history in that part of Africa. They were both surprised when Reuben said he would like to go on a hunting safari even though he had never been hunting or even picked up a gun.

Marigold could see the changes taking place in her son but she was not concerned. She saw them as pieces of the puzzle, which would, over time, reveal the true picture of her son. The leader who would be in charge of all the businesses her family had been developing for over a century now. She could see him becoming even more aware of his ability to succeed. She knew he would create a business empire that exceeded even what she had accomplished.

In Zimbabwe, South Africa, they hunted for impala, gemsbok and Cape buffalo. Reuben quickly learned how to use the guns from the guides. Only several hours into the safari Reuben killed the first animal, an impala. His father killed a waterbuck about an hour later. Marigold didn't want to shoot anything but she watched and was happy seeing her son accomplish what she knew he had been planning to do ever since they mentioned a safari.

They ate the impala and waterbuck for dinner that night. Reuben didn't care for either meat, but he didn't tell anyone. He knew his mother and father were enjoying it, and he loved listening to the guides talk about past safaris and how dangerous hunting for Cape buffalo would be. One of the guides said, "Shoot straight and always use enough gun." That's a good rule, Reuben thought, as he filed it away in his memory catalog.

The guides emphasized how important it was to kill the Cape buffalo with the first shot as the wounded buffalo was very dangerous. They were notorious for running off and then doubling back to find what had hurt them and trying to kill it. Reuben asked the main guide if anyone had ever died with them while hunting the buffalo. "No, because if you don't kill it on the first shot, we will kill it with the next shot. Several of our competitors never learned that. A few of their customers were injured and even died. They learned the hard way that an injured or dead customer is bad for business. We have fewer competitors now, mate," he said as he smiled and looked over at Simon and Marigold. The thought of killing something that could kill him excited Reuben. He could barely sleep that night at the thought of the hunt the next day.

The guides ensured that Simon and Reuben had the proper guns for the hunt and made them practice shooting them before they left the camp. Though he had never shot a cannon, Reuben could only imagine he was doing so when he shot the Remington .416 Magnum and felt the recoil against his shoulder. He had continued to maintain a strength regimen after he finished wrestling which helped him keep from dropping the gun. The next time he shot it, he was ready. The lead guide came over and patted

Reuben on his back and told him he wouldn't be surprised if he got "his cape" on the first shot.

Marigold nodded her head in agreement. You underestimate him at your own peril, she thought, as they loaded up in the jeep. About a mile from the area that had been scouted earlier, they got out of the jeep and headed into the woods. When given the tap on the head, Reuben took the shot and hit the buffalo right in the shoulders as instructed. The buffalo ran for about twenty feet before it fell over, dead. His father was unable to kill a buffalo that day but it didn't matter. He was proud of what he had seen his son accomplish, shooting a "cannon" that he held in his arms.

They ate buffalo filets that night, and unlike the other meat, Reuben really enjoyed them. He complimented the chef and told his parents that they should have buffalo available to eat all the time. His parents and the guides laughed, as did Reuben, unaware that a seed had been planted within his mind that he would see grow later in life.

They did no more hunting on the trip. The guides told them they would have their trophy heads ready in about a month, but Reuben said he didn't want them. Simon wasn't interested in them either and the guides were somewhat taken aback by their response. Marigold wasn't. She knew her husband wasn't interested in hanging a large animal head in their house because it would not mesh with the antique and artistic décor. She knew her son didn't want them because he didn't need a visual reminder of what he had done.

For the next ten days, they were just explorers and tourists as they visited Victoria Falls before they left South Africa and went to Egypt, Israel, and Turkey. On the flight home, Reuben was much quieter than he had been on their return from Europe the year before.

"Are you tired son?" Marigold asked, wondering if that was preventing him from talking about their trip.

"No, not really," Reuben replied.

"Did you enjoy the trip?"

"Immensely. Amazing that people still live in that level of poverty isn't it? In fact, they not only live, some even thrive. I found that quite remarkable."

Marigold thought about what her son said. He had seen the beginning of civilization and recognized that in some ways, things had never changed, even after thousands of years. I was there with him and never even thought of that, she said to herself. He is much more perceptive than I was at his age. He sees and thinks of things differently than others. He always has, she thought as she closed her eyes and went to sleep.

Reuben continued to thrive in school and since it was his senior year, Marigold began researching colleges. She was surprised by the fact that the University of Georgia offered one of the best joint MBA and Law degree programs in the country. Only four years too, she said as she read more details. Selection for the program was very discriminating, not only based on grades but on the overall student high school experience. When she read that, she just smiled. She was certain that if some evaluator decided that Reuben didn't have enough high school experiences to qualify for the program, the financial influence that accompanied him would lead to his acceptance.

On his sixteenth birthday, his parents gave Reuben a 2003 Porsche 911 Carrera. It was the first time that Marigold had seen her son speechless. When he was given the keys to the car, he did nothing for about twenty minutes except walk around the car and inspect it. He looked at the trunk, the engine, everything about the car. He finally walked over and hugged his parents before he got in the car and drove off.

He drove around town and had to catch himself from running into the back of other cars as he looked at the people watching him drive by. This is one of the coolest things ever he thought as he drove back home, where his parents were still standing in the driveway.

"Is there something wrong?" Simon asked as he drove up and Reuben rolled down the passenger window.

"Yes, my mother and father aren't with me. Who wants to be first?" he asked.

Simon looked at Marigold and opened the door for her. "My queen," he said as Marigold did a semi-curtsy and kissed her husband on the cheek.

Reuben drove in a sedate manner until he reached Gordon Highway. Then he hit the accelerator, throwing his mother's head back, as he shifted the gears in an almost seamless manner. He reached sixty miles per hour in four seconds and one hundred miles an hour in fourth gear before his mother told him to slow down.

"You will promise not to kill yourself in this, won't you?" she said as they drove down the highway a few more miles before he turned around and headed back home.

"It has two more gears," Reuben replied. "I'm not sure I can promise that."

"Well, then just promise me you won't kill me," she said as she looked over at him and smiled.

"That I can do," he said and together they laughed and drove back onto Redbud Lane and into their driveway.

Marigold advised her husband to make sure he had his seat belt on as she closed the door and took his head in her hands and kissed him on his lips, letting the kiss linger as long as she could before her son told them enough. "Just in case you don't come back," Marigold said. She waved to them and Reuben took off. They were gone for over an hour. Reuben knew his father wanted to drive the car too and they went all the way to Waynesboro before turning back home.

Reuben loved that car and kept it spotless, washing it himself every weekend. As Simon and Marigold watched him washing it one day, Simon looked at his wife and asked her, "What are we going to give him to top this?" Marigold didn't hesitate in replying.

"The world," she said. She pulled her husband close to her and suggested to him that they get something to eat and then have some lunch. Simon laughed as he took his wife's hand and led her back to his study and locked the door.

The rest of Reuben's senior year passed by uneventfully. He excelled in his studies and graduated with a 3.9 GPA and was the salutatorian for his senior class. With all he had learned from his history tutors, he had enough American history education to qualify for a B.A. in history from any college he attended. Marigold had made sure of that from the very beginning.

Throughout his senior year, Marigold and Reuben discussed universities and colleges and visited several Ivy League schools that she thought he would like. Even though the schools appealed to his parents, Reuben showed no indication that any of them appealed to him. One of them actually did, however. He was very interested in attending Harvard, but he was waiting for his mother to tell him what school he should attend. He had never forgotten rule number one.

They also visited the University of Georgia and both Marigold and Simon were instantly impressed with their four-year JD/MBA program. Reuben saw it in his mother's face as she talked to the professors. He knew he would be attending the University of Georgia, at least in the beginning, but he still wanted to go to Harvard to study what truly interested him.

When Marigold asked Reuben what he thought about attending the University of Georgia, he told her that he thought it was a great idea, as well as an excellent program. She thought she would have more trouble convincing him to go there and was surprised that he supported the idea so quickly. Once he told her his idea with regard to Harvard, she understood why she had no trouble convincing him to go to the University of Georgia.

There were doctorate degrees available at Harvard in history and in English/American literature. They both required five to six years to complete the programs but he told his parents that he thought he could finish them both in six years. Marigold told him that wasn't possible and Reuben smiled at the expected response.

"It would be if you hadn't provided me a history tutor all through high school. I have learned so much that I won't be starting from ground zero at Harvard, at least in the history program. I know I can complete both of them. I would like to try it at least. Will you give me that opportunity?"

Reuben had very skillfully used his mother's rules as he suggested this academic endeavor. Marigold was impressed by how her son had manipulated the process. She doubted Simon was even aware of what Reuben had done. She wanted to say, "You've been planning this for six months, haven't you?" but she didn't. She knew what she wanted instead.

"It will be a difficult path, son, but I know you are capable of it. I will support it, provided you stay at home with us this summer and work. No vacation, just work. I want to show you the land in South Carolina and southern Georgia. I want you to get to know those industries and the people that work out there in those rural areas. What say you, Mr. Broadwater, soon to be Mr. Broadwater, esquire?"

"Love to, mother. Thank you both for believing in me and allowing me these opportunities. I don't know how I will ever be able to repay you."

"I do," Marigold replied. "Success and heirs. I want the Redbud Lane home to still be around one hundred years from now and for the family heritage to continue to grow and prosper. Deal?"

He had heard that question before. Right before he agreed to that restaurant/business degree challenge. This time he knew the right answer and why it was the right answer.

"Deal," Reuben replied.

They had a large graduation party for Reuben's senior class and their families. There were over three hundred people in attendance and it was talked about for many years. Government Mule performed at the party and though it cost Marigold five thousand dollars for just a one-hour set, plus travel expenses for the band, she knew her son loved it. Marigold spared no expense, with the entire party costing over forty thousand dollars, but she didn't care. She wanted to make a statement to the town about their place in the social world of Augusta. She did.

That summer, Marigold and Reuben traveled for weeks at a time visiting the agricultural and timber businesses. Marigold wanted Reuben to understand how hard both those industries were. So, they worked in the farming fields and timberland alongside the people who worked them on a daily basis.

Marigold explained to Reuben how these fields were started by his grandfather Jack Sumpter and how his grandmother Katherine had helped him acquire more land in South Carolina, as well as the timberland in Georgia. She also shared what she knew about his great-grandparents, Absalom and Hephzabah Wood.

Just as expected, Reuben wanted to know more about the family. "Did my great-aunt Meredith have any other siblings besides my grandmother?"

"Yes, four other brothers. Two of them, Lemuel and John, were killed in World War II. The other two, Mark and Daniel, opened up bars in Savannah and Atlanta. They were both killed in bar fights. Neither one of them married and my mother sold both of the bars after they were killed."

Marigold chose not to tell Reuben about the family's liquor business in the 1930s and didn't mention the tunnel that her uncles and her grandmother had built. For a reason she couldn't explain, she didn't believe that Reuben ever needed to know that. Perhaps it was because her mother had sold the bars so quickly after her brothers were killed. She knew liquor had led to their success and their death.

Though her mother never actually told her that, she certainly didn't hide her contempt for the federal government and their interference in people's lives, right up until the very day she died, smoking a cigarette. But something was bothering Marigold; as if her mother was reaching out to her beyond the grave when her son asked these questions. Something that had been developing over time in her own mind now told her to keep that story hidden. So, she listened to those voices and avoided that discussion when her son continued to ask questions.

"You told me how my grandmother Katherine died, but how did my grandfather Jack die?" Reuben asked.

"Rattlesnake bite," Marigold replied. "The rattlesnake was about as big as him and he was almost six feet tall."

"Uh, do we need to be looking around for rattlesnakes while we're on this trip?"

"It's not a bad idea. Especially when we go out into the forests down in Georgia. Not so much here in the farmland, but even so, they are out here too. But they prefer the absence of humans and don't frequent the farmland as much, seeing how there are tractors and people and dogs out in the fields most of the time. It's the copperheads that will sneak up on you. You never see them before you step on them."

"Shouldn't this have been something we discussed before I asked about how my grandfather died?" Reuben asked as he checked out the ground.

Marigold started laughing. "Copperheads won't kill you, most of the time. Unless you are very young or very old or sick. But it won't feel good. Have had a few of the migrant workers step on a copperhead and they lived. They told me it was muy doloroso when I saw them in the hospital."

"Though I haven't studied Spanish, I am assuming that means very painful."

"Bueno, hijo," Marigold replied as she laughed.

"Good to know," Reuben said as he pulled out his phone and started searching for poisonous snakes in Georgia. She put her arm through his and started walking him back to the farmhouse.

"I know you will be distracted for the next hour or so as you learn all about snakes in Georgia so I'll lead us back to the farmhouse. Tomorrow we'll go down to south Georgia. I think you've seen all you need to for now here in South Carolina."

The next day, they got up early and had breakfast with the farmer who was in charge of all of the operations in South Carolina. Just before they left, Marigold asked, "How are things going Jimmy?"

"Good. Got a good crew working for me. They are happy and work hard. I couldn't ask for much more," Jimmy replied.

"And this will be your tenth year with us, right?"

"Yes, ma'am."

"And you have met all the production goals each year except one, correct?"

"Yes, ma'am."

"I thought so," Marigold said. She pulled out some paperwork and handed it to him.

"A lot of that is legalese but it says what I promised you ten years ago. Meet the goals and you acquire ten percent of the property after ten years. That will be yours and your family's for perpetuity. Congratulations, Jimmy. Good job."

"Thank you, Mrs. Broadwater. Thank you so much," Jimmy said as he stood up and held out his hand.

"After ten years, Jimmy, and on this occasion, we can do more than just a handshake," Marigold said and gave him a big hug. "Read over those papers. Sign them and make a copy. I'll be back sometime later in the year to pick them up."

Reuben shook Jimmy's hand and as they walked to the car, they both could hear his wife screaming. "He just told her, didn't he?"

"I would think so," she said. "Or she just stepped on a copperhead."

Reuben and his mother laughed as they got into her black all-wheel drive Land Rover and took off for Georgia. Reuben bombarded her with questions along the way about the farming industry as a whole, the different types of agriculture, the profit margins, the workforce, and the deal that she had made with Jimmy.

"Why do you think I made that deal with him?" Marigold asked.

"Loyalty. Farming is hard work. I know the answer to this without even asking but I'll ask anyway. Aren't most of the laborer's illegal aliens?"

"I'd say about half of them during the year. More during harvest time," Marigold replied.

"Then it's important that you have someone steady at the helm of that ship. Weather and workers are not guaranteed. And then there's the government. At times helpful, at times ignorant, and at times detrimental to the success of the farm. It's important that someone knows how to make all that work. When you offered up the deal ten years ago, it made him immediately vested in the success of the farms. Now, even more so. "

Marigold was impressed with her son's response, especially when he added to it.

"I noticed that they used a lot of pesticides on the farm. I've seen a trend that I think will continue to grow each year. And that is organic farming. More and more people want organic food and are willing to pay for it. Look at what's happening in California and is starting to pop up even down here, primarily in the bigger cities, but it's coming. I would suggest that we start moving in that direction. I think we can improve the margins and beat our competitors to the punch."

Underestimate him at your own peril, she said to herself, as she smiled at her son. She agreed that was a great idea and promised she would discuss it with some of her attorneys and a few valued advisers that she trusted in regard to agriculture trends, and of course, with Jimmy.

In Georgia, they stayed in a beautiful cabin in the woods. The owner was her foreman for the timber industries that they owned. Reuben loved the wood exterior and how it extended into the interior of the home. I think I will have one of these homes in the mountains one day, he told himself, as he learned about the timber industry over the next week.

They even saw a rattlesnake out in the woods while they were there. Reuben watched as the foreman shot it with a pistol he carried on his belt. Reuben saw how the logging industry was much more dangerous than farming, and it wasn't just because of the presence of large poisonous snakes. A mistake out there could kill more than one person and that's why Marigold made sure that the foreman was always with them while they were out in the woods. She had remembered the warning her mother gave her father.

On the way back home, Marigold asked Reuben what he thought of the timber business, expecting a lot of questions from her son, similar to what he had after seeing the farms. He didn't. He only had one.

"Who do we sell the wood to?"

"Paper mills," she replied. "About seventy percent paper mills. The other thirty percent to the home building industry."

"I suggest you sell all of that property now while it is still very profitable. I think over time the paper industry is going to dry up as more and more things become electronic. Just look at how computers have changed our life. E-books and getting news and information from the internet are becoming more popular and that will just continue to grow. If I had just been able to think of the internet before Al Gore, we would be millionaires."

Marigold laughed and then thought about what her son said. Again, it showed how perceptive he was. He saw things that others didn't, and in this case, figuratively saw the forest through the trees.

"We are millionaires," she said.

"You are. I'm not yet," he replied. "But I've had a pretty good teacher and I think I will be someday."

Rules one, two and three, Reuben thought as he looked over at his mother. He wanted to say something like, "What do you think, huh? Pretty smart, huh?" but he didn't. He just took a great deal of satisfaction with the expression he saw on his mother's face which he believed was reflective of his insight and intellect.

His mother shook her head. He was right. She could tell he wanted her to tell him that, but she refrained from doing so. I hope he is able to keep himself in check when he goes to college, she thought. She remembered how a lot of her classmates wanted to make sure everyone heard and saw how smart they were. And she hated that. All it did was make her want to show them they weren't as smart as they thought. She had been very successful in doing that her entire life.

Reuben learned everything Marigold wanted to teach him that summer sooner than she expected. So for the rest of the summer, Marigold spent time with Reuben and Simon at home or at the beach on long weekends and it was September before she realized it. The University had a rule that all freshman must live in a dorm, but she managed to have that rule changed for her son. She bought a condominium for him. Once they had him moved in, she and Simon said goodbye and drove away.

She cried on the way home and in the past, she might have tried to hide that from Simon, but she didn't that day. She didn't care. She just held his hand as she cried and he kept holding it until she stopped. She didn't tell Reuben when to call them or when to come back home since he was only about an hour and a half away. It would be up to him from this point forward. She knew he needed to grow up, even though he was still only sixteen years old. That is probably what prompted the "waterworks", she said to herself as she thought about her son at college. He was still only sixteen years old.

Reuben excelled in college even more so than in high school. The dual law and MBA degrees were very difficult and he had never been challenged in school like that before. Whatever the assignment was in either discipline, he exceeded what was expected of him. He didn't spend time watching TV or searching the internet unless he was researching an assignment. He studied day and night and he loved reading books at the library about whatever topic they were studying at the time.

He even asked the professors for suggested additional reading. At first, they all thought this was some smart-ass who was trying to make a false impression, but they soon learned they were wrong. This young man was smart and genuinely inquisitive. He soaked up the information in an osmotic manner that impressed his teachers. His instructors agreed that Reuben was very smart and extremely confident of his abilities, and he was also a very likable student. That's because Reuben still remembered Rule #1. They were his bosses for now. But he knew that was just a temporary situation.

Reuben returned home frequently during his freshman year and always went home for the holidays. He and Marigold discussed what he was studying and learning and she always made sure to have an executive summary for him to read regarding all of their businesses. In the middle of his sophomore year during Christmas break, she told him that they had made the switch to all organic corn farming but hadn't done so with the soybeans or tobacco. She had decided it wouldn't matter with those crops and Reuben agreed with her. He did point out that he thought it would be important with the peach crops. She said they were working on that, but it was taking longer to implement with the peaches as there were more issues with insects and diseases. Reuben nodded his head and made a mental note to research that later.

When he returned home from his sophomore year, he found a new red Corvette Stingray sitting in the driveway. As he went into the house, he hugged his father and mentioned what a cool car that was out front and that he was surprised that mom let him buy it. "I didn't think she liked sports cars."

"She doesn't," Simon replied. "But you know, sometimes a man just has to be a man."

Reuben looked at him and was not certain that he had heard his father say what he did. Though he loved and respected his father, Reuben always knew who made the decisions around the house. He had been told that in an emphatic manner by his mother and he couldn't believe that things had changed in the two years that he had been away at school. His mother smiled as she came out of the kitchen and hugged him.

"You are more handsome each time I see you," she said as she stood back and looked at him. He had inherited both of his parents' good looks and he was now a six-foot-tall, eighteen-year-old young man with an athletic build and the face of a male model.

"What do you think of your father's new car?" she asked.

"Damn nice car," Reuben replied.

"I know. I really like the black color, don't you?"

Reuben looked at his mother in a confused manner.

"The Cadillac, CTS- V. Down in the garage. You said you thought it was a nice car. You look confused," Marigold said. "Oh, you weren't referring to that red Corvette in the driveway, were you? The one that you need to drive your Porsche to the dealer to so that we can complete the deal and then the Corvette will be yours?" Marigold asked as she held out the keys in her hand.

"Shit," Reuben said as he looked at his parents smiling at him.

"Is that the type of language they are teaching you in law school?" Marigold asked.

"No, that comes from the MBA program. Lawyers are more prone to say words that start with f and end in k or i-n-g. Along with a reference to God and his ability to send things to Hell."

Marigold and Simon laughed as their son grabbed the keys from his mother's hand and ran outside to the car. And just like the day he got his Porsche, Simon opened the door of their son's new car for Marigold and watched them drive away.

Reuben didn't want to get out of the car that afternoon and after following his father to the Chevrolet dealership to drop off the Porsche, he and Simon drove about halfway to Macon before they turned around and started back to Augusta.

That was the best summer Marigold had experienced since Reuben left for college. They had fun together as a family. She didn't talk about business with her son. Not one time. She didn't feel that she needed to and she didn't really want to. Though her little boy was never a little boy, she knew that three-foot little man was gone and was never coming back. She couldn't wish him back, but she could have moments with him during that summer that would make her remember and smile.

The curriculum became more time consuming during his junior year. He didn't go home as much and at times he struggled with completing all of his classwork in addition to the extra reading that he expected to complete. He only went home for five days at Christmas.

Something felt different to him now. He noticed it at school and even when he was at home for the Christmas holidays. He told his parents that he needed to spend the break time studying and catching up and then trying to get ahead. Marigold could see the changes that were taking place in her son, and she knew that she only had herself to blame. The need to be successful was a genetic trait that had been passed down to her and she had now passed on to her son. She couldn't fault him for it, but she regretted some of it now as she watched him leave. "Call us when you can," she told him and hoped that the calls would be frequent even though she had more doubt than hope when she said it.

Reuben heard his mother's request and he told himself on the drive back to school he needed to remember to do that. Don't forget rule number one or two he told himself. She is your mother. Don't create a wall where there is none. He said the words in his mind several more times as he pressed down on the gas pedal and revved the Corvette up to 150 mph before slowing down. I believe this is faster than the Porsche he thought. The Porsche had a little more initial punch but it wouldn't be able to keep up with this.

He smiled at the thought. Just like the Porsche, he wasn't able to keep up, but now things were going to be different. New car, new focus, renewed desire to win. You've always won at anything you put your mind to, now do it again he said as he looked up in the rearview mirror. He swerved off the road for a moment as he thought he saw someone in the back seat. But it was just his eyes. Yeah, everything is changing, he told himself. But you're ready. You were born ready.

Reuben completed his junior year at the top of his class and told his mother that if he stayed through the summer semester, he could probably finish his degree by March, about four months early. She loved the idea and asked him if he had applied to Harvard yet. He told her no, but he was in the process of doing so. He asked her how the businesses were doing and she told him that she had sold all their timberland. She added, sarcastically, that she would be able to afford his college education at Harvard now and Reuben laughed. He told her that he would see her and dad during Christmas break but he ended up coming home in the fall. For his father's funeral.

Simon was a scratch golfer and had played all over the world. He loved playing at Hilton Head and went there at least a dozen or more times during the year for long golf weekends. He always played at the Harbour Town course in Sea Pines. On this particular day in September, he had about 180 yards to the green and his ball was on a downward slope next to one of the large water hazards. He was focused on his shot and didn't notice what was coming toward him. Just before he could swing, the alligator leaped out of the water, grabbed his legs and pulled him down into the pond. His friends rushed over to him but all they saw was his TaylorMade 5 iron and one of his arms floating on the surface of the pond. The alligator was captured and killed. That was mentioned in the story about Simon that was published in the Augusta Chronicle and the Hilton Head Island Packet.

They recovered other parts of his body and sent them to the funeral home in Augusta where Marigold had them cremated. Reuben never saw his mother cry during the funeral in Augusta or on their way to Hilton Head where she wanted to spread the ashes.

"He loved playing golf there. He told me if he died before me, he wanted to be cremated and placed in one of the sand traps at Harbour Town. He liked knowing that he would be part of at least one more golf shot when he was dead," Marigold said.

"I wonder what the golfer would say if they knew that not all of that sand was sand," Reuben said.

"I think they would be okay with it," she said. Reuben wasn't so sure about that, but he didn't argue. The more he thought about his fathers' ashes flying up into some golfer's face or falling into their socks and shoes, he started laughing and when he did, Marigold laughed too and hugged her son. They sprinkled Simon's ashes into the sand trap and Reuben raked them into the sand. They stood silently for a few minutes as each of them remembered the husband and father.

Marigold asked Reuben to stay with her that night and he did. They sat outside on the porch for a long time. His mother drank a lot of scotch and he drank a lot of beer, though Marigold made him toast his father with a scotch several times.

They reminisced about the time they went to Disney World when Reuben was only four years old and Reuben learned that was his father's idea. Marigold told Reuben that she didn't think he would like it, but she was wrong. Reuben smiled as he realized that was the first time he had ever heard his mother say she was wrong. I wonder if she ever told you that, Dad, he thought as he looked up and tipped his beer toward the sky.

Reuben recalled all the trips to Hilton Head with his father. He didn't really like golf, but he enjoyed riding in the golf cart when he was very young. As he got older, even his father knew Reuben was bored on the golf trips so he stopped taking him. But they still went on frequent father and son trips, usually to a place with some historical reference, and he remembered how his father always made each of the trips so much fun.

They talked about the European trip and the African safari and Marigold told Reuben how proud his father was of him when they were in Africa; how he looked so grown up and impressed all those guides. Reuben smiled and wished his father had told him that but he was at least glad to hear it now.

Reuben told his mother that Dad gave him his first beer, the night before his first date with Sarah and made him brush his teeth and use a lot of mouthwash before he went out. Marigold laughed and said that sounded like him. She then told Reuben about the time he got drunk and was arrested early in their marriage. When asked what she did, his mother just smiled and said she got him out of jail and kept it out of the newspapers. She avoided telling him what she did with the fire poker.

"He was a good man," Reuben said and he heard his mother agree, "Yes, he was, a very good man." Reuben remembered what his father said when they drove into Zambia to see Victoria Falls that day. He didn't hesitate. He said it as soon as he saw them. "Looks like something that would be in heaven," and he felt his father's hand on his shoulder. He knew right then, whenever he thought of his father, he would imagine those falls and he hoped his dad got to see them every day.

The next day, Reuben asked his mother if she would be okay alone or if he needed to stay another day. She could tell he was anxious to get back to school. She wanted him to stay but wouldn't tell him that. "No, I'll be fine alone. Just call me when you can."

Reuben called his mother every week until the end of November when he got away for the holiday break. This time he stayed with his mother for the entire five weeks and again Marigold minimized the discussion of work while he was there. She did take him to visit the farms in South Carolina and they went by the stores in Augusta once but that was all. He made a few comments to her about how she should look into some things regarding tax credits, especially for the farming properties, but that was the extent of their business related talks.

They toasted Simon several times during the holiday break and even went to Hilton Head once. He and his mother poured a very expensive bottle of Scotch into the ground next to the sand trap where they had spread his ashes.

It made them both smile and they enjoyed the rest of the time they spent with each other, having fun, and not worrying about business or school.

Reuben finished his JD/MBA in March of the following year as he said he would. Marigold wanted to celebrate with a big party but he told her that he would prefer she didn't. He asked her instead if she would accompany him to Harvard to meet with the school enrollment counselors and the dean of the history department, and then afterwards they could go to Boston and spend a few days. He had always wanted to visit Boston and Marigold was thrilled with the idea. She loved spending time alone with her son.

The enrollment counselors told Reuben that it would be very difficult for him to get a Ph.D. in English and American literature and history at the same time. In fact, they weren't aware of anyone even attempting it before. Hearing that only made Reuben more eager to prove to them how wrong they were.

Marigold recognized that look on his face as soon as they said it. Don't underestimate my son's abilities she said once again in her mind. Even if he was only doing this just to prove that he could, he would still succeed. But he is passionate about these subjects and the degrees associated with them, and he will get them. He has been groomed to succeed from a very early age and I know he will complete all the course requirements, probably before the expected timeline.

The dean of the history department was nice and cordial to Reuben and Marigold, but he also reiterated that what he was trying to do would be nearly impossible. However, after talking with Reuben for thirty minutes he finally said that if anyone could do it, he could see Reuben being the one that might be able to accomplish it and that he wouldn't stop him from trying it.

Reuben was accepted into Harvard and slated to start in September. And just as she knew he would, he asked if it was okay for him to get a place in Cambridge and start on his course work ahead of time. Marigold agreed but told him that he needed to sell his condominium in Georgia before they could look for one in Cambridge.

Without question, Reuben knew this to be a test in his mother's eyes and he had already done a full pictorial layout of the condo and placed it on multiple internet websites for homes before he even asked her. He had already researched pricing of similar housing in Athens and he knew what his mother paid for the condo four years ago. After she gave him the go-ahead, he had it painted and upgraded the appliances. He sold it in ten days and made a $10,000 profit even after factoring in the improvements, which considering the downturn in the current housing market at the time, was a very good profit.

"Not bad, huh?" Reuben said when he called his mother from Athens to tell her about selling the condominium. "I am mailing the paperwork to you to sign. You won't have to be at the closing. I've already taken care of that. Just mail the signed papers back to the attorney. I'm on my way to Cambridge. I've found a townhome there that we can purchase, about six blocks from the school in a very good location. It's a little smaller than the condo but I can still use all my furniture. It's only about $250,000 more than the condo, which I believe to be a very smart purchase considering the Boston/Cambridge market. And I assure you, even if this down housing market lasts when we go to sell it, this townhome will be worth double what we pay for it now. What do you think? Impressed?"

"I always have been, son," Marigold said as they talked a little longer, working out the specifics of the payment for the townhome. "I look forward to seeing it." She held onto the phone for a minute as she thought about the conversation she just had with her son. He wants the verbal acknowledgment now, she said to herself. Doesn't he see that people don't like braggarts? You have a lot to brag about son, but it will do you no good to do so. Except in rare business or scholastic situations. If this starts to get out of hand, I will just have to reign it in, she reminded herself.

As she walked away from the phone, she continued to think about her son and what may be required of her. It's not like you haven't done that before with other people she thought. But she knew if she had to do it with Reuben, it was going to be more difficult even though that wouldn't stop her from doing so. He needs to learn, she said as she went out to the sun porch and drank a glass of tea and looked at the flower garden that was still in bloom.

The first year at Harvard was hard. Reuben had doubts many times, even though he studied ten to twelve hours a day. It was difficult and he knew he needed to find a way to allow his mind to rest. His brain never seemed to turn off, even at night. One of his classmates in the doctoral program for literature offered Reuben a joint to try when they were discussing his lack of sleep. His friend, Tom, claimed it always made him relax and he was even able to study, provided he didn't get too stoned.

Reuben liked the idea of still being able to study if he needed to, so he tried it, only smoking a quarter of it that evening. It felt odd at first, but his classmate was right. It did allow him to rest and he found that he was still able to concentrate. The next day, he asked where he could buy a bag of it, and Tom told him he would take care of it. The bag would cost $250 but that should last him a month. He even included a glass pipe with the bag of marijuana the next day, and just as predicted, it was a month before Reuben was wanting more.

When he gave his friend the money that following month, Tom also suggested some stronger drugs. Reuben shook his head no, even though he stood there and listened to him talk about it.

"I'm telling you man, a little push of that golden stuff into your veins and you will see Lord Bryon or Washington Irving in a whole new light. I think it actually gives me some insight into what they were writing at the time. I just do it every once in a while and I always do it with some particular project or piece of literature I am working on. Every time I come out of that high, man, it takes me at least thirty minutes to write down everything I thought about when I was out there floating among the rainbows. Granted, some of it isn't worth shit, but some of it's damn good. Wrote a paper the other day comparing 'The Legend of Sleepy Hollow' to the ineffective government and the lack of courage that voters had in holding those elected responsible for not doing their job. Got an A on that one. Professor loved it. Surfing the rainbow, man. That all came from surfing the rainbow."

Reuben smiled and told him no, that the marijuana was sufficient and Tom just shrugged and said "no problem" as he handed over the baggie. That evening after smoking half a joint, Reuben was reading a history assignment on the various immigrant migrations to America. He began thinking of the neighborhood that was across the street and about a block away from his home in Augusta; an area that everyone in his family chose to ignore. None of his family ever talked about that neighborhood except to say how terrible a place it was. It was built in the early '70s for the poor as a government-subsidized housing project and had, over time, become a place where crime flourished and where hope gathered behind a locked door.

Drug use was prevalent in that neighborhood and Reuben began to formulate a plan of how he could capitalize on their need. Marketing supply and demand, he said to himself, as he lit up the pipe and took another puff. We don't need to ignore the neighborhood. We need to embrace the neighborhood and improve the lives of those that live there. Addressing their needs, he said as he smiled. He wondered what his mother would say as he laid back on the couch and thought about his ideas.

He completed his first year at Harvard before he came home. He had made the Dean's List in both of his disciplines and he made sure that Marigold knew. Reuben didn't tell his mother how exhausted he was and that he really needed a break and was looking forward to doing nothing as he allowed his brain to shut off. He wanted to just enjoy the weather and his home and sleep and eat, and perhaps have a few beers and a joint or two. All of that sounded good he thought as he got in his Corvette and headed toward Augusta.

Marigold tried to control her emotions when she saw Reuben, but it had been almost a year since she had seen her son in person. They had talked quite a bit via Skype but that didn't compare to seeing him in person. He looked tired, but she mistook stoned for tired, although it didn't matter to her right then as he walked into her outstretched arms. She couldn't stop the tears from falling as she held her son close to her.

She took him by the hand and led him to the sunroom. She asked him if he would like anything to eat or drink and he said he would love some popcorn and a coke. Marigold couldn't remember Reuben ever saying he liked popcorn that much, but she knew tastes changed over time. So, she just smiled and told him to sit down and she would be back in a few minutes with his request.

Reuben laid down on the wicker sofa and closed his eyes. He could hear and smell the popcorn. He smiled when his mother told him to get up and scoot over. She placed the popcorn between them and started to share it with her son. She told him that she was proud of him making the Dean's List. She knew he needed that affirmation from her again and he smiled when he heard her say it.

"By the way, I liked Skype so much that I put it on my manager's computers in all the stores and even out on all the farms in South Carolina. It works really well."

"Yes, it does," Reuben replied as he tried to control the manner in which he was engulfing the popcorn.

"Haven't had anything but breakfast," he said as a cover-up and he saw his mother nod her head as if she understood. "Mom, didn't you say my great-uncles started bars in Savannah and Atlanta?"

"Yes, why?"

"Did they ever do anything during the prohibition era?"

This was a question that she didn't think she would ever answer and she hesitated. Before she could reply, Reuben continued with his thoughts. "I've read a lot about the prohibition era and how people made a ton of money. I was just wondering if you were aware of them distributing whisky during that time."

She knew he would find out sooner or later so Marigold told Reuben the truth about how her uncles made their fortune during prohibition. She told him about the tunnel that his great-grandmother allowed them to build, and how they moved whisky in and out of the tunnel.

"Why didn't you tell me any of that before?" Reuben asked.

"I'm not sure," she replied even though she knew why she didn't. Her fears were confirmed with the next sentence.

"I bet if we were smart, we could re-use that tunnel as a way to sell marijuana to the neighborhood a block away from us. There is a very strong demand for it over there. I'm sure that it would give us access to other areas in town. It would be safe, with the right people and the right set-up."

"It's not the same thing, Reuben. Times are significantly different today than they were 70 years ago. Primarily, the ability of money and one's standing in society to influence those that need to look the other way has changed. Influence used to allow a few indiscretions and even ensure that a serious crime could be ignored and or forgiven. The influence we possess today, would not cover up what is considered a very serious felony and a crime that every politician makes a part of their platform. It doesn't matter if they are city, state or national politicians. They all make the same types of promises with regard to making the drug problems go away. And they like getting their picture in the paper with a successful drug bust. One where they give all the credit to the police and federal agents when talking to the media about it, but always remind people at election time, how all that happened under their watch."

"Actually, it was the same in the 1930s but the politicians and the police were indeed a lot more corrupt back then. That has certainly changed. They are still there, just not as obvious. But regardless, most politicians actually accomplish very little and what they say is still a lot of false bravado," Reuben replied. "You know that. Those in government follow through with very little that they say they are going to do. You even alluded to their hypocrisy as you were arguing against the idea. I'm not sure there's been a president in almost 40 years; not since Lyndon Johnson, who by the way was a drunk and a racist, that's done anything as significant for the country as he did. Medicare. Medicaid. Civil Rights, food stamps. Four pretty big things for him to hang that big fat hat of his on. And he didn't do that because he cared about the neighborhoods that are like the one a block over from us. He did everything with a political motive, believing what he was doing was helping the Democratic Party. He was right about that. And though people may argue Reagan defeated communism, I would just say he helped move the needle in the direction it was already headed. That 'famous wall' he talked about was coming down with or without his help. But I have to admit, he did make America feel good about themselves and considering everyone else that has held that office of late, that is saying something."

Boy, he is good at channeling his great-grandmother and grandmother, Marigold thought. And he's so damn smart. A lot smarter than either one of them but too damn smart for himself right now. He needs to be hit in the head with the fireplace poker and Marigold began talking to her son as if she was talking to Simon when she hit him twenty years ago.

"You are not going to go into the drug business. We are just not going to do it. You have a law degree and an MBA. We have a twenty-million-dollar business operation and at least that much invested in stocks and such. You would lose all of that, and I won't allow that to happen. Am I making myself understood?"

Reuben heard the tone in his mother's voice and he knew he could go no further on the subject today. He nodded his head and smiled at her. The smile would let her know it was forgotten, even though it wasn't going to be. I just need to do some more research on the subject, he told himself. Starting today.

"Okay, I get it. But would it be okay for you to show me the tunnel?"

"Yes. After you drive me over to our floral shop. I want to get some flowers for the dining room and sunroom." And introduce you to Melissa, she added to herself.

"Sure, let's go," Reuben said. He finished off his coke and got another one from the kitchen. As he walked toward the car, he realized that it probably smelled like pot and he wasn't ready to have that discussion now. Especially not now. Shit, he said to himself. Think Reuben.

"Hey, do you still have Dad's Cadillac?'

"No, I traded it in on a Cadillac Escalade. A black one. I didn't tell you that, did I? I just never think about cars the way you and your Dad did. Want to drive it?"

Perfect, Reuben. Perfect.

"I'd love too," he said as his mother handed him the keys and they went through the kitchen door to the garage.

"Damn nice, Mom," Reuben said, backing the large SUV down the driveway. He looked back at the neighborhood on the other side of Mercy Street, a little over a block away, and said "untapped market" to himself before he turned onto Redbud Lane and headed toward the floral shop.

Reuben was going to wait in the car, but Marigold asked him to come in with her to meet some of the new staff. Ah yes, Reuben said to himself as he got out of the car. Employer-employee relationships. The keys to success.

They walked through the back door of the floral shop and Reuben watched his mother say hello to everyone she met, introducing her son to those that didn't know him. None of them asked what he was doing these days, and he was surprised his mother didn't mention that he was at Harvard. Maybe she's in a hurry he thought.

"Marigold! What a nice surprise," a woman said as she came over to his mother and hugged her. Reuben remembered she was the manager of the store. He checked his file-cabinet memory and saw the bouquet he attached to her name as a memorization tool, as he held out his hand. She pushed it away as she took him into her arms.

"Hello, Mary," Reuben said. "How have you been?"

"I have been wonderful and let me look at you," she said as she stood back from Reuben and then looked over at Marigold. "My, he's a handsome young man, Marigold. But you know that don't you?"

Marigold simply smiled.

"And you are at Harvard now, right?" Mary asked Reuben.

"Yes, just completed my first year."

"Do you like it?"

"Very much so."

"Hated school work. Always wanted to go outside and get in the garden with my father. I loved those times with him," she said as she looked off into the distance for a moment. "But enough of that. What can I do for you, Marigold?" Mary asked.

"I want some fresh flowers for the dining room and sunroom. Can you put some together for me?"

"Happy to. Melissa!" Mary called out and Reuben saw a beautiful young woman with long black hair pulled back by a scarf turn around and smile. "Can you help me please for just a moment?"

The young woman put down her cutting shears and left the arrangement she was working on. She held out her hand as she approached Marigold and Reuben.

"Hello, Mrs. Broadwater. Good to see you again. Hello," she said as she looked up at Reuben. "I'm Melissa."

Reuben took her hand and smiled as he looked at her face, almost forgetting to tell her his name. He felt like he was looking at a young Elizabeth Taylor. The one that was in the movie "National Velvet." He and his father enjoyed watching old movies and he never forgot how beautiful she was in that one. He had never seen anyone as beautiful since then. Not until today.

"Can you put together a bunch of those lilies - the tiger lilies and the swamp lilies - and several varieties of the alstroemeria? And we can add in all those pretty irises we just got in. You'll love them, Marigold," Mary said as she and Melissa walked away.

Marigold watched her son stare at Melissa as she worked on the flowers for them.

She leaned over and whispered in his ear, that he needed to watch himself or he would start drooling. Reuben looked down at her as he reached up and wiped his face as discretely as possible.

"Thank you, Mary, and thank you, Melissa," Marigold said as she took the bundle of flowers from both of them. "They're beautiful. They will look lovely in the house. And the lilies smell so nice."

"Don't they?" Mary said as she watched her daughter pretending to look at the flowers and not Reuben.

"When I get these in the vases at home, I'd love to have you and Melissa come out for lunch and tell me how I did. Would you two be able to do that?"

"Just name the day," Mary replied. "I never turn down a free lunch."

"Good. We'll see you later in the week then," Marigold said as she turned to walk away.

Reuben told Mary it was good to see her again and told Melissa it was a pleasure meeting her. He started to ask her if she was free for dinner but he didn't. As he followed his mother to the car, he told himself he was stupid for not doing so. Women didn't intimidate him. Why did that happen he wondered?

While they were driving home, Marigold asked Reuben what he thought. Reuben replied that he thought the business looked like it was thriving and Mary looked good.

"That's not what I'm talking about and you know it," Marigold said. "What did you think of Mary's daughter?"

"Her daughter? Her daughter is Melissa?"

"Yes, she is."

"She is very pretty," he said as he realized why his mother asked him to come into the store.

"She's more than pretty. She is a knockout. And I can tell she is interested in you. You should ask her out. She isn't dating anyone. She's in college. Works there for her mom during her breaks. She is studying to be a nurse and will be starting her clinical rotations in the fall. She's very smart. Smart and beautiful."

"*For the moon never beams without bringing me dreams, of the beautiful Annabel Lee. And the stars never rise but I feel the bright eyes of the beautiful Annabel Lee*," Reuben said as he opened the door for his mother.

"That's lovely," his mother said.

"It is, isn't it?" Reuben said as he closed the door. "It's a poem, 'Annabel Lee,' written by Edgar Allen Poe. About his dead wife Virginia. It's one of my favorites."

"I remember now," Marigold replied. "You read it to us many times when you were in high school. But I never heard you quote poetry after meeting a girl. I think that may be a first."

Reuben didn't say anything but he knew she was right. He had never been prompted to recite poetry because of a girl he had just met or had dated.

"So, when do you want me to set up lunch?" Marigold said.

"As soon as possible," Reuben replied and together they laughed as they drove home.

Reuben stayed a week longer than he anticipated that summer. He and Melissa had started dating. The sex with her was unlike any that he had ever had before. Now I understand why there are poets in the world he thought as he looked at her body lying next to his.

Reuben loved listening to her talk and was, for once, uninterested in telling her of his school accomplishments and what he was currently doing. But she wanted to know. She asked him to tell her all about what he was studying. He described the degrees he was pursuing and also about the degrees from the University of Georgia that he already had.

"How old are you?" she asked as she looked at him like he had farted.

"Twenty-one," he replied.

But instead of being repelled by the imaginary fart, she stared into his eyes and pulled him closer to him. As soon as his body felt her breasts, he felt himself getting hard.

"You're some sort of fricking genius, aren't you?" she asked as she reached down to touch him.

"I'm not sure," he said as he tried to remain humble but as soon as she put him inside of her, he smiled and changed his comment. "Yeah. I am," he said and the words were like some aphrodisiac fairy dust that sprinkled down on her as her body consumed him.

Neither of them was able to talk for a minute as they rested on the bed in each other's arms. As soon as she got her breath back, she wanted to know more about what he had been doing at school, the literature he had read and the history he studied. He had never been with a woman who wanted to know what truly interested him. They lay together and talked for hours and she never looked away or seemed bored with anything he said.

He wasn't sure if he was dreaming but when she got up and went into the bathroom and he heard the toilet flush, he knew it wasn't a dream. You don't hear a toilet flush when you are dreaming about beautiful women.

Reuben and Melissa were almost never apart that summer and he never gave another thought to the neighborhood that he saw, but ignored, when he drove into his driveway. He never smoked a joint or even thought about it.

He even forgot about the tunnel entrance that his mother showed him when they got back from the floral shop that day. He never noticed the fresh flowers that were in just about every room of the house because his mother and Mary saw each other every week, exchanging information about whatever they heard their son or daughter say about the other one.

When the time came for him to return to Boston, he invited Melissa to come and visit whenever she could. When she asked him if he really needed to leave so soon, he was almost convinced to stay by the look on her face.

But he knew it was necessary to get back because the second year would be more demanding and he needed to start studying even before the semester began. He told her that she would always be on his mind, which he added, was not a good thing considering it was all he could do to just get by the first year studying ten to twelve hours a day after attending four to five hours of class. She "one-upped" him by telling him that he would always be on her mind and that wasn't good a good thing either, considering that she would soon be putting needles into patient's arms and placing large tubes up men's penises.

"I'll be thinking of you, darling," she said, "as I grab hold of that man's dick and start shoving that plastic tube up through his urethra and into his bladder. The grimace on his face will remind me of some of those expressions you made when you were inside of me."

He burst out laughing as he pulled her into his arms.

"*Take this kiss upon the brow, and in parting from you now, thus much let me avow, you are not wrong, who deem, that my days have been a dream,*" he said as he kissed her forehead.

"Wrong place," she said as she pulled his head down and placed his lips on hers, letting them linger there for a moment before she opened her mouth and kissed him in a much more vigorous manner.

"I knew if I could get you to recite me poetry, you would be all mine," she said as she looked up at him and smiled. "That's my litmus paper test."

"Oh really?" Reuben replied. "You have a lot of men reciting poetry to you?"

"Not a one," she said as she smiled and looked into his eyes. "You are the first and I've got to say, it made my body get a little tingly inside."

Reuben smiled. "Edgar Allan Poe can do that to you. By the way, you do wear gloves when you are putting a catheter in someone don't you?"

"I wasn't planning on it, but I will. Just because you asked."

He laughed and pulled her even tighter toward him and before he knew what he was doing he said it.

"I think I am falling in love with you, Melissa."

"It's because I mentioned the catheter isn't it?"

"I'm serious. I have never felt this way before. Not with a woman. A few men maybe."

"You shithead. I don't have to think. I know I have fallen in love with you, Reuben Broadwater. And I'm pretty sure you will probably break my heart one day, but I'm willing to give it to you, even knowing that. I am unable to stop myself."

"So, what do we do now?" he asked.

"You go back home and pack for Harvard and spend the night with your mom so she doesn't start hating me because you spent your last day in town with me. And I'll go inside and start texting the hell out of your phone. I suggest you put it on vibrate unless you want to hear it chime every few seconds. I will do the same thing tomorrow when I know you're on the road. I will tell you that some of those texts, might be very sexual so I wouldn't try reading them and driving. And don't pull off in a rest stop and start beating off. I can't tell people my boyfriend was caught at a rest stop beating off. Nobody would believe that I dated someone that did that, *Again.* And then I wait. I will wait about thirty minutes and call you and tell you that I love you and miss you already. That's what we do, Mr. Broadwater."

"I do love you, Melissa," Reuben said as he held her face in his hands.

"I know you do," she said as she kissed him one more time before she let go of him. He stood at the bottom of the driveway until she walked into the house before he drove away.

He received ten texts from Melissa on the way home and told her that even though he didn't want her to stop, he was at home now and was going to turn off the phone. She said she understood just as she sent him a picture of her eating a banana. He replied that he was glad to see that she was eating fruit and then said, "I love you," as he turned off his phone. He found his mother in the kitchen and asked her what she wanted to do for the day. She told him that she just wanted to stay home and spend time with him, maybe order a pizza later if that was okay. Perhaps they could watch an old movie like he used to do with his father.

Reuben thought that was a great idea and went into the den and started searching the channel guide on the TV. He couldn't believe what he saw was coming on at 3:00. "Casablanca" and after that, "The African Queen" and then after that, "The Big Sleep." It was a Humphrey Bogart marathon. He began to think his mother had planned the afternoon too. That when she said in a casual manner "watch some old movies," she knew what was coming on. Yeah, she knew, he laughed. Hell, she probably even knows Ted Turner and called him up to suggest those movies. His mother came into the den and asked him what was so funny.

"I'm laughing because I am happy. Very happy. How did you know?"

"I had a hunch. You love her, don't you?"

"I do," Reuben said as he sat down beside her on the sofa. "I wasn't expecting it and didn't think it would ever happen so soon, but it did. As if there was some unseen force that I couldn't control. Sort of like some person I know," he said as he looked at Marigold. She just shrugged her shoulders and smiled.

"I've never felt like this around a woman before. She is not like any other woman I have ever met. She likes what I like. I love talking to her and she likes listening to me ramble on. She is smart. Witty, in fact, damn right funny. Charming. Enchanting. Sensual. Beautiful. And I'm sure I could throw out some other adjectives but I think you understand how I feel."

"I do. I loved your father in the same way."

Reuben thought that might have been the way she felt about his father, but he knew that all stemmed from him also knowing who was in charge. He wanted to tell her that Melissa wasn't like that, but he realized that would do nothing but hurt his mother. She was in love with the memories she had made of his father and he wouldn't do anything now to disrupt her version of the past.

Reuben sat back on the sofa and turned up the TV volume as the movie was about to start.

"You do know that while filming the movie "Casablanca," Humphrey Bogart hated working with Ingrid Bergman. And she, him. They avoided each other and only came together when they had to be in a scene. They both thought the script was stupid and that the movie wouldn't amount to much."

"Yet now it's considered a great love story," Marigold said as she looked at her son and smiled.

"He doesn't win Ingrid in the end. He gives her up. For the war and for the love of a more noble man."

"It's just a movie."

"Yes, it is," Reuben replied as the movie started.

They watched movies all afternoon, talking during commercials. They talked about the past and about the future. They had a few drinks as they talked and then ordered a pizza just as "The African Queen" was coming on.

"Bogart hated filming in Africa. But Katherine Hepburn and John Huston loved it. They were in real danger there too. From catching dysentery to poisonous snakes, crocodiles. Amazing movie."

Marigold smiled as she listened to her son discuss the movie. Now was the time to tell him.

"Reuben, I am glad Melissa likes hearing you talk about the things you know. As I do. But you need to be careful. Some people may view your knowledge of everything as arrogance. And you don't want people to think that way about you."

Reuben nodded his head but didn't reply to his mother as he thought about what she said. I can't help it if people think it's arrogance when you have something interesting to say that they don't know. I'm not just throwing out words that have no meaning in regard to the subject. But I hear you, mother. I still remember rule number one.

They watched "The Big Sleep" but Marigold didn't see the end of it. She fell asleep and Reuben tapped her on the shoulder when the movie ended and he turned off the TV.

"Time to go to bed mom," he said and she nodded her head. "Did Bogey get the girl in the end?" she asked as she followed him up to their bedrooms.

"He did. In the movie and in real life."

"I like that," Marigold said. She kissed her son on the cheek and said good night to him.

Reuben left early the next morning. His mother was already up and had some biscuits and bacon ready for him, along with a large cup of coffee. He told her thanks for everything and was on the road by 6 a.m. He drank his coffee as he drove, knowing that he would need a lot of caffeine to make it to Boston. It was a long fourteen-hour drive and he already felt a little tired, because he didn't get a lot of sleep. But after receiving his first text from Melissa that morning, any tired feelings went away like disappearing ink as he read the very sexual message. With the subsequent messages, he doubted he would have any trouble at all staying awake for the entire trip.

His second year at Harvard was what he expected. Even more demanding. He spoke with Melissa every day though, via text or a short phone call. She talked about her clinical rotations in the Children's Hospital at the Medical College and how much she loved working with the pediatric patients. She told him it was very difficult to watch them die, and she considered leaving that rotation because of it, but that the miracles that occurred every day helped her work through the losses she witnessed. That and prayer.

When he heard her say that, he immediately thought of C.S. Lewis and provided her with a quote.

"Miracles are a retelling in small letters of the very same story which is written across the whole world in letters too large for some of us to see."

He heard her voice waver as she told him she would never forget that quote. She told him it gave her strength and she loved him for sharing it with her. She then composed herself and asked him what he was working on. He could have talked for hours but he knew they both needed to get back to work, so he told her he loved her and would talk to her tomorrow.

After he hung up, he remembered what his mother had warned him about sharing information, whether it was from the great writers of the past or from some aspect of history that only he and few others knew. His mother was wrong. What he had told Melissa today helped her. Granted, Melissa is an amazing woman but I think you are wrong, mother, he said to himself as he went back to his work.

Even though he was working harder, he felt like he was falling behind. If not for the marijuana, he wasn't sure what he would have done. It helped lessen his anxiety and slow his mind that was stuck on the gerbil wheel spinning around and around his class assignments.

It's funny how things can change, he thought as he took a hit off the pipe. He had imagined he would be smoking a lot of marijuana and relaxing at home over the summer break but when he met Melissa, he had never given it a thought. Nor the neighborhood a block away and the tunnel that led to it. Interesting, he thought, as he lay down on his sofa and listened to the album "Dixie Chicken" by Little Feat. I love the old Southern rock bands, he said to himself as he drifted off into the music and thought of nothing else.

As the semester continued, Reuben told Melissa that it was impossible for him to get away for a long weekend, and though she was disappointed she told him she understood. It would just make things that much better when they saw each other over the Christmas break and he promised he would be home then. She is always the optimist he thought.

When he told his mother, she also said she understood and told him he needed to do what he thought was necessary in order to succeed. After all, it wasn't anything she hadn't heard before but she had to admit, she didn't expect it this time knowing how he felt about Melissa.

But as she thought more about it, she knew how driven her son was. You were the same way at his age, she thought. You need to let him do what he needs to. He will come back soon she told herself. I know he will come back soon she said again, this time out loud as if she was talking to someone there next to her. She poured herself a scotch and after several more of them, convinced herself that everything would be all right over time and then marked off another day on the calendar.

Reuben finished the semester on the Dean's list but he only had one week off at Christmas before school started again in January. He flew to Augusta and spent Christmas with his mother and Melissa. Marigold asked Reuben if he wanted to show Melissa the farms over in South Carolina and he thought that would be a great idea. They went up there for the day and though they didn't plan on it, Jimmy invited them to stay and have a holiday dinner with his family, which they did.

Marigold threw a lavish Christmas party and Reuben was often asked about the young woman he was with. He couldn't talk about her enough and it pleased Marigold to hear him talking about Melissa instead of himself. She is so good for him she thought.

Both Marigold and Melissa took Reuben to the airport and said goodbye to him. On their way home Marigold couldn't hold back any longer. She wanted to know exactly what Melissa thought about her son. "Melissa, I only know one way to say this. What do you think of Reuben?"

"He's smart. Handsome. And he loves me."

"Do you love him?"

"He's okay, I guess."

Marigold looked at her in a strange manner, swerving off the road as Melissa warned her to watch where she was driving.

"I was just kidding. I love your son. Very much. I've never met anyone like him."

"He said you had a hell of a good sense of humor. Did he tell you I didn't?"

Melissa looked a little shocked and started to say she was sorry when she heard Marigold laughing.

"I'm so happy for both of you," she said with a devious grin on her face.

"So, the score is 1- 1 for now," Melissa replied.

"Yes, I suppose it is," Marigold said as she laughed some more and drove her home.

Reuben finished his second year at Harvard, again on the Dean's List. He was going to stay in Boston and start his third year early, but Melissa was graduating from nursing school and he needed to be there for her graduation. Again, he flew to Augusta, as he didn't plan on spending much time there. He had other ideas.

After the party that his mother threw for Melissa, Reuben asked her if she had a job yet. She told him she had been offered a position at the Children's Hospital in town and planned on taking more courses and training that would help her get into the pediatric intensive care unit.

"What would you think about working at Mass General Children's Hospital?" Reuben asked.

"Are you kidding?"

"No, I'm not. I don't know if you know this or not, but they are nationally ranked in pediatric diabetes and endocrinology, pediatric gastroenterology and GI surgery, pediatric pulmonology and pediatric urology. I think it would be a tremendous opportunity for you."

"Oh my God. Of course, it would. But, where would I live?"

"I know of a place up there. You might know the guy that lives there. In fact, he is standing right here in front of you. What do you think?"

"What are you saying? Are you asking me to marry you or move in with you?"

"I am asking you to move in with me. I know this sounds like a cliché, but I think we need time around each other. Times when we aren't at our best and we'll see if we can tolerate each other when that occurs. Believe it or not, I do have bad days. Sometimes really bad days when I'm not too pleasant to be around. Maybe you will change that, maybe not. But I want you to at least know if it's something you can live with."

"I can be a bit bitchy at times too, Mr. Broadwater. So, what you are asking may not be something you really want."

"I'll take the chance if you will."

Melissa reached up and kissed him. "I still think you will break my heart," she said as she wrapped her arms around him and then she realized something.

"How do I know…" and before she could complete her sentence, Reuben interrupted her.

"The Dean of the History program happens to be very good friends with the CNO at Mass General. He got me in to talk to her and I told her all about you. I can be quite charming when I have to be. She said she would be glad to meet with you. And personally, considering how charming and persuasive I was, I think you will get the job. Provided you pass the drug screen and background check. You haven't been convicted of any felonies, have you?"

"Convicted? No, not convicted," she replied as Reuben started laughing.

"Let's go tell the moms," Reuben said as he pulled on Melissa's arm but she pulled him back to her.

"How do I know you just don't want me up there for sex whenever you want it?" she asked as she reached into his pants.

"Because I'm going to pull your hand out of my pants, wait a few minutes for the bulge to subside and then we're going in there and tell our mothers."

"Well, then I will do it, provided you understand that when I want sex you have to be able to deliver, Mister. Can you handle that?" she asked.

"I wash my own laundry. I'm sure I can do that other stuff you are referring too."

"You know when I said that, I meant once a month or maybe every other month," Melissa said as she tried to keep from laughing but she couldn't. Reuben smiled and laughed too as he lifted her off her feet and swung her around before they went inside to announce their plans to their mothers.

Marigold and Mary were thrilled to hear that they wanted to be together. Mary told Melissa privately that she really wished they were getting married, but she wouldn't hold that against her. She understood people did things differently these days. Melissa started to say that the sex was the same as in her day but she knew her mother didn't want to hear that. So, she refrained and hugged and thanked her for her support and everything she had done for her.

Marigold told Reuben this was one of the best decisions he had ever made and that she was happy for him. She warned him again about overdoing conversations with subject matter, and Reuben just nodded his head, instead of telling her that she was wrong. I can't tell you that you are wrong, mother. Not yet, because of rule number one. But there is a day coming.

Reuben arranged to have Melissa's belongings sent to his townhome as they flew to Cambridge the next day. He spent the next several days introducing Melissa to Boston. He loved showing her the history of the town and the vibrant downtown area with the old restaurants and bars mixed in with the new. She loved listening to Reuben tell her about the city and seeing it through his eyes. She even said she loved his townhome and wouldn't change a thing about it. He thought she was just being nice so he told her that she could change anything she wanted as long as she didn't touch his computer workstation or move it from its location in front of the window.

It was sitting on an old wooden rolltop desk that he had found in Boston, dating back to the 1800s. Melissa just looked at him and smiled and told him that she loved it too. He had impeccable taste and she knew he got that from his mother. She realized that the first day he took her into their house. Everything about the house was beautiful - the antiques, the art, the architecture. There was nothing she didn't like. Reuben just smiled and picked her up and took her into the bedroom where she saw the vase full of beautiful cut lilies.

"Those are all the lilies you arranged for my mother the day we met," Reuben said.

Marigold pushed him back onto the bed and started taking her clothes off.

"Those flowers just moved sex up to twice a month," she said as she jumped on him and they rolled around in the bed like two little kids before the hormones that flowed through their adult bodies suggested other things they could do which would be even more fun.

The next day, Reuben took Melissa to Mass General to meet the CNO and the director of the pediatric unit. He studied downstairs while they talked and about an hour later, he saw Melissa walking toward him. Something wasn't right, he thought, as he looked at her. When he asked her what was wrong, she told him they did offer her a job but that they didn't want to pay her what she thought she was worth.

He looked at her and told her that she didn't need to worry about money, but then she started laughing.

"No, I don't need to worry, because they offered me $20,000 more than I thought I would be making!" she screamed as she jumped into his lap and put her arms around his neck. "I can take you out tonight for dinner, my treat."

"Are you sure? I have very expensive tastes."

"Well, if I don't have enough money, we'll just have to figure out something else I can do to pay for the bill. Can you think of anything?"

"Yes, but if I do, I won't be able to stand up," he replied.

That first year in Boston together was one of the best years of Reuben's life. He loved everything about Melissa and she loved everything about her job and being around Reuben. They were both "neat freaks" and both a little OCD, so they got along very well living with each other. Even so, school work was still very stressful and Reuben pulled out some pot one evening and started smoking it.

Melissa looked at Reuben a little strangely and said she didn't think he did drugs. He replied that he didn't; he only smoked a little pot every now and then because it helped him turn his brain off for a couple of hours and helped him handle the stress of school. He asked her if she wanted to try any and she shook her head no. She said she didn't care if he smoked some every now and then, as he said, but she asked him if he would do it outside. If she got any second-hand smoke she might fail one of the random drug screens at work. Reuben said that wouldn't be a problem and did as she requested.

Though Melissa said she didn't care about Reuben smoking pot, she really thought there were better ways to relieve stress and she began researching ways to do that. She didn't feel comfortable asking anyone at work about it, so she did a lot of research online. She knew regardless of whether they were a friend at work, as soon as she said she was researching it "for a friend" that some of them would think that friend was her. She didn't want that level of scrutiny even though she was doing nothing wrong. She had learned that perception was reality early on in her medical career.

She knew Reuben loved history and would be more prone to listen to her if she had data to back up her assertion that whatever she found was better than smoking pot in relieving stress. She started out researching marijuana and how it affected the brain. There were many articles that suggested what Reuben said was true with just as many articles saying the long-term effects were detrimental, and also articles that stated there was not enough data to support either side of the argument. She knew there had to be alternatives and when she googled a combination of stress relief and science she found information on yoga and meditation.

This is perfect she thought as she learned more about how yoga and meditation complement each other. She read that some yoga exercise regimens could be very intense and she thought Reuben would be interested in those, considering how he liked to stay in shape. She found several programs online that she thought he would be interested in trying. She knew exactly how she would present this idea to him and on the way home from work the next day, she stopped to purchase a book that would help her convince Reuben to try what she was suggesting.

That evening before dinner she told Reuben that she had been looking for other ways to relieve stress and tension. She informed him that yoga had been around for over 5,000 years and had been traced back to the Indus-Sarasvati civilization in India. She then showed him a You-Tube video of a very intense yoga exercise session and he had to admit to her that it looked intriguing. She also talked to him about meditation techniques and how they began back in the second century and though she had never practiced it, she had seen it used in the hospital, in particular with adult cancer patients.

She then gave him the book she bought. It was a book on Kama Sutra and she said if he was interested in doing the yoga and meditation with her, she would make sure that they tried every one of the positions in the book. She didn't tell him to stop smoking pot, she just showed him what alternatives were available. Reuben smiled and said she had him as soon as she mentioned the Indus-Sarasvati civilization and asked when they could start. She told him it would have to wait until tomorrow because she needed to study the book a lot more and he started laughing.

The next day, they tried a yoga workout and a meditation exercise that they found on the Internet. The Kama Sutra position they tried after the workout only lasted five minutes as it was one they were already familiar with and they were both a little sore and didn't feel like standing on their heads.

They continued with the yoga and meditation exercises every evening and Reuben had to admit they did relax him and take his mind off of school. They didn't have sex after each exercise session, but they did explore the Kama Sutra diagrams so that they could decide if that was something they really wanted to do. He stopped smoking pot and their life together continued to be one they truly enjoyed. He loved listening to what she did at work, and she loved listening to him talk about English or American literature or whatever he was currently studying in history.

It was Christmas before they knew it and Reuben suggested that they invite their mothers to Boston for the holiday since neither of them could take much time off. Melissa thought that sounded nice, but she knew her mother would want her to come home so she could be with all her cousins and aunts and uncles. She also wasn't even sure that her mother could be off during Christmas since it was very busy at the floral shop during that time. Reuben realized that Melissa was right. He had never considered work an issue before in making a decision about a vacation.

But he then remembered that he wasn't unfamiliar with how some aspect of work had always been part of the decision-making process with him and his mother. He remembered the restaurant business his mother gave him to run and what he learned and how it required him to get his law degree and MBA. He remembered the summer she kept them from going on vacation so he could learn the farming and timber business. He remembered the condominium he was required to sell before he could move to Harvard. And he remembered the tenderizing mallet. Though he had yet to have a true job, work had meaning in his life and now he realized another important lesson. Not everyone could just pick up and leave and go on vacation when they worked. Even though he had been around hundreds, if not a thousand employees in his life, he had never really thought about that before now.

They spent Christmas in Augusta and his mother hosted another large party and invited all of Melissa's family, in addition to the stalwarts of the Augusta societal hierarchy. Reuben watched his mother and marveled at how she still managed to work in some business deals while mingling with the guests during the party. Reuben got to meet Melissa's entire family. He counted all of them and there were sixty-three cousins, aunts, and uncles. He found it interesting that he had none, except on his father's side of the family, and there were only five of them.

He thought about how his family tree, on his mother's side, could be traced back to the late 1800s. It was a very big family, but now, there was just him and his mother. Everyone else was dead. "I wonder if our family is cursed," he suggested to Melissa that night after the party. She told him they weren't cursed; they just lived colorful lives. He smiled at her and remembered what she had said about him coming home the last Christmas break - "how being apart would just make things all that much better when they saw each other." Always the optimist, he thought, as he kissed her and tried to remember a Kama Sutra move but as he did, they fell off the bed and couldn't do anything else that evening besides laugh and then go to sleep.

Reuben finished year three on the Dean's List once again, and by that time, Melissa had worked at Mass General for a year. This time he asked her how much vacation time she had and where she would like to go that she had never been before. He thought she would say something like Paris or London but she didn't. She said she had always wanted to go to Alaska and though he was surprised, he loved the idea.

"Did you know, we purchased Alaska from the Russians in 1867 for about two cents an acre? Can you believe that? It's believed that there is more oil in that one state than in all of the Middle East. But bad decisions by oil companies in the past, and ignorance within our government have allowed us to access only a small portion of it. Not many people know this but Japan occupied two Alaskan islands in World War II, Attu, and Kiska. For fifteen months, can you believe it? No one teaches that in high school and they also don't teach that the war was a lot closer to the US than people thought. During World War II, German U boats attacked and destroyed 397 ships along the east coast and the Gulf of Mexico. The waters off Cape Hatteras earned the nickname, "Torpedo Junction" because of so many ships that were destroyed off of North Carolina's Outer Banks. The US government kept all that information classified so that people wouldn't panic and to this day, not many people even know about it."

Melissa came over and sat in Reuben's lap. "How do you know all of this stuff? Doesn't your brain get flooded so that nothing else will go in there?" she said as she tapped on his forehead with her index finger.

He just smiled and said, "Velma Wallis is probably the most famous author from Alaska. She is an Athabascan Indian and one of thirteen children. Her book 'Two Old Women' reminds me of Hemingway's 'The Old Man and the Sea.' Tales of survival. Great books for the young and old. Though I'm afraid, the young today and certainly of tomorrow will not be exposed to such good reads. And 'The Leatherstocking Tales.' That would be a good book to read on our Alaskan cruise. I could re-read that and you could read 'Two Old Women.'"

"Did you say Alaskan cruise?"

"I did. I need to get working on it. You do know my mother will want to go and I'm fine with that. What about asking your mother? They seem to like each other a lot and would help us sneak away, you know, in case you want to read another book."

"I have been reading that book without you, you know. I think you may be very surprised with what my nimble body is capable of doing now,"

Melissa said as she kissed Reuben. "Come in the bedroom and I will show you." If the walls at their townhome were thin, the neighbors would have heard Reuben yell out, "Holy Shit," several times but the walls were fairly soundproof.

They called their respective mothers and suggested the Alaskan cruise and both of them were very excited. Marigold told Reuben that she would take care of the plans and he was fine with letting her do that. He also wanted to tell her everything he had told Melissa about Alaska's purchase and World War II history and how she enjoyed hearing it, but he didn't. There was no need to start something when it wasn't necessary.

He did recommend Velma Harris' book to read on the cruise. He thought the book would remind her of her great-grandmother and grandmother, as it was about two very strong older women. He didn't add that it would be reflective of her too, but perhaps she would recognize that herself. He would let her tell him that though.

The trip was more than any of them imagined. The scenery of the Alaskan mountains was a postcard picture no matter where they went. They saw seals and even a brief glimpse of some Orcas before they disappeared. They saw bald eagles and even took a trip to see Grizzly bears that left all of them speechless. They watched them in the wild, unafraid of anything around them and ready to let the odd-looking animals that they smelled, know not to come any closer by a menacing look that was understood by everyone on the tour.

Melissa and Mary couldn't thank Marigold enough for the trip of a lifetime and she said she was so glad they were able to do it. In a private moment, she held onto Reuben's arm and rubbed it as she looked up into his face and told him how wonderful Melissa was and how happy she was that they were together. Reuben agreed and thanked his mother for everything. Just before they said goodbye, she told him that he was right about the book. He laughed as he got on the plane and held Melissa's hand while they flew back to Boston. She slept on his shoulder as he finished reading "The Leatherstocking Tales."

The fourth year at Harvard was the easiest that Reuben had encountered. Perhaps it was Melissa. Perhaps he just understood more of what his professors wanted. Or perhaps it was just because he loved what he was doing so much and who he could share it with. If asked, Reuben would have said it was all of the above. Though he didn't really need it, there were times he smoked a little marijuana to lay back and consider certain aspects of a book he was studying. It was so infrequent that Melissa never even brought it up.

When he saw what his fifth-year curriculum would consist of, Reuben understood he didn't really have time for a summer vacation and suggested that they bring their mothers up to Boston for a few days, but Melissa could see that wasn't really anything he wanted to do. She knew he wanted to get started on his classwork and really didn't want to entertain people, even if it was their mothers. She suggested to him that he stay in Boston and start on his studies and that she would go home to Augusta and visit with everyone. She told him she wanted to go home anyway and Reuben pressed his finger against her brow and asked her how she got so smart. Melissa laughed and said all women were like that but that most men failed to see it. She was impressed he noticed and he laughed and just shrugged his shoulders.

Reuben called Marigold to explain why only Melissa would be coming home that summer. Marigold simply told him to "call me when I can," just as she had said many times in the past. Reuben didn't think anything about it until he hung up and realized he thought he had heard her say "call me when I can," and that she sounded tired. He told Melissa about the phone call and she said that he had probably just misunderstood her. Perhaps he had, but he asked her to make sure she checked in with her several times while she was there. Melissa said she had every intention of seeing his mother as much as her own and Reuben kissed her and thanked her.

Melissa reached out to Marigold as soon as she got to Augusta and asked if they could have lunch one day during her visit. Marigold said she'd love to and for her to just pick the day. Melissa suggested tomorrow but Marigold told her tomorrow wouldn't work as she had to go to South Carolina for the day. When Melissa suggested the next day, Marigold said that wouldn't work either because she had some meetings about her restaurants. Finally, Melissa asked her what day would be good and Marigold told her she didn't have anything planned for Saturday. Around 3:00 would be good. She explained to Melissa that she ate late lunches these days. She preferred having a big lunch in the middle of the day instead of a big dinner.

After ending the call, Melissa asked her mother if she had noticed anything different going on with Marigold. Mary said she thought she was having a hard time these days. It was the fifth anniversary of Simon's death and Reuben hadn't been home much, at least in a permanent sense. She thought she was just missing them both and perhaps drinking a little more than she should. She added, "She does that sometimes."

Melissa thought that was a strange statement coming from her mother, but she nodded her head and didn't say anything more about it. On Saturday she arrived at Marigold's right at 3:00. The maid answered the door and announced that Marigold was outside waiting on her. That was odd, Melissa thought. She never has the maid open the door. What is going on, she asked herself as she walked toward the sun porch, and found Marigold sitting there on a beautiful floral print sofa. She had a drink in her hand and was wearing sunglasses and a large hat. It was a pretty summer hat, but she had never seen her wear anything like that before. She told her it was a beautiful hat as she walked over and hugged her. She could smell the alcohol on her body as if it was a perfume, and as they talked, she could quickly tell she was drunk.

Marigold asked a few questions about how she and Reuben were doing and then began talking about how Simon had been dead for five years now and that her son had been gone for eight, soon to be nine years this fall. She missed them both dearly and Melissa listened to her talk of things that she and Simon and Reuben had done in the past; the trip to Africa and the safari and seeing Victoria Falls. She remembered how excited Reuben was when they went to Egypt and how perceptive he was. In fact, she talked a lot about how smart Reuben was. If she mentioned Reuben, she mentioned smart somewhere in the sentence.

Melissa wasn't sure if she could get her to talk about anything other than the past and each time she tried to change the conversation, Marigold would somehow re-route it back to something she remembered happening years ago. Though Melissa didn't know it, Marigold believed that she was having a few scotches because they served as a connection to her past and to her husband, but in reality, all she was doing was connecting herself to bottles of very expensive single malt scotch.

Melissa wasn't sure what to say but she knew she needed to say something. She searched for a way to prompt Marigold to understand that she needed help and to let her know she would be there for her when she did. "Marigold, I am not sure how to say this, other than to say it. You are drunk and it's not even 3:15 in the afternoon. I am worried about you. I think you need help."

Marigold looked over and smiled at Melissa as she picked up her glass of scotch and took another drink.

"I am, what they say in the drinking world, on a bender," Marigold replied.

"That is just a euphemism for alcoholism."

"Euphemism, is it?" Marigold said as she pulled off her glasses.

Melissa was startled when she saw Marigold's eyes. Unaware, she recoiled back into her chair as if she had just learned Marigold had the Ebola virus. Her eyes looked as if they were bleeding and like she could have been auditioning for a horror movie. Her hoarse demon-like voice only added to that characterization.

"Don't sit over there in that chair and pretend to lecture me. Ever!" Marigold growled. "You know nothing of my life and the world I grew up in. If I wasn't strong, not just a few minutes of the day, but every fucking minute of the day with the people I dealt with, they would have stepped on me like some cockroach and after hearing the crunch of my body, wiped me off the bottom of their shoe on the curb of the street.

"Men didn't respect women in business. Especially strong women that had money. They hated me and tried to destroy me. But they learned fast, that like a cockroach or dog shit, I am just not that easy to get rid of. Yes, they've gotten better, over the years, as they have learned, but it is still a difficult world out there for women in business because there are still way too many pricks out there. To be a female leader in business. To be their equal, to be their boss even, takes a lot out of you," she said as she went to the bar and poured some more whisky in her glass. "And I don't need this fucking hat on me!"

When she threw the hat off, Melissa saw the stitches that extended around her forehead.

"Don't try and fix a drink without the lights on. After you have sat there and watched the sun go down and thought about those that had meaning to you in your life and are gone now, or not living here anymore. Don't do that, Melissa, because there's a good chance you will fall and crack open your head on the tile floor."

She took another drink and continued to talk in a very loud and intimidating manner.

"My head is fine. I won't die from a head injury. My skull is too fucking thick. Reuben has the same thick skull and very thick skin. He doesn't care what people think of him, to his credit. I did and have tried to teach him, that you have to establish relationships in business. He knows that now. He's smart. Smarter than me. Smarter than you and I put together and I am pretty damn smart. I think you are smart too. And you know if you hurt Reuben in any way, you will be hurting me too. And people that hurt me, find out that's a bad idea for their future."

Melissa was shocked and unable to speak. She had never seen Marigold act like that. She had never seen anyone act like that. She didn't know, regardless of what shape she was in, Marigold was still Marigold. She didn't understand Rule number one.

"Now, are you interested in lunch? I think Frances made her chicken salad for us. I asked her to do that so I am sure she did. It's very, very good. Probably the best in town. I really need to look at selling that in *The Fifties*. I don't know why I didn't think of that earlier. I'll have to get her to give the recipe to the cooks downtown. I'm sure that she made more than that too. Always does. And I told her to make that coconut pie you like. So, shall we go into the dining room and eat?"

It's as if nothing happened, Melissa said to herself. How can that be? What am I supposed to do now?

"You might as well eat. I won't berate you anymore. And this," she said as she pointed to the glass in her hand, "will pass. It always does."

"Um, I appreciate the invitation for lunch, Marigold, but I can't stay. I just remembered that I need to do some things before I fly back tomorrow. I'm sorry."

"That's fine, but let me say one more thing before you leave. Don't ever lie to me again. If you wanted to leave, just say so. That's why I didn't invite you over here until Saturday. I didn't think you wanted to see me in this state. Reuben doesn't like it either. But he was gone most of the time when it happened. Tell Reuben that I love him and I do think you are good for my son, Melissa. But you need to learn a few things about life. You're still a very young woman and yes, you are still gorgeous. An absolute beauty. Reuben was right when he said you looked like a young Elizabeth Taylor. You do. Have a good flight," Marigold said as she turned and walked away toward the dining room.

Melissa couldn't get out of the house fast enough. She drove home and told her mother what happened. Her mother again said that she wasn't surprised.

"Have you seen Marigold act like that before?"

"Once," Mary replied. "Only once. She didn't like the money I spent on Christmas ornaments one time. Said they were too expensive and people wouldn't buy them. She was right. But she still was able to sell them the next year. We made them part of the floral arrangements and marked up the price a little. She trusts me now though and I don't have to go through her to make what I think is a smart purchase for the store. She gave me five percent of the store three years ago. It helped me pay for your college. We are friends now. Good friends. But you don't want to cross Marigold, especially when she is in one of those states that she's in now."

"Mom, she is an alcoholic."

"Probably," Mary replied. "But she will not change and there isn't anyone here that can change her. Reuben might be able to if and when he comes back to town, but he is the only one."

"I can't talk about it anymore. I'll talk to Reuben about it when I get back. So, let's go get something to eat. I'm starved."

The next day, Melissa flew back to Boston. After she unpacked, she sat down with Reuben and told him about his mother.

"I was afraid of that. I could tell when I was talking to her. That's why I wanted you to check in on her."

"Reuben, I wasn't really able to check in on her. I was only with her for about thirty minutes and then I left after she scolded me several times. Telling me I was ignorant of what she had gone through and how she missed your father and you. Reuben, she is an alcoholic and needs help."

"She's gone through these phases her entire life. Most of the time, Dad and I were away, but I have seen them before. It takes her about a week and then she is back to normal. There is nothing to do, Melissa. When you came to live with me, I told you that there would be things about me that you wouldn't like. Well, you met one of them the other day."

"Reuben that wasn't you. That was your mother. If you don't do anything, you are just enabling that behavior. She had a huge cut on her head from falling down. Drunk and falling down. You need to do something. She is your mother, for God's sake."

"Melissa, let me tell you something you need to know. There are lessons in life my mother taught me - Life Lessons, that are really teachable moments for people. Rule number one is to know who is boss. And in our family, my mother is the Boss. As such, there is nothing I nor anyone else can do. Except understand and accept it."

"As a medical professional, I don't know how to accept that. I see someone hurting and I have to help."

When Reuben looked at Melissa, she could see nothing but his eyes, and though they were not blood red, they still scared her as much as when she looked into Marigold's eyes.

"Don't lecture me on this subject again. If this is something you cannot live with, then I encourage you to leave as you will never be happy. I cannot fix my mother and neither can you. This will pass. It always does. I hope you can let it pass because I love you very much, but you don't understand my family. "

Reuben turned around and told her he was going to the library and would see her later and left. Melissa sat alone, not knowing what she should do. She looked up alcoholism on the internet and read some information about Al-Anon and considered going to a meeting. She went back and forth in her mind as she thought about Reuben's mother. What if she was a racist instead of an alcoholic? Would you stop dating Reuben she asked herself? No, you wouldn't. Reuben was right. She couldn't fix his mother. She would be there for Reuben and his mother and told herself she would just have to pray every night for her. She didn't know it but she had just become a Broadwater. They had rationalized away things that were wrong their entire life.

The fifth year was very difficult. Reuben again didn't go home at Christmas. But this time, Marigold came to Boston. Melissa spent some time with her family in Augusta before she came back and spent a few days with Reuben and his mother. Marigold was her old self. Happy. Friendly. Not depressed or melancholy. In fact, Melissa only saw her drink a few times the entire time she was there. Reuben was right. I don't understand how this works but she was willing to try and find out.

Reuben had very good grades the fall semester but fell just short of the Dean's List, so he studied even more. By the spring he was once again at the top of his class. He had already spoken with both department heads regarding the dissertation topics he was considering for next year and they had both given their approval. He was exhausted but he wanted to celebrate and he called up his friend, Tom.

He told him he still didn't want any IV drugs, but he asked Tom about Ecstasy. After all, Aldous Huxley's Brave New World's Soma drug was his reference to LSD. His favorite writer, Poe, smoked opium all the time. And though Lewis Carroll didn't write "Alice in Wonderland" as a psychedelic trip as many thought, he did take laudanum, which was a combination of opium, morphine, and codeine.

Tom said he could certainly get some but before he did, Reuben peppered him with numerous questions about the drug. He asked him if he was sure that the drug was pure MDMA and not filled with cough syrup, or pseudoephedrine or any other drugs that would be harmful to his body. He had done his research and in appropriate quantities, the drug MDMA was un-harmful to the body. Tom told him it was pure and that he would have a great trip. Even though he heard him say it, he asked him one more time. "Are you sure? I've never done anything but marijuana."

"Yeah, man. Yeah. I'm sure. I wouldn't give you anything that wasn't pure. I've done it numerous times and it was a nice cool trip. Was at a jazz concert, David Sanborn and David Benoit. Wow. The colors. The music. I could see the music, not just hear it. I saw the fucking notes."

So, Reuben tried it when Melissa went to work. She was going to do a twelve-hour shift that weekend and according to his friend, the drug would only last at most eight hours.

Thirty minutes after taking the drug, Reuben was in a euphoric state and found himself talking to Ralph Ellison about his book, "The Invisible Man." They talked about the struggle of black Americans which made Reuben think about the neighborhood near their house in Augusta. They were then joined by President Johnson telling Ralph and Reuben that he understood how the blacks in America struggled and how much he had done to help them.

Ralph looked at President Johnson and laughed telling him he was just a painter. A painter who made paint by mixing black pigments to achieve different shades of white tones. They heard Lyndon describe his Civil Rights program and then saw his two dogs Him and Her speak up saying how it was their idea for Medicare and Medicaid. And then up above them, they saw the President's wife, Lady Bird, sitting in a tree, flapping her arms saying over and over, "don't forget the food stamps, Lyndon. Don't forget the food stamps" and then fly away.

Reuben argued with the President saying that all he did was ensure that the money he provided to the poor would only keep the wealthy rich and the poor, poor. Poor and Democrat. The President said that wasn't true, that his programs would help provide a way for the poor to escape poverty and Reuben said he was a liar.and that all he gave them was a crutch that would enable them to walk to the voting booth and vote for whatever Democrat was running for office.

Reuben then noticed John Steinbeck had joined them, telling Reuben that what Lyndon did was right. And Reuben started laughing. "How the hell do you know? You were a rich kid in California with maids and servants. You wrote about the poor but you never lived it."

"You don't have to live it to know it," Steinbeck replied. President Johnson agreed with him.

"I think the only person in here today who said anything of value was Ralph and I am going to help them, Ralph. The black people you spoke of by providing them jazz. Jazz that lets them improvise with new homes and a new start and a way to forget their troubles for a while. Everyone needs to forget their troubles for a while," Reuben said as he got up and put on The Doors "L.A. Woman" album.

When he turned around, all the people were gone and he smiled and thought about what a productive conversation had taken place. He lay down on the sofa and floated into the music. It felt like he was right there at the concert. Standing just in front of the stage and he loved it as he kept looking around for Melissa.

She is missing one hell of a good concert he told himself. He closed his eyes and though they were closed, he could see right through them as if they were transparent covers. That's pretty cool, he thought. He got up from the sofa for a beer and some marijuana and took a couple of puffs. He put on the Beatles "Abbey Road" album and laid back down and listened to the music and thought how good he felt. He was close to achieving what he had worked so hard for and he knew he was going to be very successful. By the time, Melissa got home, he was no longer high, but he was drunk. They ordered some pizza that night from one of their favorite places to celebrate the completion of his fifth year at Harvard.

The next day, Reuben announced that he was going to go home for a few days and check on his mother. If Melissa could take some time off when he got back, they could fly to the Cayman Islands for a long four or five-day weekend. Melissa hugged him and told him that sounded wonderful but she probably needed some new swimsuits. Reuben just smiled and nodded his head.

His mother greeted him at the airport and told him how happy she was to have him home. She asked how Melissa was doing and he thought that was a good sign. He wasn't sure what to say when he saw the silver sports car parked right outside of the garage.

"It's a 2012 Audi R8 with a 5.2 liter V-10 that puts out 520 horsepower. Now, that's all I know about it except that it looks like a sports car, it's very expensive, and probably shouldn't even be allowed on the road. What do you think?"

"You really drive this?" Reuben asked.

"Of course not. It's for you. I showed the dealer pictures of your Corvette and they were good with the value that I assigned to it without having to see it. They do want it though and will be coming up to Boston in the next week to drive it back to Atlanta. I hope you're okay with that."

Reuben hugged his mother and she dropped the keys in his hand and he took her for a ride. He told her many times that night how much he enjoyed the car. It was his favorite and she smiled as she looked out the window on her way to bed because he was just sitting out there in the car. I believe he truly meant that she said to herself and laughed as she went into her bedroom.

Reuben and his mother spent the next three days going on short trips to Charleston, Savannah, and Columbia, to allow his mother to shop and for him to drive the car. They realized very quickly there wasn't a lot of trunk space for some of the antiques, and even some of the clothes she bought, so she had to have them shipped to Augusta.

"Thanks for a perfect weekend," Marigold said. "I am so proud of you. This is your last year and then you will be finished with all of your school. A law degree, MBA, and not one, but two, Ph.Ds. Not many people can say that. I am guessing you can count them on one hand, maybe even one finger."

Reuben smiled and said he would see her soon and left for the long trip back to Boston. But, he didn't care about the drive this time; he was just enjoying his new car. He hadn't told Melissa about it, but he said that he would pick her up at work. When she saw him in the car, she screamed, "Really? Really? You go home and you get this?"

"What can I say? She loves me."

"She likes having control of you," Melissa said and as soon as the words came out of her mouth, she pretended to reach up in the air and grab them back and put them in her mouth.

"Here is she. Got it. There are likes and having," she said as she pretended to swallow them. "And then control, of and you. Damn, those were hard to swallow. In fact, they are making me nauseous. I may puke in your new car, so I better walk home," she said as she started to walk away.

Reuben let her walk across the street and then beeped his car horn and waved for her to come back. She smiled and threw him a bird as she started running across the street. She never saw the large Mercedes hit her. It knocked her to the street, running over her with the front tires and then the back tires before it stopped in the middle of the road.

Reuben cried out, "No!" as he ran over and bent down and tried to help Melissa. He didn't hear the elderly man telling him how sorry he was and how she just jumped out in front of him. Reuben wanted to pull Melissa out from beneath the car but he was afraid if he did anything, he would only make things worse. Even though he really knew he couldn't make things worse. Part of her spine was sticking out of her back and her head was turned in a way that wasn't possible for a human head to turn.

Reuben laid there and held her hand as he cried. He felt numb and broken and for the first time in his life, unsure as to what to do next. He didn't move until the ambulance and police cars came and someone helped him up, though they had to sedate him before he would let go of Melissa's hand.

The funeral for Melissa was a week from the time of the accident. Marigold told Mary that she would take care of all of the arrangements. There were over 1,000 people at the funeral. Some of her coworkers even came down from Boston. The paper said there was such a large crowd at the funeral that it looked like a princess had died. When they showed her picture under that comment, they added that one had.

Once the funeral and reception were over, Reuben sat in the sunroom with a picture of Melissa in his hand. His mother told Mary it would be best if they let him sit there alone. He heard his mother whisper that to Mary and he wanted to tell her that was probably a good idea. He didn't want to be around anyone for a long time.

The next day, he told his mother he was going back to Boston and that she could tell the dealer where she purchased the Audi to come get it. He didn't want it. He took her car to go say goodbye to Melissa's mother and told her that he loved her daughter like nothing else in his entire life. She wasn't able to talk to Reuben or provide him any comfort. She just held onto his body for a moment, before he removed her arms in a gentle manner and left.

He told his mother that he would see her after the school year was over. He would not be coming home during any of the breaks. He flew back to Boston and went to his townhome and just sat. As he looked around the house, he saw many things that reminded him of Melissa, but seeing them was comforting and so he told himself that he would leave everything as it was for the rest of the year.

Reuben studied and read for days without sleeping, catching up on sleep on the weekends after smoking a joint. He was at the top of his class that fall semester and called his mother during Christmas to tell her about it. He talked for almost two hours about what he had studied. She was surprised that he talked with her as long as he did. He never asked about Mary or talked about how he was feeling and he just said he would see her as soon as the school year was over.

His dissertation in history was titled *European and African Immigration: Which culture had the greatest impact on America?* In it, he described the innovations and inventions that changed America which were the result of European and African ideas and work. He concluded that America's success overall was impacted more by the scientists, engineers, and inventors of European heritage, but wondered, if given the same opportunity for education and money that the Europeans were provided, would African immigrants have been just as successful. He gave numerous examples of how African scientists had changed America such as George Washington Carver, Katherine Coleman Goble Johnson, whose calculations of orbital mechanics were critical to the US manned spaceflights, and Mark Dean, who at IBM developed the system that connected computers to printers.

He then examined the impact of Europeans and Africans on American culture as a whole, excluding the changes that came about from inventions and scientific knowledge. He noted the tremendous impact of music on American culture in general and that the greatest influence of all of that music, regardless of what you called it, could be traced back to African immigrants. Almost every form of music had its roots in the blues and the European invasion of the Rolling Stones, The Beatles, Led Zeppelin, Eric Clapton, brought all that to light; even though artists such as Nat King Cole, Count Basie, Ella Fitzgerald and, later Aretha Franklin, Stevie Wonder, and James Brown, and others in their respective decades and eras, through their combination of jazz, soul, gospel and love songs, did enjoy significant acclaim in what was still very much a white and black society.

Within business, he again found that the Europeans had the greatest impact but that was because blacks were restricted significantly from managing that change. Their labor was just as important as any provided by the hands of Europeans. In the areas of food, art, and clothing he concluded Europeans had made a greater contribution and overall impact but stated it would be an injustice to conclude that African immigrants didn't have some influence in the growth and changes that occurred, and argued that perhaps today, they had even more. In the end, his dissertation denoted that the America of today, would not be truly American without acknowledging the significant influence of both cultures and the innovation, the ideas, the artistic ability, and the labor of both.

After completing his history dissertation, Reuben needed a break and he called his friend Tom once again and asked for some more marijuana and a couple of hits of ecstasy. His friend brought them over and they smoked a joint together as they discussed what they were doing for their literature dissertations. Tom said that his would be on the European poets and writers and how it led to the porn trade of today and Reuben laughed until he cried. He told him he wanted to read that after he finished it to see how he made that argument and Tom just smiled.

Tom asked Reuben what his dissertation topic was and he said it would be about his favorite American author, Edgar Allen Poe, and the national media. Tom said that sounded cool and left before Reuben could discuss much more about it. Reuben was glad that he left. He was still formulating his thesis and he believed if he took some ecstasy, it would help him collect all of his ideas and form a coherent strategy and theme. So, the next day he got up late, ate breakfast and put on some soft jazz and took a hit of ecstasy.

Again, after about 30 minutes, Reuben realized the effects of the drug when he looked over and saw Edgar Allen Poe sitting across from him with his feet on the ottoman smoking a pipe. He asked Reuben if they would be the only ones in this opium den as he took a puff on the pipe and leaned back in his chair. Reuben replied that he wasn't sure but if someone else showed up, he was certain that they would be trustworthy. Poe nodded his head and took another puff on the pipe. Reuben then asked Poe what he was thinking when he wrote "The Bells" and Poe sat up and looked at Reuben in a strange manner.

"How do you know about that poem?" he asked. "It hasn't been published yet."

"You were talking to me about it the last time you were here," Reuben said.

Poe looked at him with some disbelief but the opium he was smoking took away his concerns. He told Reuben that it was just a poem to try and move you from one emotion to the next. At first, bells on a sleigh, a happy, tinkling sound. Then, golden bells at a wedding with joyful noise. Then brass bells denoting a fire. Then iron bells that make people sad to hear them. Though the ones ringing the bells, ghouls, are happy and delighted by the misery that they bring to those hearing them ring.

Reuben nodded his head. I thought so. "What about 'The Conqueror Worm?'" he asked.

"Isn't it obvious?" Poe replied. "It's about the inevitability that you will die and you will meet the lowly worm, regardless of your station in life."

"There's more to it though, isn't there?"

"You are an insightful soul. I don't recall you providing me your name, yet you know me as if we have been friends for many years," Poe replied.

"It is Reuben. Reuben Broadwater."

Poe nodded his head toward Reuben and then took another puff. "Excellent opium, Mr. Broadwater. I assume this is your establishment."

"It is."

"Would you have any absinthe, perchance?"

"No but I have something you might like," Reuben said as he got up and got Poe a beer. He popped the top and poured the beer into an ice-cold mug and brought it to him.

Poe looked at the mug with bits of ice on the side of the glass and in the beer and wondered how that was possible. He took a drink of the beer and smiled. "I will return to this establishment more often. This is the most refreshing drink I've ever had.

"Twas noontide of summer, and mid-time of night; And stars, in their orbits, Shone pale through the light, Of the brighter cold moon, Mid planets her slaves, Herself in the heavens, Her beam on the waves."

"Evening Star," Reuben replied.

"Yes, my new good friend, Reuben. You recognize the poem. Thank you. And thank you for this drink. This cold drink made me believe I had the effects of the cold moon in my hand and I never knew I would be able to taste its influence on an ale, but perhaps I should attribute that to the opium," Poe said as he started to laugh.

Reuben laughed too and asked again about "The Conqueror Worm."

"My good friend, Reuben, human life is mere folly. Always ending in a hideous death. The universe is controlled by dark forces that man cannot understand. And the only supernatural forces that might help are powerless spectators."

"Yes, I agree. You're going to like this," Reuben said as he put Black Sabbath "Paranoid" on the stereo and turned up the volume. When Reuben turned around, Poe was gone but he saw the empty mug on the table and smiled. He lay down and listened to the entire album. He had all the information he now needed for his dissertation.

Reuben's dissertation in English and American Literature was titled: *The Melodic and the Melodramatic; Edgar Allen Poe and the World Media.* In it, he described the way Poe looked at life in his poems and short stories and compared it to the way that the media reported the news. Regardless of what they were reporting, the way in which they reported it reflected the dark nature of life.

He said that Poe's reason for the manner in which he wrote, reflected the darkness that surrounded his life. Death was a common theme for him because the deaths of those he loved in real life impacted him greatly. He suffered most of his life from either being poor or from addiction. There were few good moments in his short life and his use of imagery and the specific nature in which he chose his words, all reflected that bleak view. Though the media didn't have that same life experience, they reported news in the same manner, with words reflecting the somber outcomes of what they were reporting, whether they had actually happened or could possibly happen.

With references to story after story and poem after poem by Poe, Reuben easily made his argument. At the very end, he stated it was ironic that government-controlled media was often the most positive in the way they reported the news, considering it was within those environments, people suffered the most. And where the disparaging words or manner in which events were described in the free world or in Poe's world, would be more appropriate.

Reuben was awarded a Ph.D. in both subjects and the Deans applauded him for his work. Reuben smiled and said he appreciated their support. They both said they looked forward to seeing his family at the graduation ceremony and Reuben told them that he was sorry but neither he nor his family would be able to attend. Both deans looked surprised by Reuben's response, but they did not inquire further. Reuben's demeanor suggested they shouldn't.

Before he left Boston, Reuben placed his townhome on the market and sold it within three days. He sold it as is with all of Melissa's clothes, and all the furniture, excluding his 1800s roll-top desk, and agreed to be out of the house in three days. The buyers accepted all the terms and though he didn't double his mother's investment as he had predicted, he looked forward to showing her the $290,000 profit.

He kept only one item of Melissa's. It was a silver necklace he had bought for her when they went on the Alaskan cruise. It had a dark onyx stone interlaced with Alaskan Jade, or as he found out before he bought it, Siberian nephrite, which was dark spinach green in color with black graphite inclusions. Melissa loved it and neither of them had ever seen anything like it. She wore it every day and was wearing it on the day she was killed.

He called his friend Tom and said he needed to talk to him before he left. Tom thought he was calling to discuss their dissertations, but when he got to Reuben's home, he realized he had something more serious to consider. He asked Tom if he knew of anyone he could talk to that could help him establish a distribution market for marijuana and ecstasy in Augusta. He told Tom that he suspected there was a high level of demand within the Augusta market that wasn't being met, and he was certain that high demand and insufficient supply would allow for great profits.

Tom smiled as he looked at Reuben and pulled out a joint. "Let's talk a little more about that," he said as he lit the joint. "You got a beer?"

Tom's discussion with Reuben that day was only a formality regarding his ability to cover the cost of doing the type of business he was talking about. He already knew how much money Reuben had. He came from "old money" and Tom was very familiar with that term. His reason for talking with him that day was to determine just how serious Reuben was about getting into the drug business. He found out that day he was very serious.

Tom gave Reuben a piece of paper with a phone number but no name on it. He said to call that number and that person would tell him where to meet in Atlanta. He told him it didn't matter when he called. "Just tell him that you are Reuben Broadwater and the man will know who you are. I will make sure of that."

"I won't be calling for two years," Reuben said and Tom looked at him in a strange manner.

"Two years?"

"Yes, it will take me that long to establish the presence I need to have in Augusta. To establish an identity in the community that is above suspicion. If that isn't acceptable, I'll have to work with someone else."

Tom just smiled. "Two years. No problem, man. I will make sure he knows that. Don't lose that number. I don't recommend you put it in your phone. Just memorize it. If the number changes within two years, I'll get hold of you and let you know."

"But you don't have my number," Reuben replied.

"I'm sure I'll be able to find you in Augusta. It appears you won't be that hard to locate considering what you just said."

"True," Reuben replied.

As Tom got up to leave, Reuben asked him how his dissertation turned out. Tom said, "The professor loved it. He wants to make it into a book. I'm considering it. I'll email it to you. Just give me your email address."

"It's SweetMelissa87@comcast.net," Reuben replied. "I look forward to reading it."

"Would you mind sending me yours?" Tom asked. "My email is TomJacksonwinsitall@yahoo.com."

Reuben nodded and shook his hand. Just before Tom left, he cautioned Reuben not to discuss anything illegal via the internet. No phone numbers. No names. It was too easy to be discovered and Reuben said he understood.

That afternoon, Reuben arranged for the movers to come get the rolltop desk and watched as they packed it and then loaded it on the truck. He took what clothes he wanted, Melissa's necklace and left everything else. He got in his Corvette and left Boston knowing that he would never return to that city again. Reuben took his time driving home, stopping anyplace that looked interesting to him. Spending the night in towns where he had never stayed. Each time he stopped, he thought about how Melissa would have liked where he was and it made him sad. After a few days, he realized that he couldn't do that anymore. When he got home, Marigold was waiting for him at the door, and hugged him and told him that she was so glad he was home.

"Home for good now, right?" Marigold asked, not sure what Reuben had planned.

"Home for good," Reuben replied. "Tomorrow I would like for you to help me start meeting important people in the community. I want to do some things to make this city better. Over time it will be well worth it to give back to the town."

"That's fine, son. I'm sixty-five now, retirement age you know, and I would like to start handing over the businesses to you. We can start all of that tomorrow. Deal?"

There is that word again. And for now, you are still the boss, but you won't be for very much longer, Reuben thought. But for now, he smiled and replied. "Deal," and then asked if they could go down to *The Fifties* and get something to eat.

Marigold said sure, but they only had about fifteen minutes before they closed, although she thought they might still serve them if they got there a few minutes late. She thought that would make Reuben laugh but it didn't. He just looked straight ahead and told her that they made two hundred and ninety thousand dollars on the sale of the townhome. Marigold reminded him that was not double their money and then Reuben looked at her and smiled.

"No, not quite, is it?" was all he said. Then he told her he was expecting a rolltop desk to arrive tomorrow or Friday and asked Marigold where he could put it.

"Why don't you put it in your father's study? I use another place to work, by my bedroom. It's an anteroom that gives me access to my bedroom. I built it about a year ago, knowing that when you came back, you would need an office. Your father's study is perfect for you."

She is always thinking, Reuben said to himself, but she's right. "Yes, I would love to take over Dad's study. Thanks, Mom."

The next day, Marigold took Reuben to meet some of the city commissioners and the mayor. She always started the introduction by saying this was her son who just graduated from Harvard with two PhDs and then somewhere during the discussion, sneaking in the fact that her son also held a law degree and MBA from the University of Georgia.

At a different time, that would have bothered Reuben, but now he wanted those that he met to know of his education. It reflected his drive to succeed and indicated to them he was very smart. When he met Mayor Parkland he talked to him about a plan he had for urban renewal, something that he had thought about at school. He called it the ICE program, which was an acronym for Inner City Enhancement. Through that program, they would build nice new houses on Laney Walker Boulevard, in conjunction with Habitat for Humanity and a generous donation that would come from the Broadwaters. He told the mayor he could use that idea and state it was his own, provided he placed him in charge of the program.

"How many houses?" the mayor asked.

"Five there and one in the Royal Manor government housing neighborhood across from our home and Mercy Street. Those houses will cost seven hundred and twenty thousand dollars to build and furnish and that will come from a two-million-dollar donation to the city. Leaving the city 1.28 million dollars to be used at your discretion. For studies needed for other improvements."

Reuben knew that the mayor understood that last sentence meant that he and the commissioners could spend that money in discretionary ways where some of it was always lost. On things like studies that studied other studies regarding the improvements needed downtown. Money that became lost in plain view for programs which had less than a ten percent chance of being completed, but made everyone on the commission look concerned and often richer in one way or another.

"Welcome aboard, Mr. Broadwater. I look forward to working with you on my new ICE program," Mayor Parkland said as he held out his hand.

Reuben shook the mayor's hand and said that there was one more thing he would appreciate from him. He asked if some of the money could be spent on changing the name of Red Bud Lane to Tamer Lane. The street was only a block long, and with just three houses on the entire block, it shouldn't be that difficult to change. Reuben would make sure the residents who lived there were compensated for their inconvenience. It would mean a lot to him if the name was changed.

"Why Tamer Lane?" the mayor asked.

"My dissertation at Harvard was on Edgar Allen Poe and the Media. I am very fond of that author. This road name is taken from the first book he had published in 1827, called 'Tamerlane and Other Poems.' There are only twelve known existing copies, which, considering there were only fifty published originally, is not surprising. One of those twelve was last auctioned at Christie's four years ago for $662,500, a record for a work of American literature."

"Interesting. How do you spell that?"

"T-a-m-e-r Lane. The book title was spelled as one word. It's a play on words."

The mayor smiled and said that he would put that on the agenda along with his new ICE program. He told Reuben it would be nice for him to attend the commission meeting and say a few words about it so that the press and the public knew what was about to happen. Reuben said he would be happy to oblige.

"The meeting is in seven days. Be there at 4 p.m.," the mayor said as he shook Reuben's hand again and hugged Marigold before he left.

Marigold turned to Reuben when they were in the car. "What in the hell are you doing?"

"I am beginning to change the narrative."

"The narrative of what?"

"Of our family and family name."

"Who said you could do that?"

"You did. Thirteen years ago, when you started teaching me how to manage the companies. The day you showed me how Rodrigo would respond to a tenderizing mallet. And you were right. You opened my eyes that day. They were opened even wider at Harvard."

Reuben knew his mother was mad but he had been preparing for this conversation ever since he left Boston.

"Where are you going to get two million dollars? Just because I said I am getting ready to retire doesn't mean I am ready to give up control over everything."

"Then you will have wasted over a million dollars in sending me to school." He realized that sentence alone would paralyze his mother for a moment as she thought about it. She didn't like losing money at any level.

"We need to sell the peach farms. It is too difficult for them to become organic. I have calculated that we will get $3.7 million for selling all five of them. That will pay for the donation to the city and will allow us to start the bison farms. We will be the first in the state to sell bison burgers and steaks at our restaurants. After three years, we will have doubled our money by moving from the peach business to the bison business. And the $290,000 that I made on the sale of the townhome, along with the $1.7 million in profit will allow us to buy five hundred acres of land and five hundred bison.

"You don't need barns for them. They prefer to stay outside all year round. They eat most grasses and eat less in the winter. All they really need is good water and good grass to feed on. Organic. Healthy. Better tasting and less fat, so it's better for you and best of all, more costly for the consumer. But they won't care. And thus, more profit for the owner of the farm and the restaurants," Reuben explained.

"We can't get that much money for the peach farms. At best they are worth $2.5 million. And where are you going to find that much land at that price with everything you need to raise bison? If you can do all that, then I will sign the papers. But only then. Deal?" his mother replied.

"Deal," Reuben said. He didn't let his mother know that he had already sold the farms to some wealthy farmers he had met in south Georgia. Or that he had already found the farmland he wanted to purchase out in Barnwell and Bamberg counties. She will learn, Reuben said to himself. Underestimate me at your own peril, he thought and smiled.

Three days later, Reuben brought his mother the paperwork for the sale of the peach farms. It was the exact price he had told her. He then took her to see the five hundred acres of land that he wanted to buy for the bison farm. The land had several ponds and a stream running through rolling hills that was fed by an underground well. Marigold realized the property was perfect and she agreed to the purchase. With that taken care of, Reuben turned his thoughts to the commissioners' meeting. He decided his mother should present the check at the meeting; the oversized type of check that was always photographed at public events. Marigold liked the idea of making the presentation to the mayor and her son was very aware of that.

Mayor Parkland announced the Inner City Enhancement program to the commissioners. They knew none of the specifics and were uncertain of how to respond. He then introduced Dr. Reuben Broadwater, detailing his vast educational background and said that he would explain what the ICE program entailed.

Reuben thanked the mayor and then turned to his mother and thanked her, telling everyone that without her, he would not have the abilities or the education he needed in order to fulfill the grand plan of the mayor's ICE program. In that one initial sentence, he had made the two most important people in that meeting unable and disinclined to do anything but support Reuben in his efforts.

Reuben described his dissertation at Harvard and the European and African immigrant's impact on America. He stated that Europeans had made a greater impact on science and technology, but he wondered if African immigrants would not have been just as successful if given the same opportunity for education and money? And as he did in his thesis, he cited the contributions of George Washington Carver, Katherine Coleman Goble Johnson, and Mark Dean to justify the reason for that question.

He stated that within business, the European immigrants had once again made the greatest impact, but he felt that was largely because blacks were restricted significantly from managing that change. That was unfair because their labor was just as important as any provided by the hands of Europeans. When considering the American culture in general, Europeans had once again made a greater contribution, though it would be an injustice to conclude that African immigrants didn't have some influence in the growth and changes that occurred over time.

He told the group that when he and the mayor first talked about the ICE program, he immediately thought about one of his favorite books, Harper Lee's "To Kill a Mockingbird," and one of his favorite quotes from the book: "I think there's just one kind of folks. Folks." He said that in America, in Augusta, everyone deserved the same opportunity to succeed and to live the American dream. That was what he believed the ICE program to be. That opportunity. That chance.

As he looked around the room, Reuben knew he had the attention of everyone. All eyes were upon him and waiting for his next word. He savored that moment as he continued.

"Abraham Lincoln once said, 'In very truth he was, the noblest work of God – an honest man.' But in our America, our Augusta, there are many honest men who are not given a chance to succeed, just because they were born poor. That is not fair. In fact, it is an injustice. With the beginning of the ICE program, we will give the poor our hand and help them stand up. We will build new homes they can be proud to live in. Give the young access to the arts, and a reason and opportunity to do something positive instead of being destructive. And give those that have the ability and desire, the access to learn how to be successful in business and life.

"We are not a bad community, but we can be a better community. This ICE program will enable us to do that. Through Habitat for Humanity and from a two-million-dollar donation from my family, we will build five new homes on Laney Walker Boulevard and one new home in Royal Manor. And once they are built, we will build more homes and create more programs by relying on those within our community that believe now in the Mayor's vision, and on those that will believe later, once they see the vision become reality. As Dr. King once said, 'Every man must decide whether he will walk in the light of creative altruism or in the darkness of destructive selfishness.'"

Reuben sat down and for the first time ever, a speaker in a city commission meeting received a five-minute standing ovation. Reuben had to stand up and wave to the crowd several times before they would stop. The euphoria he felt was like a hit of Ecstasy. Photographers took pictures of Marigold presenting the large check to the mayor and all of the commissioners wanted a picture next to the mayor and Reuben. After Reuben and Marigold left, the commission returned to the city's business. The request to change the name of Red Bud Lane to Tamer Lane was approved with no dissent.

On the way home, Marigold complimented Reuben on his speech, but let him know she was still apprehensive about giving away so much money. Reuben didn't want to say anything that would start an argument so he just nodded his head. He was proud of himself and knew he had accomplished everything he had set out to do that day.

He knew his speech had contained the right combination of truth without offending those minorities he spoke of. Accomplishing that in the city commissioners' meeting, was like walking through a sculpted garden maze of firethorns blindfolded. When you emerged from the green labyrinth, you did so because you had become most familiar with the pain that those thorns inflicted. His mother's words were just the first indication that he had made it through the maze.

The next day, Reuben met with Mayor Parkland, Habitat for Humanity leaders, and several commissioners and began working on the plans for the home construction. Within weeks, the permits were all signed, the people in Royal Manor were notified of the move by the commissioners, and every day a new article appeared in the paper describing the progress of the ICE program.

The first several articles mentioned Marigold, but after that, the stories were all about Reuben and how he was changing the landscape, literally and figuratively, within Augusta. He rented out a bowling alley one day for the kids in Royal Manor. He hired buses to take those same kids to the Columbia Zoo. He was there on the job site, helping build the homes. The Augusta Chronicle loved Reuben Broadwater and Marigold Broadwater was jealous.

She started drinking early one morning and had finished a bottle of scotch by the time Reuben came home that evening. She asked him how his day was and he told her it was very good.

"Exactly what needed to happen today, happened," he replied. He realized his mother was drunk and he wanted to avoid interacting with her, so he excused himself, telling her that he needed to get ready for dinner that evening with the mayor. He spent a long time getting dressed, hoping that his mother would just pass out, but she didn't. She was still sitting out on the sun porch, holding a drink in her hand, when he came back downstairs and she asked him to sit with her before he left.

"When do you plan to take your bar exam?" she asked. He was unprepared for that question. He hesitated for a moment but told her the truth. "I don't plan on taking the bar exam. I don't need it. It could just be used against me later on down the road. I don't need any negative publicity that I have been disbarred."

"Then why the hell did I send you to the University of Georgia to get a law and MBA degree?" Marigold asked angrily as she walked over to the bar.

Before Reuben could reply, she turned and hit him with a fire poker. The iron hit him in the head with such force that it almost knocked him unconscious. Reuben tried to protect himself but she had caught him by surprise. He held his arms up over his head and could feel her beating him over and over until he heard her scream as she dropped the iron poker onto the floor.

If she hadn't been so drunk, she would have recognized the irony in what she had just done. Now, she was the drunk and using a fire iron instead of beating a drunk with a fire iron. If the long-term staff had not been so terrified of Marigold and had leaked any of this information about Reuben or his father to a glib reporter, the headline would have made itself: "Iron Becomes Ironic in Socialite Bludgeoning." But no one ever spoke of it again after that night.

His mother stepped back and stumbled into a chair and Reuben heard her sobbing. As he tried to clear his head, his mother began apologizing for what she had done. She said over and over that she hoped he would forgive her and that she never meant to do this.

As anger built up inside Reuben's body, his pain disappeared. He sat up for a moment to steady his equilibrium, and then walked to the bar, wrapped a towel in ice and placed it on the large cut on his head. He pulled a chair over and sat down in front of his mother who was looking at him with the eyes of a demon; almost absent of any color except red, created by the amount of alcohol she had consumed and from crying as she gazed at what she had done.

"What do you mean, you never meant to do this?" Reuben asked.

Marigold wasn't sure what he was asking and didn't respond.

"Don't fool yourself, mother. You have created the person you always wanted me to be. You should know that by now. You wanted me to get that law degree and MBA. You made sure of it by ensuring I failed at the restaurant. But you never said I had to pass the fucking bar exam. Did you? I never agreed to that. You just assumed that would happen, but you should have known better. You taught me to never assume anything. You taught me to create the answers you want. And with your own son, you failed to do that.

"But you will see how much I have learned from you over the next year when you take me around to each of the businesses and tell them that I am now in charge. You will also give me access to all of the money in the Cayman Islands. You can inform the lawyers sometime in the next week about the title change in management for the companies and line up whatever I need to access that money.

"Don't worry. You, more than anyone else, will appreciate it when you are able to see your son take ten million dollars and turn it into forty million in two years. Impressive, don't you think? Yes, just nod your head. That's fine. Oh, and I won't touch the stocks or bonds or any of that money. You can do with that as you need, but I will be using the money in the Caymans. By the way, how much is in those accounts now?"

"About sixteen million," Marigold replied.

"Good. It will take a few million to open up that tunnel your uncles built during the prohibition. I will have need of it in the very near future."

Even in her drunken state of madness and sorrow which was now bordering on psychosis, Marigold thought she understood what Reuben meant by that last statement but she was afraid to ask any additional questions for clarification. She just nodded her head and then tried to reach out and touch her son's face, but he pulled back.

"If you ever try and hurt me again, physically or in any other way, I will destroy everything you have worked for. The reputation and name that you have cherished for so many years will be nothing. I will tell everyone of the family history and how we made so much money, how you abused your staff and beat your husband and your son, and that you are a dangerous alcoholic. But let's not dwell on the bad things that could happen.

"Let's look at this as a new beginning. A teachable moment, so to speak. You shouldn't be worried about the past. I am positive that none of that will ever reach the outside of these walls. You have done your job well. You taught me a long time ago it was okay to color outside of the lines and you will be amazed at the artist I have become," he said as he walked away to assess the damage to his body.

Reuben had to cancel his dinner with the mayor that night explaining that his mother was ill and he didn't think he could leave her. She was bad about not taking her medicine and she would only listen to him. The mayor said he understood because he had a grandmother like that. Reuben thanked him and said they would do it another time.

Marigold's personal doctor came over to stitch up his head. The doctor had been there so many times, he didn't bother asking how it happened. He did what was required and left. Reuben didn't leave the house much for several weeks as his wounds healed. When someone asked him about the cut on his head, he just said it happened when he wasn't paying attention while walking around the job site late at night. He said he wouldn't do that again and that was all the response that was needed.

Over the next twelve months, Reuben became very well-known in the Augusta area. The press loved him. The TV reporters, describing him as a young JFK, vied for live interviews. He was on talk radio several times discussing the latest developments in the ICE program. In addition to the bowling and zoo outings, he provided fishing guides to help the kids catch fish at Thurmond Lake. He even took them to Six Flags over Georgia. One of the young female reporters at the television station accompanied them on that trip. She wanted to report on how much fun the children were having, but she also wanted to try and get to know Reuben in a more intimate manner.

Reuben was aware of the reporter's intentions and even though he wasn't interested in that type of relationship with her, he did nothing to squelch her desire, nor anything to encourage it. He was only interested in the publicity, and in as polite a manner as possible, he told her emphatically that work was all consuming for him. The reporter inferred from the polite and assertive rejection that he was probably gay. She knew, however, if she tried to suggest that in some negative manner, she would be crucified by her coworkers within the press. But if given the chance, when her bosses said that they needed a story on the ICE program or Reuben, she always asked for and received the assignment. She told herself she could be wrong and she wanted to find out the truth, whatever it was.

Marigold and Reuben went to "*The Fifties*" restaurant to tell Rodrigo that Reuben would now be in charge of the operation. Rodrigo smiled and shook his hand.

"Muy Bueno, Mr. Reuben. Su Madre makes a good life for me and my family. I look forward to working with you. I hope, Senora, that you will still come by."

Marigold nodded her head yes and smiled.

"You can't get rid of me that easy, Rodrigo. I love eating here and I think I will love it even more after my son tells you what he has planned."

Reuben explained that he was establishing a bison farm in South Carolina and they would soon be offering bison burgers at the restaurant. He told Rodrigo that they would sell for $2.00 more but not to worry, he was certain people would buy them. Rodrigo smiled and said, "si."

Reuben asked Rodrigo if he knew of any good construction workers because he wanted to build a very large wine cellar. He told Rodrigo that it didn't matter if they spoke English, which was code for telling him he didn't care if they were illegals. He also added that they had to be very skilled at working underground and making sure that the ground wouldn't fall in on anyone. Rodrigo told him he understood and said that his cousin, Florentino, was an engineer and he would make sure he was there.

Utilizing drawings from Reuben, the engineer and nine other men soon began the work of reopening the tunnel. Reuben stressed that the tunnel needed to be structurally sound. The walkway would lead under the house to a safe room with a six-inch metal door. He told Florentino that the walls needed to be at least six inches of concrete over two rows of cinderblock and reinforced with rebar. He wanted oak planks put up over the walls. Not laminate, but solid oak boards at least two inches thick, along with solid oak floors. He didn't care what it cost and promised Florentino that if the job was completed in six months, he would receive a $10,000 bonus and all the other men, a $3000 bonus each. Florentino smiled and said it would be done in five.

When the houses were finished, a ceremony was held to showcase the homes to the press and the families who would be moving into them. These families would be displaced from the Royal Manor apartment building which was being torn down to build the new home inside that neighborhood. The press and the families were astonished at what Reuben had accomplished in so little time and asked him to give a speech. Reuben had been certain that they would ask and he was prepared.

"Thank you for allowing me to speak today, but it really should be the mayor or my mother up here speaking. They are the inspiration for what you see behind me." He wanted to stop there and explain to everyone what he had just done by saying that, but he couldn't. So, even though his mind was laughing at how clever that sentence was, his body language displayed humility as he continued.

"Six months ago, on an afternoon downtown, we talked about the vision for the mayor's ICE program. Now you see, in physical form, what that program looks like. But it's not just the homes. Talk to the families. Talk to the young children who have been to the zoo for the first time, or fishing for the first time, or even to the amusement park or bowling for the first time. When you do, remember what Dr. King said: 'The time is always right to do what is right.'

"Augusta, look around you. What we have started was always the right thing to do. The mayor had the idea and my mother had the generosity within her to give us, and I mean all of us, the two million dollars to get the program started. I say all of us because we all benefit from this program, not just the five families that are moving into their new homes, or the family moving into the new home that will be built in Royal Manor. We did something positive for our community that we can all be proud of. Mark Twain said it best when he said: 'The two most important days in your life are the day you are born and the day you found out why.' Today we all found why."

At that moment in time, if Reuben had wanted to run for governor of Georgia, he would have won in a landslide. But he had other plans. The governor's job would be akin to picking peaches on the peach farm, compared to what his ambitions were. After the clapping had died down, Reuben had another surprise for the crowd and for his mother. He could tell she was ready to drown in all the attention she was getting and would have passed away with a smile if all of those accolades were indeed water.

"One final thing before you leave today. I wanted to tell you about something my mother wants to start, above and beyond what she has already done. So today, we have established a scholarship program that will provide fifty thousand dollars to some deserving young man or woman that desires to better themselves by going to one of our fine universities within the state, or even to one of the fine technical colleges we have all around us. That scholarship will be called the Marigold Broadwater Enrichment Scholarship and I hope many, many people who have never felt they had the opportunity in the past, find that they do now. Thank you, Augusta, for your support.

Thank you, Mayor, for the idea and the opportunity to lead this endeavor. And special thanks to you, Mother, for your selfless acts of generosity."

Marigold understood what her son was doing, but she still enjoyed all of the attention she was getting from the crowds. She didn't care if her son was sincere or not; in her mind, on that day, he was sincere. And that was all she needed to put things in the past and savor the moment.

People came up to shake her hand and thanked her over and over. More pictures were made of the mayor with the families, the families with Reuben and Marigold, and of course the mayor with Marigold and Reuben. Reuben told Mayor Parkland that he would leave the process for awarding the scholarship up to him and the commissioners. He found it very interesting, as time passed, that the scholarship winner was often a son or daughter of a friend of someone in city government, though there were a few awarded to students from Royal Manor. I suppose to keep things honest, Reuben laughed. But it didn't matter to Reuben who won it. He only wanted the name recognition that the scholarship brought him. It was worth more to him than the money.

The tunnel had been completed and led into the new house in Royal Manor. Access to the home came through a back bedroom from under a door in the floor. It was opened by an electronic switch that moved the door and single bed that was on top of it. It was an ingenious design and Florentino had no questions when asked to build it. Reuben had built his reputation up to such a degree that no one had reason to question when a crane was used to place a large metal door down into the ground before the construction on the Royal Manor home had even begun.

After the door was in, the house went up quickly. Florentino told Reuben he appreciated everything he was doing for the city and that he understood that people with his kind of money needed an escape room. Reuben paid him an extra $5000 on top of his $10,000 bonus and Florentino promised he would be available to build anything else he ever needed. Reuben was doing just what his mother had taught him, giving the person "ownership" in the business. In this case, that ownership was an extra five thousand dollars, not a deed. But it achieved the same effect. He had remembered that you don't always need a mallet to ensure loyalty.

The tenant he found for the house in Royal Manor was perfect in Reuben's mind. He deemed it divine intervention. Frank Miller was a seventy-two-year-old ex-felon who had served thirty-five years in jail for armed robbery and assault on multiple occasions. He was also an alcoholic. Both elements were key in Reuben's mind as to whom he needed to live in that particular house. He didn't want a drug addict to live there. He knew they couldn't be trusted. But an alcoholic, especially one as old as he was and who had seen the darker side of life, knew better than to screw up what Reuben was offering him.

Reuben told Frank that if he kept the yard groomed, the flowering plants growing and the yard looking like it belonged on the Augusta National grounds, he would make sure that he never ran out of alcohol. He also said he would need to ignore people coming to and from the back bedroom. He told Frank that "illegal was in the eye of the beholder" and that within his family and circle of friends, the beholders often had their eyes closed or looking in another direction. Frank winked and gave him a thumbs up, telling him he knew exactly what he meant. He even smiled when Reuben told him about his family and how they had used this house as an entry and exit during the prohibition era.

"Wish I could have been back there with them, Mr. Boss Man. Just one question before you leave, though," Frank started. "Is it okay if I keep Ole Blue?"

"Old Blue? Is that a dog?"

"No," he replied as he reached around the door and pulled out a sawed-off 12-gauge shotgun. "This is Ole Blue. I use it as a suggestor."

"A suggestor?"

"Yes, sir. It helps when those fucked up young assholes come around here and think they are going to do something to me or steal something from my house. I suggest they change their mind with Ole Blue and it seems to clarify things for them."

"Well, Mr. Miller, are you aware that it is illegal for an ex-felon to have or own a gun?"

"I was told that illegal was in the eye of the beholder."

Reuben smiled and patted Frank on his shoulder. "It is indeed, Mr. Miller. It is indeed," he said as he walked away.

As soon as he heard that question from Frank, Reuben knew he had checked off several important boxes of his mother's life lessons. He now had an ex-felon with loyalty to his boss. A boss who would always make sure he had a nice roof over his head, meaningful work in a beautiful garden, and the comfort of never again having to worry where or when he would be able to get his next drink. Reuben didn't even mind that he preferred expensive single malt scotch. He actually liked that about Frank. No sense in not being aware of what good whisky was just because you lived in a government housing complex.

Eighteen months after he left Harvard, he pulled out the slip of paper that Tom had given him and placed the call. He told the man on the phone that his name was Reuben Broadwater and the man said he wasn't expecting his call for another six months. Reuben laughed and just said he got things done sooner than he expected. The man said to meet him at the Varsity restaurant at noon on Saturday. It would be very busy and he suggested that Reuben might enjoy a hot dog and some onion rings because they were the best in town. After getting his food, he should go into the seating area and they would find him there.

Reuben noticed he said "they" at the very end of the conversation and that bothered him. He placed one of his father's smaller revolvers, a four-inch .357, into a leg holster before he left that morning. He walked into the Varsity at 12:01 and the place was extremely busy. The lines were long, but they moved quickly and he ordered a hot dog with chili. And though he didn't like onion rings, he ordered them anyway to show whomever he was about to meet that he listened to them. They were the boss for now, after all, and Reuben didn't want them to think otherwise.

As he came into the seating area, he saw Tom waving to him. He was sitting with two large black men. Reuben sat down across from Tom and next to the larger of the two men.

"Reuben. Damn glad to hear from you. I've been reading about you. You've made quite a name for yourself in Augusta. Some of it is even starting to trickle up here into Atlanta and across the state."

The large man sitting next to Tom looked at Reuben and told him it was cool what he did with those houses and the scholarship. Real cool.

Reuben thanked him and before he could ask him his name, Tom started making introductions. "Reuben, these two very large men are some of my best friends. Trayzon is the man you are sitting next to and the man sitting next to me is Enoch."

They nodded their heads toward Reuben and continued eating their lunch.

"Go ahead and eat Reuben. We'll talk about what you want to do. No one will be listening to us. They can barely hear each other at their own table and I have a scrambler device in my pocket, which is quite effective at garbling our conversation to anyone trying to listen."

With those words, Reuben understood. He knew that Tom was the boss. Smart. At Harvard, he had acted like just a go-between, but he was the boss. He bit into his hot dog and it was better than he thought. "I have to admit, Tom, this hot dog is really good. I've never been here before, even though I've heard of the place for years."

"Who the hell is Tom?" Trayzon asked.

Reuben looked confused.

"Tom Jackson doesn't exist, Reuben. My name is really Henry Fielding."

Reuben nodded his head. He wasn't going to let those sitting next to him know that wasn't Tom's real name either. Tom knew Reuben would recognize the name, Henry Fielding. In fact, it made him smile. Henry Fielding was an author he had quoted throughout his thesis and wrote "Tom Jones." He also wrote "A Journey from This World to the Next." Appropriate name for a drug dealer, he thought.

"So, you are interested in becoming an antique dealer?" Henry asked.

"I am. Very interested," Reuben replied.

"High-end antiques?"

"Yes, ten million-dollars-worth. I have a very large store I need to fill and I think the market demand for antiques is very high in Augusta and the surrounding areas."

"That's a lot of money," Trayzon stated.

"I have it. All I need to know is what account you want it deposited in; preferably an off-shore account. Once I have the antiques, the money will be there."

"We can do that," Trayzon replied.

Reuben found it interesting that Trayzon was the one responding and not Henry. Did I miscalculate something, he asked himself.

"Trayzon and Enoch do most of my antique sales here in the south. Here is an account number," Henry said as he slipped a piece of paper to Reuben. "I'm going to leave now, and Trayzon and Enoch can let you know how things will proceed from here. Good to see you, Reuben. I think you'll enjoy the antiques. A lot of them are very valuable. Hope to see you soon," he said as he got up and walked away.

Trayzon and Enoch told Reuben to finish his lunch and then they would go look at the antiques. Reuben nodded his head and ate his hot dog and waited for them to finish their food.

"Aren't you going to eat those onion rings?" Trayzon asked.

"No, I don't like onion rings," Reuben replied.

"Then why buy them?"

"Because my host suggested I do that."

Trayzon laughed and reached over and punched Enoch on his shoulder. But Enoch wasn't laughing. He was studying Reuben. Trying to understand everything he could about him. Trayzon may be the boss for Henry in the south, but Enoch is the one with the calculating mind, thought Reuben.

"I like you already, man," Trayzon said as he looked at Reuben and smiled. "You got street smarts for somebody that's an old money dude."

An old money dude. Henry has told them everything about me. That's okay, he thought. "Would you like them, Trayzon?" Reuben asked.

"Damn right I want them! I'll eat them on the ride. Let's go take a look at those lamps."

They followed Reuben to his car. Good thing I brought the Escalade, he thought, as they all got in the car and Trayzon directed him where to go. They drove out of downtown Atlanta and headed west toward Birmingham.

"What kind of gun do have holstered on your leg?" Enoch asked.

Reuben didn't hesitate in replying. "A .357. It's good at short range."

"Yeah, it is," Enoch replied.

They didn't ask for me to hand it over to them, so that's a good thing, Reuben thought. And if they killed me, they'd never get the money. Only my mother and I know the code, but I guess they could try and torture me to get it, which doesn't concern me. I'll shoot at least one of them in the head before any of that happens.

"Are either of you familiar with the Revolutionary War?"

"Yeah, a little bit," Enoch replied.

"So, you've heard of Ethan Allen?"

"You mean the furniture store guy?" Trayzon asked.

"He had nothing to do with the store, but yes, it is named after him. He was captured by the British and remained a prisoner of war for three years. They put thirty-pound irons on his legs and feet. He sat on a chest for days and nights at a time while being guarded round the clock. He and thirty-three other prisoners were kept in a twenty by twenty-two feet enclosure as they took them to England. They had to eat and piss and shit in that small dark room. They had lice, diarrhea, fever by the time they got there. Some died in their own excrement. But he survived. Upon arriving in England, they argued against hanging him, afraid that Americans would start hanging British officers as revenge. So, they loaded him up and shipped him back to America, where he caught scurvy. He almost died before they got to New York and released him, placing him on house arrest. He was finally freed when General Burgoyne retook Fort Ticonderoga. Which I find very interesting because he and Benedict Arnold captured that same fort years earlier from the British before Arnold became a traitor for trying to give West Point to the British."

"What's with the history lesson, man?" Trayzon asked.

"He's telling us that he isn't afraid of us," Enoch replied. "That he isn't afraid of dying."

Enoch is very smart, Reuben thought. Very smart. I wonder why he lets Trayzon run things.

As Trayzon finished the onion rings, he said, "Man if we wanted you dead, you would have been dead an hour ago. We're going to make sure you get those antiques and help show you the man you'll have to kill in Augusta if you want to take over that market. Take the next exit, Professor."

Reuben did as instructed. They traveled about 20 miles more before turning onto another road that took them deep into the country. They drove to a farmhouse with several large barns. Trayzon directed him to park beside one of them. Inside the barn, he revealed a thousand bales of marijuana that he would be purchasing. The bales were very large, at least five feet by five feet. Reuben realized that he would never be able to fit them into his tunnel. Even if they were broken apart, he still wouldn't be able to do it. He knew he needed another plan.

"So, you got a place to put all this shit?" Trayzon asked.

"What if I said I wanted heroin instead? How many of those bales would my ten million buy me?"

Trayzon smiled. "Five of those sized bales. You can break them apart a lot easier too. They're all packed up and could fit in a large U-haul. Make you more money too. But you still got to deal with that man in Augusta. He handles all the product down there and he's a scary dude. He's fucked up a lot of people over time. I think he'd try and fuck me over if Enoch wasn't always with me. We never go anywhere without the other. In our business, you can't take chances and you can't do things by yourself. I doubt you would even get to that gun on your leg before he nailed you to the wall and sliced you up like a pig going to slaughter. I'm not sure you are cut out for this business, Professor."

"Call Henry and tell him I want to change the order. Let's see what he says."

Trayzon did as requested and Reuben couldn't tell what Henry was saying as Trayzon ended the call.

"You and Henry must go way back," Trayzon said. "He said he could have it for you in a week. You cool with that?"

Reuben nodded his head.

"Me and Enoch will bring it down to you in a U-haul. We'll get to your house at 1:00 in the morning. Be ready for us to store it. After we unload it, we'll get us a place to stay and come get you the following evening and take you to meet Zeus. That's what he calls himself. Zeus. Stupid fucking asshole."

Reuben walked back to the Escalade. Trayzon and Enoch followed him but didn't get in.

"I'll call you the day before we comc. Be ready for us," Trayzon stated. "You can GPS yourself out of here. We're going to stay for a while. We'll get a ride later. See you in a week, Professor."

Just before he got in the car, he heard Enoch call out his name and he turned around.

"You made a much better decision. The heroin will make you four times your investment. You might make more on volume if you cut it, but you don't want all that volume. Not that way."

"Do I need to cut it with something?" Reuben asked.

"Not our stuff. Sell it as is. If you do, you will get all the repeat business you can handle. That dumbass punk Zeus cuts the shit all the time even though we told him he'd make more money if he didn't. But he's a wise-ass dope-head who thinks he knows everything. You can't use this shit and sell it too. At least not every day like he does. His time was coming whether it was you or from the shit he puts in his body. Hope you're ready for what you say you want. There ain't no turning back once you drive off this farm. Don't matter how much old money you got."

"Have you ever read 'Invisible Man' by Ralph Ellison?" Reuben asked Enoch.

"You mean that dude that makes himself invisible?" Trayzon asked.

"No, that's a book by H. G. Wells, a very good English writer of science fiction stories. The book I'm referring to is about the experience of a man growing up black in the 1920s and '30s. You should read it. It's considered one of the best books by a black American author ever written."

"Why you telling us to read that shit?" Trayzon asked.

"He's telling us that he's ready to take the next step," Enoch replied before Reuben could.

Reuben smiled at Enoch and then got in his car and drove away analyzing everything that had just happened. It didn't matter if he sold marijuana or heroin, he told himself, from a legal perspective. Either way, he would get the same sentence if caught. The only difference was, he would be selling a product that people could become addicted to.

Could is the key word, Reuben thought. They don't have to become addicted. They choose that. You are letting them escape. To enjoy the jazz. You are helping them, just like you told Ralph you would do in that dream you had back in school. You would give them all a way out. Which door they chose was up to them. And in a matter of a few moments, Reuben had rationalized away the selling of narcotics to the people in the neighborhood down the street from his house. After all, he was a Broadwater.

The U-haul arrived a week later just as Trayzon said. Reuben had them back into the driveway up to the garages. He had given his mother a four-hundred-dollar bottle of scotch earlier that day along with several valiums before helping her upstairs. She would not hear a thing that evening. The staff no longer spent the night in the house since he had returned home, so he didn't have to worry about them either. He was certain no one would be able to see what they were doing as they unloaded the heroin and took it down through the renovated tunnel and into the storerooms. They filled up the room under the house and had to use the additional room behind the steel door, but there was more than sufficient space.

"Pretty damn cool place you got here, Professor. Damn nice," Trayzon said as he lit up a joint and offered it to Reuben. Reuben shook his head no. He had more work to do that night and needed to have a clear head. Trayzon shrugged his shoulders and offered it to Enoch who also turned it down.

"Shit man, that's cool. Just more for me." Trayzon took a couple more hits before he put it out and placed the rest of the joint into a metal cigarette holder. "You ain't the only one that got antiques," Trayzon said as he showed Reuben the cigarette holder. "From the '30s. Copper and bronze and silver. Cool, ain't it?"

Reuben nodded his head.

"Are you ready for tomorrow?" Enoch asked.

"Yes," Reuben replied. "Go to the front gate of Phinizy Swamp at midnight. The gate will be open and just drive straight in. You'll see my car and I'll be there waiting for you. We'll need to take him into the swamp about a mile, so I suggest you wear some waterproof boots or snake boots if you have them."

"Snake boots?" Trayzon cried. "Shit, I hate fucking snakes."

"All the more reason to wear snake boots," Reuben replied.

That night, Reuben transferred the money into the account that Henry had given him and then burned the piece of paper with the account number on it. He laid down on the couch and thought about what he needed to do tomorrow. He remembered the safari he went on with his parents and the way he had killed that Cape buffalo with one shot. He remembered how the guides told him that wounded buffaloes had killed people before and that wasn't good for business. Cape buffalo, drug dealer. Not much difference he told himself. Either they died or he died and he didn't plan on dying.

He didn't sleep much that night, but when he did, he dreamed of the concentration camps in World War II and saw picture after picture of the bodies that were tortured and starved to death and piled up in heaps like refuse. It was sickening to him and he woke up in a sweat. He went into his father's study and stayed there reading about all of the wars that America had been involved in until it was time to go to the swamp.

Zeus was wearing plastic handcuffs and a sack over his head when Enoch and Trayzon dragged him out of the trunk and began following Reuben.

After they had walked a mile, they reached an area where the water was about a foot deep. Reuben told them to put Zeus down on the ground and to stand back. Reuben pulled out the katana sword that had been unnoticeable in the black sheath hanging from his waist in the minimal light he had used to get them through the swamp.

He had been out to this place several times before. He knew that alligators were all around them, about one hundred yards away and that they would take care of the body. He had sharpened the sword that was in his father's study and practiced with it every day for a year. Trayzon and Enoch saw just how sharp the sword was as Reuben removed Zeus's head from his body with a swing so hard that it would have sliced through a four-inch tree.

He pulled out a trash bag and placed the still-covered head into it and handed it to Enoch. He then pushed the headless body away from him into the water. As he walked back to Enoch and Trayzon, he could hear movement in the water that sounded like large rocks had been thrown into it and he knew the alligators had found Zeus.

He cleaned the blade in the water with a rag that he would burn later and placed the sword back in its sheath. He took the head from Enoch and led them out of the swamp back to their cars. The only words he said to them were to go back to Atlanta and that he would call them when he needed some help with the distribution of the product.

They silently followed him out of the swamp and watched him lock the gate before they drove off. The next day there was a story in the Augusta Chronicle about a known drug dealer who had been killed in a brutal manner. They failed to mention in the article that his head was stuck onto a three-foot piece of rebar that had been driven into the ground in front of his house.

The police looked for clues regarding Zeus' murder for over two weeks but there were no leads. There were no fingerprints anywhere. There was no way to link the rebar to any one place and there was no DNA evidence of any kind. Reuben knew all of this because the mayor told him about it. He thought he should know since Zeus had lived in a house on Ellis Street, just a few blocks down from Royal Manor and only about three blocks away from Reuben's home. The mayor told Reuben that the police assumed that the people who supplied Samuel Johnson, the real name of Zeus, were upset with something he had done and sent in some professional killers who left a message. They didn't think they would ever find who killed him, but they weren't going to be upset about it if they didn't. Reuben knew that meant that the investigation was over. The press would talk about it for a few more weeks, but the story would eventually disappear.

The katana blade used to kill Zeus was hanging back up in his father's study after being cleaned with hydrogen peroxide and a bleach solution. The rags and trash bag had been burned. Nothing on that sword would provide any evidence. The only evidence of what had been done with the sword was in Reuben's mind as he looked at it every day. It made him remember how that young boy had beaten him in the wrestling match. And he would walk away and not think about it anymore.

Even so, Reuben knew he had now done more than just cross over a line when he left that farm that afternoon. He had known it as soon as he had made that call to Tom, or Henry, as he was now called. The call. The farm. The heroin. Zeus. They all led him into another world. It was as if he had just stepped into the boat guided by Charon, the ferryman on the river Styx. But he knew he wasn't by himself on that boat. Many others in history had done the same thing as he did. History was filled with those moments.

The white settlers killed and murdered the indigenous tribes because they wanted their land. The soldiers from the Citadel, firing on Fort Sumter in Charleston Harbor, started the bloodiest war in American History. Brothers killing brothers. Entire families wiped out. Indian, Northern or Southern. It didn't matter. Families were destroyed by someone who believed they had to do it.

History was full of people who did things cognizant of the fact that a bad outcome was a possibility. When he met Melissa, he had let himself believe he might escape the world that had been created for him. But when she died, he knew what that meant. He knew it as soon as he looked under the car. He would be pulled into a dark world that he could never escape from again. He wondered how history would remember him. He believed he couldn't do any of the good that he wanted to do without doing some of the bad that was required of him. History told him that. He would have to accept that fate and move forward. The Broadwater blood within him would allow nothing else.

Over the next six weeks, Reuben had Marigold accompany him to the rest of their businesses so she could inform them that he would be assuming management. She no longer had any desire to stop it. It was difficult for her to maintain her composure and act in a friendly manner as she shared the news. And it wasn't because she was handing everything over to her son. It was because she knew what she had done to her son.

People only saw a handsome, friendly young man as Marigold presented Reuben to the staff. But, behind the friendly demeanor, Marigold saw a change in her son. He was driven, more than he had ever been, and she feared what that would do to him. When they were by themselves, she felt alone. As if he wasn't there. Just a shadow that reminded her of her son.

She knew it wouldn't matter if she apologized every day. She would have to live the rest of her life with the gnawing feeling in her gut that reminded her she had made her son into what she now saw. She had seen the items stored down in the tunnel and though she wasn't completely certain what they were, she knew they were some type of illegal drugs. She saw the metal door and had been unable to open it. But she didn't really need to see behind it; she had already seen enough.

She would never forgive herself for what she did to her son and she knew she would never be able to question what he was doing. After all, she told herself, it was in his genetic make-up and she couldn't fault him for that. Like he had told her the day she had crossed the line and beat him with the fire iron, he was only doing what she had taught him to do his entire life. Succeed.

Two months after Zeus had been killed, Reuben notified Trayzon and Enoch that he was ready to start distributing the product. They came the next day to set things up. Reuben introduced them to his mother and she just smiled at them and said she wasn't feeling well and was going upstairs to lay down. That was her polite way of excusing herself from having a conversation. She thought she was being discrete, but she wasn't.

"What's wrong with your mom? I know she seen black people in this house before," Trayzon said.

"She's never seen drug dealers. At least not in her house, even though they are all over the neighborhood just a block away," Enoch replied. "And she doesn't want to talk to them. I doubt she even talks much to her son anymore. We're all just invisible men to her now."

Reuben looked at Enoch and nodded his head. He read the book by Ellison I suggested. He is extremely smart and perceptive. Why does he allow Trayzon to lead? I don't understand that. There is more to this than I'm seeing right now, he thought.

Reuben led them out on to the sun porch and offered them a drink.

"I'll have what your mother drinks," Trayzon said.

"You have good taste," Reuben laughed as he poured the scotch over some ice and handed it to him.

Enoch said he preferred a beer and Reuben got them both a Heineken.

"Man, this is some smooth shit. What is it?" Trayzon asked.

"Macallan Rare Cask Single Malt Scotch," Reuben replied.

"How much does a bottle cost?"

"About $300."

"Oh, hell yes," Trayzon said as he downed his drink. "Mind if I fix me another?"

"Help yourself."

Before Reuben could ask, Enoch told him they had the network set up and ready to go. "And the little picture you painted with Zeus; hell, that got people talking. All over town and even in Atlanta. Ain't nobody going to fuck with you. We have twenty dealers we trust ready to go. They will each take twenty-five pounds a month. That's a quarter-ton a month. That's two million dollars a month. In a little under two years, you will have made thirty million. You got a way to handle all that money?" he asked.

"Yes. I need you and the dealer's agents to meet a man named Frank over in Royal Manor. I'll take you there in a few minutes. They'll need to come into the neighborhood in a discrete manner, as if they live there. Don't draw attention to themselves. Have cars with Georgia tags, even if they don't live in Georgia. Frank will let them into the room with the metal door. Their twenty-five pounds will be there waiting for them. They take it and leave the money. They each come on a separate day of the month, only at night. Since there are twenty of them, it will be the first twenty days of the month. I don't need to know who is coming on which day. You work that out with them, but they need to stick to their assigned day, whether it's the first day or the second or third or the twentieth. If they come after the twentieth day, there will be nothing there.

"Also, they must always come after dark, but before 11 p.m. If they ever come onto my property, I will make sure that they don't ever do that again. In fact, they shouldn't even know where I live. Tell them the dealer is a person named Bix and that's all they need to know besides what he did to Zeus."

"Bix. What the hell kinda name is that?" Trayvon asked.

"It's a nickname for a jazz cornetist and pianist. His name was Leon Beiderbecke."

"Ellison liked jazz," Enoch commented. He understands everything, Reuben thought.

"And If they take the product and don't leave the money, I will make sure they never deal with me again. I'll just call you to find out who was assigned to that day and ask how I can introduce myself to them. Make sure they understand that. Are you two good with that?"

"Yeah, we real good with that," Trayzon said. "Damn, mind if I take that bottle with me?"

"It's all yours," Reuben said as he took them down through the tunnel and showed them how the entry into the Royal Manor house worked.

"Shit you're a fucking double zero, ain't he, Enoch? You got a license to kill?" Trayzon hit Enoch on the shoulder and laughed as he looked at Reuben.

Reuben knew that he was referring to James Bond but he wasn't interested in what Trayzon said. He was interested in what Enoch thought. Reuben introduced them to Frank and explained to Frank what would be occurring every month. Frank said that was good with him. He showed Trayzon and Enoch his "suggestor" and Enoch smiled at the sight of it.

After meeting Frank, Enoch asked Reuben to show them the five houses he had built for the poor. Reuben took them by the homes and Enoch was impressed. Trayzon was half drunk and all he said was "little pink houses for you and me" and started laughing.

Before leaving that afternoon, Enoch admitted to Reuben that this was one of the best setups he had ever seen, but that he needed to be prepared for anything to happen. "When you deal with thieves, expect to be robbed," he warned and Reuben nodded his head as he watched them drive off.

Within a week, the operation was up and running. Reuben placed the twenty-five pounds of heroin in the room each day himself and took the money that was left there. Every other month, a trusted family lawyer took the money to the Cayman Islands on a private charter plane. Nothing looked any different to anyone who had dealt with the Broadwater's in business or to the neighborhood where drugs were bought and sold just about every hour of the day.

While the money amassed in the bank accounts, Reuben wanted to make sure the ICE program was still in the news on a monthly basis for something new that he initiated or completed, with a picture of him and the children having fun, or him and the mayor or a commissioner talking about the positive impact that the program was having on the community.

Six months after starting the business with Trayzon and Enoch, Reuben found a face jug, made by the slave David Drake, at an auction in Atlanta. The jug prompted a new idea and he had to have it. It cost him $25,000, but he didn't care. As soon as he got home, he contacted several local artists and asked if they would be interested in helping with his idea and they said they would be honored. He found a cheap empty warehouse downtown and gave the artists the money they needed to carry out his vision.

Once the warehouse was ready, Reuben called the mayor and told him he had something exciting to share with him involving the ICE program. The next day, the mayor, the press and five commissioners were at the warehouse with Reuben, the artists, and about a dozen children from Royal Manor.

Mayor Parkland introduced Reuben to great applause, and once again Reuben thanked the mayor and his mother. He said she was unable to attend as she wasn't feeling well, but her spirit was there with him. Reuben displayed the face jug he had purchased and explained to everyone what it was. He told them about David Drake, who was born a slave in 1801 and had five owners throughout his life. He lost his leg as a young man from a train accident. Having only one leg made him unfit for field work, but well suited for the work that required sitting, such as pottery.

Reuben continued the story by telling how another slave by the name of Henry, who was missing both arms, sat across from Dave and moved the potter's wheel with his legs, while Dave sculpted enormous containers and other small jars and face jugs. Together they produced thousands of jugs, jars, and pitchers and today, for those fortunate enough to own one, they are worth thousands of dollars.

"Now, Mr. Drake, being a slave, was never able to enjoy the fruits of his labor. We have the same problem today with our children living in our poor neighborhoods. They are enslaved in a world of poverty with no access to a world that would allow them to tap into their unrecognized artistic ability.

"Dave and Henry would be millionaires today if they were alive and making the pottery that they made over 170 years ago. This jug that I bought recently at an auction cost twenty-five thousand dollars. The large jugs they made, those that stood four or five feet tall, would cost three to four times that. Imagine that. Take a moment to calculate twenty-five thousand dollars by one thousand. You don't need to get out your phones. I can tell you the answer. Its twenty-five million dollars. That's what Dave and Henry would be earning today. That is astonishing, isn't it?

"Just down the road, in Edgefield County, the clay present in the ground, made it a center of pottery making in the early 1800s. Those pots are also worth thousands of dollars today. I ask you, why can't Augusta become a center for pottery in the 2000s? I say it can! Under the ICE program, we will provide lessons one day a week for any impoverished child who has an interest and demonstrates an ability to make art. I will personally pay professional artists for their time to train these young students. I have purchased this building to house the program and will provide all of the materials needed.

"They will create real art, not little ashtrays. Art that will sell and will provide them money for what they created. With their own two hands, mentored by artists, but created by them. Half of all the money they earn in this new ICE Pottery Consortium will go to the young artist and the other half of that money will go back into the ICE program for Habitat for

Humanity. The program will never run out of funding. My mother and I will guarantee that. And the world will never tire of seeing the work of new artists. History has proven that."

The crowd's applause was loud and long after Reuben's speech. But after everyone was gone, the mayor took Reuben aside and told him that the slave references were a little too strong. He understood what he was doing and that it was a good thing, but he needed to tone down the slave references in the future.

Reuben looked at the mayor and said that everything he had told the public was true. There was nothing that couldn't be researched and proven as facts. If the truth hurt some people that was too bad. What he was doing was more important than the feelings of a few black commissioners.

Mayor Parkland had never heard Reuben speak like that to anyone, especially him and he wasn't sure how to take it. He chalked it up to the fact that his mother was sick, but he issued Reuben a warning: his knowledge could be deemed as arrogance if he didn't understand the crowd he was talking to. Just before he got in his car, he called out, "Great job, Reuben" so the press that still lingered could hear him. Reuben smiled and waved to him and then went home. He found his mother on the sun porch drinking a scotch and he got himself a beer. He told her about the new piece of pottery he had purchased recently and the new program he had started.

"I never have liked those face jugs," she said as she got up and walked away. "They remind me of blissful ignorance which doesn't exist anymore."

Blissful ignorance. If only people knew, Reuben thought, and then yelled out, "Everyone's an art critic!" as he sat and admired the jug. And then added, "Or doesn't understand history!" as he looked up toward his mother's bedroom.

"And you know what art critics can't do?" he asked as if someone was still sitting there. "Make art. And you know what happens to those that don't understand history? They are doomed to repeat it. Well, by God, guess what? I bet the consortium makes art and makes money. And there will be other Dave's discovered. Only this time, they will be able to earn money. I'll show you both. Wait and see!" Reuben yelled as he finished off his beer and got another one.

It took almost a year, but the warning Enoch had made came true. Someone stole the product and Reuben had to make a phone call to Trayzon to find out who it was. Trayzon gave him a name and also informed him that he lived right there in Royal Manner.

Reuben knew the neighborhood was a convenient place to live for someone who liked to sell and use drugs, but he was aware there was a risk to him living so close to a dealer and being the supplier of those drugs. He needed to eliminate that risk. So, he installed a gate at the entrance to his house and he killed the dealer and placed his head on another rebar pole in the middle of the community.

The gate would have more of an aesthetic value to it than one of creating a barrier, but it sent a signal to everyone that he had concerns about what was occurring several blocks away from his house. The real protective barrier would be created by fear. The severed head on a spike had been used for centuries to create fear which was very difficult to forget. Though no one knew he was the dealer, it created a psychological protective barrier around his home, the home in Royal Manor where Frank lived, and the neighborhood itself. One that would be difficult to overcome, even by one with a drug-addled mind.

The severed head revealed to the police that the dead person was not just a drug addict, but actually a drug dealer and that he had apparently done something wrong to his suppliers. There was no evidence that gave them any clues and the police once again assumed it was a professional hit performed by killers that were long gone. To a certain degree, they were right. After several weeks with no suspects, the story disappeared from the minds of the media. The image was, however, burned into the minds of the Royal Manor residents and to those who dealt with someone that they only knew as Bix. A new dealer was found within a week and the process continued uninterrupted. The dead dealer's theft was like an acorn falling into a large pond; the ripple within the revenue stream was barely noticed.

Reuben believed he was immune to everything that he had done, but he wasn't. His friend, Edgar reminded him of that in his dreams. One night as he slept, he saw the two heads of the drug dealers on the rebar poles looking at him. Edgar was sitting between them in a rocking chair, smoking opium and smiling at Reuben. The mouths of the drug dealers opened and began to speak.

"With light like hope to mortals given;
But their red orb, without beam,
To thy weariness shall seem
As a burning and a fever
Which would cling to thee forever.
Now are thoughts thou shalt not banish:
Now are visions ne'er to vanish;
From thy spirit shall they pass
No more, like dew-drops from the grass."

Reuben screamed, "No!" and shot up on the edge of his bed. He repeated the poem from his dream and as he did, he heard someone saying, "Very good. You know the poem very well. 'Spirits of the Dead.' Appropriate, don't you think, my good friend, Reuben?"

Reuben looked into the corner. He saw no one in the shadows, but he could hear a rocking chair creaking back and forth. He knew who it was, even though it wasn't possible. He had to still be dreaming. When he got up and turned on the light, Edgar Allen Poe was in the rocking chair, smoking opium, looking at him.

"Sometimes the images never go away," he said as he rocked back and forth smoking the pipe.

"No, I expect they don't, but that is something that I will have to live with," Reuben stated.

"It won't be easy. I can promise you that. I was haunted my entire life. I do not envy your sleep. I am sure we will see each other again," Edgar said as he took one more puff and the smoke from the pipe engulfed him. When the smoke was gone, so was he. Reuben could still hear the rocking chair creak back and forth and he covered his ears and ran out of the room.

He went downstairs to the study and lay down on the leather sofa. He closed his eyes and tried to sleep. The creaking sounds were gone, as were the images and he fell asleep and did not dream about anything. It was just blessed darkness and he allowed it to embrace him for several hours before he got up and took a shower.

It was almost 2 p.m. before he came down the next day and he told his mother that he was going out to the French Market Grille to get some lunch. He wasn't sure why, but he asked her if she wanted to come with him and she said yes. As they drove to the restaurant, Marigold asked him how his pottery project was doing. The question surprised him and even if the interest was not real, he appreciated the attempt by her to ask.

"It's going well. They've already identified five students, the youngest being 10 and the oldest being 15, who have significant talent. They are creating some great stuff. The consortium has only been open three months and they have sold five thousand-dollars-worth of pottery. Considering the time, I don't think that's bad. I hope it makes that much each month. That would be amazing, don't you think?"

"They aren't making those face jugs, are they?" Marigold asked.

Reuben laughed. "No, I haven't seen any of those yet. They have been making some very pretty vases and urns. We can go by there later if you want to see what some of their work looks like. That is, if you're interested."

"Yes, I would like to see them."

"Good," Reuben said as they pulled into the parking lot. He was even more surprised by how pleasant lunch was with his mother. She only had one drink and they enjoyed a nice conversation while avoiding the topics of work or what was going on beneath their house. She said she would like to go by and see the houses they had built on Laney Walker Boulevard and Reuben reminded her that she had never seen the one in Royal Manor. She said she didn't expect she would ever see it since it wasn't safe to go in that neighborhood. He reassured her it was perfectly safe during the day and that she would enjoy meeting the man who lived there.

After lunch, Reuben took Marigold to the art warehouse and she mentioned that she really liked the sign. He wasn't surprised. Marigold Art Consortium. He told his mother that her flowery name was perfect for an art enterprise. Inside, she found a beautiful piece of raku for sale and asked Reuben about it. He explained how raku was made as Marigold turned the vase around within her hands to see the different colors that seemed to move as the light hit it.

Reuben paid the clerk fifty dollars for the vase and handed it to his mother. She thanked him and put her arm through his as they walked out to the car. Though it felt somewhat awkward, Reuben liked having his mother hold his arm and he opened the car door for her as she held onto her vase.

He took her by the homes on Laney Walker and then drove into Royal Manor to the house where Frank lived. Marigold got out of the car still clutching the vase. Reuben told her it would be safe in the car, but she shook her head, telling him that she would prefer to keep it with her. She admired the yard with so many flowers and azaleas and the large Japanese Maple trees on opposite ends of the house.

Frank came out of the house to meet them, saying hello to Reuben and tipping his hat to Marigold. "Hello, Mrs. Broadwater. I know we haven't ever met, but I seen your picture in the paper so often and I know Reuben so well, that I feel like I know you. My name is Frank, Frank Miller. What do you think of my house and the yard?"

Marigold took an instant liking to Frank and she told him that the yard was beautiful and the house looked nice too. He invited her to come in for a tour. As they walked around the house, Marigold spotted the bottle of Macallan Rare Cask Single Malt Scotch sitting out on an antique bar in the living room. "You have very good taste, Mr. Miller," she said as she walked over to inspect the old oak bar.

"Would you like a drink?" Frank asked.

"Maybe one. Just over some ice."

"A woman after my own heart," Frank said. He poured their drinks as she and Reuben sat down.

Marigold and Frank talked for a long time, getting to know each other. Frank even admitted that he had been in jail for much of his life and Marigold just smiled at Reuben when he said that. He remembered what I taught him, she said to herself. Though that memory brought a smile, it also brought back thoughts that made her uncomfortable. She finished her drink and announced that it was time to get back home.

"I hope we can meet again, Miss Marigold. I really enjoyed talking with you," Frank said as he led them to the door.

"As I did with you. Perhaps you can come over for lunch one day."

"Just tell me the day and I will be there."

"How's this Friday at one?" she asked.

"Let me check my calendar," Frank said. He pulled out a small note pad that Enoch and Trayzon had given him filled with the code names of those who would come by each night. "Yes, I'm free," he said and laughed.

Reuben thanked Frank for the hospitality and for doing such a good job. Frank replied, "Glad to do it, boss man."

When they got to the car, Marigold didn't want to ask, but she couldn't help herself. "What did you mean when you said thanks for doing a good job? What does he do?"

"He takes care of the yard. I wanted a showcase yard for the neighborhood. Something that others here could walk by and take pride in and perhaps inspire them to take better care of their own homes. Frank is very good at doing that and making friends within the community. He is excellent at it, as a matter of fact."

"Oh," Marigold replied, but she knew the other answer to the question that Reuben didn't say. Just like her uncles had done. It was intuitive for him. He needed someone to watch the place. The place where they get the whisky. For a moment she thought she was back in the 1930s, listening to her mother tell her about the tunnel and everything that occurred. She wasn't going to start a fight with Reuben about the illegal hooch down in the cellar. There was no need to. It wouldn't accomplish anything except to drive another wedge between them and she didn't want that.

"Frank is a good choice to have over there, son. He seems like a very nice man. I look forward to getting to know him."

Reuben smiled. She knows, but she accepts it. "Yes, I think you two will get along very well," Reuben said and told himself that he needed to go by the liquor store before Friday as they walked into the house.

Though the business Reuben had started with Enoch and Trayzon was very successful, Reuben knew he would end up killing Trayzon. He didn't know why or when, but he knew it would happen. He began to dread waking up each day, wondering if this was going to be the day and how that killing would manifest itself. He remembered the letter Poe wrote talking about his beloved Virginia's death from tuberculosis. "I became insane with long intervals of horrible sanity." That will become me, I fear. His escape became pulling out books from his library and immersing himself into the words to try and keep himself from thinking about it.

He began reading Ezra Pound's "Cantos" and he contemplated the poet's life. He doubted very few people knew how much the American expatriate had influenced poetry and writing in both England and America, because of his political beliefs and activism. Becoming a fascist and a follower of Benito Mussolini during World War II would do that. "Brilliant stupidity," Reuben said out loud and decided that would be a good title for an analysis of his work and life. Before he could get started on it, he heard someone buzzing at the gate. He recognized the voice on the intercom and jumped up from his chair. He greeted Henry Fielding with a hug as he welcomed him into the house.

"Your name is still Henry, isn't it?" Reuben asked.

Henry laughed. "For the time being. My throat is a bit parched. Would you have a glass of water?"

"Certainly," Reuben said and went over to the bar.

"Would you mind adding some scotch in there with the water?"

"Certainly," Reuben laughed. He knew that meant he really wanted scotch with just a little water and he accommodated his request. He brought the bottle with him as he handed Henry his drink.

"Laphroaig, twenty-five-year-old single malt," Henry said and tipped the glass toward Reuben. "That's about five hundred dollars a bottle isn't it?"

"When did you ever care about what things cost, Henry?"

"Oh, perhaps my first two years in college. After that, I somehow found a way to supplement my expensive tastes."

Reuben understood what that meant as he remembered what he had been trying to forget before he arrived. Why is he here now?

"Reading Pound? What are you contemplating - leaving the country or committing yourself to a mental institute?"

"Three weeks in a six by six metal cage would wear on most people's minds," Reuben replied.

"He shouldn't have been such a vocal fan of fascism. He should have realized America would and was winning the war."

"Others didn't care. Eliot, Joyce, Frost, Hemingway. He mentored or influenced all of them in some way."

"Those writers weren't in charge of freeing Europe of the Nazis and Fascists. It's okay to have an opinion on government but be careful how you express it. Extreme expression in any form is dangerous to your career and often to your own life."

"Why are you here, Henry?" Reuben suddenly asked.

Henry finished his drink and poured another as he leaned back in his chair and looked at Reuben.

"You've been busy over the past several years, haven't you? Terrific what you have done with all the publicity. That ICE program is genius and I know the Mayor didn't think of that. That was you. All you. I saw the homes that you built as I was driving around. And the process you set in place is brilliant, as Enoch told me. I suspect you have close to twenty-four million in the bank and probably two tons to go. Is that about right?"

Reuben nodded his head without saying anything. It didn't matter that he knew the exact number. He wasn't even really surprised that he did. He only wanted to know one thing. Why was he here? He knew he needed to just go along with the conversation and he would eventually find out. But now there was something else circulating in his mind as he sat and looked at Henry. Could he believe him? He heard the words from his friend Edgar whispering to him: "Believe nothing you hear and only one half that you see."

"I'm afraid I have something to tell you that you will not like, but it's better that I tell you than you be the subject of a story in the local newspaper. Trayzon, as is often the case, was high and drunk the other evening when we were together. He talked about how easy it would be to rob you and take the two tons that you have left. I told him that he could not do that, but I'm afraid he'll do it anyway."

Henry paused for a moment as he took another sip of his drink and then continued.

"He has put me in bad positions before. Situations that could have been quite harmful to my well-being. I'm afraid he's becoming even more reckless in his behavior. But I can't do anything to him. If I did, it would, should I say, make some people unhappy with my actions. And as such, impact my reputation. If you were to do something to him though, because you knew he planned to rob you, that would not be seen in a negative light at all. In fact, it would be deemed most appropriate. Even saluted by those within the industry. You know, 'honor among thieves' and that type of thing."

"Why are you telling me this?"

"Because I like you, Reuben. Always have. You have accomplished things very few people have. And you will continue to do so. You have not just become rich. You were rich before you even started down this new path. You have become a positive force within your community, knowing that in order to do so, you had to do what we know history demands of those given the opportunity to create real change. Trayzon is just a drug dealer. He will never be anything but a drug dealer and I would hate to see him kill you. But don't doubt that he would. He would not hesitate."

"What about Enoch?"

"Enoch will not be happy, but he understands the nature of the business. Just don't expect him to help you. He would not. You will have to be careful how you go about taking any action. Placing Trayzon's head on a pole would not be a good idea, but I love how you did that to Zeus and how you disposed of his body. Is that the sword you used hanging on the wall above the bar?"

"I'm not sure what you are referring to, Henry," Reuben replied.

Henry smiled and finished his drink. "I see that it's time for me to go. Thank you for your hospitality, Reuben. I hope we can talk later."

He escorted Henry to the door. "Did you ever write that book?" Reuben asked.

"No, I didn't want to talk to the publisher about my background and I wasn't really sure what name I would use as the author."

Reuben nodded his head. I should have known that he thought.

"Remember, Reuben. 'An idea that is not dangerous is unworthy of being called an idea at all,'" Henry said as he got into his car and drove away.

He leaves with an Oscar Wilde quote. How very appropriate, he thought as he turned around and walked back into his study.

One week later, Reuben was hiding in the woods behind the farmhouse where Trayzon and Enoch had taken him just outside of Atlanta. He had pulled off on a nearby road and parked the rented RV. It was a five-mile hike through the woods to the farmhouse and Reuben made that hike every day for a week, living in the RV at night until Trayzon and Enoch showed up at the farmhouse.

As Reuben knew he would, Trayzon came outside alone to smoke a joint. As soon as he walked away from the farmhouse, Reuben fired the arrow from his crossbow. The arrow tip entered through his nose and exited out the back of his head, severing his brain stem. He fell to the ground and died in less than a minute, as his body forgot how to breathe. Reuben left as soon as he saw Trayzon fall, assured of the outcome.

Enoch found Trayzon dead about twenty minutes later. When he saw how he was killed, he knew who the killer was. He knew that the killer probably practiced making that shot on a coconut for days, if not weeks until he was sure he could hit that target ten out of ten times at a certain range. He knew why he did it too. Trayzon shouldn't talk shit like he did when he was high. He had always known that would get him killed one day.

For several weeks after killing Trayzon, Reuben didn't leave the house. He wasn't sure if it was fear or the fact that people would ask him if he was ill and he didn't want to answer those questions. His mother could tell Reuben was not well but she didn't mention it. She was afraid to say anything because she was terrified that he would tell her he was using the drugs down in the tunnel. He certainly looked like a drug addict she thought. When Frank came over one day for lunch, she asked him what he would do if he found out his child was killing himself doing drugs.

"Well, Miss Marigold, that's a good question, but I am afraid I don't have a good answer for you. First of all, 'cause I ain't got no children. And second of all, 'cause for me to lecture any child on drug abuse, would make me a hypocrite. And I ain't no hypocrite. Always told the truth. I ain't ever going to stop drinking and I reckon one day, I might even die from it, but I been in jail half my life, so I don't really care. I have a good time every day. Meet nice people. See some not so nice too, but I ain't afraid of them and they don't bother me. Get paid for keeping up my house and yard and I truly love my new house and my garden. Never thought I'd ever have anything like this. And I really love the scotch your son provides me every week. Ain't too many people in this town, probably in the entire damn state, that drinks the kind of fine whisky I do every day. I ain't got to worry about anything and ain't got anything to complain about. So, you see Miss Marigold, I don't think I'm the right person to be asking such a question."

Marigold smiled and looked down at her hand, wrapped around her scotch. He's right. Neither he nor I have any moral ground on which to stand and lecture someone about addiction, but that still bothered her. She didn't like not being able to impose her will on someone and she felt that familiar feeling in her gut again. That gnawing feeling, but this time it was even worse, as if there was really something inside of her abdominal cavity, gnawing on her organs, and clawing at her skin, looking for a way out.

She knew she would have to leave. She couldn't stand not being in control of everything and she was certain if she stayed, the pain in her gut would only get worse. Whether psychological or physiological, she didn't want any doctor telling her something she didn't want to hear. She, like Frank, also knew it was too late for her to change. She thanked him for his candid answer and told him how much she enjoyed his company and that she hoped they could continue to have these lunch dates for a very long time to come. He said as long as he could walk, he'd be there. She didn't tell him that she may have to send a car for him. For on that day, she decided that she would build another house for herself to live in. One that overlooked the Savannah River. She always liked the river.

She announced her plan for building a house on the river to Reuben that night. He just looked at her and quietly said that was a good idea. She was looking in his eyes as he talked to her and she could see he wasn't even there in the room. His eyes appeared vacant and as if they were looking off into another world.

In a voice just above a whisper, he told her that he knew she had always liked the river and building a house there would be something special. "A nice place to live," he mumbled, as he walked by her and into his study. He wanted to tell her that he wished he could move with her, but he couldn't leave even if he wanted too. There were too many other people living here now that he had to deal with. Others, less informed, would suggest that he just needed some rest. But they would be wrong because they didn't understand what it meant to live in a haunted house. A house haunted by a dead author obsessed with death and with the images of those people he had killed. All of them and, now, Melissa.

At first, he wasn't sure what he was seeing. Just a shadow from the window out of his peripheral vision. When he turned his head to look, there was nothing there and he thought he must have imagined it. Eventually, the images became clearer, and he saw her, standing at the doorway of his study. She watched him reading before she disappeared, walking away without making a sound on the wood floors. Sometimes she sat next to him while he slept, so that when he awoke, he saw her, for just a brief moment before she faded away like morning fog.

He saw her in every room of the house. Always there for just a second to make sure he was aware of her presence before she disappeared. He yelled at her asking what she wanted, but she never responded. She never even moved her lips. She was just there. Watching him from a distance.

"You were wrong," he cried out to her one day when he saw her in his study. She didn't move. She just stood there silently and looked at him. "You said I would end up breaking your heart, but that was not the case. You ripped mine out of my chest. Now, what do you want from me? You know I can't give it to you. Whatever you want, I am incapable of giving it to you. But, tell me anyway. Tell me what you want! Your presence is not comforting. And if you are here on an angelic mission, I'm afraid you will be disappointed!"

Her head twisted around so that it mimicked the way it looked on the day she died. He felt the anger within his body growing and he picked up an antique copper paperweight and threw it against the wall where she was standing. The paperweight went through her image and penetrated the wall, wedging itself there for a moment, before it fell. He heard it hit the floor and he laughed.

"That was our first fight, Melissa," Reuben said out loud to the now empty room. "Our first and last fight. I will leave that hole in the wall as a reminder and I will not ask you again why you haunt me. Though it seems rather obvious, I learned from my mother long ago to never to assume anything. So, I ask, even though most of the time I already know the answer.

"But be forewarned, I have other visitors within this house and like you, they come and go like smoke," he said as he began laughing again.

"Like smoke, but not your father's tobacco smoke. It's a different kind of smoke and I suggest you stay away from it and from them. They will frighten you. My mother is leaving this house and soon it will just be me and whatever else decides to pop in here and announce its presence in some form. But so be it; '*for a man is never more truthful than when he acknowledges himself as a liar.*' You can find that quote in an autobiographical book over there on Samuel Clemens, next to his 'A Connecticut Yankee in King Arthur's Court.' Both very good reads," he said as he left his study and went looking for something to eat.

For the next six months, Reuben immersed himself in expanding both the family businesses and the ICE program. Focused on work, he was not haunted by his past or by anything or anyone in the present and his spirit was uplifted and unencumbered. When the Cayman account balances reached forty million, he reminded his mother that was originally a ten-million-dollar investment.

"I didn't exactly double the money on the sale of the house in Boston, but I did make good on my promise to you that I would make thirty million on the ten-million-dollar investment. Didn't I?"

She simply nodded her head. She didn't want to say anything that would encourage him or make him angry. So, she said nothing.

"You should be happy, Mother. That didn't happen by accident. It took a lot of foresight and planning, by me and by you. You had the foresight to make sure that I got my MBA and a law degree. I had the foresight to see an untapped market that was full of demand. Better than peaches, don't you think?"

"Yes," was all Marigold said as she forced a smile and tried to control what she really wanted to say.

"Yes? That's all you can say? I'd think you would be very proud of your accomplishment."

Marigold felt the animal clawing within her stomach. Before she could say anything, she glanced toward the fireplace and noticed the fire iron. She immediately felt the fire in her stomach disappear, almost as if she had been doused in water. She gathered herself, changed the subject and told him that her house was almost finished and he should come see it. She would be ready to move in about another month.

Reuben told her that was wonderful and suggested she should have a big party once she moved in. They could use it to announce his new plans for the ICE program. She said she would prefer not to do it there. She didn't want a lot of publicity about her new home. In fact, she didn't plan on telling anyone else about her new location except Frank and Mary. He said he understood and would try to go by soon and take a look at it.

Marigold said her idea of a perfect housewarming party would be to have a picnic at the new house with him, Frank and Mary. She would plan everything. She was so excited as she told him about the view from up on the bluff. The entire back of the house was glass and looked out over the river.

"You know what they say about living in glass houses, don't you mother?"

His mother nodded her head.

"Make sure you keep the stones hidden, especially if you are drinking," he said as he walked away.

And just like that, the excitement she had about the picnic was gone. She walked into the sunroom and poured herself a scotch. She stared out the window into the gardens. I want a lot of roses up there around the patio, she thought. A lot of roses and tea olives. I love the smell of tea olives.

Reuben needed to keep enlarging his business footprint in Augusta so that anyone watching could see he was still growing his empire and making lots of money. He decided to focus on several businesses that often went overlooked by those with his level of education. The only problem was, he would be competing against some of the city commissioners in these business endeavors, but he didn't care. He felt immune from anything that they could do to him now that the ICE program was so successful. He could hold that up against their records on the council, should they elect to get into one of those discussions that were frequent, but went unseen behind closed doors.

He bought several car washes, one downtown and one out in Evans and renovated them, making them more of a car detailing business than his competition provided. All he needed were better wash units, better training, and an extra two hundred thousand-dollars in labor costs. He knew those costs would be more than offset by the one cost for the service. Forty-two dollars would get everyone the same high-level wash instead of charging the various prices for levels of service that the competition offered, with very little difference noticed. The service was so successful that within three months his competition had lost over half of their business.

When the owner of the other car washes confronted Reuben about it, he took a few moments to explain to him how the free market worked. If you offered a better product than what was currently available and if that better product was cost competitive and more service-oriented, for example like picking up a client's car, washing it and delivering it to them at work, then customers would most likely go where they were getting more for their money.

The commissioner stormed away while Reuben laughed telling him that he would probably make about one and a half million dollars from those two car washes in the next eighteen months. Three months later, the commissioner sold his car washes to an Atlanta businessman who was more interested in the land than the business and razed the property to prepare it for future development. The commissioner later learned that the Atlanta businessman was a friend of Reuben's.

During this same period, Reuben informed Mary that they would be ordering flowers from Central America and discontinue ordering them from the local nursery. He told Mary they could get them for a much lower price, even factoring in the transportation cost. Reuben knew that the owner of the local nursery was the brother of another commissioner, but again he didn't care. He felt impervious to anything that they could do to him.

The nursery only lost five percent of its business due to Reuben's change, but it managed to piss off another commissioner. Reuben knew that both of the commissioners were probably plotting together to try and think of something that they could do to hurt him. But like so many of their discussions on operations within the city, he knew that they would be just as unproductive.

Reuben also informed Mary that they would start selling Bonsai trees. They were very popular and he felt people would buy them if they were priced right. He had a good wholesaler in Atlanta that they would use. They wouldn't make a lot of money at first, but most of their customers would be repeat buyers and that is where they would make a profit. His best estimate was that they would make over $250,000 with those two changes to the floral shop. If he was right, he would give her a five thousand-dollar bonus and all the employees a one-thousand-dollar bonus. Though there was some grumbling at first, all of that disappeared at the end of the year when everyone was holding their bonus checks.

Just before Marigold moved out of the Tamer Lane house, she invited Frank over for one last lunch. She was planning to tell him about her new house during their visit. As usual, their lunch started out in the sunroom with a large scotch and discussions that centered on the flowers, shrubs, or trees that were in season at the time.

After the first drink, they always poured themselves another before going into the formal dining room where lunch was served. Frank told Marigold he often felt like he had died and gone to heaven when he came over and had lunch with her and that made Marigold smile. Today they were eating chicken salad made with pecans and cranberries. Marigold asked Frank if he had any nut allergies and he replied only when his family was around. Marigold laughed and immediately choked on a pecan.

She couldn't catch her breath and Frank didn't know what to do when he saw her struggling to breathe. He pulled out his phone and within a minute Enoch was in the dining room performing the Heimlich maneuver on Marigold. The pecan came flying out of her mouth, and though her breathing wasn't quite restored to normal, she was now getting oxygen into her lungs and to her brain.

Enoch knew she was having a panic attack from almost dying and asked Marigold if she took anything for her nerves. She said yes and whispered to ask Frances. Before he could ask who Frances was, Reuben came into the dining room. He was shocked to see Enoch kneeling there next to his mother and asked what was happening.

Enoch quickly explained and Reuben ran upstairs to get the valium that his mother took when the scotch wasn't sufficient to manage the day. He held her head up and gave her the pill with some water and told her to breathe slowly. He began to rub her arm and started reciting "Annabel Lee" to her.

"It was many and many a year ago, In a kingdom by the sea, That a maiden there lived whom you may know by the name of Annabel Lee; And this maiden she lived with no other thoughts than to love and be loved by me." As he finished the first stanza and started the second, Marigold's breathing was already returning to normal. But Reuben didn't stop until he had finished the entire poem. Marigold leaned over and hugged her son.

"Okay, okay, the old woman lives another day," she said as she got up and sat in the chair.

"Damn, Miss Marigold, that scared the beejesus out of me and it ain't easy to do that. I called the only person I knew that could help you and he came running. I think it's a damn miracle that he was there. A damn miracle," Frank said as he took his drink and turned it up. "Think I'll get another one, Miss Marigold. Can I get you one?"

"No thank you, Frank," she replied. "But you could introduce me to this huge man that saved my life and didn't break me in half while doing so."

"Name's Enoch, ma'am," he said as he held out his hand. "Your son and I go back a few years. We have been business partners in the past. Came up here to see him. He sure is making quite the name for himself."

Reuben had known he would see Enoch again one day. He was just surprised that it had been a whole year since Trayzon had died and now he was standing in his dining room, after just saving his mother's life. If he had wanted to kill me, he would have been here much sooner, Reuben thought. Or did he purposely wait for a whole year and then come looking for me? That would have been much smarter and Enoch was very smart. Even saving my mother's life and then killing me, that would be something Enoch would do. Listen to yourself, Reuben. Enoch didn't tell Frances to put pecans in the salad. Do not give substance to the ethereal dispositions of the past.
Yes, Henry told me Enoch would not be happy about Trayzon's death, but does he look like a threat to you or anyone at this moment? There is a calmness about him that suggests he is here for another reason besides revenge. In time, you will know. Don't show him that you are bothered by his presence. Instead, you should be thanking him for saving your mother's life.

"I'm sorry, Enoch. I let myself get caught up in what just happened. Thank you," Reuben said as he shook his hand. "We should celebrate. Should we fly to Paris, or would lunch and a beer suffice?"

"Lunch and a beer would be enough for me," Enoch replied.

"I don't think I can go out of the country, Mr. Reuben," Frank said. "Though Paris does sound nice."

"I have an idea," Reuben said. He returned in a few minutes with two Heinekens and a bottle of scotch.

"I was saving this for a very special occasion and I believe coming back from the dead qualifies as one of those," Reuben said as he gave the bottle to his mother to inspect.

"That is Glenlivet aged fifty years single malt. That bottle cost a little over forty thousand dollars, but it will be worth it today. And Enoch, here is a beer for you. I know you prefer that. Frances will be bringing more food so that we can have lunch with my mother and Frank. But first," Reuben said as he picked up four crystal tumblers, "a toast."

Reuben waited for his mother to open the bottle and allowed her to pour the drinks. He raised the glass of scotch in his hand.

"'Because I feel that, in the heavens above,
The angels, whispering to one another,
Can find, among their burning terms of love,
None so devotional as that of "Mother,"
Therefore by that dear name I long have called you…'

"And to the fortuitous presence of Enoch and another day of life. Thank you," Reuben said as they each touched their glasses.

Marigold could not prevent the tears from running down her cheeks though she tried. She smiled at Reuben and took a sip of the scotch. She wasn't sure if it was the fact that she was alive or the scotch itself, but it was the finest tasting whisky she had ever had. As she wiped away the tears, she thought about what Reuben had said and took another drink. The whisky was even better with the second sip.

"That was beautiful, Mr. Reuben," Frank said. "And this whisky. There can't be any better in Heaven. I sure as hell know there isn't any better in this world."

"That was from a poem Edgar Allan Poe wrote to a woman he loved dearly and believed was more of a mother to him than his own. And I agree with you, Frank. This is excellent scotch and I'm not even a scotch drinker," Reuben replied. He didn't have to ask his mother what she thought. He knew as he watched her pour herself a little more without offering it to anyone else.

"What do you think, Enoch?"

"It's good. Trayzon would have loved it."

There it is. He brought him up without me even mentioning it, Reuben said to himself. Just allow the conversation to continue without injecting the paranoia that continues to circulate within your brain.

"Where is Trayzon?" Reuben asked.

Enoch took a drink from his beer and paused for a moment before he responded. "He's dead."

"I'm sorry to hear that," Reuben replied. "How did he die?"

"A stroke. I thought you would have known," Enoch replied.

A stroke. What a brilliant and poetic way to tell me that you know I killed him. You are so clever, Enoch. I have always thought that. But what aren't you telling me? Before Reuben could contort any more synapses wondering, Enoch said what he needed to hear. "Yes, I thought Henry would have told you. I told Trayzon more times than I can remember that he smoked and drank too much. He was killing himself. I was right. He was a stupid dumbass who was always going to die at an early age."

“Who is Trayzon?” Marigold asked.

“My former business partner,” Enoch replied, just as Frances came in with more plates of chicken salad.

Marigold took another drink of her scotch. She didn’t want to know any more about Trayzon or Enoch or the business relationships they had with her son. She didn’t have to ask. She understood and her appetite for food was now gone. She was surprised that everyone at the table couldn’t hear what was going on in her stomach, but she knew she would be eating nothing else today. She would have to drink a great amount in order to drown that animal that was clawing at her stomach trying to get out. She reached over and poured more of the Glenlivet into her tumbler and offered Frank another drink, which he was more than ready to accept.

He’s here to talk to me about a deal of some kind, Reuben said to himself. That’s why he said “former” business partner. He always understood what I was doing. He even tried to warn me from the very beginning about what I was getting into and what I would have to do. Whatever it is he has in mind, it will probably be very worthwhile for me to listen.

“Would any of you like to see my new house?” Marigold asked as she finished her drink. “I was going to tell you about it earlier Frank, but then something happened that prevented me from saying anything. I may suggest to Frances to keep pecans out of the chicken salad in the future.”

“You’ve built a new house? You’re moving away from here? I sure will miss coming here for lunch with you,” said Frank disappointedly. “But I’d love to see it, Miss Marigold.”

“You don’t have to worry, Frank. I am moving away, but it’s not too far and I don’t want to give up our lunches together.”

“What about it, Enoch?” Reuben asked. “I’ll fill up a cooler of beer and we can sit up there and look out over the river and talk.”

“Sounds nice. Can we take some of this chicken salad with us? It’s damn good.”

“Of course,” Reuben replied. “You’ll probably be saving my mother’s life a second time by eating it all.”

Marigold grabbed the bottle of Glenlivet and in a low voice told Frank to bring the bottle of Macallan too. Reuben smiled as he heard his mother whisper. It’s not as if we can’t see you have both bottles. But you deserve whatever you wish to do today. The grim reaper can choke on his own pecans he thought and grinned as they climbed in the car.

The road that led to Marigold’s new home was unmarked. A stone mailbox at the entrance to the driveway was the only indication that a house was nearby. The road twisted and turned for half a mile through a dense forest before coming to a large bronze gate attached to a natural stone wall. Two huge weeping willows hung down over the wall and the edges of the gate.

Marigold told them that the wall wrapped around the entire property all the way to the edge of the bluff. After going through the gate, the road became less forest and more landscape. Large boulders and beautiful trees and flowers followed the curvature of the road. Several very old live oaks and a half dozen large dogwoods had been transported there by truck and planted with a crane and backhoe. A five-million-dollar budget can allow one to do things like that.

The view over the river was as stunning as Marigold had described. The scene was also beautiful from inside the house through twenty-foot windows that stretched up to the ceiling of exposed oak beams. Electric blinds enabled Marigold to block the view when she wanted and she made it a point to demonstrate how they worked. Reuben told her that was a very smart idea and complimented her on the beautiful house. She wasn't sure if it was his words or the whisky and valium combination, but she felt very content as she continued the tour for them.

Stepping out onto the marble patio, Reuben told his mother that the view was even better than he imagined. You could walk right up to the edge of the bluff and look down onto the river. This would be an easy way for someone who was drunk to kill themselves, he thought, but refrained from sharing that with anyone. One near-death experience in a day was enough for all of them to contemplate, especially his mother, whom he could see was enjoying showing off her new home.

"Damn, Miss Marigold," Frank said. "You know when I said sometimes I feel like I died and gone to Heaven when I come over to your house? Well, I believe I just got a bit closer. Might be as close as I ever get."

They all laughed and Marigold went over and patted him on his hand. "Thank you, Frank. I do love it. Why don't you make us a drink with the Glenlivet and you and I can sit here and enjoy the view?"

"Yes ma'am," Frank replied.

"I'm going to check out the house some more if you don't mind," Reuben said as he smiled at his mother. "I need to find a place for the right piece of art for a housewarming gift."

"A very large St. Claire would be nice," Marigold said.

"Of course it would." Reuben laughed and then turned toward Enoch. "Would you like to look around some more Enoch?"

"Yes, very much so."

Reuben retrieved a couple of beers from the cooler and handed one to Enoch. As they walked around the house, Reuben was amazed at the simplicity of the home when compared to the house his mother had lived in her entire life. Simple, however, did not mean cheap.

"Damn, this place looks like one of those million-dollar homes on HGTV," Enoch said.

"It does, doesn't it?" Reuben replied as he inspected the large ceiling beams. He ran his hand over the marble countertops in the kitchen and noticed they matched the marble on the patio. The floors were large panels of oak that matched the ceiling beams.

What continued to surprise him, however, was the simplicity of the design. His mother had gone from living in a forty thousand square foot mansion to what he guessed to be about a four thousand square foot home. There were only essentially three rooms: a great room and kitchen combination that looked like it belonged in a resort lodge and two huge bedroom/bathroom suites at either end of the house.

"My mother has always had very good taste," Reuben said as he looked at Enoch. "But what a hypocrite I've become. I'm standing here looking at what is at least a four-million-dollar home, but probably closer to five, and thinking how simple it is. Simple? There is really nothing simple about this house. To suggest it is simple shows how jaded I have become."

"Lots of fucking money does that to people."

"Yes, I suppose it does. What can I do for you, Enoch? Tell me what brings you here besides saving my mother's life."

"I was thinking that you might be ready and interested in helping me turn thirty million dollars into three hundred million."

"That sounds like a very dangerous enterprise, Enoch."

"It is and not a lot of people could accomplish it. But from what I know of you, I believe you can."

"Did you know that Trayzon, if spelled with an i, is Haitian Creole for traitor?"

"He would have probably killed you one day."

"And Enoch is Hebrew for dedicated and learned. Are you aware of that?"

"You like words, don't you Reuben?"

"Words have no power to impress the mind without the exquisite horror of their reality."

"Poe?" Enoch asked.

"Yes."

"Tell you what. Why don't I hang around here for a little while and we can continue to talk about my idea? I think you'll see that I can help us both achieve our goals."

"Perhaps you can," Reuben replied. "Perhaps you can. But I will need to know your last name."

"It's Jones."

Of course, it is, Reuben said to himself. He told Enoch they probably needed to get home before he had any more to drink and was unable to drive. He knew Frank and his mother would sit out there all day unless he prompted them that they needed to go.

"Man, it's such a beautiful day, you ought to let her have one more drink out on that patio. That's something to see out there. And she is drinking a forty-thousand-dollar bottle of scotch," Enoch said.

"True, and you're right. One more for the road, as they say. You know, I'm afraid I may have to hire someone to stay with her when she moves up here. If I don't, I may be writing her obituary sooner than I planned to."

Within two weeks, Marigold had moved into her new home. He tried, but Reuben couldn't convince her to hire a live-in assistant to help her with day to day activities. She knew by day to day activities Reuben meant he was afraid she would fall or drive off the bluff drunk. She told him Frances would be enough help and told herself that she would prove to him that he was wrong.

After all, she didn't show him the secret room behind the pantry, with the door that looked like a wall, complete with shelves and food on it. Inside, the room looked like a distillery showroom in Scotland. There were four rows of glass cases filled with bottles illuminated by recessed lighting. Six small alcoves lined with stained glass mirrors displayed other special bottles and made the room look more like a place of worship than a place to store liquor.

And he didn't know that she had already set up daily dinner deliveries from their restaurants. No, she wouldn't make a fool of herself and fall off her patio. She knew she would be fine. Each day she seemed to love her new home even more. And every week, she picked up Frank for their lunch date and had a taxi return him home. She even showed him the secret room and told him that he needed to keep that to himself. Frank just shook his head and said that wouldn't be a problem. Though he didn't say it, he wanted to tell her he was used to keeping secrets like hidden rooms. Must be something in their blood that makes them need to do things like that, he thought.

Each day Marigold woke up in her new home, the gnawing feeling in her gut became less and less. She realized that getting out of that house was one of the best things she had done for herself. And she spent the rest of each day convincing herself that what she thought was the truth.

Soon after Marigold moved away, Reuben called the mayor and told him he was planning a party at his house to announce some new plans for the ICE program. He asked him to invite the media, the commissioners and anyone else that he wanted there and added that he would be very happy with his announcement. The mayor warned Reuben not to embarrass him as he had already pissed off two commissioners and he didn't want another fight where he had to defend him. Reuben told him not to worry. He would be very pleased with "his" ICE program's success and the plan for the future.

Over a hundred people attended the party. Enoch stayed in the background and watched Reuben work the room. That was his idea and Reuben agreed with him but told him to be prepared to talk to the mayor and some of the leaders in the community before the night was over. Enoch said talking to drunk politicians was not difficult for him and that he would be ready.

The mayor got everyone's attention and began talking about how successful his ICE program had been. He introduced Reuben to the crowd, thanking him for his leadership. Everyone roared with approval as Reuben walked up onto the raised platform where the band had been playing.

"I can never start to speak about the ICE program without thanking two very important people. Mayor Parkland for the opportunity to lead this program, and my mother, Marigold Broadwater, for providing me with the drive and the ability to succeed."

Reuben allowed the people to clap as he glanced at the mayor and his mother, who was sitting at a table with Frank and Enoch. She had refused to come without Frank and Reuben told her that would be fine. He had already planned to invite Frank anyway because he would be mentioning him in his speech. Marigold told Reuben to make sure he didn't embarrass either one of them.

"I would also like to recognize Julia Johnson and William Lance, the first two recipients of our ICE scholarship programs. Julia recently graduated from Augusta Tech as a radiological sonographer and is already working at one of our fine hospitals, and William is doing his internship in radiological technology at another one of our hospitals. With their degrees, those two young people took themselves out of poverty into a position where they can, and will be very productive and successful members or our community. You can hear it when you speak with them and see it by the career paths they have chosen. Healthcare jobs that will enable them to help others through some of their worst days. Let's give them a big round of applause for their success and compassion."

Enoch surveyed the room and observed how Reuben commanded everyone's attention. He understood why he had been so successful running a heroin distribution center from his house. The way he had developed his persona among the leadership of the community was brilliant. But those leaders were unaware that five tons of heroin used to be fifty feet below the very floor they were standing on. And unaware that the person speaking was also known as Bix in some other circles. It made him smile as he sipped his beer.

"I would also like to give you an update on our Marigold Art Consortium. It has been operating for almost two years now. In that time the consortium has sold thirty thousand-dollars-worth of art. Fifteen thousand of that went to the artist and the other fifteen thousand has gone into our Habitat for Humanity funding project. If you haven't already met them, some of the artists are here tonight with examples of their work out on the sun porch. I encourage you to meet them and to buy some of their art. They are very talented young men and women. I promise you; you should buy some pieces now because it will only become more expensive later."

Everyone laughed before he continued. "J.R.R. Tolkien once said, 'How do you move on? You move on when your heart finally understands that there is no turning back.' I didn't know Tolkien could look into the future, but he must have had that ability because I can tell you, the ICE program is truly moving forward. I am announcing today, that instead of one fifty-thousand-dollar scholarship to any of our schools in Georgia, we will now have two each year. In addition to those, we will also offer a full four-year scholarship to Georgia Tech and another to the Savannah College of Art and Design!"

The crowd was up on their feet and cheering before the words were barely out of his mouth. The mayor was even standing, along with several commissioners he had been seated with. It seemed the whole room was smiling and happy. Except for his mother, who was sitting at her table staring at her son.

"These new scholarships could not have happened without my mother," Reuben went on. "Let's just say she 'knows' people at those two universities and has provided them financial backing when they needed it over the years. Regardless, without that woman you see sitting over there in a humble manner, Marigold Broadwater - my mother- these scholarships would not have happened."

The crowd erupted into another round of applause and Frank leaned over and whispered to Marigold to stand up. She reluctantly stood and smiled and waved to the crowd. The recognition was nice though, she thought, as she looked around the room and saw everyone smiling at her while they continued to applaud. As the applause grew, she realized it was very nice and she loved all the attention she was receiving. Reuben knew even without Frank's urging his mother would be standing up and smiling. He had framed the speech so that would happen.

"But we are not finished. As you know, when asked to help with the ICE program we pledged money for the building of six new homes. Five on Laney Walker Boulevard and one in Royal Manor. In fact, the handsome man standing next to my mother lives in the house in Royal Manor. His name is Frank Miller. I know he lives in a neighborhood that still needs improvement but I wish you would go by there and see Frank's house and garden. The house is beautiful, inside and out, and the landscape that Frank has created is amazing. Please wave to everyone, Frank, and take a most deserved bow."

Reuben's mother smiled even bigger when her son mentioned Frank and she clapped along with everyone else as he bowed and waved to the crowd. With each word, Enoch became more impressed with the way Reuben was able to create a feeling within the room. As the clapping started to subside, Reuben continued.

"As I said, we are still not finished. So, this year, my mother and I are pledging an additional nine hundred eighty-five thousand dollars to go along with the fifteen thousand from the art consortium profits for a total of one million dollars for the construction of five more new homes on Laney Walker and one more home in Royal Manor. The home in Royal Manor will be built on the opposite end of the neighborhood so that we can make sure everyone within that environment can see what is happening to it. Let everyone who lives in that neighborhood and drives along Laney Walker see and feel the changes happening that we can all be proud of. Like the others, the homes on Laney Walker will be new homes for the families displaced from the destruction of the old apartment complex in Royal Manor. But this time, the house in Royal Manor will be built as a duplex and will become homes for two homeless veterans that I have already identified with the help of the Salvation Army."

The applause was deafening as everyone stood again. All eyes were focused on Reuben as he looked over the crowd. It seemed like each one of the eyes he was looking into was like a spotlight shining back on him. Now for the finish, he said to himself, as he smiled.

"Robert Louis Stevenson once said, 'Don't judge each day by the harvest you reap, but by the seeds you plant.' I encourage everyone in this room tonight to go back home and plant marigolds in their yard, this year and every year. They are beautiful flowers and they always brighten the garden where they are planted. That's what we have done with our ICE program and just look around you to see how beautiful that garden has become."

Reuben turned to his mother and for the second time in less than a month, he could see her wiping away tears as everyone stood up and applauded. Regardless of what she thought she had done to her son, tonight she felt as if everything she had done had purpose and meaning. She had taught her son to succeed and everywhere she looked that evening, all she saw were examples of his success.

It took almost an hour for Reuben to work his way through the crowd to where his mother still sat with Enoch and Frank, accepting the accolades of the people that came by. She remembered Reuben saying he wanted to change the narrative of their family. She hadn't liked it when she heard him say it then, but she basked in the words she heard now.

"You ever think of running for office?" Enoch asked.

The mayor came up behind Reuben. "What did I just overhear and who did I hear that from, may I ask?"

"Mayor Parkland, Enoch Jones. Enoch Jones, Mayor Parkland. Enoch is a personal trainer I've just employed," Reuben said. "A personal trainer and an advocate for my well-being."

"Is that a fancy way of saying bodyguard, Reuben?" the mayor asked.

"You know me, Mayor. I am a humble man of few words but I do live in a dangerous neighborhood and Enoch's stature is sort of a suggestion to some people to re-think what they might be inclined to do otherwise," Reuben replied.

Enoch smiled. Shit wouldn't stink if it fell out of Reuben's mouth he thought.

"Pleasure to meet you, Mr. Jones. You are a very big suggestion," he said as he reached out and shook Enoch's hand. "Just how big - if you don't mind me asking?"

"Don't mind at all," Enoch replied. "Six-nine and a half and 301 pounds."

"Wow. Did you play sports?"

"No, never did. I was always afraid I'd end up hurting somebody."

Beautiful, Reuben thought. If he is indeed here to kill me, at least I will know it will be done by someone that I enjoy being around.

“And a pleasure to meet you, Mr. Miller. I have to admit I haven’t seen your house in a while and I need to get back by there and see your landscaping.”

“I’m there every day, Mayor, rain or shine. Come on by,” Frank said.

“And Marigold. My God, I don’t know how to thank you for everything you’ve done for our community. Not just with the financial resources, but for giving us this son of yours. Everyone talks about change but very few people actually create it. You and your son are within the few category.”

Slick as shit politician, Enoch thought. If someone didn’t believe human cloning was possible, they were mistaken.

“It was a helluva of a speech, Reuben. Very impressive. But I would like to talk to you if you have a minute. Is there someplace private we can go?” Mayor Parkland asked.

“Well, this house is forty thousand square feet, so I’m sure there is a place we can find some privacy. Frank, would you mind taking the mayor to the study? I’ll be right there after I talk to my mother for a moment.”

“My pleasure, Mr. Reuben. This way, Mayor,” Frank said as he led him away.

“Well, mother, what did you think?”

“You have a gift, Reuben, that very few people have. You have done what you set out to do. I doubt anyone else in Augusta could have accomplished what you have. I only hope that you haven’t sold your soul in order to achieve it.”

“‘Nearly all men can stand adversity, but if you want to test a man’s character, give him power.’ Abraham Lincoln said that over one hundred years ago. He was right. I won’t say I haven’t been tested, but so far, I’ve been able to overcome the obstacles that were placed in my way.”

Marigold didn’t want her son to define what those obstacles were. She was afraid of the answers, knowing that she would probably be on that list and even more afraid of the other things that her son would divulge.

“Thank you for the kind words, son. Now go to the mayor. You don’t want to keep him waiting.”

“I’m not worried about the mayor any longer, Mother. Like the first life lesson you taught me, I know who the boss is. He is no longer my boss. If I ran for Mayor against him, I would win in a landslide and he knows it. I allowed him to be the author of the book, but I wrote all of the words. The people would realize that fairly quickly. At least the vast majority of them would. There will always be a small portion of the public that will continue to feel they are victims and listen to those who tell them they are.”

Marigold reached over and patted her son on his cheek as Frank returned. "Frank, let me show you the house. I don't think you have ever seen all of it. I think I know where there is a bottle or two of some very good scotch. Not as nice as the bottle my son gave me the day I died, but I think you and I will enjoy it." She put her arm through Frank's as they walked away. Reuben then turned to Enoch.

"I'm not sure whose liver will shut down first. But perhaps they never will. Maybe they just both possess the genetic makeup that will let them go on forever enjoying expensive scotch."

"There are worse ways to die," Enoch said.

"Indeed there are," Reuben said. "Would you like to accompany me to the meeting?"

"I was hoping you'd ask. I'm looking forward to it. My money's on you."

"Thank you, Enoch. My money is on me too."

The mayor had been joined by the two commissioners that Reuben had pissed off. He was certain they would be there as he introduced them to Enoch and then asked the mayor what he could do for him.

"Reuben, the ICE program has just been amazing. The homes, the scholarships, the pottery consortium, and the activities you have done for the kids; all of that has been just inspiring. And now those two new scholarships, along with the six new homes. Everything is just really beyond belief."

"I hear a but coming," Reuben said.

"How much will those new homes cost?" the Mayor asked.

"Eight hundred twenty thousand, fully furnished. The construction costs have gone up and the duplex will cost a little more. So that gives the city one hundred eighty thousand in discretionary funding."

"That's a lot less than the discretionary funding that we got last time," the mayor replied.

"Yes, eighty-six percent less, to be exact."

"Well, Reuben, that doesn't sit too well with me or the commissioners. We need that money to help other people in our district and throughout the rest of the city."

"'Double, double toil and trouble;
fire burn and caldron bubble.
Fillet of a fenny snake,
In the caldron boil and bake.
Eye of newt and toe of frog.
Wool of bat and tongue of dog.
Adder's fork and blind-worm's sting,
Lizard's leg and howlet's wing.

For a charm of powerful trouble,
like a hell-broth boil and bubble.'

"Are any of you familiar with those words? Never mind, you don't need to answer. It's from 'Macbeth.' City Hall reminds me a lot of that play," Reuben replied.

"How's that?" Mayor Parkland asked.

"The discretionary funding. What did you do with it the last time besides throw it into a witch's brew that accomplished very little? For the most part, you do nothing but fight amongst yourselves, concerned that a white district gets something, then a black district needs to get something better and this goes back and forth every day, every month, every year. Being black does not entitle you to anything any more than being white entitles you to anything. But none of you see that. In fact, I'm sure if I asked one of the black commissioners to throw the eye of newt into the cauldron, they would go off looking for the former speaker of the house's eye. Not because they are ignorant, but because they have an infantile notion that would be justice. It's absurd and tiresome and I will not fund that type of idiotic victim mentality to the degree that I once did."

"Now hold on just a damn minute," the former owner of the car washes said and approached Reuben with a finger in his face.

"No, I won't hold on. Did you not learn enough about the free market when you complained about the carwashes I built? You are a preacher in a small church, but I don't believe you understand what you are reading from or what the words truly mean. You are a sanctimonious pulpit manipulated by strings of ignorance. And I would be careful the next time you approach me in a threatening manner. My friend Enoch here may believe he needs to do something to protect me and I am afraid when he does that, someone might get hurt.

"And Mayor, who do you think the people were applauding for in there - you or me? Who has done all of the wonderful things you mentioned, you or me? Who has given over a million dollars to the city to do with as they wish – and plans to give even more? I wonder what the Augusta Chronicle would say if I asked them to investigate what happened with that money. Who has built those nice homes in the worst neighborhood in town? The mayor's ICE program or Reuben Broadwater? I don't think you want to have that discussion in public."

"Mayor, we don't have to stand here and listen to this pale-ass rich son of a bitch talk to us like we are nothing," the other commissioner said.

"No, you don't," Reuben replied. "But before you leave, let me give you something to remember that Samuel Langhorne Clemens once said, 'Never argue with stupid people, they will drag you down to their level and then beat you with experience.'"

Mayor Parkland smiled through his teeth as he answered. "You are right, Reuben. Thank you for the discretionary funding and for what you're doing for our community. We appreciate it. I think it's time for us to go now gentlemen," as they left the room.

"Son of a bitch, Reuben," Enoch said as he tipped his beer toward him. "You put those fuckers in their place, didn't you? Black politicians. Just pimps, most of them. I'm telling you, you need to listen to my plan. Hell, I'm not sure if I'm looking at Reuben or Bix. They both are some bad mother-fucking dudes. Cut your head off without you even knowing it, with a sword or a sharp word. Both of them just as effective."

"'The rich rob the poor, and the poor rob one another.' Isabella Baumfree said that or as she was better known, Sojourner Truth. A woman born a slave who became a symbol of freedom and a very well-known abolitionist. She said those words over one hundred fifty years ago and they are still just as relevant today. All politicians are pimps for the most part. It's a shame that there are those who still feel like something is owed to them or think that people can only rise up from poverty with programs that are for the most part set up to prevent them from doing so. Look at the people in the new homes on Laney Walker. They are proud of what they own. They were given a hand up, not a handout. People want something that they can be proud of. Have you ever seen government housing that looked like people were proud of where they lived?" Reuben asked.

"No, but it's a helluva good drug market and I got the right product for them. I just need to show you," Enoch said. "And once we introduce it, we are going to make a shit load of money. And you can do with your money as you see fit. I just want a small piece of it. Just twenty percent."

"Twenty percent of three hundred million is sixty million."

"Yeah, it is. Got to pay the royalty fee for the idea, man."

Reuben smiled. "We'll talk about it later. I've got to get some rest. Will you watch over the house and make sure everyone gets out of here okay? Especially Frank and my mother?"

"No problem, Cube."

"Cube?"

"Reubix cube. That's what you are, man. The Reubix cube."

Reuben smiled. I never thought of that when I picked that jazz musician's name. That's clever, Enoch. Witty. Yes, I won't mind it at all if he ends up killing me. I enjoy being around this guy.

"Hey, Cube. You do know the mayor and those two pimps are going to come after you because of the way you talked to them?"

"Yes, I am aware of that. I know that there are those who call me a friend to my face, only to call me an arrogant prick behind my back. But those that mistake knowledge for arrogance or carelessness always make a horrible mistake. A mistake that becomes a teachable moment and always leaves them with a painful financial memory, so that their lapse in judgment is seldom repeated. Good night, Enoch," Reuben said as he turned and walked away.

Reuben was asleep as soon as his head hit the pillow. And though he went to sleep pleased with what he had accomplished that evening, he was awakened by accolades that arose from a restless spirit.

"Magnificent speech," Reuben heard the familiar voice say as he sat up in his bed and looked toward the corner. He could see the smoke coming out of the darkness but he could not see Edgar's image, nor could he hear the squeaking of the rocking chair.

"I fixed that nasty squeaking. Just needed a little tweaking and some resin and wood oil that a carpenter acquaintance of Virginia's told me about. I'm afraid the squeaking of the rocking chair is going to be the least of your concerns as time elapses."

"Why do you say that?" Reuben asked.

"The voices. The multitude of voices that will start to gather in your head will drown out everything else. The voices of the dead are often heard way beyond their death. I'm afraid your friend Enoch's plans will only increase the strength of that chorus."

"I have only killed three people."

"Only three people, you say, as if one is acceptable. My good friend, you have killed hundreds more. The heroin that went from your cellar into the streets was not free of risk for those that purchased it. It was, at times, the last act of a troubled life. I have seen it way too often in mine. You have been fortunate to be able to separate that part of the world from yourself, but your mind knows it exists. It always knows."

"Fucking straight as an arrow, EP," Reuben heard from the other corner of the room. Trayzon was sitting in his leather chair at his desk.

"This fucking bottle of scotch cost forty thousand dollars? Are you shitting me? Can you believe that, EP? I am going to get all up in this shit," Trayzon said as he turned up the bottle. But the severed spinal cord prevented him from swallowing and the whisky just flowed out of his mouth.

“Fuck you, double zero. Can’t even enjoy an expensive bottle of scotch ‘cause of your ass. You’re going to pay for that, asshole. I promise you, you are going to pay for that.”

“I probably will, Trayzon. But I won’t listen to either of you anymore tonight. Maybe we can continue this conversation another time,” Reuben said as he got up from his bed.

“You god-damn right we ain’t through talking, you mother-fucking ninja-freak professor white son of a bitch.”

Quite a sentence, Reuben thought as he went over to his mother’s room and opened the drawer where she kept her valium. He took three of them, followed by a large glass of scotch. Within thirty minutes he was deep in a dreamless sleep.

It was almost 10:30 before he woke up the next morning. He sat on the edge of the bed for a moment and thought about the events of the prior evening. He got up and looked at himself in the mirror and realized he needed to take a shower. I don’t know how she drinks that stuff the way that she does, he thought.

When he came downstairs, most of the house was already cleaned up and back in order from the party. He didn’t see anyone he knew except the owner of the cleaning company.

“Morning, Mr. Broadwater,” Nick said. “We should be finished in about thirty more minutes. Heard it was one heck of a party. Read in the paper what you said. Quite impressive what you are doing.”

“Thank you, Nick,” he replied. “Have you seen a very large black man by the name of Enoch? It would be hard to miss him.”

“I did and you are right. He’s a very big man. He said he was going out and that if I saw you before he got back to tell you he had something to get, but he’d be back around lunchtime. And I saw the newspaper on your lawn and picked it up for you. It’s in that sunroom if you want to read it.”

“Thanks, I appreciate it.” Reuben fixed a fruit and protein shake and sat down to read the paper and began to laugh. Only one sentence mentioned the mayor and the rest of the article about the party was about the charismatic Reuben Broadwater, the director of the ICE program. They even included the quote from Stevenson and his words about planting marigolds. When he noticed the author’s name, Melissa Grant, he dropped the paper.

“Am I going to act like this every time I see the name Melissa?” he asked out loud as he looked down at his shaking hands. Thinking of Melissa, he remembered some of the meditation exercises that they used to do. He got down on the floor and closed his eyes and tried some relaxation techniques.

He really didn't think it would help, but it did. He felt a calming presence in the sunroom with him that he welcomed. He could even smell the perfume she used to wear. He wasn't sure how long he sat there before he heard someone coming toward him. He opened his eyes and couldn't believe what he saw. The necklace he gave Melissa in Alaska was in his hand. How did it get there? He must have gotten it out last night just before he went to bed. But why didn't he remember that? He stared at it for a moment before he heard Enoch's voice.

"You okay, man?"

"Yes, I'm fine," Reuben said softly as he placed the necklace in his pocket.

"I figured you meditated. Fits in with everything else I know about you."

"I used to do it a lot more. I think I'll try to rediscover my love for it. How are you this morning?"

"I got something for you," Enoch replied. "I put it in your study. Come on, let me show it to you."

Reuben wasn't sure what to think as he followed him. If it was a Rubik's cube, he wouldn't have had to put that in the study. Unless it was a really big one. Yeah, maybe that's it.

The birdcage was at least six feet by eight feet and inside it was a very large black bird.

"That right there is a raven. Not a crow. Not a blackbird. A raven. Smart birds. Has a three to four-foot wingspan and is about two-feet from head to tail. This one has been domesticated though. It doesn't mind being in that cage, I am told. Has a lot of different sounds too. Not just that caw sound you hear with crows. I mean, you are living on Tamer Lane. You quote the man all the time. I just figured you needed something that would represent, you know."

Reuben wasn't sure what to say. The bird watched him approach without moving off its perch. It turned its head from side to side as if it was evaluating Reuben. When he got near the cage, it spread its wings out and let out a sound, unlike any bird he had ever heard. Reuben jumped back and the bird placed its wings back next to its body.

"What do you think, man?" Enoch asked. "I gotta tell you, I've not ever seen one of these in anybody's house before."

"Yes, that wouldn't surprise me in the least. I'm afraid Enoch, you are going to make me into quite the eccentric. How did you even get the cage in here?"

"Comes apart. Not that hard. You can't get to some of your books, I know, but I didn't know where else to put it. And I think it's pretty dope in here."

Reuben continued to stare at the bird as Enoch kept talking.

"Ravens are omnivores, but they prefer meat. So, I got some mice and some seeds and grains that the guy I got him from said he'd like. You need to kill the mouse before you put it in the cage. They prefer to eat dead things. Sorta like vultures in that regard. The mice are in a plastic case, just take them out of the fridge, snap their necks and throw them in there or maybe let them sit outside in the sun a while. That's what the guy said he did. So, Cube, you cool with it?"

"I don't want to say anything to offend you, Enoch, as I'm most appreciative of all the trouble you went to in order to get this. Understanding my love of the author's work and what stands before me is the representation of his most famous poem. It's very overwhelming at the moment. So, give me a day or two to adjust and then I'll tell you," Reuben said as he put his hand on his shoulder. "But believe me when I say this, I truly appreciate what you've done."

"No problem," Enoch said. "And by the way, I didn't do that to the wall over there. That hole was there."

"Yeah, I know. I put that hole there. I was having a bad day. I was reminded of some things that I'd rather forget."

"I get it. It's hard to do sometimes, man. Sometimes that shit don't ever get out of your head."

"Yes, someone else was telling me just that very thing recently. He had suffered a lot in his life and had done things he wasn't proud of. It tortured him his entire life."

"Shit. What did he do to make it stop?"

"He wrote about it and then died."

"That's fucked, man."

"Yes, it is," Reuben replied. "But enough of this morose conversation. Let's go out. Let me take you to one of my restaurants. I'm in the mood for some spicy food that I think you might be fond of."

"Oh, hell yes. You can't get it too hot for me."

"We'll have to talk to Rodrigo about that. I'll bet you he can." The bird let out a loud noise again and Reuben cringed. I'm not sure I'll be able to get used to that, he thought. "And wild and high, over hill and dale, was heard the loud cry of the Banshee's wail," he said to himself as he walked out into the sun.

Rodrigo was able to find something that was too hot even for Enoch. They all laughed together as Enoch drank several glasses of milk before he could talk again. They also drank quite a few beers before they left. When they got back to the house, Reuben walked right into the study and looked at the bird.

It didn't seem to have moved at all since they left. Reuben asked Enoch where the mice were.

Enoch showed him and Reuben grabbed one, snapped its neck and put it in the microwave for a few minutes before tossing it into the cage. The raven pounced on it and began pecking out one of its eyes. "Never let that bird out of the cage," Reuben said to Enoch. "I believe he has a penchant for eyes and I would prefer to keep mine. And remind me to get another microwave in the morning. I don't believe I'll be using the one in the kitchen for anything else except this bird."

They enjoyed a few more beers that afternoon and Reuben finally asked Enoch what his big plan was to make all that money he had talked about. Enoch said people had been trying to come up with a way to combine heroin and Ecstasy in a form that was safe enough to inject in the veins without killing you and he had finally figured it out. With that type of product, Enoch thought they would make a ten-fold profit over the cost, instead of only three times.

Reuben said that was very interesting, but he would have to think it about it some more and would let him know within a week. "But tonight, we let the banshee wail and howl at the moon," Reuben said as he got them some more beers.

"How many beers have you ever had in one sitting, Enoch?" Reuben asked as he handed him another Heineken.

"A case," Enoch said. "But I was pretty high on some other stimulants, you know."

"Yes, I can imagine," Reuben said. "Do you think we might need two or three pizzas if I were to order them later?"

"Depends," Enoch said as he pulled out a joint. "Let's do this and then ask me."

After smoking the joint, Reuben ordered four pizzas.

The next day, Reuben and Enoch went to Laney Walker to see where they would soon be building the new houses. He asked Enoch if he would be interested in overseeing the construction with him. Enoch said that sounded cool and Reuben agreed to set it up. The next day, they broke ground on the site and Reuben introduced Enoch to the foreman with instructions to teach him everything he knew.

As Enoch worked at the construction site, Reuben began researching the effects of injecting Ecstasy in the veins. Enoch was right. It was very dangerous. He heard the bird squawking as he read the information and went into the study. Poe was walking around the cage studying the bird.

"Animals have a keen insight to both the living and the dead," he said as he looked over at Reuben.

"It appears that I have that same profound insight, though I'd prefer I did not," Reuben replied.

"I do not think you will ever lose that sixth sense," Edgar replied. "Not with what you are planning with Enoch."

"How do you know all of this?"

"'Why, what care I? If thou canst nod, speak too. If charnel-houses and our graves, must send those that we bury, back, our monuments shall be the maws of kites.' I can recite 'Macbeth' too, Reuben."

"You feed the bird then," Reuben said as he left.

Later that evening, Reuben told Enoch he was going to keep the bird even though it would require some renovation of his study to accommodate the cage. He also told him that he decided he would buy ten million dollars-worth of the heroin and Ecstasy. If it performed as well as he said and they made one hundred million on the deal, he would continue with the business.

Enoch was gone for a week before returning in the middle of the night with a U-haul filled with their product. Reuben sent the money to the account he was given. "I need to try this before we distribute it, Enoch," Reuben said when they finished storing away the heroin.

"Sure, Cube. I can help you with that. I figured you'd say that. I brought my junior chemistry set so that I can mix up a batch for you. I promise you will not be disappointed. You'll be in another world, believe me."

"Oh, I do believe you, Enoch. I'll try it tomorrow morning. I don't mind exiting this world for a while and trying another one. Perhaps it will be less crowded there."

"Yeah, sure, Cube. I hear ya," Enoch said as he watched Reuben go up to his bedroom.

The next morning Reuben got up early and went out for a walk. The Royal Manor neighborhood looked like an empty Hollywood movie set. The construction of the new home just added to his initial impression as it looked like a new façade was being erected on the set.

He walked over to Laney Walker to check on that construction and smiled. These ten homes are just the beginning. And they will be just as effective a barrier around my home from any assault by the local government officials as the other more colorful images were for those that exist in a darker environment. This could be a beautiful part of town again, he thought. If only those elected to serve the people would realize that and actually do something about it.

Once he reached home, he called his mother and apologized for not calling or visiting her for a while, but explained that he had been very busy.

"It will probably be a few more weeks before I can get by there, I'm afraid. I'm working on a book and some other business and I can't be disturbed. But I should be free in about two weeks, and I'd love to take you anywhere you want. We can even fly away for the day or weekend if that's what you want to do."

"Oh, I'd love to go to Charleston for the weekend. Will you take me there?"

"Of course. That sounds perfect. It will give me a chance to buy that housewarming gift for you that I've been negligent about. And it helps so much in buying you a gift, to have you there telling me if it is indeed one you want."

Marigold laughed. "You act like I'm difficult to buy for!"

"No, you aren't difficult to buy for at all, provided I follow your directions."

"Two weeks. I'll be expecting to hear from you," Marigold said.

"Yes, two weeks. I look forward to it," Reuben said as he hung up.

Within about twenty minutes, Enoch came up from the tunnel with a straw-colored vial in his hand.

"Is that a urine specimen you're carrying around?"

Enoch smiled. "You better hope not. I'm afraid that wouldn't be very good going into your veins."

"I'm not so sure the other alternative is going to be any better."

"Believe me, man, you are going to love this shit. I call it Pandora, 'cause you are about to see some pretty wild shit."

"Very catchy name, Enoch. Did you know that it was supposedly a jar that the Gods gave her, not a box? But like her, I am just as curious. I only pray that I am not abandoning hope as she did."

"What? I don't remember that in the movie," Enoch said.

Reuben smiled.

"It's not important. Let's get started, Enoch. Follow me," Reuben said as he went into his study and laid down on his couch. "Do you notice the bird never takes his eyes off of us as we come into the room?"

"He's looking for food," Enoch replied.

"I suppose he is. Will you feed him after you take care of me?"

"Yeah, man. I got this."

Enoch cleaned off Reuben's arm as if he was about to draw blood from him. He opened the little packets of isopropyl alcohol and wiped the area in the middle of his elbow.

"Were you in the medical field, Enoch?"

"No man, never went to college."

"Why is that? I think you would have done very well in college."

"Just wasn't for me. Too many arrogant pricks there," Enoch said and Reuben laughed.

"Get ready for blast off," Enoch said. "See you when you land."

Reuben felt the warm liquid seep into his veins and within seconds his eyes were closed. He felt as if he had been administered an anesthetic, only he was awake. Awake, but in a different world. He saw colors explode within his head like he was watching a fireworks display at night. His body felt like it was floating and he could see the couch beneath him as if he had been turned around and was now suspended by some unseen cords.

Then he heard something snap like he had been cut loose from the cords, but he didn't fall. His body just continued to float. When he moved his arms one way or another, his body followed their movement like they were wings. He pushed his arms down and felt himself propelled toward the ceiling and as he touched it, he flipped over and used his feet to push himself back toward the floor.

It was then he heard a voice from above and he saw the raven. The bird flew around the room several times and then floated down toward his desk and stared at him. "Before you ask, I am telling you right now, I am not going to be saying 'Nevermore' to everything we talk about," the raven said. "That's why we stay away from college campuses. Every time someone sees one of us they yell out, 'Nevermore!' It's become quite tiresome."

"You're not real. You are just an image created by this drug. I'll have to tell Enoch that his concoction will do really well because everything feels so real. It's like I am really talking to a blackbird."

"If it's not real, try and get out of that cage," the bird replied.

Reuben realized he was standing inside the bird's cage. He tried to open the door, but he could not. He walked around the cage looking for a way out but he couldn't find one. Then another voice began talking to him. He recognized the voice and turned to see Poe sitting in a chair beside his desk.

"Will you help me get out of here?" Reuben asked Poe.

"Out of where?"

"This damn birdcage."

"That is not a birdcage. The bird suggested it and so now it is what you see. You feel trapped therefore you imagine a device that traps you. He is quite cunning, that bird. All you need to do is walk forward."

Reuben did as Poe suggested. His body moved through the metal bars of the cage and it appeared to come apart, split into sections by the bars as he walked through them, reforming and reconnecting as he found himself outside of the cage.

"That was amazing," Reuben said.

"Anything is possible within this world you have traversed," Poe said. "I have been here many times."

"It's like a dream," Reuben stated.

"Or a nightmare. It is sometimes hard to distinguish between the two. Dreams are very frustrating. At times you think you understand what they mean, only to realize you were awake the entire time," Poe said as he pulled out his pipe and lit it.

"Are you suggesting I am awake?"

"Don't listen to him," the bird said. "His brain is addled. He does nothing but lament the loss of his wife and smoke opium to try and forget. He will not help you. Only I can help you."

Poe leaned back in his chair and lit his pipe as the smoke floated over toward the bird. The bird flapped his wings and coughed as it hopped around on Reuben's desk. Just as it got close to Poe, he pulled out a fireplace poker and swung it at the bird. He squawked, flew up in the air and then perched on the edge of Reuben's desk.

"That bird can be quite peckish at times," Poe replied. "Guard yourself if you continue to speak to it."

"He doesn't have a choice," the bird said. "I am here and you are here. He will learn more from me than you. And he knows it."

Reuben sat down on the couch and put his head between his hands and closed his eyes. He then looked up at Poe.

"I do not wish for either of you to argue. I would not enjoy that."

"No, I suppose you would not," Poe said. "I will remain civil if the bird states that it will."

"I do not promise anything," the bird said.

"Birds have no honor," Poe said. "And they can be quite arrogant at times. Looking down upon us as they fly unhindered within the sky."

"I understand that feeling," Reuben said as he looked at Poe. "Do not curse the bird for it. It is not the only animal that does that."

"He awakens," the bird squawked.

"You have both said that now," Reuben replied. "Suggesting that I'm awake, but I know that I'm in a world that only exists within my mind. Influenced by the drugs that are circulating through my body."

"In some ways, you are more awake now than you have ever been," Poe replied. "But it is a tightrope you walk. Awareness can become unconsciousness and unfortunately, you sometimes realize that transition has taken place much too late."

Reuben watched the bird as its feathers started falling from its body. As the feathers fell onto the floor of the study, the bird's body began to twist and turn and Rueben could hear the hollow bones cracking as the shape became unrecognizable.

"What is it doing?" Reuben asked as he looked over at Poe.

"Changing," Poe said.

"Changing into what?"

"What it always was," Poe replied. "Death."

Reuben saw what appeared to be Pat Sajak standing next to the desk, where the bird once perched. He began looking through his books and then pulled several down from the shelves. "I always loved 'The Leatherstocking Tales,'" the man said as he turned and looked at Reuben.

"You look more like Pat Sajak than Death," Reuben said.

"I hear that a lot," Death replied. "It's always a shock when I remove the cowl and they see my face for the first time. Sort of like that scene in Star Wars when you find out Darth Vader is Luke's father. Surprise! I bet you didn't expect this, did you? That look on their face; it's priceless."

"But you are not what I envisioned Death to be."

"Hello? Did you not just hear me? That guy over there said I was a raven."

"Then this ebony bird beguiling my sad fancy into smiling,
By the grave and stern decorum of the countenance it wore,
Though thy crest be shorn and shaven, thou, I said, art sure no craven,
Ghastly grim and ancient Raven wandering from the Nightly shore;
Tell me what thy lordly name is on the Night's Plutonian shore!
Quoth the Raven, Nevermore."

"Damn, I really like all that dark symbolism. Damn good, Edgar. Damn good. But I am not a raven any more than I am Pat Sajak. I do get that comparison a lot though. It's amazing how popular that show is and even though the people are dead, the image is comforting to them, so I assume it."

"It's not comforting to me," Reuben replied.

"Want me to go back to the raven?"

"I'm not sure," Reuben replied.

"Well, while you are deciding, do you mind if I sit down and re-read a few of these books? You've got some good ones. Read them a dozen or so times, but I never tire of them," Death said as it sat down in a big leather recliner next to the bookcase.

"Then you are here symbolizing my death?" Reuben asked.

"Why, yes I am, Reuben," he said. He smiled before he tilted the recliner back and opened a book.

"This is just a warning. A hallucinogenic journey brought on by my obsession with you," Reuben said as he looked over at Poe.

Before Poe could respond, Reuben heard another voice. One he didn't want to hear.

"Reuben. Reuben. Look at me. I am here now because I loved you once," Melissa said as he turned toward her.

She sat down next to him and he could feel her hands as she held his.

"'*Miracles are a retelling in small letters of the very same story which is written across the whole world in letters too large for some of us to see.*' Do you remember saying that to me?"

"Yes."

"You never told me who the author of those wonderful words was, but I know now. It was C. S. Lewis. I have come to know him quite well. He has given me a lot of comfort since I died. He was so smart, with such a vivid imagination. In some ways, he reminds me of you. The Reuben I knew, but not the Reuben that is here right now. The Reuben that spoke those words about miracles, I loved. The Reuben that sits here with me now, I abhor."

"Don't say that Melissa. Please do not say that," Reuben said as the tears fell down his face.

"I'm sorry, but you chose this path."

"I chose it because you left me."

"Do you realize how much that hurts me to hear you say that? That I am the reason you killed people and distributed tons of heroin that killed even more people? You only say that because I'm here now talking to you. You would have always chosen the dark road you find yourself on. I came to say goodbye to you for the last time, Reuben, and to leave you with another quote from Mr. Lewis. '*Each day we are becoming a creature of splendid glory or one of unthinkable horror.*' I pray that you understand the meaning of that before it's too late," Melissa said. He felt her hands slowly leaving his until the image of her was completely gone. He looked around the room and saw that Poe was also gone. The only one left was the thing that looked like Pat Sajak sitting in the chair reading a book.

"Stop reading those god-damned books!" Reuben screamed at Death. "Bringing her back to me to speak those words is pure evil. You are not comforting at all. You are just hurtful and mean-spirited!"

Dcath put the book in his lap and shook his head at Reuben. "I am neither evil nor good; I simply exist. I am only a guide. Where we go from here, depends on you. But you already know that."

For a moment all he saw was Pat Sajak sitting in a leather recliner reading a book until another voice suddenly called out.

"I told your mother-fucking white ass that wouldn't be the last time you saw me. How have you liked this party so far, you shit-ass, white-fucking son of a bitch?"

"I haven't liked it all, Trayzon, and I'm not surprised you're here too, reminding me of how much I despise it."

"You fucking right I am here now reminding your smelly white ass of what Hell looks like. But you are just getting the visitor's tour for right now. You are about to pay full admission and get to see all the fucked-up shit that's in that fun house. And that name is really a misnomer. It ain't fun at all. And the price of admission is fucked up. But you ain't got to worry about a thing, Cube, 'cause you can afford it."

Reuben closed his eyes and thought about everything that he had seen and heard as Trayzon's words replayed in his head. Misnomer? Cube? He wouldn't even know what misnomer meant. And he never called me Cube. Those are Enoch's words. He looked up and saw a ghoulish figure laying on the sofa. It resembled the image of someone from a German concentration camp and he grimaced. The image grimaced too.

He raised his hand and the image he was looking at raised the same hand. There were cuts on the face, and on the hands and legs of the image, and though the blood looked dry, other fluid was leaking from the cuts. All Reuben could think of was Macbeth and the cauldron of the witch's brew. And then he heard Enoch's voice as he continued to look at the horrifying image staring back at him with a hollow look in its eyes.

"Reuben, that image you are looking at is you. That's your own reflection in a mirror that I rolled in here soon after I injected you with the drugs. At this point, I'm not sure how well you can see, but if you can focus, you'll see that those cuts on your body have some nasty greenish-yellow looking shit oozing out of them. Those are some real bad infections you've got.

"Your body is septic and is shutting down. You haven't had anything to eat or drink in two weeks. And I don't know how many times you pissed and shit on yourself. With all that bacteria around, well you probably aren't going to make it much longer. I'm actually surprised you lasted this long, considering all the heroin and ecstasy I've been shooting in your arms and that infection getting worse each day. Now the port that I put in your veins has tried to shut itself off several times. It's pretty infected too and I know the end is near.

"You are dying, Reuben. I'm not sure how much you can hear and understand so I will say it again. You have been on this couch for two weeks.

It smells pretty fucking bad in here and I just came in one more time to wake you up with a little meth. I wanted you to have a few lucid moments before you died so that you would know who did this to you. Your smart, arrogant ass always thought it knew what was going on, even right up to the end as you tried to lecture me on mythology, but you didn't know shit. Jar. Box. Who gives a fuck? Tom's real name wasn't Henry. It was Raymond Moss and he worked for me. He came to you about Trayzon because he wanted you to kill him. He knew what I would do when I found out you killed my brother.

"He knew I would eventually figure out who told you, but he was betting on you killing me before I got to him. But that dope-head made a fucking bad bet on that plan. I placed his head on a pike at one of the movie sets where they film 'The Walking Dead.' Got that idea from you since you had already done that down here. I knew they would just think the murders were linked to the same killer. So, I appreciate that. Hell, they didn't even find it for three days and when they did, they fucking freaked out. I know a little about chemistry and made sure it didn't really start smelling for seventy-two hours. Easy enough to do and easy enough to get on the set without them knowing anything. Stupid mother-fuckers thought it was just something they had made. Several of the set designers put a load in their pants that day, I heard. Wish I could've seen that.

"Once they figured out who it was, the GBI didn't really pursue it, just like they did with the head here in Augusta. They knew Raymond to be in the drug trade and figured he had pissed off the boss. They were right about that. He pissed me off when he told you about Trayzon. I was going to let Trayzon rob your ass, but I told him not to kill you. Fuck you up good, but not kill you. But then things changed. You changed the narrative. I knew from the very first time we met you didn't believe Trayzon was the boss. You always thought it was that fucker, Raymond, just because he was the white guy that I allowed to look like he was the boss. You see what you want to see. You have known that your entire life, but you ignored it.

"You talk about the life lessons that your mother taught you and one of them was knowing who the boss was. But in the end, it appears you didn't learn shit. All that fucking education. Two fucking PhDs. Well, I got several PhDs too. They are called Google that shit, mother fucker!

"You like words so much that you even tried to lecture me about the meaning of Trayzon's name. You arrogant asshole. He was named Tray after my uncle that was killed in Nam and the 'zon' just happened because my mother thought it sounded good with Tray. That's it. No Creole Haitian bullshit.

“And then you went even further after I looked interested in what you were saying. Telling me what the Hebrew meaning of Enoch was. You dumb mother-fucker. That’s not even my real name. My real name is Gideon P. Jones. Let me tell you what those words mean. First of all, Gideon means Destroyer. Second of all, The P stands for Pharaoh which means King. And last but not least, you put them all together and you have Gideon P. Jones, which means you are going to fucking die.

“The good news for you is that no one but me knows who killed Trayzon. Hell, in my world, you could have a hundred or more to choose from. That’s why a picture of your stinking rotting ass isn’t all over the internet. I don’t need to show them what I did to the person that killed my brother. You know, creating that psychological protective barrier of fear around me and those that fuck with me. Yeah, I know about that shit too.

“I suspect the only person that will see your rotting ass will be your mother and the people she pays to remove it. I can’t wait to read what she says you died from. I know there will be an article in the paper glorifying your death and saying that you died way too soon. That pimp-ass mayor and all his friends will say how sorry they are to see you go when all they will be sorry about is seeing your money go away. I doubt your mother will be as generous in that regard. She ain’t trying to create some image that hides what she really is. She don’t give a fuck anymore. Man, that is some nice house she made up there looking over the river though. I’m going to have something like that one day. Not sure where yet, but now I know what it will look like. I’ll add a few fountains though. I like fountains and waterfalls.

“I do have to give you props for how you created your image. Never seen it done better. You were fucking incredible at creating that philanthropist shit and you actually did some good things. Those houses and the art consortium and taking those kids out on nice trips. That was good, man. Real good. The kids got the money from their art. The houses are fucking nice. And those trips. Hell, I bet that was the first time some of those kids had ever done the things you took them to do. And Frank. Yeah, Frank. That was good too. Good man, Frank. It’s a good thing you introduced him to your mother. She will need his ass once she finds your rotting corpse.

“But those scholarships. I know why you did it, but you knew what would happen as soon as you put them out there. And you were right. Commissioner Moe and the three stooges made sure who those scholarships went to. They weren’t stupid enough to give them to relatives, but you and I know they went to kids of people that knew the assholes. And I’ll bet you, the families didn’t even really need the money. It just helped the son of a bitch spend less and paid off a favor of some kind. Regardless, you did some things right.

Even so, you and I both know your heart and mind weren't concerned with doing the right thing. There ain't no way the ends justify the means here. You are way too fucking smart to not know that.

"I hope you can appreciate everything that I've done for you. If you weren't the main character in the story, I think you would have loved it. 'Cause just before I get the fuck out of here, I'm going to let four vultures out of that cage I brought into your study to house that fucking raven in for a few days. I knew you'd eat that raven shit up since you loved that crazy-ass author so much. Hell, you even changed the name of your street to Tamer Lane, after one of his books. You think 'cause you got the money you can do whatever the fuck you want. Well, you probably could have, if you hadn't decided to go ghetto and get in the drug business.

"Those birds have been getting real antsy in that cage over the past few days. They know you are almost dead because they can smell your rotten ass. Too bad you don't have any neighbors that give a fuck about you because as soon as they would knock on the door, they would smell the putrid stench that is leaking out of your body like shit from a pig farm. It's revolting to me, but it's making those fucking birds real hungry.

"Oh, by the way, don't worry about them finding any drugs here. I took that shit out of the house a long time ago. I may retire after I sell that shit for about forty million. Yeah, pretty sure I will. But here's one last quote for you. Reuben. 'No matter how smart you think you are, there is always some asshole who is smarter.' That's a quote from Gideon P. Jones. All it cost you to hear it was forty million dollars. That and your fucking life."

Reuben heard the scraping of metal and the birds screeching as they were released from the cage and began trying to fly around the room. They were fighting with each other in such a small space and soon realized that they could not fly. They also soon realized there was no need to. Instinct suggested that they continue to fight with each other, but the familiar scent of death filled the room and they all began moving toward it in a tentative but determined manner.

Reuben saw them approaching and could no longer see anyone else within the room. The person that was in the recliner reading 'The Leatherstocking Tales' was gone. The other images he once saw in the room were also gone and all that remained were the ugly heads of the large birds that moved closer to him.

He felt the first one peel away some of his skin. He tried to scream, but nothing would come out of his dry mouth. And because the first one met no resistance, the others soon joined in. He felt them tearing away flesh and then his fingers and toes. He closed his eyes to try to block out what was happening.

One of the birds pulled away some of his stomach and intestines, and suddenly he saw something that took away his pain. He was standing next to his father at Victoria Falls. He turned toward him and told him he was sorry and hoped he would forgive him. His father smiled and warned him to be careful because he was walking too close to the edge of the falls. Reuben fell down into the tons of water that poured into the river. He felt the power of the spectacle just before it threw his body against the rocks, shattering it apart as if it was glass.

Marigold found Reuben's body on October seventh, sixteen days after she had last talked to him. Though sickened by what she saw, she knew what she needed to do. She placed a towel around her face, retrieved her shotgun from her old bedroom, and went to Reuben's study and shot each bird. When she was sure they were dead, she walked back to each one of them and shot them again as she cursed them. She then called Frank and requested his help. He came over and removed the segments of birds and burned them in his back yard. No one questioned what he was burning.

Marigold called a physician friend at the medical college and told him that her son was dead and she needed some help in taking care of his body. She said he had died of cancer that no one was aware of and had taken his own life, rather than suffer what would be a debilitating and painful process. She did not want the community to know how he died and he told her he understood and that he would take care of it.

Her physician friend signed the certificate of death and Marigold had Reuben transported to a funeral home that cremated him immediately. She made sure that the attendants who picked up her son from the house were well paid and would continue to be so each year, provided they said nothing about the state of her son. Both they and the director, a person who was very familiar with what Marigold could do, never revealed anything about the condition of Reuben's body.

Several days after the cremation, Marigold informed Mayor Parkland of her son's death. She had arranged a press conference by the homes on Laney Walker and thought he should be there. The mayor extended his sympathy and said he would make sure that he and all the commissioners would be there as she announced the death of her son to the city.

The media was curious when they were asked to come to the Laney Walker development and were shocked when Mayor Parkland introduced Marigold and she told them why they were there. They all wanted to know what had happened and Marigold was as eloquent as her son as she described the cancer that was eating away at his body. She said he had fought it in silence, but unfortunately, had been unable to overcome the disease.

The tears that fell down her face were real and when asked about the funeral, Marigold said it would be a private affair. She thanked everyone for their prayers as she left with Frank at her side. The newspaper reports were kind in their descriptions of Reuben, as they praised his life's accomplishments and mourned his early death from an incurable disease.

Marigold and Frank were sitting on her patio drinking scotch when Frank told her he had an idea. She should make the old house on Tamer Lane a museum. An art museum, filled with the poetry and literature that her son loved so much. Marigold was touched by what a beautiful image that was and thanked him for the idea. She thought it was perfect. Frank did mention that she would definitely have to renovate the study if she was going to turn the house into a museum because it was still an awful mess.

Marigold went to Mayor Parkland and explained what she wanted to do with the house on Tamer Lane. She described Frank's idea, though she presented it as her own, stating that the home could be a landmark destination in Augusta. She promised to make it into the best art museum in the state, not only with the art collection itself but by the way in which the museum would operate. Live actors would portray authors and bring their books to life. It would be unique and constantly changing, and thus would be something that people would come back to over and over.

There were other museums in the country where actors portrayed one author or a figure from history who had lived in a particular area, but this would be better. You would be able to talk to Edgar Allan Poe, James Fennimore Cooper, Mary Shelley, C.S. Lewis, Oscar Wilde, Mark Twain, Ernest Hemingway, Velma Wallis; the list could go on forever and she would make sure there was funding to enable that.

Each room inside the house would either have art or an author, sometimes both. She would make sure that each actor was well versed in the history of the author and his writings, and ready to take questions from the audience. The art within the home would be first class and the envy of even larger cities.

Mayor Parkland nodded his head and said it sounded like a good idea but he had concerns about whether people would actually want to go there, considering the house was so close to Royal Manor.

Marigold started to call him a slimy piece of shit, but she refrained from doing so. She did what she knew she had to do in order to address his concerns. She asked what he wanted in order to make the house into a museum that the city would recognize and promote. He told her that he hoped the ICE program would continue and she replied that she could make that happen to a certain degree.

She would not build any more houses or lead outings with students as her son did. The Georgia Tech and SCAD scholarships were also not going to happen, but she would allow the art consortium to continue and she would give the city one hundred and fifty thousand dollars each year for scholarships. The mayor had dealt with Marigold many times before and knew she would not negotiate with him, so he agreed to her terms. Both of them knew that fifty thousand of that scholarship money would go right into the city's discretionary funding, but Marigold didn't care.

She also expected a concrete historical marker to be erected outside of the museum with her choice of inscription. He agreed and said it would be in place when the museum was ready to open.

After the study had been rebuilt, Marigold invited several interior designers to the house to explain what she envisioned. As they went through the house, Marigold found a letter on her vanity that she had never seen before and placed it in her pocket. After they had toured the home, she told them that she expected their design plans within a week and they assured her that they would be ready.

Marigold went into the sunroom and poured herself a scotch as she sat down and opened the letter.

"Dear Mother,

I fear that my life is coming to an end because of some of the reckless decisions that I have made. I would hope that you will forgive me for that. I never wanted to disappoint you and I am afraid that by dying a premature death, I will have done so. Please understand that you are no more responsible for my demise than the birds that fly south for the winter are the cause for the change in seasons. Believing one can control nature is folly.

I would ask that you give this necklace to Melissa's mother and give her three million dollars that I have put away in the account listed here. Please tell her that I loved her daughter more than life itself. As I did my parents. I would leave both you and Mary with a quote that I believe is most appropriate for this occasion. It is from Samuel Clemens and is as follows: 'Let us endeavor so to live so that when we come to die even the undertaker will be sorry.' Appropriate, but in my case, I fear unobtained.

I know I perhaps use too many quotes at times, but I find comfort and guidance within those words that I steal for a moment from their authors. I do not pretend that they make me more intelligent. I know they only demonstrate that I have a better memory than others.

With Love, Reuben"

Marigold read the letter over and over and tried her best to fight her sorrow with scotch, but on that day, the bottle lost. The next day, she tucked the letter in an envelope and put it away in a table next to her bed. For the rest of her life, she read that letter at least once a week and thought about her son and their time together.

She gave Mary the necklace, along with the money and ownership of the floral shop. Mary thanked her and donated all the money to pediatric cancer research. For several years, Marigold came to the store each week and worked alongside Mary making floral arrangements. When Mary died, she sold that store, but transferred ownership of every other business she still owned to the current store manager, making them all very rich and making her feel much better about herself.

She and Frank changed their weekly get-together to an every evening get-together. With each dinner, regardless of the weather, they sat on the balcony and drank and ate and drank some more as they often reminisced about Reuben. It took her almost a year to transform the house into a museum. The final piece was the marker she had inscribed to read:

The Broadwater Museum

This grand estate was built in 1908 by Absalom Wood, grandfather to Marigold Broadwater and great- grandfather to Reuben Broadwater. The estate was the home to Marigold and Reuben Broadwater for many years and over time, they became two of the most prominent philanthropists in Augusta's history.

***"Let us endeavor so to live so that when we come to die even the undertaker will be sorry"* - Mark Twain**

The museum opened with a speech by Mayor Parkland, once again thanking Marigold for her generous manner and thanking Reuben for all the things he had done for the community, many of which were still continuing to enrich people's lives. As people poured into the museum, they marveled at the beauty of the home, the art, and being able to interact with Edgar Allen Poe, James Fennimore Cooper, and Velma Wallis. Though the other actors changed every few months, Edgar Allan Poe had a permanent "home" within the study.

She stopped to read the concrete marker with Frank as they toured the museum almost every day. No matter how many times she came, she always saw or learned something new and Frank told her that he did too. He laughed and said that was because they were both getting pretty old. They both knew he was only partially right. Age and drinking lots of expensive scotch are quite effective in promoting the decline of one's memory.

Over time, Marigold found one of the original twelve editions of the Tamerlane books. She bought it for $800,000 and had it placed in the study with the Poe actor. It was encased in clear, heavy plexiglass that allowed those who came to the museum to see it but ensured its safety and value.

Marigold was right about the museum's success. It became a destination point in the Augusta area and the city advertised it almost as much as the Masters tournament. That gave Marigold a great deal of satisfaction. Ten years after she had made the museum a reality, Frank died and Marigold had no one else that she enjoyed being around. She left her house only on rare occasions, except to go to the museum. When she did go to some function the mayor wanted her to attend, she did so begrudgingly, staying just long enough to hear her name, before she left and returned home to her patio and scotch.

When Marigold was ninety-eight, she heard a young boy talking to his mother one day as he read the concrete marker at the museum. The boy asked his mother if the house was a grand estate built back in 1908, did that mean the people that lived in it were grand too? His mother said that was a very smart question and that they certainly were. The concrete marker stated so.

Marigold smiled at the mother's response. It made her think of her own mother and how she loved to smoke. So, she started smoking cigarettes and enjoyed it so much that she began having a cigarette with each drink. She smoked half a pack a day.

Marigold lived to be ninety-nine years old. Her only friend was old age but he offered her none of the attributes usually associated with friendship. Instead of happiness, he offered loneliness. Instead of a helping hand, he offered a mallet of arthritic pain. Instead of someone that listened to her concerns and offered her words of support and encouragement, he listened with a deaf ear of indifference and reminded her of disappointment and loss.

Shortly before she died, Marigold donated eleven million dollars million to charity. She set up a trust fund so that the money would be around for many, many years, and if not mismanaged, would last almost indefinitely. With her last remaining five million dollars, she set up another trust fund that would run the museum in perpetuity.

Upon her death, the newspaper ran a long article about her and the Broadwater family, describing the long-lasting changes to the city of Augusta which were due to the hard work of her son, Reuben, and the programs that were started as a result of his initiative; and of Marigold's generosity that would help thousands less fortunate for many, many years into the future. Her physician at the time was quoted as saying that she died from complications due to smoking.

I-75

He hated driving on Interstate 75 South through Atlanta. He was certain that the road to Hell was an unmarked exit ramp somewhere along that part of the interstate. He didn't want to stop for gas but he knew it would be better than to run out somewhere in the middle of that traffic and the gas gauge suggested he needed to get off now. He should have planned better but he was in a hurry.

He didn't recognize anything as he turned off onto the ramp and came to the stop light. The street that he needed to turn on became very dark while he was sitting there waiting for the light to turn green. He didn't think it was supposed to rain today, but it wouldn't surprise him if it did. It seemed like it rained every time he needed to drive through Atlanta.

There were street lights along the road, but they weren't on. The only light he could see flickered on and off from the buildings that aligned the road. He thought it looked like candles were burning in the windows making it seem as if he was driving along a road in the early 1900s before electricity became a common element in people's homes.

He had been intrigued by the ad in an email he received. It said that he should come to Jasmine Trail off of I-75 if he wanted to find out the truth. He didn't know what that meant but he was somewhat captivated by the simplicity of the statement. That was all it said. If you want to know the truth come to Jasmine Trail. No address, just the name of what appeared to be a street. He wasn't even sure if it was a street, but it sounded like one. He only hoped it wasn't some fucking politician or political group. That would be a waste of time if it was.

As he drove along, the houses disappeared and he found himself climbing up what looked to be a mountain road. How is this possible he asked himself? Is there really undeveloped land this close to Atlanta? Shit, was his answer as his car sputtered, running out of gas. He pulled off onto the shoulder of the road.

He got out and started walking though he wasn't sure if he should go forward or backward. At least if he went backward, he knew there was civilization but he hadn't seen any gas stations. So even though it looked uninhabited, he started walking forward, thinking he would run into a neighborhood eventually. It would be impossible not to. Not in Atlanta, where there must be thousands of communities and suburbs.

Walking along the road he smelled the woods and also what seemed like stale water though he saw no water anywhere. Maybe there are some ponds behind these trees, he thought. They were probably filled with decomposing leaves and perhaps some dead animals, by the way the smell started worsening the further he walked. It became even darker too. Soon he couldn't even see the trees anymore. He activated the flashlight on his phone so he could continue to see where to walk.

Then he saw it. It glowed blue and green like one of those animals that live in the dark depths of the ocean and lights up the area around them by some sort of bioluminescent organ or bacteria. The shimmering colors outlined the body and he recognized it as a female form but that was all. He couldn't see that she was smiling until she was just a few feet from him and she stopped and pointed toward two benches that were out in the woods.

A fucking ET and no one's around with me to prove it, he thought. No one's going to believe this. He snapped a picture with his phone for proof and then walked toward one of the benches. He jumped back when he stepped on something that was moving. He could hear whatever it was skittering through the leaves away from him. He sat down on the bench and waited for the woman-like thing to join him but she had disappeared. He was there all alone. Sitting in the dark. Waiting.

Then he saw the sign. It was dark, but it was there on the other bench. It said Jasmine Trail. Shit, he thought. This is getting way beyond weird. It's fucking Twilight Zone weird. He wasn't sure if he should wait around for Rod Serling but thought what the fuck. I'm here. What's the worst thing that can happen? A glowing female alien can put a probe up your ass is what can happen, you dumbshit. But his rational mind overcame the one prompted by the shot of adrenaline and he continued to just sit there, unmoving, as he looked around.

And then he started yelling. "What's the fucking truth?" After several minutes of yelling the same thing over and over like an obnoxious drunk, the glowing female looking alien reappeared. She was sitting across from him on the other bench. The one with the faded Jasmine Trail on it. Smiling at him.

"That's a good question," she said. "I hope you can find the answer this evening. Because if you don't, I am afraid that there isn't too much hope for your soul."

"You have got to be shitting me," he said. "My soul? The next thing I guess you are going to say is that you are the devil or some demon and that I have to do something with you in order to save my soul from eternal damnation."

"You are not as stupid as you look," she replied.

"Then you aren't very smart because I don't believe in this bullshit."

"Why did you come then?"

"I had nowhere else to go."

"I know that's not true. You had a choice."

"I am not so sure I did. And by the way, you never told me your name."

"My name is Abaddon."

He looked down at the phone in his hand. "Is that with two d's?" he asked.

"It is."

He googled the name and read what it said out loud.

"Abaddon – The Destroyer. Said to be the chief of demons. Sometimes regarded as the destroying angel."

She nodded her head.

"Well, I have to admit that since everyone in my life who meant anything to me has either died or left, I guess your timing couldn't have been any better."

"We pride ourselves on that."

"Who is we?"

"All of us in the Rotary Club."

"You're telling me the Rotary Club is actually a bunch of demons?"

"Just kidding. Not all of the Rotary Clubs are demons. But we are in just about every club or organization. Everywhere but the KKK. They don't need us to seduce them with the benefits that we can offer. They know all they need to know about that. There are some really fucked up souls, in that little outfit, and they will all be coming to live with us one day. They aren't going to like their burning little crosses then, I promise you.

"Oh, and I almost forgot. We are not in that Scientology church. I mean, come on. Who in the hell would believe in that shit? Amazing. Simply amazing what people will believe. We don't want to tarnish our reputation by being around them. Just a bunch of crazy nut-jobs that believe humans are immortals called thetans which evolved from extraterrestrial cultures. That's really out there for someone not taking medication. Wait till they undergo one of our audits. Failing an audit with us doesn't mean you wash the bathroom or do the laundry. It means you lose a finger or a limb or an organ. You should watch one of them. But I have to warn you, the screaming can get quite loud."

"Good to know. But I don't belong to any clubs or to a church."

"Yes, I know. That's why we are talking here now."

"Ok, if we are here to talk about me, why in the hell are we sitting here in the dark, like every cliché book or movie about demons and lost souls? It's really cold too. It wasn't this cold when I left my house or I would have brought a warmer jacket."

"Because this is the environment that you expect. It's different for other people, but for you, this is what gives our little meeting the atmosphere that you have created in your mind. It was either that or a dark cave, but I knew with your claustrophobia, you'd never walk into the cave. And the cold, well that's something I did just for my own entertainment. I like watching you sit there shivering. Suffering. It's the demon part of me that makes me all warm and fuzzy inside."

"I appreciate your thoughtfulness with regard to the cave. Very considerate. But fuck you for the cold."

She smiled again as she looked at him and when he saw her face this time, he could see a burning fire within her eye sockets.

"Really? Flaming eye sockets? Like that hasn't been done a thousand times before. Can't think of anything more original?"

"How's this?" she asked as something really foul smelling started dripping from her eyes down her cheek. It looked and smelled like diarrhea.

"The flaming eyes, the flaming eyes. Go back to the flaming eyes," he yelled as he turned his head and covered his nose, trying to keep himself from throwing up.

Her eyes returned to normal and she told him to turn back around.

"You have a real sick sense of humor for a demon."

"I am not sure that statement is correct. Just how many demons do you know?"

"Good point." For a moment neither one of them said anything while he continued to look around the darkness. He felt something bump into his feet and he jerked them up into the air. "Snakes, I'm supposing?" he asked.

"Of course. They are the perfect demon accessory. Goes all the way back to the Bible you know. The snake thing and humans. It's a love/hate thing. But I know for you, it's a really bad hate thing. So I wouldn't think too much about walking off into the woods. There are a lot of snakes out there."

"Spiders too, I would imagine."

"Of course. That one on the arm of the bench getting ready to crawl into your lap is the Goliath bird-eating tarantula."

"Are you fucking kidding me?" he said as he looked over and screamed. He swiped the spider with the back of his hand and jumped off the bench. He heard the spider fall onto the ground and move off.

The demon was laughing and he threw a bird at her. The sound of her laugh reminded him of Vincent Price laughing at the end of the Michael Jackson video "Thriller." Of course, he told himself. A female demon that laughs like Vincent Price. Makes perfect sense.

"I didn't know you were in the Rotary Club," she said.

"Yeah. I know all the secret handshakes."

"I thought so. I don't know why humans are so afraid of tarantulas. Even the one that was just on the bench. It looks scary because it can get as big as a foot across but its venom won't kill you. I am pretty sure that there hasn't been one human death due to the bite of a tarantula. But on the other hand, that black widow and brown recluse on your shoulders, those can kill you."

Though he wanted to jump, he looked at the spiders on his shoulders and told himself he wasn't going to move. He wasn't going to jump from point A to point B all night because of what sat across from him amusing herself. When she saw that he wasn't moving, he felt the spiders crawl down his arm and then down his leg until they went off into the darkness.

"Impressive," Abaddon said. "Congratulations. You just passed the spider test."

"So, what happens next?"

"Depends on you."

"Then I would like to just leave and go on back home."

"You say that, but I know you don't really want to leave. You don't want to go until you know the truth. You want to know what will happen to you when you die."

She said when I die. Shit, I thought I was already dead. I wonder if she can read my thoughts.

"Yes, I can to some degree. If there is any anger or fear associated with them, I can tell you everything that you're thinking."

"So, I just need to think happy thoughts and you won't know a damn thing, huh?"

"You are not capable of doing that."

She hit the nail on the head with that statement. Too many deaths over the past five years. Your depression and anger have led you here. I don't think this is a dream.

"No this isn't a dream. You have been having a lot of bad dreams though, haven't you? Familiar locations where ghosts or death haunt you."

"Maybe."

She smiled when he said that.

What do you say next? What can you do to get out of here? Think Joseph.

"I thought it was just a matter of truly believing. That if you believed you were saved."

"For most people it is. But not for everyone," she said and smiled. Then her mouth opened and wasps flew out of it toward him, stinging his hands and face as he tried to swat them away.

The more he swatted, the more stings he felt until he realized he needed to just stop. Just put down his hands and sit there. When he did, the wasps flew around him but they were no longer stinging. When she realized he was not going to move anymore, he watched her flip her hand and the wasps disappeared.

"Don't tell me. I just passed the wasp test."

She started laughing. "This is going to be a lot more fun than I thought."

So she doesn't know the outcome. That's good. Stay calm, Joseph. Stay calm. "You said that for most people just believing was enough, but not for everyone. How? Who? Why?"

"If you play with fire, you get burned," she replied.

"What the hell does that mean?" he yelled. Suddenly, he felt an intense jolt of pain in his hand. When he looked down at it, he saw his fingers being pushed back until several of them cracked. They dangled from his hand as if the seam in his skin had been torn apart like stitching in a shirt.

"Fuck you, goddamnit!" he yelled. He felt that same pain in his hand again and another finger cracked and hung limply from his hand.

He tried to block out the pain but it was so intense that it consumed his entire body. Then he remembered the tarantula and he thought about it on his hand. Within a few seconds, he looked down and watched it sink its one-inch fangs into his hand. But he felt no pain. The venom made his hands numb and actually gave him relief from the broken fingers.

"Oh, yes, this will be a good night," she said as he looked over at her. "That was very smart. I am impressed."

He smirked as he regained control over his pain. He asked her again what she meant by her last comment.

"If you write about demons, you get to experience demons. You write about demons all the time. You think it's just fiction and it's what your readers think too, but it doesn't seem like fiction now, does it?"

You have got to be fucking kidding me, he thought. This can't be real. It's just a dream. Well, not a dream but a nightmare. Perhaps even a hallucination brought on by all the death you have experienced, along with the new antidepressants interacting with all the other medicine. And maybe watching "The Descent." That damn movie you watched the other evening; the one your niece recommended. And you followed that up with re-watching "The Exorcist" and "Jaws." Perhaps that wasn't a such a good idea, even if you couldn't sleep.

"So, if we follow your line of thought, Clive Barker and Stephen King really saw demons. Is that what you are saying?"

"Yes."

"So again, just so I can be perfectly clear, what you are saying is there is no fiction, everything is non-fiction. That all the writers actually see what they are writing about?"

"Not all writers. There is a cut-off. But if you are writing about horror, then yes."

"I didn't hear you mention sci-fi writers or fantasy writers. Why not them? It seems like that would be the perfect trifecta."

"It's because of the Scientologists. Their entire line of books is sci-fi and fantasy. Thus, those writers of good sci-fi and fantasy are exempt."

Wake up, Joseph. Wake the fuck up.

"Oh, and I forgot about cookbooks. They see what they are writing about too."

"Yes, they do, but I don't ever see them noting at the end of the recipe to make sure they put the red velvet cake in a locked cabinet so it doesn't come into your bedroom that evening with a cake knife and impale it into your skull."

"That would make for a more exciting book, don't you think?" Abaddon asked.

"Well, a lot of horror books could be considered fantasy. And ghost stories. Come on, some of those are just love stories. Granted there are those ghosts that do sneak into your bedroom and impale you with a cake knife, but there has got to be some gray area there, don't you think?"

"Gray area, ghosts. Nice. But what you are trying won't work. You can't trick a trickster."

"Did you bring a pen and some paper? I would like to write that last line down."

"You don't need a pen. I'm certain you will remember it."

"Certain because you know the future or certain because you know I have a great memory?"

“I told you earlier, I am not sure what will occur tonight. But I can tell you this. What terrifies you becomes a part of you.”

“Again, it sounds like you’re telling me I have no choice in the matter of what we began discussing hours ago.”

“You have a choice. Most everyone has a choice, excluding those two groups I mentioned earlier.”

Think Joseph. Think.

“Why just the Jasmine Trail address without a number? I always thought 666 was the mark of the Devil.”

“If I had put down 666, would you have come?”

“That’s a good question. Not sure. Maybe,” he said as he paused for a moment to think. “Yeah, I think I would have. Anyone that has 666 as their address has got to have some balls. Or is certainly out there. Either way, I figure I would have a chance to meet someone really strange or as fucked up as I am.”

“Do I not fit that description?”

“Please don’t tell me you have balls. You are a female, right? But you are a fucking female demon, God only knows what you have there between those, what I have to admit are. very nice-looking legs.”

“God is not the only one that knows.”

“What does that mean?”

“I think you know that answer. Do you really want to play you show me yours and I show you mine?”

“No, no, God no. Even if you didn’t have a dick and testicles, I’m sure there is something else weird down there. Live some Venus Fly Trap looking thing, only with sharper teeth.”

Abaddon laughed. “You should save that for your next story, should you find a way out of here.”

She keeps saying if I find a way out of here so that means there is a way out. But what the fuck is it? Wait a minute don’t use that word fuck when you are thinking. It lets her in.

“Yes, it does let me in.”

“You do realize that if you had made yourself look like Katheryn Winnick, I probably would have taken a chance with that show me yours-mine thing.”

“I can do that if you like. But beware of what you ask for, as the saying goes.”

Joseph sat for a moment as he thought about her proposal and then realized it would not be what he envisioned. That would be too easy and she wasn't here to make things pleasurable for him. But maybe that's it. Maybe you turn things around. How do you make things unpleasant for her?

"Our Father who art in Heaven, hallowed be thy name," Joseph started. He heard Abaddon began to growl.

She doesn't like this. Go on Joseph. Go on. "Thy Kingdom come, thy will be done, on earth as it is in Heaven."

Abaddon howled and screamed when he said "Heaven."

It's working, Joseph told himself. Finish it. "Give us this day our daily bread and forgive us our trespasses as we forgive those who trespass against us, and lead us not into temptation, but deliver us from evil."

Abaddon was writhing on the bench, clawing at her body. With each swipe of her hand, a part of her skin fell to the ground and something oozed out onto the strips of flesh.

"For thine is the Kingdom, and the power, and the glory, forever and ever, Amen."

At the word Amen, Abaddon's body started to disappear as if he had just broken apart a large Etch A Sketch and the aluminum powder that formed her image, spilled out onto the ground in front of the bench, until there was nothing there but a pile of silver and black powder.

"Take that, you Demon bitch," Joseph said as he jumped up. "If you only exist because of me, then I can make you go away. So, it's been fun and everything but let's just say we don't share the same interests and call it a day. Didn't really learn the truth either but, you know, maybe another time. Like never."

Before Joseph could take one step, he heard Abaddon laughing. The pile of powder began to swirl around and within a few seconds, the image of Katheryn Winnick was there. Standing right in front of him.

"Honey, I'm home," she said as she grabbed him in her arms and pulled him close. He felt something snapping at his dick and saw Katheryn's eyes turn black and the skin on her face start to melt away until there was no head. Just a hole on top of her shoulders. From that hole came a smell that was so overwhelming it made him throw up. The smell seemed to blanket his entire body and though he tried to get out of her arms he couldn't.

All he could do was stand there and continue to throw up into the cavity where the head once was. The body that was holding him, gripped him even tighter until he had trouble breathing. Just when he felt like his spine was going to snap, the body released him and he found himself sitting back on the bench across from Abaddon.

"Demonology for $600, Alex," Abaddon said. "And the answer is: A prayer that means nothing to a demon when they are in the tormented realm."

"Well, thanks for ruining "Vikings" for me for the rest of my life. And tormented realm? You have brought me to fucking Tuscaloosa?" Joseph asked.

Abaddon laughed. "You know Joseph, I have been doing this for thousands of years, and I just don't think it ever gets boring. Isn't that amazing?"

"Yeah, fucking amazing. So, does this have an ending?"

"It does."

"And I guess if I ask, you will say it depends on me."

"Very good. Would you like to try Demonology for $800?"

"No, I don't, but I do want to explore some things with you if that's all right."

"I have all the time in the world."

"Yeah, I get that. But let's retrace something I've been thinking about. I came here looking for the truth. And then you tell me I'm here fighting for my soul. As if I am here to find out whether the path heads up or down, and if that analogy is even appropriate - is that correct?"

"It is."

"Sorta like hiking up to Mt. LeConte in the Smokies, huh?"

"If that makes things more germane for you, then yes. Your life is indeed a journey and yours is nearing an end."

"Germane? Fuck, who in the hell uses that word? Just tell me, what is it I am really fighting for? What does a soul look like?"

"It is a shadow within a shadow."

"So I guess when Peter Pan lost his shadow, he lost his soul."

Joseph looked down when he heard the rattling sound next to him. The large rattlesnake lunged and bit him on the arm, and then his shoulder and his neck. It felt like someone sticking burning hot nails into his body and he felt his heart racing. Calm down, Joseph. Make yourself calm down. This isn't the end. That thing across from you is having too much fun to end this. He closed his eyes and tried to think of something that reminded him of better times.

He remembered how his dog greeted him each time he came home. It was always as if she was seeing him for the first time. He remembered how she lay down at his feet while he wrote. His time with her was special and he then realized the burning pain was gone from his arms and face. He opened his eyes and looked over at Abaddon. She was smiling.

"I am pedantic with regard to what is funny and what isn't. And when I am not amused, I find other ways to amuse myself. Watching that rattlesnake bite you was amusing. If that is germane to you or not."

"Good words. Pedantic and germane in the same conversational exchange. I'm impressed."

Abaddon turned her head and for a moment Joseph heard the rattling again at his left but he didn't look down and it soon went away.

"So, this soul you talk about. That you have said is some sort of shadowy element within the body. When you are at the journey's end as you said in such an elegant manner, can you feel it? Can you touch it? Do you know that it's there?"

"Not in a tangible manner as your questions suggest. But let me help you. It is a key."

"A key?"

"Yes, a key that links you to God or to NeoGod."

"NeoGod. Do you mean Satan?"

"He's trying out a different name. He's known by many, you know."

"Yeah. Never heard that one though, but I bet that's a hit with the Neo-Nazis."

"They like it, yes."

"Ok, but let's get back to what you said about your soul being a key."

"Yes, that's correct. You have free choice, remember?"

"Okay, then I choose Heaven. Glad you could clear things up for me. Tell you what though, I never want to come back here. So, if you will just show me the way to get out of here, I will be going."

"I can't tell you how many times I have heard that before. Well, I can, but the number is undecipherable by you. And it's just so damn predictable. Just as you know you are dying, you reach out to God, but unfortunately, many fail to realize, it has to be a true plea for forgiveness. It's not like calling the cable company to fix your TV. And yes, before you ask, there are hundreds of demons that work there."

"I fucking knew it!"

Abaddon smiled and the colors that outlined her body, changed from a blue and green to a dark red with pink and orange hues at various places on her body.

"I am assuming by your response that my verbal choice is not sufficient. So, what next? Lawn Darts?"

"We could play Lawn Darts, but I don't think you would like the way I play it. We would be throwing darts at your dog."

'YOU FUCKING BITCH," Joseph yelled as he leaped off the bench and grabbed her neck. He squeezed as hard as he could and watched her face turn red as she seemed to lose the ability to breathe. He squeezed even harder and heard her gasp and close her eyes, only to open them a second later and smile.

He was suddenly thrown back with his arms and legs spread out and strapped onto a circle of wood. The circle began revolving and it picked up speed as he heard something hitting the wood all around him. Something sharp pierced his dick and nailed it and his balls against the wood. He screamed in agony.

"Want to keep playing?" he heard Abaddon ask and he screamed "No!" He felt the wooden circle slowing down, as it righted itself and him. He looked down and watched the dart disappear from his crotch and the excruciating pain vanished as if nothing happened.

"Fuck you. Why don't you go join a fucking circus?"

"I don't like clowns. They frighten me."

"Who the hell does? I bet there's a whole army of them in Hell, isn't there?"

"You do not want to be around them when they are having a party, believe me. They will scare the shit out of you and then make you eat it."

"You sure have a thing about shit, don't you?"

"As they like to say, the shit is just the icing on the cake," Abaddon said and smiled. "It's a very effective tool in getting your point across to those we interact with on a routine basis."

"Well, please don't do that eye thing with the diarrhea again," and Abaddon nodded her head as if she would acquiesce to his request. But standing there, still strapped to the circle of wood, he tasted something sickening in his mouth and threw up. He was puking shit and the thought of it, as well as the texture and taste of it, made him even sicker. If this was a taste of Hell, he began to cry thinking of an eternity of this. As soon as he started crying, everything stopped. His mouth was clean. Everything around him was clean.

"It appears you are beginning to understand the truth," Abaddon said.

"I know that I don't want to ever experience that again," he replied. "So, if you are doing things to me now to let me know that I want to stay away from here, consider mission accomplished."

The straps holding his wrists and ankles disappeared and he stepped down to the ground. As he walked toward the bench, he felt many things that he couldn't see touching his legs. He stopped and took a deep breath as the unseen animals moved up and down his leg before they moved away and he started walking again. He prayed he didn't step on anything and he could hear Abaddon laughing as he made his way back to the bench and sat down.

"I want to ask some more questions, Abaddon. Questions that I hope will help me find what I came here seeking."

"Good. Go ahead. Ask."

"What about the Charlie Mansons and Ted Bundys? And Hitler. The Idi Amins of the world? Do they get the full shit treatment too?"

"Yes, on Bundy and ole Charlie and any other serial killers that you refer to. The actions that they took when they were alive, are the actions that they endure in Hell. Only worse because they are forced to endure them every day. They scream in pain and anguish until we allow them to sleep and to believe that their life is again their own. Then we take it away from them again as we start anew with enhanced versions of the evil things they did when alive, now being done to them.

"And when they cry for water, we give them water. The kind of water that you smell around you. Filled with shit and other things that will grow in their body and make them sick. The torment is unspeakable. But every once in a while, we get surprised by someone. Someone like Charlie. He was so fucking crazy he started to like eating the bowl of shit we fed him every morning. He was like a fucking dung beetle so we had to find different ways to torture him. So, we started feeding him his own body. He doesn't appear to like that as much. And with regard to Hitler or Amin, you don't want to know what goes on with them, but just know they relive it every day and it's worse than the Hell they created on Earth. A thousand times worse," answered Abaddon.

"Abortion and the Catholic church. Well, any church really. How does one reconcile themselves with going through that and still believing in God and what the church teaches?" Joseph asked.

"First of all, aborted babies are untouchable. Pure innocence. We are unable to touch them. Regarding the mother, she, like you, has free choice. The abortion is not necessarily the end for her. She can seek forgiveness and receive it. It may or may not be something that comes under review at the end.

"Regarding the church, those who surround themselves in piety and harm the innocent; well, we have a special place for them. Very few of them find true forgiveness. The church itself, regardless of what type of church, it depends. Sometimes it is just another conduit for us. We might as well be there sitting in the front pew, considering some of the things they do in there. Like those nuts that handle serpents and drink poison. We are there encouraging them to do it. We find it quite entertaining.

"On the other hand, the church can be very helpful for many. Acts of unselfishness are unassailable. But even in that environment, we can be very seductive as we offer a mechanism for people to fool themselves. Going to church one day and listening about how to live, is a lot different than performing actions that show you understand what Jesus is saying. We read the Bible in Hell. We love the Old Testament stories. Not so much the New Testament ones except for Revelations. I could read Revelations every day. Love it."

"So, helping your fellow man, helping the poor are things you should do. Things that will help you at the end, right?"

"You don't do them to help yourself at the end. You do them because they are the right thing to do. Helping your fellow man from a pureness in your heart is one of the best ways for you to avoid having this discussion with me. And the poor. We don't bother the poor. They have enough problems. Well, we don't bother them, you know, unless they give us reason to. But just between you and me, always help the poor. The working poor, who still believe and follow the teachings of Jesus, they will indeed sit in a special place in Heaven."

"You keep speaking about the fact that we have a choice. But it doesn't sound like we do," he said.

"You have a choice, but that is not the same as free will. There is no free will in the world in which you live. There are consequences to your choices and requirements for many of them."

"So those that abuse themselves, they are lost?"

"Drug addicts and alcoholics, we love them. They often do themselves in before they have a chance to ask for forgiveness. It's not one hundred percent. But with regard to their end, consider Hell like Vegas. The house usually wins."

"What about the mass shooters or those who commit suicide?"

"If anyone doubted that evil was present in the world around them, all you have to do is look at the news and count up the mass shootings that occur. Here's your gun and welcome to Hell we say as we let them start shooting. Only they do not like what they are shooting when they come into our world. They try to resist but they cannot and their tears and screams are delicious. They all have something they loved at one time in their life. And the regret they feel within their body rips them apart. Figuratively and literally. It never gets old watching that.

"Those who commit suicide; that is an interesting phenomenon. They are stuck between the world of the living and the world of the dead, but they cannot enter either. Their regret and desire to die is overpowering and maddening. You would think you would be unable to scream after a while, but that is not the case. Like the mass shooters, it never gets old watching them being tortured by their decision."

"But what about God's love? Isn't that given freely?"

"It is not free. You know the Ten Commandments, correct?"

"Yes."

"Well, you are asked to follow them, correct? And I can tell you, that they are impossible to follow 100% of the time. You will screw one or two or maybe all of them up and the more you screw up, the harder it is to find your way back. And the longer you wait, the more we are able to creep into your life. Bringing along doubt or arrogance with us and then we begin the game."

"The game?"

"The game of Life - It's not just a board game anymore. I suggested that to NeoGod as a mission statement for all the new demonic spirits. He liked it. We still use it on occasion. Anyway, you need to live your life according to those commandments, in order to receive God's love. So, you see it's not free."

"But he forgives you when you ask, does he not?"

"He does. If you are honest in your heart when you ask. But most are not. They find God at the times when they feel like they are going to die and then it's just like spending a weekend in Vegas. The odds go up that we will be able to sneak in and snatch your ass to Hell."

She said the odds are there. As if there is still a chance, Joseph said to himself. She even alludes to doubt about what she's doing. She says I have a choice. I cannot doubt myself. Believe Joseph. You must truly believe.

"I believe I can find my way back. I have had a good life. I have no reason to be depressed or sad. I have loved and been loved. I believe God has been there with me all the time. Seen the bad and the good and I believe he will forgive me and welcome me home. That is what I believe, Abaddon. So, I will just get my keys and you can do whatever you have to do to send me back home," Joseph said. He pulled out his key ring with the little squirrel foot on it, swaying back and forth, that he had bought at Spencer's Gifts.

"No!" Abaddon yelled as she burst into flames. "Put it away! Put it away!" she screamed.

Joseph looked confused. Put what away he asked himself as he looked at his hand.

"Squirrels?" he asked out loud and began laughing. He pulled the squirrel's foot off the key ring and threw it toward Abaddon. He heard a loud explosion and felt as if his body was being torn into pieces as he was sucked back through the darkness. When he opened his eyes, he was sitting at his desk staring at his computer. Looking at the ad questioning anyone that read it, if they wanted to know the truth. He walked over and looked out the window.

"Man, I need to get out of the house more," he said as he wondered what had just happened. He went over to his chair and picked up the book he had been reading: "Elvis is Dead and I Don't Feel So Good Myself," by Lewis Grizzard.

"Lewis would have kicked your ass, Abaddon," Joseph said as he picked up reading where he had left off last night. "Thank you, God," he said as he closed his eyes for a moment. When he did, he saw his wife and dogs for just a second. Next to his friends and family. They were all there. Waiting.

He was asleep in the chair. He didn't know how long he had been asleep but it felt like it had been several years. The children playing at his feet woke him up. When they saw that he was awake they ran to him, asking to hear stories of his travels. They loved listening to stories of his travels. He looked down into their eyes and smiled. They looked like burning flames.

"You both have the eyes of your mother," he said.

"Tell us the story about Wheeler Road or Walton Way or Holston Avenue. Or do you have some new ones now that you have been gone? Tell us the ones that will make us laugh the most."

The roads that they mentioned were ones he had been dreaming about. Those, as well as some new ones. All the roads he dreamed about had meaning. He had traveled all of them when he went on the dream journeys, and some of them he kept coming back to because he had fond memories of them. He had paused to watch what occurred on some of them. He had stayed to cause what occurred on the others. He had to admit one thing though. His children were right. Humans were funny. Very funny when they were scared or being tormented. He liked the way they screamed. It made him laugh every time he heard it.

It bothered him though about Abaddon and that damn squirrel's foot. It was unfortunate that happened, but squirrels are dangerous animals. He would have to make sure Jasmine Trail was free of squirrels the next time he visited there.

One of my dogs died during the writing of this book. I thought it would only be appropriate that you get to meet her, seeing how she was an important member of our family for a very long time. Though death comes to all things, by writing this story about her, it helped me deal with the loss. I hope you can find as much strength in the story as I did from writing it.

The Old Brown Dog

We never knew her true age. We weren't there when she was born. She just showed up at our house. I saw her that morning when I was leaving for work, sitting there in our front yard, as if she knew this was a safe place to rest. I stopped the car and looked at her. I could tell she had left wherever she was because she knew if she didn't leave, she may not be able to do so later.

She was dirty and brown, a scrawny looking dog, with one ear standing up and the other pointing down. A filthy old gray rope with frayed ends was hanging around her neck, indicating that she had pulled herself away from wherever she had been. She looked pitiful and scared but I didn't think she looked dangerous. I went back inside and got some turkey or some ham, I don't remember now which. She looked at me with suspicious eyes as I approached with the meat. I threw it to her and she jumped back for just a second before she ran over and gobbled it up.

I had done my good deed for the day and drove on to work, knowing that brown stray would probably move on and I didn't think anything more about it. She was gone when I got home that evening but the next morning, there she was. Sitting almost in the same place as the day before. Right there in the front yard as if she knew the exact time when I would be leaving for work. I got some more food and tossed it to her and this time she didn't back away, she just gulped it down and looked at me with what I imagined was a grateful look. I smiled knowing I had once again done my good deed for the day. This time as I drove to work, I thought about her and I hoped she would be okay wherever she ended up. I had no idea that my life was about to change.

I was unaware of it, but that pitiful scared dog had found another friend that first day when she came to our house, and she was sitting there at his feet when I drove home from work that evening. I didn't know that my son had also been feeding the dog and taking care of her. He had cleaned her up and she looked like she was his dog before I even got out of the car. My son was a freshman in college at the time and had never had a dog before.

We had just moved into our new house. We had watched it being built from the time they cleared the land - our dream house out in the country. I think I may have said at one time, that when we moved into our new house in the country, my son could have a dog. I was reminded of that as soon as I got out of the car. But even if he hadn't reminded me, I don't think it would have mattered. As soon as he asked if we could keep the dog, there was only going to be one answer, even though I made it appear otherwise when I responded.

"If she doesn't have any diseases, then, yes, we can keep her," I said. The empathy for the poor animal oozed from my mouth, I know, but I was trying to maintain a level of distance. I wasn't sure what the vet would find, and I didn't want my son or myself to be disappointed. So, we took her to the vet. The doctor said she was very malnourished and might have been abused, but other than that, she was fine. That's when I knew, we had just adopted a stray dog. A stray dog that had a new name: Maggie.

In some ways, Maggie reminded me of my dog Cindy that I had when I was growing up. They were both brown mutts, but unlike Maggie, Cindy was just a puppy when we got her and she didn't come from an abusive environment. I was also much younger than my son when Cindy came into our family. I was only ten years old when we had moved to the country, but just as I had done, my father made me the same promise about moving to the country and getting a dog. I suppose it must be some sort of ancestral decree that has been passed down from fathers to sons for centuries: When one moves to the country, the eldest son of the family shall request and be given a dog.

I have no idea where I came up with the name for my dog. To this day, I don't know. There were no Cindy's in my life. There wasn't a Cindy on TV that I fawned over. It just happened. Not so, with my son. In fact, he had probably named the dog as soon as it showed up in our yard, but if he did, he never told me. My son was a huge fan of the Simpson's television show and he named the dog after the Simpson's baby character, Maggie. Looking back, it couldn't have been a more appropriate name. Just like the character on the television show, our new dog was strong, smart and very lovable. I don't think Maggie, the cartoon character, ever met a stranger and Maggie, our dog, was just the same. She never met a stranger, whether it was another dog or another human. But that didn't happen overnight.

Maggie was scared of everything in the beginning, even to some degree of the young man that had fallen in love with her as soon as he saw her. At first, she always tucked her tail when you walked up to her as if she was afraid you were going to hit her or do something bad to her. It took her a while to realize that no one in her new home would hurt her. When she understood that, she became the dog that I am sure God meant her to be.

The dog who loved being around other dogs and interacting with children. The dog whose tail wagged as she smiled and played with all of them. The dog who loved going to the dog park and had as much fun meeting all of the dog's owners as she did meeting all of the dogs. The dog who loved to go for car rides, with her head hanging out the window. The dog who loved being outdoors; running, walking, and later swimming. The dog who loved to nap, free of concerns. The dog who loved to eat, even though she gulped down her food in seconds. Looking back, I think I understand why she ate so fast. I don't think she lost that feeling of wondering when or if she would ever eat again. It was just her natural instinct to survive that was never going to be suppressed, regardless of how many cookies and dog treats she received in her new home.

When we first got Maggie, I was concerned about a dog ruining our new carpet with her bathroom needs, but interestingly enough, house training for Maggie was not difficult at all. She was very smart and quickly understood that she wasn't supposed to pee or poop in the large building she now considered a home. She learned all she had to do was go over and scratch on the door or look out the door and then look back at you and she could get someone to come over and let her outside.

My father had taught me that house training a dog just required a rolled up newspaper, and/or, rubbing the dog's nose in the soiled spot. And like my father once again, I educated my son on how we would house train Maggie. I realize now that there are better ways to train a dog, and as I sit here and reflect on his advice, I think it sounds rather inhumane.

But my father didn't know any better and I didn't either. That's what he had been taught and so that's what he taught me and so that's what I taught my son. I never liked the idea of putting the dog's nose in their waste and resisted doing so, but I did occasionally use the rolled up newspaper and or magazine. With Cindy, it worked very well and it worked with Maggie, but I regret that I didn't know better with her. I feel now that the sight and sound of that rolled up paper reminded her of the past and though it helped her become housebroken, it probably scared her too, and I am sorry for that. Thankfully, Maggie learned quickly.

Actually, I should have been somewhat suspicious of all the "sage" advice that came from my father, but I was only ten years old when he told me how to housebreak a pet. Perhaps if I had been older, I could have offered up some other options reminding him that he thought it was perfectly okay for me to lay up in the flat space beneath the rear window of the car and the backseat while he was driving. And even though I was never injured, I am sure he would have been interested in looking at other advice from experts in the field.

As time progressed and Maggie realized she was a member of the family, she learned how to shake hands, sit down, and speak, all for a treat, of course. She loved doggie treats. She loved other non-doggie treats too. She just loved to eat. She would even eat food I have never seen other dogs eat. All kinds of vegetables - green beans, carrots, peas. Just about anything and everything except lettuce and pickles. She didn't like lettuce and I certainly understand her discriminating taste with regard to that. I don't like anything except iceberg lettuce and in today's world, good luck on finding just that in a salad. Regarding pickles, I get it. Not everyone likes pickles.

Maggie also ate things she shouldn't have, but as I said, I don't think she could help herself. It was all instinctive. So when she found some dead animal out in the woods, she had no problem with helping herself to the gamey treat. We usually found out that she had indulged in these pleasures when she threw it all up sometime in the middle of the night. But there was no sense in trying to tell her that there were some things you shouldn't eat. If it was out there and she could find it she was going to eat it, or if there was nothing there left to eat, she would settle for just rolling around in it. When she came home with that distinctive aroma and traces of her "treat" around her neck and body, she got a bath and we just crossed our fingers that was all she had done with what she had found.

That thin dog who arrived at our house with her ribs showing, gained weight with regularity not only because she loved to eat, but because she was one of the best beggars I have ever met. She learned very quickly that when we sat down at the table to eat, there was a good chance she would get something to eat too. At first, she sat there at your feet, peering up at you with her soulful brown eyes and a smile on her face, but over time, she would brush her paw across your leg and let out a soft whine, reminding you that she was there and would appreciate some "love from up top." I have to admit, I made things worse as I actually put her in a seat at the dinner table a few times and let her eat from the plate, so I have no one to blame but myself. But regardless, no one that encountered her could resist her "starving act" and she always got the food. Always.

Maggie enjoyed being outdoors. She loved her walks every day, morning and evening. Walks provided her a chance to smell all the new things in the neighborhood and if she was lucky, she would get to see a neighbor's dog, or even better, the neighbors themselves. She always had a greeting for them, and they for her. When anyone petted Maggie their first comment was always, "she has the softest fur." And she did. One of her favorite things was to simply lay in our driveway and feel the sun on her back and she would do that for hours. Perfect contentment. And then, there was swimming.

When we added a pool at our new house, I think Maggie believed we built it just for her. She loved to run and splash through the creek that developed after hard rains on our property, so when this large body of water appeared in the back yard, she didn't hesitate to jump in. She especially loved the pool after taking a walk in the summer. If you weren't watching her and the gate was open, she was jumping in the pool. Her regular routine was to swim around in several circles and get out, shake herself off, and then slide down the small grass hill next to the pool, rolling over and back as if she was receiving an exotic spa treatment at some hotel.

Pool parties with my son and his friends were exciting events for her because they involved swimming, people and food – three of her favorites. It would be hard to say who enjoyed those most. When it was just the two of us, she would chase me around the pool, waiting for me to jump in, so she could jump in after me and then together we would see who could get to the other end of the pool the fastest. She won every race. I made sure of that.

We are big college football fans in our house. Maggie wasn't. In fact, she didn't enjoy the college football season in our house at all. Whether our team was winning or losing, Maggie didn't like the shouts of joy or the shouts of disappointment. And unfortunately, over the past 10 years, there have been more sounds of aggravation and misery than elation, watching our alma mater, Tennessee. Though I have to admit, beating Georgia with a Hail-Mary pass on October 1st in 2016, will be one of the greatest feelings I have ever experienced watching a football game. For all of you non-SEC college football fans, you may not ever understand what I am saying, but that's okay. I don't understand the fervor that some people have for Soccer and Hockey or even Baseball. Zero to zero games or 1-0 games don't excite me.

And I don't understand the excitement for NASCAR at all. And I grew up in Bristol Tennessee, so it is probably heresy for me to put this down on paper, but so be it. I like the idea of drinking beer at a sporting event, but there isn't enough beer in the world to get me through three hours of loud cars going around and around in a circle.

Maggie would have hated the loud cars because she didn't like loud noises. And it always got loud when we were watching college football. Just as soon as I started to suggest the other team had nefarious characters on their team in a loud and disgusted manner, she would get up and go into the back bedroom and wait for the game to be over. Once the yelling had subsided, she would come back out and look at me as if to say, "Are you done now?" And I was. Most of the time. And if I wasn't, she let me know by another quick exit.

Maggie just didn't like loud noises. I think it may have had something to do with her early life, but there are many dogs that don't like loud noises. Cindy didn't like them either. Both of them hated the fourth of July celebrations and the sound of the fireworks. When those started going off, they would both run for cover. Cindy often went under the bed and would stay there panting and shivering until they stopped. Maggie would do the same thing, but there were times we would find her in the back of the closet, trying to hide and no amount of coaxing would bring her out. Neither of them would leave their shelters until the loud noises ceased. It took Cindy a little while to get her anxiety under control after the noises had stopped, but for Maggie, once the loud noise ended, it was if it had never happened.

Maggie was good about that. She never let things bother her for long. Even when her best friend moved away or when she got a sister that she didn't ask for. My son moved out of the house while he was in college. He still lived in the same town though, and being much smarter than his father had been at his age, he came home on a much more frequent basis.

With each visit, he sought out his friend and Maggie rejoiced in those reunions. For her, it was as if he had never left during those short periods when he was home. But over time, she learned that her best friend would only be coming home every now and then, so she looked toward another to become her best friend. She found one in my wife. Especially after I adopted a dog that I saw in a newspaper picture over the Thanksgiving holidays.

Her name was Oreo and because of my last name, I didn't see how it could be anything but fate that led me to that picture in the paper. Oreo Doriot - the t is silent in my last name so the name rhymes with Oreo. I was certain that could not be a coincidence. And though one would have thought Maggie would be jealous of Oreo, another dog in the house, she wasn't. She welcomed Oreo into the house even though the welcome wasn't reciprocated. Over time, we realized that Oreo just tolerated other dogs although there were some occasions when she would cuddle up with her older sister.

Nevertheless, Maggie just went on being Maggie. If Oreo wanted to play, that would be fine. If she didn't, that would be fine too. I can't tell you the exact day or time when it happened but eventually, Oreo became my dog and Maggie became my wife's dog. My wife would tell you it happened the first day I brought Oreo home and perhaps it did. Oreo and I formed a bond that Maggie formed with first my son, and then my wife. And while Oreo could be jealous of my attention, Maggie never was. She accepted the change in our relationship as she knew the other dog had appropriated much of the attention she used to get from me, and she turned her devotion toward my wife.

Oreo followed me around like she was my shadow and was clearly "my dog." One day I jokingly referred to Maggie as the "old brown dog" when talking about the two of them. It was never meant to be a derogatory term because I still cared very much for Maggie. It was just a joke that I made as I referred to my wife and the "old brown dog" that followed her around, like her shadow. My wife defended Maggie and accused me of calling her old, seeing how I called her shadow old, and I endured a lot of grief for that for some time. Deep down, she knew it was just a joke but nevertheless, the term stuck and I often referred to Maggie from that point forward as the "old brown dog."

Age crept up on the "old brown dog" faster than we anticipated, and before we knew it, the scared little dog who had become the nicest and the friendliest dog I ever met; the dog who was full of energy and wanting to play every moment she was outside, couldn't do it as easily as she once had.

The changes in Maggie were never more prominent than in her last year with us. She could no longer jump up on the bed or the sofa and didn't like to go outside quite as much as she used to. It was hard for her to even get up and down and she walked with a severe limp in her hind legs. But if you looked at her face, all you would see would be a few more white patches where there were once brown ones. You would never see that those changes to her body were bothering her because I think in her mind, she never believed that they were issues. They were just changes that slowed her down.

She still wanted to go on her daily walks, and she always wanted to go all the way to the end of the street, even though her body just wouldn't let her do it. So she would go as far as she could and then lay down in the middle of the road and rest. If cars came down the road, they would just have to go around her, and our neighbors were always willing to accommodate that need. Once rested, Maggie would know it was time to go back home and so she would get up and start the walk back. If another rest was needed, she would stop and rest. She did this until the very last day of her life, and even then, she still wanted to go all the way down to the end of the street. The will of the dog that broke free from a rope wanted to keep going but her body couldn't accommodate her desires.

Maggie passed away on October 26, 2018. I told my wife the night before that I thought she was dying. She was having even more trouble getting up and down and was really struggling to walk. Even so, she went outside to do her business and did her best in eating her meal that evening, although her appetite had diminished over the past week. When Maggie didn't finish the food in her bowl, you knew something was wrong. She could eat her full bowl of food in less than a minute and then look at you wondering where the rest of it was.

I called my wife at work as soon as I got up that morning and found Maggie lying on her bed. Though I called out her name, she didn't respond. She just lay there. Unaware and unresponsive. That scared and pitiful looking dog had returned, only this time I was more frightened than she was. My wife rushed home and rode with her in the back seat as I hurried to our veterinarian's office. When we got there, a staff member came out to the car and gently carried her into the office. Within a few moments, my wife and I were escorted into a room that we had never seen before, and we both knew what that meant.

The doctor came in and told us they had helped ease her breathing but they had found a large mass on her spleen and would not be able to do anything for her. She wouldn't have survived the surgery. In an empathetic manner, she told us what we both knew when we got in the car that morning. It was time to let her go.

They brought her in the room and placed her on my lap and my wife and I petted her and talked to her as she lay there. Our vet bent down to administer the drugs that would enable her to rest and be free of the pain that we knew existed every time she got up or down or tried to walk.

I heard the vet whisper that she was gone and my wife and I could not control our sorrow, even though I knew that "old brown dog" had broken free again. She had broken free of the rope again, only this time the rope had been created by age and declining health. Even though her heart was physically weak, it never stopped wanting to be with the family she had adopted so many years ago. I never imagined how much it would hurt to lose her as I sat there, continuing to hold her body and stroke her soft fur. At times I couldn't even see her because my tears wouldn't allow me to, but I hoped she could still hear me saying over and over again, that she was a good dog and that everything was okay.

I really didn't understand what it was like to lose a dog even though I told you I had one when I was growing up. When Cindy died, I had been away at college for four years. On those occasions when I returned home, Cindy barked at me, thinking I was an intruder. She had aged so much and it had been too long between visits so it would take her a while to recognize my voice and smell and then she would finally wag her tail and welcome me home. When my mother called to tell me that the vet said it was time to put her down, I didn't understand what she was feeling, because I was immature and had forgotten all of those special times I had spent with my friend while I was growing up.

I told my mother that I was sorry at the time, but I didn't truly understand the grief she must have felt to lose her companion. The dog that had been bought for me when I was ten years old and had lived with her for thirteen years and had become her loyal companion. Cindy helped fill the void created by her last child growing up and moving away. She was there when my father died, nine months before I left to go to college. Cindy was a connection to the past that helped make a home less lonely for my mother. Maggie taught me what it truly meant to lose a companion like that.

I now understand the grief that one feels when you lose a dog who touches your heart and exposes it to the world when they leave you. I opened up my heart to Maggie as soon as my son asked if we could keep her and she took a part of it with her when she passed away. But that's okay. My heart is still functioning. In fact, I think it may even be a little stronger because of that "old brown dog." The memories of my time with her have repaired that hole in my heart better than a cardiologist could ever hope to accomplish.

As I sit here and reflect on that first day she came to our house, I don't think it happened by chance. I think she came to our house for a reason. She knew we needed her as much as she needed us. She was there for my son at first and taught him what unconditional love was. When he moved away, she was there for me, and even more so for my wife because she provided that connection to the past. The past that reminded her of the times when our only son lived with us.

I am not sure how old Maggie was when she came to live with us, but she was with us for fourteen years. Fourteen years where she showed us how happy she was to see us every day. And even if she couldn't say the words out loud, no one ever doubted her love for everyone that lived with her.

I have always believed that if you go to Heaven that you will be reunited with your loved ones. To suggest that a dog would not be a part of that group, well, I just can't see how that could be called Heaven. I miss Maggie and I am hoping with all my heart that she is there in Heaven, waiting on her family to come see her.

I hope she and Cindy are friends now. Cindy would be able to show Maggie how to chase rabbits and Maggie could show Cindy how to chase deer, though neither of those two dogs ever came close to catching what they were chasing. But, that's not the point. The fun is in the chase.

I doubt Cindy or Maggie would have even known what to do should they have ever caught what they were chasing. It was just something instinctive that linked them to their past; the wolves that they descended from who hunted for their food. Maggie and Cindy didn't ever need to hunt for their food. It was always there for them in their bowl or in a hand that was held out to them under the table.

I hope there are a lot of other dogs in Heaven that Maggie can make friends with. And if she is there, I know she will be in the middle of them and the children, reminding all of them how much fun it is to run around and play.

I still feel Maggie's presence in our house. I look over at Oreo as I am getting ready to feed her and wonder for a moment where Maggie is. And then I remember. Sometimes I even walk in the living room and I think I see her laying over there on the couch or chair, asleep and happy. It's only for a second and perhaps it's just wishful thinking, but I think it is more than that.

I even see her outside sometimes, laying on the ground next to the pool. Or laying in the driveway in the sun. Again, perhaps it's just the images created by the shadows of the trees but I think it isn't. I believe her spirit will never leave this house and I welcome the four-legged ghost each time I think I catch a glimpse of it.

I miss the "old brown dog," and I hope I'll see her again one day. Waiting for me at the gate (the pearly white one), with her tail wagging and ready to go for a walk, or for a car ride or to get something to eat. I hope there are all of those things in the afterlife, especially the food part. Not in particular for me but because I know where Maggie will be. Sitting there at my feet. Pawing at my leg, telling me not to forget that she was there and that she would like something to eat too. And I would get to feed her again. She would like that. I would like that too.

Run free, girl. Play with the other dogs. Chase the deer. Enjoy your naps. Enjoy your food. I also hope that they allow us to watch college football games in the afterlife. If they do, I promise that when I watch them with you, I will be more careful with my enthusiasm and my language. I am pretty sure that there are guidelines that I will have to follow with regard to that.

Otherwise, they may kick me out and I would end up in that hot place somewhere in southwest central Alabama.

Acknowledgements for quotes, character and title references:

"Harry Potter" – created by J.K.Rowling in 1997

"The Twilight Zone" – created by Rod Serling in 1959

"Apocalypse Now" - directed, produced and cowritten by Frances Ford Coppola in 1979

"The Godfather" - book written by Mario Puzo in 1969, movie directed by Frances Ford Coppola in 1997

"Star Wars" - created and directed by George Lucas in 1977

"Robocop" - movie directed by Paul Verhoeven in 1987

"The Walking Dead" - created by Robert Kirkman, Tony Moore, Charlie Adlard, first aired on TV in 2010

"Tamerlane and Other Poems," "A Dream Within a Dream," "The Bells," "The Conqueror Worm," "Evening Star," "Spirits of the Dead," "Annabel Lee," "To My Mother," "The Raven," "The System of Dr. Tarr and Prof. Fether," "The Narrative of Arthur Gordyn Pym" - written by Edgar Allan Poe 1809-1849

"Macbeth" – written by William Shakespeare in 1606

"The Banshee" – written by Henry Wadsworth Longfellow in 1876

"Avatar" - directed, written, and produced by James Cameron in 2009

"The Descent" – written and directed by Neil Marshall in 2005

"Jaws" - written by Peter Benchley in 1974, directed by Steven Spielberg in 1975

"The Exorcist" – written by Peter Blatty in 1971, directed by William Friedkin in 1973

"The Little Rascals" – created by Hal Roach and directed by Robert F. McGowan in 1922

"A Christmas Carol" – written by Charles Dickens in 1843

www.ingramcontent.com/pod-product-compliance
Lightning Source LLC
Chambersburg PA
CBHW070636310726
48982CB00001B/294
9781733252850